IMMORAL

IMMORAL

BRIAN FREEMAN

**Doubleday Large Print
Home Library Edition**

ST. MARTIN'S MINOTAUR ✄ NEW YORK

**This Large Print Book carries the
Seal of Approval of N.A.V.H.**

For Marcia

The distance that the dead have gone
Does not at first appear—
Their coming back seems possible
For many an ardent year.

—EMILY DICKINSON

PROLOGUE

Darkness was a different thing in the north woods than it was in the city. He had forgotten.

The girl was invisible—no more than a ghost under the midnight sky—but he knew she was there, very close to him. He clutched her warm wrist in his hand. Her breathing was soft and measured; she was calm. Her perfume, always familiar to him, filled his nostrils again, a lingering, unusual essence of spring flowers. Lilac, he thought. And hyacinth. He remembered when that perfume alone, just the smell of it, could arouse him. He had missed her scent and her body. Now here they were—together again.

A fist of dread gripped his insides. A wave of self-hatred washed over him. He didn't know if he had the courage for what came next. Waiting, planning, wanting, he had fantasized about this night. She was so much a part of his mind that when he looked in the mirror, he could actually see her behind him, like a dark raven on his shoulder. But after all the anticipation, he hesitated at the threshold.

One last little game, he thought.

"Let's get it over with," the girl hissed, betraying irritation and impatience. He hated to hear any hint of disapproval in her voice. But she was right—she was always a step ahead of him. They had been outside in the frigid air for too long. The barn was a magnet for lovers. Someone might interrupt them in their hideaway, ruining everything.

He felt wolfish eyes upon him. They were alone, but even so, he felt as if strangers were hiding behind the skeletal birch trees, stalking him. He took a deep breath, trying to rein in his fears. He couldn't wait any more.

He dug his left hand into the pocket of his coat, letting his fingers caress the blade.

Time to play.

*   *   *

He had waited for her in the darkest section of the street, along the route he knew she would come. Cold pellets of sleet, blown horizontal, rained down on the car, gathering like snow on his windshield. He shivered, pulled his light coat tighter around his shoulders, and nervously eyed the mirrors.

He had arrived early, much earlier than was wise. But the neighborhood was quiet. His watch said ten o'clock. *Soon,* he thought.

Each minute passed with excruciating slowness. He squirmed, his bowels like water. It occurred to him for a horrifying moment that she might not come. All the waiting, all the sacrifice, would be for nothing. As cold as it was in the car, he began to sweat. He chewed his upper lip between his teeth. The longer he sat, counting the seconds in his head, the more he felt his fears grow. Would she come?

Then she appeared, seemingly out of nowhere, looking ethereal under the pale glow of a streetlight. He gasped at how beautiful she was. His pulse raced, and more sweat gathered in a clammy film under his arms and on the back of his neck. His mouth was so dry he couldn't swallow. As she glided closer, his eyes drank her in. She had full red lips and black hair falling in wet strands below her shoulders. The cold brought a ruby flush to her cheeks, startling against the creamy alabaster of her skin. A single hoop earring dangled in a glint of gold from her left earlobe, and a gold bracelet hung loosely on her right wrist. She was tall and took long, hurried strides. She wore a white turtleneck over her slim torso, its damp fabric clinging to her body. Her black jeans fit snugly.

He imagined what it was like to be so powerful and confident. He could almost feel himself inside her skin, keenly aware of her body: the taste of rain on her lips, the singing and biting of the wind in her ears, and the wanton, supple sensation between her legs.

Her eyes found him. He knew she couldn't see him inside the car, but he could feel her stare anyway. And he knew those eyes, intense and green, like sea foam in which he wanted to drown. She was coming straight toward him.

He knew what to do—stay in the car, wait, let her come to him. But the aching in his heart was too much. His eyes flicked up and down the street, checking to see if they were safe. Then he opened the car door and called to her, his voice barely louder than a whisper.

"Rachel."

Now, miles away, she was running. Trying to escape. He reached out, grabbing for her shirt. He snagged a fistful of her turtleneck, but she slapped his hand away. Slipping, he lunged again for her wrist, but his gloved fingers yanked on her bracelet instead. She wriggled free, the bracelet tumbled away, and she galloped into the tall weeds.

He followed, barely two steps behind her. But Rachel was like a gazelle, fleet and graceful. He felt clumsy, slowed by his big shoes and the sticky grasp of mud and brush. She widened the gap. He called her name, pleading with her to stop, and she must have heard him. Or maybe she stumbled in the rutted ground. When he clawed out blindly with his hands, he felt the soft flesh of her shoulder. He squeezed hard and spun her around. Their bodies collided. He held her tight as she wriggled in his grasp, her chest heaving. He smelled her sweet breath.

She didn't say a word.

He hooked his right foot around her ankle,

trapping her, and pressed their hips together. He tugged her shirt. The fabric
bunched in his hand, and he brought up his
other fist, the one with the knife. With just the
point of the blade, he sliced the shirt like butter, hearing the cloth tear and fray. He cut
the shirt again. And again, turning it into
rags. He let his fingers touch her skin, feeling the swell of her breasts, which rose up
and down, up and down, like a roller coaster.

He put the point to her chest, right where
the heart must be, somewhere deep inside.
If she truly had a heart. She struggled, playing along. A dying game. He knew she
wanted him to do it. This was never about
him, he reminded himself. This was all about
Rachel.

He pushed. A gasp finally escaped her
lips. Something wet ran on the blade. That
was all it took, and they were free.

PART ONE

PART ONE

1

Jonathan Stride felt like a ghost, bathed in the white spotlights that illuminated the bridge.

Below him, muddy brown swells flooded into the canal, spewing waves over the concrete piers and swallowing the spray in eight-foot troughs. The water tumbled over itself, squeezing from the violent lake to the placid inner harbor. At the end of the piers, where ships navigated the canal as delicately as thread through a needle, twin lighthouses flashed revolving beams of green and red.

The bridge felt like a living thing. As cars

sped onto the platform, a whine filled the air, like the buzz of hornets. The honeycomb sidewalk vibrated, quivering under his feet. Stride glanced upward, as he imagined Rachel would have done, at the crisscross scissors of steel towering above his head. The barely perceptible sway unsettled him and made him dizzy.

He was doing what he always did— putting himself inside the mind of the victim, seeing the world through her eyes. Rachel had been here on Friday night, alone on the bridge. After that, no one knew.

Stride turned his attention to the two teenagers who stood with him, impatiently stamping their feet against the cold. "Where was she when you first saw her?" he asked.

The boy, Kevin Lowry, extracted a beefy hand from his pocket. His third finger sported an oversized onyx high school ring. He tapped the three inches of wet steel railing. "Right here, Lieutenant. She was balanced on top of the railing. Arms stretched out. Sort of like Christ." He closed his eyes, tilted his chin toward heaven, and extended his arms with his palms upward. "Like this."

Stride frowned. It had been a bleak October, with angry swoops of wind and sleet raining like bullets from the night sky. He couldn't imagine anyone climbing on top of the railing that night without falling.

Kevin seemed to read his mind. "She was really graceful. Like a dancer."

Stride peered over the railing. The narrow canal was deep enough to grant passage to giant freighters weighted down with bellies of iron ore. It could suck a body down in its wicked undertow and not let go.

"What the hell was she doing up there?" Stride asked.

The other teenager, Sally Lindner, spoke for the first time. Her voice was crabbed. "It was a stunt, like everything else she did. She wanted attention."

Kevin opened his mouth to complain but closed it again. Stride got the feeling this was an old argument between them. He noticed that Sally had her arm slung through Kevin's, and she tugged the boy a little closer when she talked.

"So what did you do?" Stride asked.

"I ran up here on the bridge," Kevin said. "I helped her down."

Stride watched Sally's mouth pucker unhappily as Kevin described the rescue.

"Tell me about Rachel," Stride said to Kevin.

"We grew up together. Next-door neighbors. Then her mom married Mr. Stoner and they moved uptown."

"What does she look like?"

"Well, uh, pretty," Kevin said nervously, shooting a quick glance at Sally.

Sally rolled her eyes. "She was beautiful, okay? Long black hair. Slim, tall. The whole package. And a bigger slut you're not likely to find."

"Sally!" Kevin protested.

"It's true, and you know it. After Friday? You know it."

Sally turned her face away from Kevin, although she didn't let go of his arm. Stride watched the girl's jaw set in an angry line, her lips pinched together. Sally had a rounded face, with a messy pile of chestnut curls tumbling to her shoulders and blowing across her flushed cheeks. In her tight blue jeans and red parka, she was a pretty young girl. But no one would describe her as beautiful. Not a stunner. Not like Rachel.

"What happened on Friday?" Stride asked. He knew what Deputy Chief Kinnick had told him on the phone two hours ago:

Rachel hadn't been home since Friday. She was missing. Gone. *Just like Kerry.*

"Well, she sort of came on to me," Kevin said grudgingly.

"Right in front of me!" Sally snapped. "Fucking bitch."

Kevin's eyebrows furled together like a yellow caterpillar. "Stop it. Don't talk about her like that."

Stride held up one hand, silencing the argument. He reached inside his faded leather jacket and pulled out a pack of cigarettes that he had wedged into the pocket of his flannel shirt. He studied the pack with weary disgust, then lit a cigarette and took a long drag. Smoke curled out of his mouth and formed a cloud in front of his face. He felt his lungs contract. Stride tossed the rest of the pack into the canal, where the red package swirled like a dot of blood and then was swept under the bridge.

"Back up," he said. "Kevin, give me the whole story, short and sweet, okay?"

Kevin rubbed his hand across his scalp until his blond hair stood up like naked winter trees. He squared his shoulders, which were broad and muscular. A football player.

"Rachel called me on my cell phone on

Friday night and said we should come hang out with her in Canal Park," Kevin said. "It was about eight-thirty, I guess. A shitty night. The park was almost empty. When we spotted Rachel, she was on the railing, playing around. So we ran up on the bridge to get her off there."

"Then what?" Stride asked.

Kevin pointed to the opposite side of the bridge, to the peninsula that stretched like a narrow finger with Lake Superior on one side and Duluth harbor on the other. Stride had lived there most of his life, watching the ore ships shoulder out to sea.

"The three of us wandered down to the beach. We talked about school stuff."

"She's a suck-up," Sally interjected. "She takes psychology and starts spouting all the teacher's theories on screwed-up families. She takes English, and the teacher's poetry is *so* wonderful. She takes math and grades papers after school."

Stride silenced the girl with a stony stare. Sally pouted and tossed her hair defiantly. Stride nodded at Kevin to continue.

"Then we heard a ship's horn," he said. "Rachel said she wanted to ride the bridge while it went up."

"They don't let you do that," Stride said.

"Yeah, but Rachel knows the bridge keeper. She and her dad used to hang out with him."

"Her dad? You mean Graeme Stoner?"

Kevin shook his head. "No, her real dad. Tommy."

Stride nodded. "Go on."

"Well, we went back on the bridge, but Sally didn't want to do it. She kept going to the city side. But I didn't want Rachel up there by herself, so I stayed. And that's where—well, that's where she started making out with me."

"She was playing games with you," Sally said sharply.

Kevin shrugged. Stride watched Kevin tug at the collar around his thick neck and then caught a glimpse of the boy's eyes. Kevin wasn't going to say exactly what happened on the bridge, but he clearly was embarrassed and aroused thinking about it.

"We weren't up there very long," Kevin said. "Maybe ten minutes. When we got down, Sally—she wasn't . . ."

"I left," Sally said. "I went home."

Kevin stuttered on his words. "I'm really sorry, Sal." He reached out a hand to brush her hair, but Sally twisted away.

Before Stride could cut short the latest spat, he heard his cell phone burping out a polyphonic rendition of Alan Jackson's "Chattahoochee." He dug the phone out of his pocket and recognized the number for Maggie Bei. He flipped it open.

"Yeah, Mags?"

"Bad news, boss. The media's got the story. They're crawling all over us."

Stride scowled. "Shit." He took a few steps away from the two teenagers, noting that Sally began hissing at Kevin as soon as Stride was out of earshot. "Is Bird out there with the other jackals?" he asked.

"Oh, yeah. Leading the inquisition."

"Well, for God's sake, don't talk to him. Don't let any reporters near the Stoners."

"No problem, we're taped off."

"Any other good news?" Stride asked.

"They're playing it like this is number two," Maggie told him. "First Kerry, now Rachel."

"That figures. Well, I don't like déjà vu either. Look, I'll be there in twenty minutes, okay?"

Stride slapped the phone shut. He was impatient now. Things were already moving in a direction he didn't like. Having Rachel's disappearance splashed over the media changed the nature of the investigation. He needed the TV and newspapers to get the girl's face in front of the public, but Stride wanted to control the story, not have the story control him. That was impossible with Bird Finch asking questions.

"Keep going," Stride urged Kevin.

"There's not much else," Kevin said. "Rachel said she was tired and wanted to go home. So I walked her to the Blood Bug."

"The what?" Stride asked.

"Sorry. Rachel's car. A VW Beetle, okay? She called it the Blood Bug."

"Why?"

Kevin's face was blank. "Because it was red, I guess."

"Okay. You actually saw her drive off?"

"Yes."

"Alone?"

"Sure."

"And she specifically told you she was going home?"

"That's what she said."

"Could she have been lying? Could she have had another date?"

Sally laughed cruelly. "Sure she could. Probably did."

Stride turned his dark eyes on Sally

again. She hooded her eyes and looked down at her shoes, her curls falling over her forehead. "Do you know something, Sally?" Stride asked. "Did you maybe go see Rachel and tell her to lay off Kevin here?"

"No!"

"Then who do you think Rachel would have gone to see?"

"It could have been anyone," Sally said. "She was a whore."

"Stop it!" Kevin insisted.

"Both of you stop it," Stride snapped. "What was Rachel wearing that night?"

"Tight black jeans, the kind you need a knife to cut yourself out of," Sally replied. "And a white turtleneck."

"Kevin, did you see anything in her car? Luggage? A backpack?"

"No, nothing like that."

"You told Mr. Stoner that she made a date with you."

Kevin bit his lip. "She asked if I wanted to see her on Saturday night. She said I could pick her up at seven, and we could go out. But she wasn't there."

"It was a game to her," Sally repeated. "Did she tell you to call me on Saturday and lie to me? Because that's what you did."

Stride knew he wasn't going to get any more out of these two tonight. "Listen up, both of you. This isn't about who kissed who. A girl's missing. A friend of yours. I've got to go talk to her parents, who are wondering if they're ever going to see their daughter again, okay? So think. Is there anything else you remember from Friday night? Anything Rachel did or said? Anything that might tell us where she went when she left here or who she might have seen."

Kevin closed his eyes, as if he were really trying to remember. "No, Lieutenant. There's nothing."

Sally was sullen, and Stride wondered if she was hiding something. But she wasn't going to talk. "I have no idea what happened to her," Sally mumbled.

Stride nodded. "All right, we'll be in touch."

He took another glance out at the looming blackness of the lake, beyond the narrow canal. There was nothing to see. It was as empty and hollow as his world felt now. As he pushed past the two teenagers and headed to the parking lot, he felt it again. Déjà vu. It was an ugly memory.

2

Fourteen months had passed since the wet August evening when Kerry McGrath disappeared. Stride had reconstructed her last night so many times that he could almost see it playing in his head like a movie. If he closed his eyes, he could see her, right down to the freckle on the corner of her lips and the three slim gold earrings hugging her left earlobe. He could hear her giggle, like she had in the birthday videotape he had watched a hundred times. All along, he had kept an image of her that was so vivid, it was like she was alive.

But he knew she was dead. The bubbly

girl who was so real to him was a hideous, flesh-eaten thing in the ground somewhere, in one of the deserted acres of wilderness they had never searched. He only wanted to know why and who had done it to her.

And now another teenager. Another dis-appearance.

As he waited at a stoplight, Stride glanced into his truck window and found himself star-ing into the reflection of his own shadowy brown eyes. Pirate eyes, Cindy used to say, teasing him. Dark, alert, on fire. But that was then. He had lost Kerry to a monster, and a different kind of monster had claimed Cindy at the same time. The tragedy deadened the flame behind his eyes and made him older. He could see it in his face, weathered and imperfect. A web of telltale lines furrowed across his forehead. His black hair, streaked with strands of gray, was short but unkempt, with a messy cowlick. He was forty-one and felt fifty.

Stride swung his mud-stained Bronco through potholes to the old-money neighbor-hood near the university where Graeme and Emily Stoner lived. Stride knew what to ex-pect. It was eleven o'clock, normally a time when the streets would be deathly quiet on

Sunday night. But not tonight. The blinking lights of squad cars and the white klieg lights of television crews lit up the street. Neighbors lingered on their lawns in small crowds of spies and gossips. Stride heard the overlapping cacophony of police radios buzzing like white noise.

Uniformed cops had cordoned off the Stoner house, keeping the reporters and the gawkers at bay. Stride pulled his Bronco beside a squad car and double-parked. The reporters all swarmed around him, barely giving him room to swing his door open. Stride shook his head and held up his hand, shielding his eyes as he squinted into the camera lights.

"Come on, guys, give me a break."

He pushed his way through the crowd of journalists, but one man squared his body in front of Stride and flashed a signal to his cameraman.

"Do we have a serial killer on the loose here, Stride?" Bird Finch rumbled in a voice as smooth and deep as a foghorn. His real name was Jay Finch, but everyone in Minnesota knew him as Bird, a Gopher basketball star who was now the host of a shock-TV talk show in Minneapolis.

Stride, who was slightly more than six feet tall himself, craned his neck to stare up at Bird's scowling face. The man was a giant, at least six-foot-seven, dressed impeccably in a navy double-breasted suit, with cufflinks glinting on the half inch of white shirt cuffs that jutted below his sleeve. Stride saw a university ring on the forefinger of the huge paw in which he clutched his microphone.

"Nice suit, Bird," Stride said. "You come here straight from the opera?"

He heard several of the reporters snicker. Bird stared at Stride with coal eyes. The floodlights glinted off his bald black head.

"We've got some sick pervert snatching our girls off the streets of this city, Lieutenant. You promised the people of this city justice last year. We're still waiting for it. The families of this city are waiting for it."

"If you're running for office, do it on someone else's time." Stride unhooked his shield from his jeans and held it in front of Bird's face, jamming his other hand in front of the camera. "Now get the hell out of my way."

Bird grudgingly inched away. Stride bumped his shoulder heavily against the reporter as he passed. The shouting continued behind him. The crowd of reporters dogged his heels, up onto the sidewalk and to the edge of the makeshift fence of yellow police tape. Stride bent down, squeezed under the tape, and straightened up. He gestured to the nearest cop, a slight twenty-two-year-old with buzzed red hair. The officer hurried eagerly up to Stride.

"Yes, Lieutenant?"

Stride leaned down and whispered in his ear. "Keep these assholes as far away as you can."

The cop grinned. "You got it, sir."

Stride wandered into the middle of Graeme Stoner's manicured lawn. He waved at Maggie Bei, the senior sergeant in the Detective Bureau he supervised, who was doling out orders in clipped tones to a crowd of uniformed officers. Maggie was barely five feet tall even in black leather boots with two-inch heels. The other cops dwarfed her, but they snapped to it when she jabbed a finger in their direction.

The Stoner house was at the end of a narrow lane, shadowed by oak trees that had recently spilled most of their leaves into messy piles. The house itself was a three-story relic of the 1920s, solidly constructed for the Minnesota winters with bricks and pine. A curving walkway led from the street to a mammoth front door. On the east side of the house, overlooking a wooded gully, was a two-car detached garage, with a driveway leading to a rear alley. Stride noted a bright red Volkswagen Bug parked in the driveway, not quite blocking one of the garage stalls.

Rachel's car. The Blood Bug.

"Welcome to the party, boss."

Stride glanced at Maggie Bei, who had joined him on the lawn.

Maggie's jet black hair was cut like a bowl, with bangs hanging straight down to her eyebrows. She was tiny, like a Chinese doll. Her face was pretty and expressive, with twinkling almond-shaped eyes and a mellow golden cast to her skin. She wore a bur-gundy leather jacket over a white Gap shirt and black jeans plucked from the teen racks. That was Maggie—stylish, hip. Stride didn't spend much money on clothes himself. He kept resoling the cowboy boots he had worn since he traded in his uniform to join the De-tective Bureau, and that was a long time ago. He still wore the same frayed jeans that he had worn through nine winters, even though coins now sprinkled the ground through a tear in his pocket. His leather jacket was similarly weather-worn. It still bore a bullet hole in the sleeve, which aligned with the scar on Stride's muscular upper arm.

Stride shifted his gaze to the windows fronting the Stoner house and saw a man inside carrying a drink into a back room. The crystal glass caught light from the chandelier and glinted like a mirror sending a message.

"So what do we have here, Mags?" Stride asked.

"Nothing you don't already know," she said. "Rachel Deese, seventeen years old, senior at Duluth High School. The jock, Kevin, says he saw her Friday night around ten o'clock driving away from Canal Park. Since then, nothing. Her car is parked in the driveway, but so far no one saw her arrive home on Friday or leave here on foot or with anyone else. That was two days ago."

Stride nodded. He took a moment to study Rachel's Volkswagen, which was surrounded by officers doing an exhaustive search of the vehicle. It was flashy red, cute, and clean, not the kind of car a teenage girl would willingly leave behind.

"Check for bank ATMs on the route from Canal Park to the house," Stride suggested. "Maybe we'll get lucky with a security tape from Friday night. Let's see if she really was heading home, like Kevin says."

"Already being done," Maggie informed him. She arched her eyebrow as if to say, *Am I stupid?*

Stride smiled. Maggie was the smartest cop he had ever worked with. "Graeme's her stepfather, right? What about her natural father? I think his name was Tommy."

"Nice try. I thought about that, too. But he's deceased."

"Anyone else missing? Like a boyfriend?"

"No reports. If she ran off, she either did it alone or with someone from out of town."

"People who run off need transportation," Stride said.

"We're checking the airport and bus station here and in Superior."

"Neighbors see anything?"

Maggie shook her head. "So far, nothing of interest. We're still doing interviews."

"Any complaints involving this girl?" Stride asked. "Stalking, rape, anything like that?"

"Guppo ran the database," Maggie said.

"Nothing involving Rachel. Go back a few years, and you'll find Emily and her first husband—Rachel's father—in a few scrapes."

"Like what?"

"Father was often drunk and disorderly. One domestic abuse report, never formally charged. He hit his wife, not his daughter."

Stride frowned. "Do we know if Rachel and Kerry knew each other?"

"Rachel's name never came up last year," Maggie said. "But we'll ask around."

Stride nodded blankly. He put himself in Rachel's shoes again, re-creating her last night, tracing what may or may not have happened along the way. He assumed she made it home on Friday. She was in her car, and now her car was at home. Then what? Did she go inside the house? Was someone waiting for her? Did she go out again? It was sleeting and cold—she would have taken the car. Unless someone picked her up.

"Time to talk to the Stoners," Stride said. Then he paused. He was used to relying on Maggie's instinct. "What's your gut tell you, Mags? Runaway or something worse?"

Maggie didn't hesitate. "With her car still parked outside the house? Sounds like something worse. Sounds like Kerry."

Stride sighed. "Yeah."

3

Stride rang the doorbell. He saw a shadow through the frosted glass and heard the click of footsteps. The carved oak door swung inward. A man about Stride's height, smartly attired in a V-neck cashmere sweater, a white dress shirt with button-down collar, and crisply pleated tan slacks, extended his hand. In his other hand, he swirled the ice in his drink.

"You're Lieutenant Stride, is that right?" the man greeted him. His handshake was solid, and he had the easy smile of someone accustomed to country club cocktail parties.

"Kyle told us you would be arriving shortly. I'm Graeme Stoner."

Stride nodded in acknowledgment. He got the message. Kyle was Kyle Kinnick, Duluth's deputy chief of police and Stride's boss. Graeme wanted to make sure Stride understood the juice he had at city hall.

He noted the discreet wrinkles creeping along Graeme's forehead and around the corners of his mouth and calculated that the man was about his own age. His chocolate brown hair was trimmed short, an executive's haircut. He wore silver glasses with tiny circular rims. His face was broad and soft, without noticeable cheekbones or a protruding chin. Even late at night, Graeme's beard line was almost invisible, which caused Stride involuntarily to rub his palm against his own scratchy stubble.

Graeme put a hand on Stride's shoulder. "Let me show you to the den," he said. "I'm afraid the living room felt rather exposed with the crowd outside."

Stride followed Graeme into the living room, furnished with delicate sofas and antiques, all in brilliantly varnished walnut. Graeme pointed at a mirror-backed china cabinet, stocked with crystal. "May I offer you a drink? It needn't be alcoholic."

"No, I'm fine, thanks."

Graeme paused in the middle of the room and appeared momentarily uncomfortable. "I must apologize for not raising concerns with you earlier, Lieutenant. When Kevin stopped by on Saturday night, I really wasn't troubled at all that Rachel hadn't come home. Kevin gets very excitable about Rachel, you see, and I thought he was overreacting."

"But you don't think so now," Stride said.

"It's been two days. And my wife rightly reminded me about that other girl who disappeared."

Graeme led the way through the main dining room and then through French doors into a sprawling den, warmed by a gray marble fireplace on the east wall. The white carpet was lush and spotless. The north wall was framed entirely in full-length windows, except for two stained glass doors that led to the darkness of a back garden. A series of brass lanterns, mounted at intervals on each of the other walls, lit the room with a pale glow.

To the right of the garden wall, one on either side of the fireplace, sat two huge matching recliners. Lost in one was a woman holding a bell-shaped glass of brandy.

The woman nodded at Stride from the chair without getting up. "I'm Emily Stoner, Rachel's mother," she said softly.

Emily was a few years younger than Graeme, but not a trophy bride. Stride could see she had once been very pretty, although she hadn't aged gracefully. Her blue eyes were tired, overly made up, with shadows underneath. Her dark hair was short and straight and hadn't been washed. She wore a plain navy sweater and blue jeans.

Seated near Emily on the hearth, holding the woman's left hand, was a man in his late forties, with graying hair combed to protect a thinning hairline. The man got up and shook Stride's hand, leaving behind a clammy residue that Stride tried unobtrusively to rub away. "Hello, Lieutenant. My name is Dayton Tenby. I'm the minister at Emily's church. Emily asked me to be with them this evening."

Graeme Stoner took a chair near the garden windows. "I'm sure you have many questions for us. We'll tell you everything we know, which I'm afraid isn't much. Incidentally, let's get the unpleasantness out of the way up front. My wife and I had absolutely no involvement in Rachel's disappearance, but we understand that you have to clear the family in these kinds of situations. Naturally, we'll cooperate in every way we can, including taking polygraphs, if necessary."

Stride was surprised. Usually this was the ugly part—letting the family know that they were suspects. "To be candid, yes, we do like to run polygraph tests on the family."

Emily looked at Graeme nervously. "I don't know."

"It's routine, dear," Graeme said. "Lieutenant, just send your questions to Archibald Gale. He'll be representing our interests in this matter. We can do it tomorrow if you'd like."

Stride grimaced. So much for cooperation. Archie Gale was the most feared criminal defense lawyer in northern Minnesota, and Stride had tangled with the suave old goat many times from the witness stand.

"Do you feel it's necessary to have a lawyer involved?" Stride asked, his voice chillier.

"Don't misunderstand," Graeme replied, as calmly and cordially as before. "We have nothing to hide. Even so, in this day and age, it would be reckless of us not to retain counsel."

"Are you willing to talk to me now, without Gale present?"

Graeme smiled. "Archie is flying back from Chicago. He reluctantly agreed we could review the facts without him."

Reluctantly. Stride knew Gale, and that was probably an understatement. But he wasn't about to lose his chance—it might be the last opportunity to talk to the family without an attorney screening every word.

Stride slid a notebook from his back pocket and uncapped a pen. Immediately on his left was a rolltop desk. He pulled a swivel chair out from behind the desk and sat down.

"When did you see Rachel last?" Stride asked.

"Friday morning before she went to school," Graeme said.

"Did she take her car then?"

"Yes. It was gone when I arrived home Friday night."

"But you didn't hear her return overnight?"

"No. I was in bed by ten. I'm a sound sleeper. I never heard a thing."

"What did you do on Saturday?"

"I was in the office most of the day. That's typical."

"Mrs. Stoner, were you at home during this time?"

Emily, who had been staring into the fire, looked back, startled. She took a long swallow of brandy, and Stride wondered how much she had already had to drink. "No. I only got back early this afternoon."

"And where were you?"

She took a moment to focus. "I was driving back from St. Louis. My sister moved down there several years ago. I started home Saturday morning, but I was too tired by evening to go the rest of the way. I stayed overnight in Minneapolis and got into town around noon."

"Did you talk to Rachel while you were gone?"

Emily shook her head.

"Did you call home at all?"

She hesitated. "No."

"When did you start getting worried?"

"After Emily got home," Graeme answered. "We still hadn't heard from Rachel, so we started calling her friends. No one had seen her."

"Who did you call?"

Graeme rattled off several names, and Stride jotted them down in his notebook. "We also called people from the school," Graeme added. "And several of the clubs and restaurants her friends mentioned. No one had seen her."

"Does she have a boyfriend?" Stride asked.

Emily looked up. She pushed a lock of hair from her face. Her voice was weary. "Rachel goes through lots of boyfriends. They don't last."

"Is she sexually active?"

"At least since she was thirteen," Emily said. "I walked in on her once with a boy."

"But no one special?"

Emily shook her head.

"Have you checked with relatives? People she might go to?"

"We don't have any relatives here. Both my parents are dead, and Graeme is from out of town. There's no one but us."

Stride wrote: *How did these two hook up?*

"Mrs. Stoner, what kind of relationship do you have with your daughter?"

Emily paused. "We've never been very close. When she was little, she was her daddy's girl. I was the wicked witch."

Dayton Tenby frowned. "That's not fair, Emily."

"Well, that's what it felt like," Emily snapped. She spilled a little of the brandy and dabbed at her sweater with her fingers. "When her father died, Rachel drifted even further away. I hoped when I married Graeme, we might start becoming a family again. But as she's gotten older, it's only gotten worse."

"What about you, Mr. Stoner?" Stride asked. "How is your relationship with Rachel?"

Graeme shrugged. "We were relatively close right after Emily and I got married five years ago, but as Emily said, she's grown more distant as she's gotten older. Today it's the same. Cold."

"We tried to reach her," Emily said. "Graeme bought her that car last year. I guess it seemed to her like we were trying to buy her love, and I suppose we were. But it didn't help."

"Has she ever talked about running away?"

"Not in a long time," Emily said. "I suppose it sounds crazy, but I always thought she felt she could cause more trouble for us by staying around and making us miserable. It gave her a cruel sense of satisfaction."

"Was she suicidal?" Stride asked.

"Never. Rachel would never have killed herself."

"Why are you so sure?" Stride asked.

"Rachel liked herself too much. She was always cocky and confident. It was us she despised. Or me." Emily shook her head.

"Mr. Stoner, did anything happen while your wife was gone? An argument, a fight, anything like that?"

"No, nothing. She ignored me. That was routine."

"Did she mention meeting anyone new?"

"No, but I don't suppose she would have told me even if she had."

"Did you notice unusual cars in the driveway or on the street? Or see her with anyone you didn't recognize?"

Graeme shook his head.

"What about your personal situation, Mr. Stoner? You work for the Range Bank, is that correct?"

Graeme nodded. "I'm the executive vice president for the bank's operations in Minnesota, Wisconsin, Iowa, and the Dakotas."

"Have you received any threats at home or at work? Strange phone calls?"

"Not that I recall."

"You've never felt in danger?"

"No, not at all."

"Is your income at the bank widely known?"

Graeme frowned. "Well, I suppose it's not a secret. I have to file as an officer with the SEC, so it's a matter of public record. But it's not the kind of thing that makes the papers."

"And you've received no contact of any kind that would lead you to believe Rachel has been kidnapped."

"No, nothing," Graeme told him.

Stride flipped his notebook shut. "I think that's everything for the moment. I'll need to talk with you further, of course, as the investigation continues. And I'll be in touch with Mr. Gale."

Emily opened her mouth, then closed it. She obviously wanted to interrupt.

"What is it?" Stride asked.

"It's just that—well, it's one reason we were so concerned. The reason I insisted Graeme call Kyle."

"Kerry McGrath," Tenby murmured.

"She lived so close," Emily exclaimed. "She went to the same school."

Stride waited until Emily looked back at him, and he held her stare, putting as much compassion as he could in his eyes. "I won't lie to you. We'll be looking for connections to Kerry's disappearance. We would be remiss if we didn't. But just because there are surface similarities doesn't mean that Rachel being missing has anything to do with Kerry."

Emily sniffled loudly. She nodded her head, but her eyes shone with tears.

"If I can answer any questions for you, please call me," Stride said, extracting a card from his coat and placing it on the rolltop desk.

Dayton Tenby rose from his place near the fire and smiled at Stride. "Let me show you out."

The minister guided Stride back through the house. Tenby was a nervous, effeminate man, who seemed intimidated by the up-scale trappings of the Stoner house. He walked gingerly, as if his aging brown wingtips were leaving dirty footprints. He was small, around five-foot-eight, with a narrow chin, tiny brown eyes set closely together, and a pinched nose. Stride sized him up as a holdover from Emily's past life. BG— Before Graeme.

Stroking his chin, Tenby glanced curiously outside at the lights and crowds gathered there. "They're like vultures, aren't they?" he observed.

"Sometimes. But they can be useful."

"Yes, I suppose. I appreciate your coming here, Lieutenant. Rachel is a difficult young girl, and I would hate to see any harm come to her."

"How long have you known her?" Stride asked.

"Since she was a child."

Stride nodded. *BG,* he thought. "When did she begin to have troubles?"

Tenby sighed. "As Emily mentioned, it was after her father's death. Rachel was utterly devoted to Tommy. She couldn't bear the loss, and I think she turned all her anger and grief against her mother."

"How long ago was that?"

Dayton pursed his lips and stared at the vaulted ceiling as he thought back. "Rachel was eight when he died, I believe, so it was about nine years ago."

"Tell me, Reverend, what do you think

happened here? Could Rachel have left on her own? A runaway?"

Dayton Tenby seemed divinely sure of himself. "Maybe it's wishful thinking, but that's what I believe. I really think you'll find, when all is said and done, that she's out there somewhere, laughing at us."

4

Emily downed the last swallow of brandy and pushed herself off the recliner. As Dayton Tenby returned to the room, she held out her empty glass. "I need another."

Tenby took the glass and returned to the living room to refill her drink. Emily watched him go, then spoke to Graeme without shifting her gaze. "I'm sorry I didn't call."

"That's all right. How's Janie?"

"She's fine," Emily said. "I meant to call."

"I told you it doesn't matter."

Emily nodded, feeling hollow. "I thought you'd be angry."

"Not at all."

"Did you miss me?"

Graeme waved his hand, dismissing the question as if it were nothing. "What a stupid thing to say. You know I'm lost without you. Yesterday, I wanted to go hiking, and I couldn't even find my tennis shoes."

"Shoes," Emily murmured, shaking her head.

Tenby reappeared. The portion of brandy in the glass he carried looked smaller than the last one. Emily took the glass and finished it in a single swallow, ignoring the burn that the liquor caused in her throat. She handed Tenby the glass and turned away. She wiped her eyes, but it was too late. She knew he had seen the tears.

"She's doing it just to punish me," Emily said. "It's a game with her."

"It may be more about Tommy than it is about you. Even after all these years," Tenby said.

"Tommy," she said bitterly.

"Emily, he was her father," Tenby reminded her. "She was eight years old, and her daddy could do no wrong."

"Yes, everybody loved Tommy," Emily said. "And I was always the bitch. No one ever understood what he did to us."

"I did," Tenby said.

Emily took his hand. "Yes, I know. Thank you. And thank you for coming over here tonight. I think I would have gone to pieces without you around."

Graeme stood up. "I'll walk you out, Dayton," he said, a veneer of politeness in his voice. "I'll make sure the press doesn't hassle you along the way."

Tenby was dwarfed by the larger man as the two of them retreated from the porch. Emily watched them go, listening to their footsteps, hearing the noises of the crowd outside as the front door opened, then the tomblike silence of the house as the door closed.

She was alone.

Even when she was with Graeme these days, she felt alone.

He said all the right things, and treated her well, and gave her the freedom to lead her own life, but he didn't pretend that there was any passion between them anymore. She wondered if he felt anything at all for her. She had deliberately not called from St. Louis, wanting to make him angry, wanting him to yearn for her enough to call her himself. If he called, if he missed her, if he screamed at her, at least she would see some of his emotions.

But he didn't need her. Except when he couldn't find his shoes.

And then to come home and find Rachel was gone. For years she had expected it, wondering when her daughter would leave her a note and run away. Sometimes she had even wished for it, as a way to end the hostility and restore some peace to her life. She had never realized how empty she would feel when it really happened, when all she could do was think about the missed opportunities that had kept them divided. She had long since accepted that Rachel would never know how deeply Emily loved her, in spite of the venom the girl had directed at her for so many years. Even when she tried to stop loving her, she couldn't.

Gone.

What if she hadn't run away? What if she ended up like that other girl, snatched off the street?

"Where are you, baby?" she said.

Emily heard noises in the front hall as the door opened and Graeme returned. She didn't want to see him. She couldn't balance all of it, her estrangement from Graeme, her grief over Rachel. Emily got up quickly and fled through the kitchen to the back stairs. She listened as Graeme returned to the porch. She imagined him glancing at the empty room, realizing she was gone. Emily didn't expect him to follow her, and he didn't. She could barely make out the tapping of keys as he sat down at his desk and worked on his computer. She hurried up the stairs to the second floor.

She wouldn't sleep in their bedroom tonight. He wouldn't miss that, either.

Emily went to Rachel's room. She smelled strangers there, the sweaty aroma of the police who had pawed through Rachel's desk and dresser that night. In truth, the room itself was a stranger to her, because she had hardly stepped foot inside while Rachel was home. It was her daughter's private fortress, and Emily of all people wasn't allowed.

The room was largely barren. There were no posters up on the walls, only a pale coating of yellow paint. Her dirty clothes were piled in the corner, in and out of a white basket. She had a stack of schoolbooks, some open, some closed, spread randomly across the desk, with wrinkled notepapers, half-filled with Rachel's scrawl, sticking out of the pages. Only her bed was carefully made—the one part of the room Rachel allowed the maid to touch.

Emily lay down on the bed, pulled her legs up, and curled her arms around them. She saw the photo, placed lovingly on her daughter's nightstand, of Rachel bundled up in her father's arms. Emily reached out with one hand and tipped the frame over, so she didn't have to stare at it.

As she looked at the nightstand, however, she realized she couldn't escape the past so easily. Next to the clock radio, perched on its hind legs, was a stuffed pink pig, adorned with black plastic sunglasses. A souvenir from the Minnesota State Fair.

Nine years later, and Rachel still kept it by her bed.

"Tommy," Emily sighed.

Tommy hoisted Rachel onto his shoulders. Now taller than everyone around her, Rachel opened her mouth in wonder at the sight of all the people, crammed together shoulder to shoulder, from one side of the street to the other. There were tens of thousands of them, a sweaty,

squirming mass, baking in the heat and humidity of a late August evening.

"It's amazing, Daddy!" Rachel cried.

"Didn't I promise you?" Tommy said. "Isn't this great?" He lifted Rachel high in the air, swirled her around, and swooped her to the ground.

"Can we do the midway now?" Rachel sang out.

Emily had to laugh. She suspected that was the last thing Tommy wanted. All day long, she had watched Tommy and Rachel bury themselves in the fair. Tommy ate everything, swallowing deep-fried cheese curds like popcorn and washing them down with giant plastic cups of ice-cold beer. He ate corn dogs, pork chops, onion blossoms, roasted corn slathered in butter, fried ravioli, and bag after bag of minidoughnuts. And now the rides would churn his stomach like a blender. But Tommy never said no to Rachel.

By the time they reached the midway, it was a tornado of light. Darkness had turned the carnival into a fairyland, where a sea of people screamed and their faces reflected a rainbow of colors from the rides streaking overhead. Rachel wanted to do everything. It didn't matter how fast the ride went, or how high, or how many times she spun upside down with her hair tumbling below her. She took Tommy on the Ring of Fire, going up and over in circles, then the Giant Swing, then the Octopus, then the Avalanche, then the Tornado. Emily was secretly pleased to see that Tommy was looking green.

It took them nearly two hours to work their way down one row of carnival rides, then back up the next. They wandered by the baseball game, run by a seedy barker in a devil's costume, with a button pinned on his red suit that said WELCOME TO HELL. He smiled, revealing two chocolate brown front teeth, and invited Tommy to try his hand.

"Break three plates, win the grand prize," he said.

"What's the grand prize?" Rachel asked.

The devil pointed at a giant stuffed bear, fat and soft and nearly as tall as Rachel. The girl's eyes widened, and she looked longingly at Tommy, hanging on his arm. "Can you win it for me, Daddy?"

"You bet I can."

The devil handed Tommy three baseballs. Tommy juggled two in his right hand and wound up with his left.

"You're drunk, Tommy," Emily warned him. "And you don't look good."

Tommy fired the first ball into the dead center of one of the ceramic plates. The plate smashed into shards, falling amid the litter of the booth, and the ball slammed into the aluminum wall with a bang.

"You did it, Daddy! You did it!"

Tommy grinned. He let the second ball fly, and crash, bang, another plate shattered.

"One more, Daddy, and you win!" Rachel cried.

"Make a place for that bear on your bed, honey," Tommy told her.

He readied himself for the next pitch, cocking his meaty arm. The crowd gathering behind them tensed, expecting another bang, waiting for the plate to explode.

Instead, the ball dribbled off Tommy's hand, bounced on the counter, and landed on the ground with a thud. The devil laughed. The people around the booth groaned with disappointment. Tommy's knees buckled, and he grabbed his arm, screaming. His face was contorted and red.

Emily said the first thing that popped into her head and instantly regretted it. "Damn it, Tommy, you haven't thrown a baseball in years. What the hell were you trying to prove?"

Rachel shot her mother an angry stare. Tommy bit his lip so hard that a pearl of blood formed and slipped onto his chin. Rachel rubbed it away with her hand.

"I'm sorry, honey," Tommy said to Rachel.

The old man at the counter, still chuckling, waved at Tommy. "Don't forget your prize." He held up a small stuffed pink pig, with black sunglasses, and tossed it to Tommy.

Tommy looked embarrassed as he handed it to Rachel, but Rachel held the pig as if it were even better than the grand prize. "I love it, Daddy," she said, and as he leaned down, she kissed him lightly on the lips.

It was as if Emily had been stabbed in

the heart. She was jealous, and she hated herself for it. "I guess it's time to go home," she said.

Rachel had other ideas. As they wandered away from the booth, the ride known as the Ejection Seat suddenly sprang to life in front of them, a circular chair of steel tossed like a rock from a slingshot, carrying two screaming passengers. A microphone embedded in the chair carried their hysterical cries out over the fair.

"Wow," Rachel said in a hushed voice. "Do you think I could do that?"

Emily interrupted. "I don't think that's a good idea, Rachel. Your father's not feeling well, and you're too young for a ride like that."

"You don't look too young to me," Tommy said. "And I feel great."

"Come on, Tommy, don't be foolish," Emily said.

Tommy winked at his daughter. "What do we say, Rachel?"

Rachel looked at her mother and sang out in her most girlish voice, "Bitch, bitch, bitch!"

Emily was stunned. She tugged on

Tommy's arm and whispered in his ear. "You taught her to say that to me? Are you crazy?"

"Shit, Emily, it's only a joke."

"Fine, take the fucking ride," she hissed, hating herself for letting Tommy get a rise out of her.

He pretended to be shocked. "Mommy used a bad word."

Rachel held Tommy's hand triumphantly. They headed together toward the ride, and then Rachel looked back. She called out, as if it were a wonderful joke, "Fuck you, Mommy."

Emily took two steps closer, swinging her hand back, ready to strike her. She wanted so badly to slap her daughter's face. But she froze, holding back. She began sobbing. She watched them wander away, paying no attention to her as she cried, drawing stares from the people passing by. She wiped her cheeks, then pushed through the crowd toward the spectator area near the Ejection Seat. She would do what she had done all along. Cheer for them. For the husband who made her feel like an insect, and for the daughter he had taught to hate her.

As they strapped Tommy and Rachel into the Ejection Seat, a spotlight hit them, and Emily could see their faces clearly.

Rachel was beaming, fearless as ever.

But Tommy was pale, his face bone white, sweat pouring down his forehead.

A horrifying awareness began to dawn on Emily, as she realized that Tommy's condition had nothing to do with the fair and nothing to do with a pulled muscle. Instead, it had everything to do with his father, who had dropped dead at thirty-seven, and his grandfather, who had only made it to age thirty before ending up in the ground.

"Don't ask me to grow up, Emily," he had said to her once in a sober moment.

"Wait!" Emily shouted, but no one heard her.

The sensations of the night became a blur. The din of music and voices thumped in her head. Lights blinked and whirled around her. She smelled burnt grease, powerful enough to suffocate her.

"He's having a heart attack!" she screamed, as loudly as she could.

The people around her laughed. It was a joke. It was funny.

Ping. The cable released. The Ejection Seat shot upward like an arrow. The towers rattled and swayed. The microphone in the chair caught Rachel's squeals of delight. Her excitement at being shot weightless into the air was almost sexual. The giggling laughter poured out of her and washed over the crowd.

Tommy never said a word.

Up and down the chair went, bouncing and wobbling like a jack-in-the-box for thirty seconds that lasted a lifetime. Then Emily heard murmurs among the people around her. She saw people start to point. Rachel's squeals subsided.

"Daddy?"

Emily could see her husband clearly now, his head lolling to one side, his eyes rolled up into his skull like two hard-boiled eggs, his tongue hanging limply out of his mouth. Rachel saw it, too, and screamed.

"Daddy. Wake up, Daddy."

Emily clambered over the fence that kept the spectators back. The ride work-

ers managed to snag the chair and pull it back to the ground. As Emily ran toward them, they undid the straps from Rachel, who clung to her father and cried hysterically. They undid the straps from Tommy, too, but he simply slid from the chair and crumpled in a pile on the ground, with Rachel still hanging on him and calling his name.

Emily knew at that moment she had passed a crossroads in her life. Part of her secret soul believed it would be a road to something better. In many ways, living with Tommy dead was easier than living with Tommy alive. She had always been the one holding a steady job and paying the bills. During the next few years, she began to pull them slowly out of debt.

But in the most important way, in her daughter's mind, Tommy never died. He became frozen in Rachel's memory.

It began the day after the fair, as they drove in cold silence back to Duluth. The tears on Rachel's face had dried, and her grief had turned with amazing swiftness to malevolence. At one point on the highway, the little girl turned to Emily, her eyes on fire, and said with a terrifying passion, "You did this."

Emily tried to explain. She tried to tell Rachel about Tommy's weak heart, but Rachel didn't want to hear anything.

"Daddy always said that if he died, it was you who killed him," she said.

So began the war.

Emily, lying in Rachel's bed, picked up the silly stuffed pig.

"Oh, sweetheart," she said. "What did I ever do to make you hate me so much? How can I make it up to you?"

5

Stride lived in an area known as Park Point, a crooked finger of land jutting out between the southern tip of the lake and the calm inner harbors of Duluth and Superior, Wisconsin. The peninsula was just wide enough to drop a strip of houses on either side of the road. There was only one way to get to the Point—across the lift bridge over the canal—which forced the people who lived there to structure their lives around the comings and goings of the ore ships.

He gave no thought to the bridge as he glided on autopilot, his eyes barely open, toward the Point at four in the morning. At first, when he heard the raucous warning bell, he thought his tired brain was playing tricks on him. He turned down the Sara Evans song on his stereo and listened. When he realized the bridge was really going up, he accelerated, but he knew he was too late. Disgusted, wondering how long he would be marooned, he pulled to a stop at the guardrail and shut off the engine.

He got out of the car, leaning on the door, letting the cold air wash over him. He reached back inside to the cup holder, found a new pack of cigarettes, and lit one. So much for willpower. He didn't care. Smoking, exhausted, listening to the groan of steel as the bridge climbed above him—this was his life. And it had been that way for the past year, ever since the cancer took Cindy away. The city that had always been his home, and that he assumed he would never leave, had begun to feel different to him, darker and more menacing. The familiar things, like the hulking lift bridge and the smell of the lake, now seemed consumed with memories.

Back in his youth, Duluth was a one-industry town, capital of the northern region of the state known, for good reason, as the Iron Range. It was a city where trillions of pellets of taconite belched into the hulls of giant ships, which sank low in the water and then shouldered their way through the cavernous troughs of Lake Superior toward the northeast. It was a hardscrabble, hard-luck city, filled with brawny miners and seamen like his dad.

He didn't recall that life was particularly good back then, but the city had a small-town feel, and people weathered the ups and downs of the ore industry together, living fat, living poor, working, striking. For nine months every year, until the lake froze, the rhythm of the ore industry governed the city. Trains came and went. Ships came and went. The bridge rose, and the bridge fell. The raw elements of steel that built skyscrapers, cars, and guns around the world began their journey under the clay soil in northern Minnesota and eventually traveled through the seaway in the holds of the great ships.

But the taconite industry waned, eaten up by overseas competition, and so did Duluth's fortunes. Ore couldn't pay the bills anymore. So the wise men who ran the city took a look at its location on the lake and said: Let the tourists come. The ore industry became a kind of tourist attraction itself, drawing gawkers to the bridge whenever a ship slid through the canal.

Not now, though. Not in the middle of the night. Stride stood alone, taking long drags on his cigarette, watching the rust-red hull creep under the bridge. He saw a man standing on the deck of the ship, also alone, also smoking. He was indistinguishable, little more than a silhouette. The man raised his hand to Stride in a casual greeting, and Stride returned it with a wave. That man could have been him, if his life had gone as he expected when he was younger.

He climbed back into his Bronco as the bridge settled back into place. As he drove across to the Point, hearing the bridge deck whine under his tires, he glanced at the ship, which was aglow and heading into the lake. A part of him went with it. That was true every time one of the ships left. It was partly why he lived where he did.

The residents of the Point were a hearty tribe who endured tourists, gales, storms, blizzards, and ice for the privilege of that handful of idyllic summer days on which no one on earth had a better place to live than they did. They shared a strip of beach that eroded an inch or two each year, with tufts of madras grass and mature trees separating the sand from the tiny backyards of the houses. Stride would often haul a lounge chair out past the madras on a Sunday in July, set it up on the beach, and sit for hours to watch the traffic of sailboats and cargo ships.

Most of the houses on the Point, except those few that had been torn down and re-built by wealthy transplants from the Cities, were old and ramshackle, constantly pum-meled and worn down by the elements. Stride slapped on paint each spring, using whatever was on sale, but it never lasted be-yond the winter season.

His house, a quarter mile from the bridge, was barely thirty feet wide, built in a square, with the door and two steps situated exactly in the middle. To the right of the door was the living room, with a window looking out the front. There was a detached one-car garage to the left of the house, at the end of a small stretch of sand that counted as a driveway.

Stride jiggled the key in the lock, then used his shoulder to push the door inward. He shut the door behind him and stood in the hallway, sinking back against the door, his eyes closed. He smelled the musty odor of aged wood and the lingering fishy aroma of Opilio crab legs he had steamed two nights ago. But there was more. Even a year after she was gone, he could still smell Cindy in the house. Maybe it was just that he had caught that same hint of perfume and floral soap for fifteen years, and his imagination remembered it so clearly that he could still picture it as real. In the early days, he had wanted to banish the smell from the house, and he had thrown open all the windows to let the lake air wash through. Then, when the aroma began to fade, he got scared, and he shut up the house for days for fear he might lose it altogether.

He stumbled sleepily down the hall to his bedroom and emptied his pockets on his nightstand. He yanked off his jacket and let it fall on the floor, then rolled into his unmade bed. His feet throbbed, and he didn't know if he had remembered to kick off his shoes. It didn't matter.

He closed his eyes, and she was there again, as he knew she would be. The dreams had faded in recent weeks, but tonight he expected to be tormented.

He stood on a highway somewhere in the

wilderness, with miles of birch trees lining the deserted road in both directions. Across the narrow strip of pavement, divided by a yellow line, stood Kerry McGrath. She beamed at him with a happy, carefree smile. Perspiration glinted on her face. She had been running, and her chest heaved as she sucked in deep breaths.

She waved at him, gesturing him to cross the road.

"Cindy," he shouted.

The smile on Kerry's face died. She turned and vanished, running between the trees. He tried to follow, hurrying down the slope behind the shoulder of the road and into the forest. His legs felt heavy. So did his left hand. When he looked down, he realized he was carrying a gun.

Somewhere, he heard a scream.

He stumbled along the trail, wiping sweat from his eyes. Or was it rain? Water seemed to filter down through the leaves, turning the trail into mud and matting his hair. Ahead of him, he saw a shadow pass across the trail, something large and menacing.

He tried to call Kerry's name again.

"Cindy."

Through the maze of trees, he realized someone was stopped, waiting for him.

It wasn't Kerry.

Rachel stood there, naked. She confronted him on the trail, her arms in the air, balanced against two birch trees, her legs spread casually apart. The rain fell in spatters on her body, dripping off her breasts and running in silver streams down her stomach and into the crevice between her legs.

"You'll never find me," she called to him.

Rachel turned and ran, and her body was enveloped by the forest. He could see her gliding away. Her body was beautiful, and he watched as it got smaller and farther away. Then, as before, a menacing shadow crossed the trail and disappeared.

He raised his gun. He called after Rachel.

"Cindy."

He made his way into a small clearing, where the dirt under his feet was mossy and wet. A stream gurgled toward the lake, but the water tumbling over the rocks was bright red. The crackling and rustling in the forest got louder, almost deafening, a thumping in his ears. The rain sheeted down, soaking him.

He saw Rachel on the opposite side of the clearing. "You'll never find me," she called again.

When he stared at the blurry image on the far side of the stream, he realized it was no longer Rachel who stood there.

It was Cindy. She stretched out her hands toward him.

He saw the shadow again, moving behind her. A monster.

"You never do," she told him.

Stride lay sprawled in bed with his head engulfed in his pillow. He was half asleep now, slowly growing aware of his surroundings. He heard the rustle of paper somewhere close by and smelled burnt coffee.

He opened one eye. Maggie Bei sat a few feet away in his leather recliner, her short legs propped up, a half-eaten cruller in one hand and one of Stride's chipped ceramic mugs in the other. She had opened the curtains halfway, enough to reveal the early morning view of the lake behind her.

"That coffeepot of yours stinks," she said. "What is it, ten years old?"

"Fifteen," Stride said. He blinked several times and didn't move. "What time is it?"

"Six in the morning."

"Still Monday?" Stride asked.

"Afraid so."

Stride groaned. He had been asleep for ninety minutes. It was obvious that Maggie, who was still wearing the same jeans and burgundy leather jacket she had worn last night, hadn't slept at all.

"Am I naked?" he asked.

Maggie grinned. "Yeah. Nice ass."

Stride pushed his head off the pillow and glanced behind him. He, too, was wearing the same clothes from last night. "I hope you made enough coffee for me."

Maggie pointed at his nightstand, where a chocolate old-fashioned doughnut lay neatly placed on a napkin. A steaming mug of coffee was beside it. Stride grabbed a bite of the doughnut and took a sip of coffee. He ran his hand back through mussed hair. He finished off the doughnut in two more bites, then began unbuttoning his shirt. He yanked the belt from his jeans.

"It gets ugly from here," he said.

"Don't I know it," Maggie replied. She continued calmly eating her breakfast.

"Yeah, you wish."

He joked, but Stride knew he was on sen-

sitive ground. He and Maggie had worked together as a team for seven years. She was a
Chinese immigrant whose vocal participa-
tion in political rallies during her student
days at the University of Minnesota had left
her without a home to which to return. When
Stride hired her right out of school, she
proved to be a quick study. In less than a
year, she knew the law better than he did,
and she had demonstrated her instincts
by seeing details in crime scenes—and
suspects—that most officers missed. Stride
had kept her at his side ever since.

The longer they worked together, the
more Maggie blossomed. She became fun-
nier, bolder, willing to laugh at herself. Her
face became expressive, not a somber
mask. She learned to speak English with no
hint of an accent and with a healthy sam-
pling of sarcasm and profanity.

Along the way, she fell in love with Stride.

It was Cindy who broke the news to him.
She had spotted Maggie's feelings immediately and warned him he was going to break
Maggie's heart into little pieces of Chinese
porcelain if he wasn't careful.

When Cindy was gone, Maggie made her
one and only play for his affections. Six

months ago, when Stride was at his loneliest, Maggie had let herself into his house on a frigid spring morning and slid into bed beside him. He had awakened and never seen so much love in another person's eyes. It was tempting, because he needed someone badly, and she was warm and willing.

But he remembered Cindy's warning, and he thought of those little pieces of Chinese porcelain, and he said no. Last month, she thanked him. He was right, she said; it would have destroyed their friendship and never worked as a romance. He wondered if she really believed that.

"How did you enjoy your visit with the Stoners?" Maggie asked.

Stride opened the bathroom door and continued undressing, then stepped into the shower, shivering as the cold water slowly warmed. He called back to Maggie.

"The mother says there's no chance of a suicide. What do you think?"

"Mothers never think there's any chance of suicide," Maggie said. "But I think if this girl wanted to blow herself away, she would have done it in front of them and made sure there was a lot of blood on their nice carpet."

Stride smiled. Maggie had pegged Rachel

already. This wasn't a girl who would slip away to die.

"How about Mommy and Stepdaddy?" Maggie called out. "You know the rule. Family first."

"They volunteered to take polygraphs," Stride replied. "But we have to run the questions through His Holiness Archie Gale."

He heard the sound of Maggie gagging. "Damn, I hate rich parents. Call the lawyer first, then the cops."

Stride grabbed a towel and used it to dry his damp hair, then rubbed it over his body. He wrapped it loosely around his waist and returned to his bedroom.

"We have to be careful," he said. "Check them both out, but be discreet. Graeme made it clear he knows K-2."

"Yeah, he told me that, too. Handball every week. I can't imagine K-2 playing handball. Not on a regulation court, anyway."

Stride laughed. K-2—Deputy Chief Kyle Kinnick—was no taller than Maggie. Even the mayor sometimes called him "the leprechaun."

"We got a hit on one of the ATM cameras," Maggie added. "We got a glimpse of her car zooming by shortly after ten o'clock."

"Score one for Kevin. Was she alone?"

"No one else is visible in the car."

Stride donned a pair of tan Dockers, buttoned up a white shirt, and shrugged into a navy sport coat.

"Come on, I need more coffee," he said.

Maggie followed him into the kitchen. Stride opened a window. The morning air smelled like frost, and he felt cold needles pricking his damp neck.

"Do you always need to open a window when it's freezing outside?" Maggie complained, shivering.

Stride poured coffee and sat down at the butcher-block kitchen table. He saw Maggie glance in the sink, which was half filled with dirty dishes. She pushed aside a stack of newspapers and three days of junk mail and cleared a small spot for her mug.

"You live like this?" she asked.

Stride shrugged. "What?"

"Nothing," Maggie said.

"Let's keep going," Stride said. "We think she made it home, because we've got her on tape heading there, and the car is parked right where it should be."

"Nothing strange in the car. We're running prints, but I wouldn't expect much."

"Next question is, did she go inside? How about her bedroom?"

Maggie shook her head. "We know what she was wearing that night. No clothes matching that description were found in her room. We talked with Emily about whether anything was missing. She wasn't much help. Even so, the drawers were full of clothes, and Rachel had lots of personal stuff in her desk. If she left by herself, she traveled light. She wasn't dressed for running, either—not like Kerry."

"How about a diary?" Stride asked. "I know, I'm dreaming."

"You're dreaming," Maggie said. "I checked her computer. Very few personal files. I loaded her Web browser to see if she might have been talking with some psycho on the Internet, but there was just some school-related stuff in her e-mail, and she hadn't bookmarked any weird Web sites. We'll run it through forensics, in case there's stuff we can recover."

"How about the neighbors?" Stride asked.

"A handful of people remember seeing folks out on the street that evening, but it was dark. Not many faces. A couple people saw teenage girls walking outside, but no one resembling Rachel. We had one report of an unknown car parked that night about four blocks away. The witness couldn't remember many details—dark, maybe blue or black, four-door sedan, might have been out-of-state plates. We checked with neighbors near where the car was seen. No one claimed it, and no one had visitors from out of state."

"Interesting," Stride said. "Except for a few thousand tourists in town."

"Right."

"How about the other ways of getting out of town? Any luck there?"

Maggie shook her head. "Nothing. There were no flights out of Duluth after ten o'clock on Friday until early Saturday morning. We'll be doing interviews with personnel at the airport this morning just in case. Ditto at the Greyhound station both here and in Wisconsin."

"She could have hiked down to the highway and hitched," Stride speculated.

"I thought of that. We've faxed her photo and info to police and highway patrols throughout the state and in the border states as well. Guppo has set up a page on our Web site. We're asking the state police to check in on fast food joints and gas stations along the interstate. The media is all over it, thanks to Bird Finch, which at least will get her photo in front of the whole region quickly."

Stride could imagine the phone ringing off the hook on the hotline. They had received nearly two thousand leads during the search for Kerry McGrath, placing the teenager everywhere from New Orleans to Fresno. With help from around the country, they had methodically sifted the leads by priority and tracked down each one. They all led back to the same place—nowhere.

"How about the pervs?"

Maggie sighed. "Five level-three sex offenders in the city. A few dozen ones and twos. We'll be paying a visit to each one."

"Okay." Stride felt a headache squeezing his temples. It wasn't just the lack of sleep, it was the bitter sameness. The disappearance. The search. The clues. He didn't know if he had the strength to do it all over again, or to face the possibility of another failure. This time, too, he would go through the hell alone. Without Cindy.

"Boss?" Maggie said, as he drifted away.

Stride smiled thinly. "I'm here. Look, if this

girl ran away voluntarily, she had to have help. She must have talked to someone. You direct the search today and keep me posted on the cell phone. I'll go to the school and check out her teachers and friends. Let's see if we can find out what made this girl tick."

6

Stride had been at the school for two hours, and he needed a cigarette.

It was an expensive habit the way he indulged it. He would buy a pack, smoke one or two cigarettes, then get angry at himself and throw away the rest. A day later, he would feel the craving again and buy another pack.

The high school was prominently labeled a tobacco-free zone. He saw an exit at the rear of the main foyer, tucked between rows of fire-engine red lockers, leading to the back of the school. Stride went through a set of doors and headed for an empty soccer field across the road. He passed a teachers' parking lot and wound along the side of a separate building labeled as a technical center.

Stride reached the corner of the building and stared down at the deserted field, which was filled incongruously with dozens of seagulls. He extracted a pack of cigarettes and a lighter, then slapped the pack until one cigarette jutted out from the others. He cupped his hands and tried to light it in the wind. It took several tries. Finally, the end of the cigarette smoldered, and he took a long drag. The smoke, filling his lungs, comforted him like an old friend. He relaxed, feeling some of the tightness escape. Then he coughed long and hard.

"Those things will kill you," a voice said behind him.

Stride felt guilty—a high school student again, caught smoking behind the school. He turned and saw an attractive blonde woman on a short set of gray steel steps leading up to the back door of the technical center. She, too, was holding a cigarette. Stride smiled at her, acknowledging their common vice.

"At least we'll die happy," he said. He took

a few steps closer, leaning against the railing by the stairs.

"I keep wondering whether it's better to smoke or be an alcoholic," the woman told him.

"Why not both?" Stride asked.

"I've thought about that. But I haven't committed to either one."

She was in her midthirties, with a red fleece jacket zipped to her neck and new, starched black slacks. She looked like an ex-cheerleader, with a trim body, athletic build, and short, layered blonde hair. Her eyes were pale blue. She had a pert face, up-turned nose, and cheeks that had flushed red in the cold air.

She looked familiar. Stride told her so.

"We met last year," she told him. "My name is Andrea. Andrea Jantzik. I'm a teacher here at the school. Kerry McGrath was one of my students. You interviewed me when you were investigating her disappear-ance."

"Was Rachel one of your students, too?"

Andrea shook her head. "I think she took biology, not chemistry. Peggy, the bio teacher, was telling me about her this morn-ing. I didn't know who Rachel was."

Stride dug in his pocket for the crumpled piece of paper the registrar had given him, with the listing of Rachel's classes and grades. "You didn't have her in an English class a year ago?"

"That would be Robin Jantzik. He teaches—taught—English here. But if you really want to talk to him, I'm afraid you'll have to look him up with his new wife in San Francisco."

"Husband?" Stride asked.

"Once upon a time."

"I'm sorry," Stride said. "Would it help if I told you that men are pigs?"

Andrea laughed. "Nothing I don't already know."

She had a cynical smile, which was like looking in a mirror. He recognized the walls she had built around herself, because he had done the same thing. He could see it in her face, too, as he looked closely: the frown lines creasing her lips, the deadness in her eyes, the heavy cake of makeup trying to freshen her skin. Loss had taken a toll on her, as it had on him.

"Is that when the cigarettes came back?" he asked, making a guess.

She looked surprised. "Is it that obvious?"

"I've been through something similar," he told her. "A year ago. That's when I started smoking again."

"I thought I had kicked it a year ago," Andrea said. "No such luck."

"Did your husband ever mention Rachel?"

Andrea shook her head. "No. English classes are huge."

"What about other teachers or students? Did you know anyone who might have been close to her?"

"You might want to talk to Nancy Carver. She's a part-time counselor here. She had a lot to say about Rachel this morning in the cafeteria."

"Like what?"

"She thought the search was a waste of time."

"Did she say why?" Stride asked.

Andrea shook her head.

"So this woman counseled Rachel?" Stride continued.

"I don't know. Nancy's not a permanent employee of the school. She's a professor up at the university and volunteers her time here working with troubled students. Girls, mostly."

"Does she have an office in the building?"

"More like a closet, really. It's on the second floor. But be forewarned. You carry a piece of equipment that Nancy doesn't exactly approve of."

Stride was puzzled. "A gun?"

"A penis."

Stride laughed, and Andrea giggled, and soon they were both laughing loud and hard. They stared at each other, enjoying the joke and feeling the subtle attraction that came with it. It almost felt strange to laugh. He couldn't recall how long it had been since he had relaxed enough to find humor in something. Or how long since he had shared it with a woman.

"At least you know what you're in for," Andrea said.

"Thanks. You've been very helpful, Ms. Jantzik."

"Call me Andrea," she said. "Or are you not allowed to do that?"

"I'm allowed. And call me Jonathan."

"You look more like a Jon to me."

"That works, too."

Stride hesitated and wasn't sure why. Then he realized that he felt an urge to say something else, to ask her to dinner, or to ask what her favorite color was, or to take the one strand of blonde hair that had fallen across her face and gently put it right. The power of the feeling suddenly overwhelmed him. Maybe it was because he had not felt even a glimmering like that in almost a year. He had been dead inside for so long that he wasn't sure what it felt like to wake up.

"Are you okay?" Andrea asked. Her face was concerned. It was a very pretty face, he realized.

"I'm fine. Thanks again."

He left her on the steps. The moment passed. But it never really passed.

Stride found Nancy Carver's office tucked into a cubbyhole, almost invisible from the corridor. When he poked his head around the wall, Stride saw a narrow door, with Nancy Carver's name etched onto a wooden block hung from a nail. The photos and brochures plastered all over the door were guaranteed to send school board members into hysterics.

There were magazine articles about the dangers of homophobia. Other articles, with graphic illustrations neatly scissored out, decried the prevalence of pornography. She had a brochure from last year's annual meeting of the American Society of Lesbian University Women, with her name highlighted, where she had been a speaker. There were also dozens of photographs of women in camping gear in the outdoors. Stride recognized the Black Hills and some wilderness waterfalls he guessed were in Canada. The photographs were mostly of teenage girls and young college-age women. The one exception, who appeared in most of the photographs, was a tiny, sturdily built woman around forty, with cropped berry-red hair and large, thick-rimmed black glasses. In most of the photos she wore the same outfit, a green fleece sweater and stonewashed blue jeans.

Stride studied each of the girls in the photographs closely but did not recognize Rachel—or Kerry—in any of them. He was vaguely disappointed.

Stride was about to rap his knuckles on the door when he heard faint noises from inside. Changing his mind, and wondering if the door was locked, he simply twisted the doorknob and pushed. The door fell inward, then thudded against a diagonal wall, leaving only a three-foot opening through which to squeeze into the office.

Stride's eyes painted the scene before the two people in the room could react. A teenager with a plump baby face and stringy blonde hair lay, eyes closed, in a ratty blue recliner that barely fit into the office. Nancy Carver stood behind the chair. Her spread fingertips massaged the girl's cheeks and forehead. Carver's eyes, too, were closed behind her glasses. As the door banged into the wall, their eyes flew open. Carver's hands flew away from the girl's skin as if it were on fire.

The girl in the chair didn't look at Stride but instead craned her neck and looked nervously back at Carver. Carver in turn stared at Stride with barely controlled fury.

"What the hell do you think you're doing, barging in here like that?" she demanded.

Stride adopted his most pleasant, apologetic demeanor. "I'm so sorry. I needed to talk to you, and I didn't realize you had someone with you."

The girl struggled to right the recliner and then to stand up. She didn't make eye contact with Stride. "I should get to class. Thanks a lot, Nancy."

Carver replied in a softer voice. "Sure, Sarah. I'll be back on Thursday."

Sarah grabbed a stack of books from Nancy Carver's desk. She clutched them to her chest and wedged uncomfortably past Stride. The girl wasted no time disappearing down the corridor.

Stride closed the door behind him. Carver remained frozen behind the old recliner, studying him as if he were an insect. Her glasses made her fierce brown eyes look larger than life. She was even smaller than the photographs made her look, but with a muscular physique.

"What do you want?" she asked.

"My name is Jonathan Stride," he began, but she cut him off with an impatient wave of her hand.

"Yes, yes, I know who you are. You're with the police, and you're investigating Rachel's disappearance, and you're taking up my time." She returned to her desk and sat down in a wooden Shaker chair. "Tell me something I don't know."

Stride looked around the tiny office. Carver's desk was standard school district issue, white laminate on aluminum legs. It was piled with hardcover books, most with obscure psychological titles, and manila folders overflowing with papers. The phone was stuck all over with little reminder notes. The chair, desk, and recliner were the only pieces of furniture in the office. The one item on the wall was a cork bulletin board, as crowded as her office door, with more articles and photographs.

Stride sat leisurely in the recliner and made himself comfortable. He extracted a notebook from his inside coat pocket, searched a few other pockets for a pen, then settled against the cushy backrest with a sigh. He flipped the notebook backward a few pages, glancing at the scribblings there and making an annoying clicking noise with his tongue. Finally, he looked up at Nancy Carver, who sat in her chair with all the patience of a ticking bomb.

"My partner tells me that I should get therapy," Stride said pleasantly. "Do all patients get the little face massage thing?"

Carver's face was etched in stone. "Sarah is not a patient."

"No? Too bad. I heard you were a doctor, but maybe I was wrong. Are you a massage therapist?"

"I have both a master's and a Ph.D. in psychology, Detective. I am a tenured professor at the University of Minnesota. But here, with these girls, I'm just Nancy."

"That's nice. So what was this with Sarah—a slumber party?"

"No," she said. "Not that it is any of your business, but Sarah has trouble sleeping. I was showing her relaxation techniques. That's all."

Stride nodded. "Relaxation is good. My partner tells me I should try that, too."

"Perhaps your partner should tell you to get to the point faster, Detective. Your little game is transparent and tedious, so why not just ask your questions and let me get back to my work?" For the first time, Nancy Carver smiled, without a trace of warmth.

Stride smiled back. "Game?"

"Game. See who can outshrink the other. Remember, I make a living at it. So let's be honest, shall we, Detective? In addition to whatever investigative conclusions you've jumped to, you've also already checked me out as a piece of meat. You've concluded that I'm not attractive enough to constitute a major loss to the heterosexual community. Nonetheless, you've noted that I have an athletic body, and based on my feisty attitude, you've figured that if you ever could get me into bed, I'd probably give you a pretty good ride. All of which leads you to fantasize about me making love to other women—and to wonder whether I'm having sex with any of the teenagers here. And you're hoping if you act flip and challenge my insecurities, you'll get me to spill some deep dark secret to you."

"That's amazing," Stride said. "Now tell me who's going to win the World Series."

Carver allowed herself another tight smile. "I'm right, am I not?"

"Well, since you brought it up, are you having sex with any of the teenagers here?"

"I do not have sex with underage persons, Detective," Carver said slowly, emphasizing each word.

"That's a good answer. It's not what I asked, but a good answer. I like the photographs on your door. You seem to take students on a lot of field trips."

"I call them feminist learning retreats."

"Do underage persons attend any of these retreats?"

"Of course. With parental permission."

"I was wondering whether Rachel ever accompanied you on one of these retreats."

"No, she didn't," Carver said.

"How about Kerry McGrath?"

"No, I never met Kerry. Are you suggesting I am in some way involved in their disappearances?"

Stride shook his head. "Not at all. I'm just looking for connections."

"And why not start with a lesbian activist, right?"

"It's amazing how you can read my mind. Did you ever counsel either of these girls?"

"I don't counsel people here, Detective."

"Well, since you've made it clear that you're not the school's massage therapist, what exactly is it you do if you're not a counselor?"

"I'm a mentor. Or simply a friend. There's no formal professional relationship involved."

"That's strange, isn't it?" Stride asked. "I mean, you have both a master's and a Ph.D. in psychology, and you're a tenured professor at the University of Minnesota, and I see a lot of books with 'ology' in the title on your desk."

"It's not strange at all, Detective. In fact, I could say that you're responsible for my being here."

"Me? How's that?"

Carver leaned forward on her desk, her hands neatly folded together, her huge brown eyes boring into him again. "Well, since you never did find Kerry McGrath, you left a lot of female students traumatized around this school."

Stride winced. "I'm not following you."

"Let me spell it out. After that girl disappeared last August, the school began to have a lot of trouble with the women here. Several of them were skipping classes, bursting into tears, engaging in self-destructive behavior. I offered my services as a volunteer counselor—not in a professional sense but as someone who could relate to them and talk to them about their fears. It's a measure of how worried the administration was that they didn't quibble about my politics or sexual preference but welcomed me with open arms. And I found I enjoyed working with the girls. So I made it into a permanent stint, two afternoons a week, and I've taken small groups on several retreats, too. I'm not their therapist, although my professional experience is certainly helpful. Mostly, I'm someone these women can talk to."

"Did you have a chance to become friends with Rachel?"

He watched her face, expecting a reaction. There was nothing, not a flinch, no attempt to hide anything, only the same level stare.

"I knew her," she said, still betraying nothing.

"How well?"

"We met occasionally. She was not one of my regular visitors. And as I mentioned, she never joined us on any of the retreats."

"Why did she come to see you?"

Carver paused. She stared calmly at Stride. "I'm not at liberty to say," she said finally.

"Why not?" Stride asked, annoyed. "You were quite adamant that these were not professional relationships, so privilege doesn't apply, does it?"

"Privilege would depend on how Rachel perceived the relationship and whether she considered me a therapist. But regardless, she told me certain things only with the condition that they remain strictly confidential between the two of us. I was to tell no one at all. And if I get a reputation as someone who betrays confidences, Detective, I can't be successful at anything I do in this field."

"But surely the situation is different now. The girl has disappeared. If something she said can help us find her, then you owe it to Rachel to tell us."

Carver shook her head. "I'm afraid that's not true at all."

"Dr. Carver, this girl could be in serious danger," Stride insisted.

"Detective, I know nothing whatsoever that could help you find her. Believe me."

"You were telling people at school today that you thought we would never find Rachel. Why? What makes you think that?"

"You didn't find Kerry," Carver replied.

"Do you have reason to think the two cases are related?"

"No, I didn't mean to imply that at all. I have no reason to think so."

"And yet you seem certain we won't find Rachel," Stride repeated.

"I'm not certain that she would want to be found," Carver said.

Stride's eyes narrowed. He pushed himself out of the recliner and leaned over the desk, with both hands gripping the edge. He towered over Carver, and he wanted her to feel every inch of his presence. "If you have information, Dr. Carver, I want to know what it is. Don't make me get a warrant for your arrest."

Carver didn't quaver. She met his eyes and glared at him. "Go ahead, Detective. You can't arrest me for speculations, and you can't make me tell you what I don't know. I told you before, and I'll tell you again. I don't know where Rachel is. I don't know what happened to her. I have no information that would help you find her."

"But you think she's alive," Stride said. "You think she left voluntarily."

"Here's what I think, Detective. In six months, Rachel Deese will be eighteen years old. At that point, even if you find her, you won't be able to bring her back."

Stride shook his head. "You're not helping her by staying silent. If she ran away—if she had reason to run away—I need to know it. Look, I've met her mother. I know what a battle royal it was between them all the time. But if she's on her own, alone, she could get into serious trouble. Do I have to tell you what it's like for most teenage runaways? How many end up homeless? How many get into prostitution?"

For a moment, he thought he might win. He saw an instant of weakness in Carver's eyes. She knew he was telling the truth. Then, like a mask, the steel came back down over her eyes.

"I'm sorry, Detective. I don't know anything that can help you. Whatever I told people, it's just my personal opinion."

"And that is?" Stride asked.

Carver shrugged. "Just like I said. You'll never find her."

7

Heather Hubble turned right off Highway 53 and onto a nondescript dirt road about ten miles northwest of Duluth. Her car rocked and bounced on the rutted surface. On the seat beside her, Lissa, her six-year-old daughter, rocked along with the car.

It was late Thursday afternoon. She wanted to take advantage of the waning light and the lengthening shadows for her photographs of the ruined barn. She had been waiting until the fall colors surrounding her were well past prime. The bright red leaves had turned to rust. The yellows were pale and greenish. Many of the leaves had already fallen and would be littering the field around the barn. That was perfect. The barn, too, was in the advanced stages of decay. The images in her photographs would reinforce each other.

"I like this road, Mommy," Lissa said, jumping up and down in her seat. "It's bouncy and it's pretty."

Lissa pushed her nose against the window, staring into the trees. There was a steady rain of dried leaves floating in the air.

"How much farther?" Lissa asked impatiently.

"It's not far now," Heather said.

They rounded a bend, and the barn loomed out of the field on the left side. It was beautiful and romantic in Heather's eyes; in reality it was a wreck, long since abandoned. Heather didn't imagine it would last another season, although she had thought that for several years. She assumed the weight of this year's snow would cave in the rest of the roof, which had already fallen through in several places, leaving jagged holes. The barn's red paint had faded, chipped, and peeled away. The windows had been broken in by teenagers throwing rocks. The entire frame seemed to list inward, the walls bowed and unsteady. She could probably come back in February and the barn would be no more than a snow-covered pile of splintered beams.

She pulled into the grassy, overgrown driveway, which wasn't a real driveway at all but had been worn down by the many visitors to the barn over the years. She parked and got out, and Lissa scrambled out, too.

"I don't think I've been to this place before, have I, Mommy?" Lissa asked.

"No, I don't think so. I think you've always been in school when I've come here."

"It's not in very good shape, is it?"

Heather laughed. "No, it's not."

"Can I look around?"

"Sure. But don't go inside the barn. It's not safe."

"It looks like the kind of place that could be haunted," Lissa said. "What do you think?"

"It might be," Heather told her.

"How do you know about this place?" Lissa asked.

Heather smiled. "I used to come out here when I was a teenager. A lot of us kids did."

"What did you do here?" Lissa asked.

"We just explored a lot. Like you."

There was no need to explain the real reason. Back then, she and dozens of other Duluth teenagers came out here to have sex. It was the hottest make-out spot in the county. It got so bad that there was even a secret sign-up sheet passed around school, to make sure there weren't too many people parked out behind the barn at any one time. Heather's first sexual experience had been out at the barn, in the back of a pickup truck, under the stars.

She wondered if today's students used the barn. There were still plenty of overlapping tire tracks leading around back. She also saw empty beer bottles littering the field. If she looked hard enough, she would probably find used condoms.

Heather looked down at Lissa again. "Don't you pick anything up, either."

Lissa frowned. "Well, that's no fun."

Heather softened. "You can pick up rocks and sticks, but no people things, okay? If you don't know what it is, don't touch it."

Lissa shrugged. "Okay."

Mother and daughter separated. Heather kept an eye on Lissa as she wandered into the brush. Satisfied that the girl was okay, Heather began scoping out her shot, tramping in the field to find an angle that satisfied her. When she settled on a location and began her setup, she saw Lissa dart behind the barn.

"Be careful back there," Heather shouted. Lissa called something in reply, which Heather couldn't hear.

She knelt down, looking through the camera's viewfinder, seeing the image in the frame take shape. The sun, behind her, was approaching the level of the tallest trees. Heather felt a jittery jumping in her stomach and a quiver in her fingers, the way she always did when she knew she was going to get exactly what she wanted. She took a few seconds to measure the light again and adjust the exposure. Then, ready at last, she squeezed the shutter, then again, and again, hearing the motorized whir as the film advanced each time.

"Mommy!" Lissa shouted from behind the barn. "Come look at this!"

"In a minute, sweetheart," Heather called back.

"Look, look, look," Lissa cried. She came running from behind the barn.

"Lissa, Mommy's busy now. What is it?"

"Look what I found. Isn't it pretty?"

Heather looked away from the camera long enough to notice Lissa holding a gold bracelet. "Where did you find that, sweetheart?"

"Behind the barn."

Heather frowned. "Didn't I tell you not to pick things up? People things?"

"Well, yes, but this is different," Lissa argued.

"How is it different?"

"It's not dangerous or anything. It's just a bracelet."

"Yes, and it's a bracelet that belongs to somebody else, who's probably going to come looking for it," Heather said. "Now put it back where you found it."

"You mean I can't keep it?"

Heather sighed. It was always this way with Lissa and jewelry. "No, you can't keep it. It belongs to someone else. Put it back right now."

"I don't think they'd want it anymore," Lissa complained. "It's all dirty."

"Well, then, why do you want it?"

Lissa didn't have an immediate answer. She thought about it. "I could clean it up," she said.

"And so could the person who owns it. Now no more arguing. Put it back."

Lissa gave up fighting and walked away unhappily, back toward the rear of the barn. Relieved, Heather turned her attention back to her camera. She looked through the viewfinder again.

Perfect.

Behind the barn, Lissa reluctantly put the bracelet back where she found it, which was in a muddy patch near the edge of the field. It didn't really seem fair, though. She didn't believe that anyone would be coming back for it.

"But Mommy said so," Lissa murmured to herself.

After putting it back, Lissa continued exploring. She already had a successful collection, including several interesting rocks and pretty blue flowers, all of which were stuffed in her coat pockets. She wasn't aware of time passing. It seemed only an instant later that she looked up and realized the sun had dipped below the trees.

Just then, she heard her mother calling. "Lissa, come on, it's time to go!"

For once, Lissa didn't need to be told twice. She started running out of the field toward the barn again. As she did, she had to pass right by the puddle, where the bracelet was.

"Lissa!" her mother called again.

Lissa thought about it. She really wanted that bracelet, and it was pretty careless of whoever owned it to leave it here. Besides, she could keep it and clean it up, and if the owner ever wanted it, she would be keeping it safe and sound. And she still thought maybe the person had simply thrown it away.

Mommy just didn't understand. She didn't like jewelry anyway.

Quickly, Lissa bent down, grabbed the bracelet, and crammed it deep into her pocket. "I'm coming," she called, and ran for the front of the barn.

PART TWO

8

Bird Finch paced the shadows of the studio, lifting his stiltlike legs over the cables stretched across the floor. No one talked to him. They had all learned long ago that Bird never said a word in the last few minutes before a live broadcast. He was too high. His emotions were churning. He was psyching himself up.

Tonight the ratings would be sky-high again.

After three weeks of courting them since Rachel's disappearance, he had landed the first live interview with Graeme and Emily Stoner. For the first time, they were ready to talk about losing their girl. And they wouldn't be alone. Joining them on the set was another grieving family, Mike and Barbara Mc-Grath, who had spent more than a year searching fruitlessly for their daughter Kerry. Two families would sit down with him, purge their emotions, and send the police a message.

There's a killer stalking the north shore and snatching teenagers off the street.

Find him.

Bird stopped and crossed his arms. On the brightly lit set, Graeme and Emily Stoner sat in comfortable chairs while two makeup artists fluttered around them, dabbing at their faces. He saw the McGraths walk up to the Stoners and watched the two families exchange awkward greetings.

"Two minutes," a voice on an overhead speaker announced.

Bird emerged out of the darkness of the studio and crossed the set with the grace of a large cat. He stood like a black tower over his guests, who stared up at him from their four chairs. He smiled at them, revealing paper-white teeth against his black skin. He grabbed each of their hands in turn in a crushing handshake.

"I want to thank all of you for joining me to-night," he told them in a sober, rumbling voice, which he reserved for victims. "I can only imagine how hard this is for each of you. But it's so very important that the rest of the people in this state hear your story. And, God willing, maybe your voices can reach out to your girls, or to whoever stole them away from you."

"That's very kind of you, Mr. Finch," Barbara McGrath said.

"Mr. and Mrs. Stoner, I will do everything I can to put you at ease," he said. "I don't want you thinking about the camera. Just talk to me. Tell me your story."

Bird squeezed his tall body into his usual chair. He rubbed one hand back over his shaved scalp and glanced at his suit to make sure his pockets, handkerchief, and cuffs were in place. He cleared his throat and draped one bent arm over the left side of the chair.

He gave his guests a last sympathetic smile. The red light went on.

"Good evening, ladies and gentlemen," Bird said. "I'm Jay Finch, and tonight I bring you a very special interview with two families from Duluth, Minnesota. These four people only met for the first time tonight, but they share a bond that brings them closer together as each day passes."

The camera backed up to reveal the Stoners and McGraths sitting across from Bird on the set.

"Fifteen months ago, Kerry McGrath, the daughter of Mike and Barbara McGrath, disappeared off the streets of Duluth. Three weeks ago tonight, Rachel Deese, daughter of Emily Stoner and stepdaughter of her husband, Graeme, suffered the same terrible fate. Two teenage girls who went to the same school and lived only a few miles apart. Both missing persons. We all pray for their safety, and we all fear for their lives."

Bird's voice hardened. "The police will not tell you these crimes are related. They say simply that both investigations are continuing, although they release no evidence to suggest they are any closer to solving these awful mysteries. Meanwhile, the families of Duluth face another night of uneasy sleep. Each time one of their girls goes off to school, they wonder if she will return home safely. Each time their daughter leaves them to visit a friend, they call to make sure she arrived on time. This is what fear does. This

is the price of not knowing. Because everyone in Duluth is whispering the same question: What happened?"

Bird focused his eyes into the camera, as
if he were standing in the living room of
every viewer.

"What happened? Is there a serial killer
stalking the young women of Duluth? Is
someone else in danger? Will a year pass
this time between crimes, or has the killer's
patience been exhausted? Is he back on the
street tonight, cruising in a lonely vehicle,
slowing down at each person he passes?"

The words burned on his tongue like sour
candy. He could feel the fear like a tangible
thing, and he knew he was spreading it
throughout the state. Bird didn't feel guilty.
They needed to be afraid.

"We don't know the answer to those questions," Bird said softly. "We don't know what
really happened on those two nights a little
over a year apart. God knows we all hope
that Kerry and Rachel are both safe somewhere and that in the very near future we will
see them back home with their parents. But
in the interim, the citizens of this state are
looking to the police for answers—answers
that are long overdue."

Bird turned to Barbara McGrath. "Now let's hear from the other victims of these crimes, the families who suffer and wonder. Mrs. McGrath, do you believe in your heart that Kerry is still alive?"

Emily heard the woman answer. She said the expected thing. Yes, Kerry was alive; she felt it keenly in her soul; she knew her girl was out there somewhere; she would never give up hope as long as Kerry was missing. Then this stranger next to her, Barbara Mc-Grath, turned and stared at the camera and spoke to it, pleaded with it.

"Kerry, if you're out there," Barbara said, "if you can hear this, I want you to know we love you. We think about you every single day. And we want you to come home to us."

With a sigh, her emotions overran her, and Barbara buried her face in her hands. Her husband leaned over, and Barbara let her head fall against his shoulder. His hand nestled in her black hair and caressed her gently.

Emily stared at them with a curious de-tachment. She felt far away. When she looked at Graeme, he was studying them, too, with an impenetrable expression on his face, devoid of emotion. She wondered if he was feeling what she felt—envy. She envied these people their pure, uncomplicated grief and their ability to find comfort and strength in each other. She had none of those things. That was why she had resisted the interview for so long, because she knew she would have to lie about so many things. She would have to say the expected things, even if she didn't feel them. She would say how much she missed Rachel, while wondering if she really did. She would hold Graeme's hand for support and feel nothing in his lifeless grip.

The only person who understood, who could help her, wasn't there.

Like a ghost, she felt herself floating above the set. She heard Bird Finch talking to her, his voice echoing from the end of a long tunnel.

"Mrs. Stoner, is there anything you want to tell Rachel?" Bird asked.

Emily stared at the camera and the red light glowing above it. She was frozen. It was as if she could really see Rachel, somewhere in the dark reflection of the lens, and as if Rachel could see her, too. She didn't understand what she was feeling now. The hostility had been an ache inside her for so long that she still didn't know how to live without it. Rachel was gone, and so was the bitter war. It was unimaginable that she could want it back.

Did she? Or was it really better this way?

There had been many times when she had wished that Rachel would disappear. She fantasized that her life would finally get better when the weight was lifted. Maybe she could have a marriage again. Maybe she could love her daughter better when she was gone.

What happened?

"Mrs. Stoner?" Bird asked.

Maybe she should tell them all the truth. If only they knew the secret, maybe they would leave her in peace. And the truth was that Rachel was evil.

Emily had been working two jobs in the years since Tommy died, grinding the debt down, climbing out of the hole in which he had buried them. From eight o'clock to five o'clock, she was a teller at the downtown branch of the Range Bank. Then she jumped in her car, hurried up Miller Hill, and sold romance novels and Playboy magazines from the bookstore

until the mall closed at nine. The world was a perpetual haze, in which she felt drugged by stress and sleeplessness.

The only bright spot in her life had arrived three weeks ago, when she brought home a West Highland terrier from the pound. After years of coming home to silence, or to Rachel's quiet hostility, it was refreshing to have the noise and playfulness of the dog filling the house. Originally, Emily had bought the dog with Rachel in mind, but Rachel ignored him, and Emily was the one to take him into the backyard at night to chase down the blue chew-toy she threw for him again and again.

That was when she made a surprising discovery. The little white dog, with its cropped legs and scruffy fur, had cracked her own facade. She realized she looked forward to coming home again. The dog welcomed her maniacally, as if she were the best, most important person on the planet. He slept in her lap and in bed with her. On the weekends, they walked together, the dog leading the way, tugging at the leash, pulling her up and down the streets.

Rachel didn't offer any names. So Emily called him Snowball. He was small, white, and fast, and his cold nose on her face in the morning felt like winter.

Driving home, even half asleep, she began to smile. Thinking of Snowball did that to her. Only when she thought of Rachel did the lines of worry creep back into her face and the smile fade into a weary frown. In the early days, after Tommy's death, she had taken Rachel to a psychologist, but the girl refused to return after a few sessions. Emily talked to her teachers. She talked to Dayton Tenby at church. They were all sympathetic, but no one had been able to reach her. As far as Rachel was concerned, the hurt of Tommy's death would never go away, and the only solace seemed to be to punish her mother over and over again.

Emily pulled the car into the narrow driveway of their tiny house, two stories with two bedrooms upstairs, with a yard that had long been neglected. The driveway had deep cracks with grass sprouting in tufts through the cement.

Inside, she expected to hear the thunder of paws as Snowball pounded to greet her.

"Snowball," she called. Emily listened for a distant bark, assuming that Rachel had banished the terrier to the backyard.

She continued down the hallway to the kitchen. Her stomach growled. She retrieved a plastic tub of cut broccoli from the refrigerator and munched a few florets. Emily heard her daughter clump down the stairs. Rachel joined her in the kitchen but didn't greet her. The girl tucked her sweatshirt underneath her, slumped in one of the kitchen chairs, and sifted out a Victoria's Secret catalog from the pile of mail. She reached into Emily's bucket and retrieved a piece of broccoli.

"Looking for a Wonderbra?" Emily asked, smiling. Rachel looked up and gave her mother an unpleasant stare. Emily was feeling tired enough not to care what she said.

Emily pushed her nose up against the back window. "It's getting cold," she said. "You shouldn't leave Snowball outside."

Rachel turned a page in the catalog.

"He's not outside. He got loose out front earlier."

"Loose? How?"

"He ran through my legs when I came home."

Emily realized she was frantic. "Well, did you look for him? Is he lost? I've got to go find him!"

Rachel glanced up from the catalog at Emily. "He ran into the street. A car hit him. Sorry."

Emily fell against the back door. Her hands flew up to her open mouth. A giant pit welled in her stomach, and she felt her chest heaving. Then the sting came to her eyes, and she sobbed uncontrollably, tears flooding down her cheeks and through her fingers. She bit her tongue and ran out of the kitchen. When she tried to suck air into her lungs, nothing happened. She staggered to the front door, tore it open, and fell against the porch railing. She hardly noticed the cold wind. Leaving the door open, she stumbled into the driveway, then felt her knees give way under her. She sank down on the cold pavement and leaned against the car, which was still warm. She closed her eyes.

Emily wasn't sure how long she lay crumpled in the driveway. By the time she thought to move, the car was cold again, and so was she. Her fingers were stiff. The tears had frozen into icy streaks on her face. It was only a dog, she told herself, but that didn't matter at all. At that moment, she felt worse than if she had come home and found that Rachel had been the one to die in the street.

She wandered aimlessly down the driveway. There was no evidence of the accident in the street. She slid back to her knees and stared vacantly ahead. She was so distracted, and the streetlight was so dim, that she barely saw the tiny thing nestled on the opposite curb. It was almost invisible, like a piece of junk that had fallen from a garbage can and been left there. She almost missed it, but something about it caught her eye and held it. Through her tears, a puzzled expression crept onto her face. Then the puzzlement turned to horror.

She knew what it was. But it couldn't be.

With a burst of strength, Emily pushed herself to her feet. She crossed the rest of the street hesitantly, not wanting to look into the gutter, but she couldn't tear her eyes away. Finally, she stood over it and shook her head, still not believing. Even when she bent down, picked the dirty thing off the street, and held it loosely in her hands, she wanted to be wrong.

Then her hand curled around it into a fist.

The grief subsided and became rage. She had never felt such basic hatred filling her soul. It wasn't just Snowball. It was years of cruelty coming to roost in a single crystallized moment. Emily trembled, almost washed away by the flood of anger inside her. Her jaw clenched. Her lips tightened into a thin line.

She screamed, dragging the name out into a wail. "Rachel!"

Emily sprinted back across the street, up the driveway, and into the house, slamming the door behind her with such ferocity that the whole frame of the house shook. She didn't care if the neighbors could hear. She kept bellowing her daughter's name. "Rachel!"

With deadly intent, she stormed into the kitchen, where Rachel was still calmly flipping pages in the Victoria's Secret catalog. The girl looked up, utterly unfazed by Emily's screams. She didn't say anything. She just waited.

"You did this!" Emily shouted in an agonized voice. "You did this!"

Emily stuck out her hand and uncurled her fingers, in which lay the grimy blue chew-toy that Snowball happily fetched on command. "He didn't get loose," Emily hissed. "You let him out in front. And then you tossed the toy for him when the car was coming. You killed him!"

"That's ridiculous," Rachel said.

"Don't give me that innocent shit," Emily exploded. "You killed him! You heartless fucking little bitch, you killed my dog!"

The years of restraint gave way. Emily bent down and yanked Rachel bodily out of the kitchen chalr. She swung her arm back and slapped the girl fiercely across the face. "You killed him!" she screamed

again, and then hit Rachel again, harder.
"How could you do this to me?"

She hit her again.

And again. And again.

Rachel's cheek was beet red and
streaked with the imprint of Emily's fingers. Blood trickled from her lip. She
didn't fight back. She stood there, her
eyes cold and calm, not flinching as each
blow pounded her face. She absorbed
the punishment until Emily finally ran out
of fury. Emily staggered backward, staring at her daughter, then turned away and
buried her face in her hands. The room
was suddenly quiet again.

Emily nursed one hand in the other.
She felt Rachel's eyes boring into her
back. Then, without another word, her
daughter stalked out of the kitchen. She
heard Rachel climb the stairs, then heard
the clanging of pipes as she ran water in
the bathroom.

It was the one thing Emily had sworn
to herself she would never do, no matter
how bad things got between them.

And she had done it.

* * *

"Mrs. Stoner?" Bird Finch repeated. "Is there anything you'd like to tell Rachel right now?"

Emily stared hollowly into the camera. Tears filled her eyes and burst onto her cheeks. To everyone watching on television, it was the pain of a mother faced with the ultimate agony—the loss of a child. They didn't need to know the truth.

"I guess I'd tell her I'm sorry," Emily said.

9

Stride sat alone in his basement cubicle at city hall on Friday night. The chrome desk lamp cast a small circle of light over the files he was trying to read. He had returned to his office in order to catch up on paperwork and review reports on the other crimes that had occurred in the weeks since Rachel disappeared. Most were straightforward domestic disputes, auto thefts, retail break-ins—the kind of investigations he could delegate to the seven sergeants he supervised. But the sheer volume was catching up with him. He couldn't see the pockmarked wood of his desk underneath the files and papers.

The downstairs headquarters of the Detective Bureau was quiet. His team had gone home. Stride liked it here at night, when the silence was complete and the phone didn't ring. He only had to worry about the buzzing of his pager, like a mosquito biting him to alert him to bad things happening in the city. He didn't spend much time in his office during the day. The bureau was small, and he had to share the weight of serious investigations himself. That was fine. He liked being in the field, doing the real work. He squeezed in the administrative half of his job at odd hours when he wouldn't be interrupted.

The city didn't pay for plush quarters anyway. The foam tiles over his head were water-stained from the many times that pipes had leaked and dripped down onto his desk. The industrial gray carpet carried a faint aroma of mildew. His cubicle was large enough to squeeze in a visitor's chair, which was the only real difference between a lieutenant's office and a sergeant's office. Stride didn't bother personalizing his space with posters and family photos the way most of his team did. He had only one old picture of Cindy tacked to the cork bulletin board, and even that photo was half covered by the latest advisories from Homeland Security. It was a messy, cold place, and he was happy to escape from it whenever he could.

He heard the ding of the elevator a few feet away. That rarely happened at night. It meant someone from above, in the real city offices, was coming downstairs. He waited for the doors to open and recognized K-2's dwarflike silhouette.

"Evening, Jon," Deputy Chief Kyle Kinnick said in a reedy voice.

K-2 used an open toed walk and strolled through the open door of Stride's cubicle. He looked down, frowning, at the pile of papers in the empty chair. Stride apologized and moved the stack to the floor so the chief could sit down.

"So you think she's dead?" Kinnick asked, cutting straight to the point.

"That's the way it looks," Stride said. There was no point in sugarcoating what both men knew. "Nine out of ten don't come back alive at this point."

Kinnick yanked on the knot of his tie. He was dressed in a charcoal suit, which was baggy on his tiny frame, and looked as if he were just coming from a city council meeting. "Shit. The mayor's not happy about this,

you know. We're getting queries from the national press. Dateline. They want to know if
this is a serial killer story, something they
can run with."

"There's no evidence of that."

"Well, since when did evidence mean a
damn thing to these people?" Kinnick war-
bled. He dug a finger in one of his ears. They
flapped from the side of his small head like
cabbage leaves.

Stride smiled. He was remembering the
leprechaun parody of K-2 that Maggie did at
a bureau party the previous St. Patrick's Day.

"This funny to you?" Kinnick asked.

"No, sir. Sorry. You don't have to tell me
about the media. Bird's all over me."

Kinnick snorted. He was gruff with his
lieutenants and an easy mark for jokes, but
Stride liked him. K-2 was an administrative
cop, not a field detective, but he defended
his department fiercely with city officials, and
he made a point of meeting with every interest group in the city, from kindergarten
classes to the Rotary, to talk up the police
force. He was loyal to his team, and that
went a long way with Stride.

"You realize we don't have a lot of time
here?" Kinnick asked. He kicked his black

wingtip in the direction of Stride's overflowing desk. "You're doing way too much work on this yourself already."

Stride knew there was no point in reminding the chief that he had been the one to ask Stride to lead the case personally. It was all political and bureaucratic calculation with K-2. The city wanted this to go away—fast. "The perps are cooperating," Stride said. "There's nothing big here that needs me."

"And we both know that we're already outside the zone on this one. Odds are it's not going to clear. I'm going to have to pull you and Maggie. Give the lead to Guppo. He can take this going forward. If we find something, you're back in."

"That'll just give more ammo to Bird," Stride protested. "It's too soon. Give us a few more weeks. We don't want to look like we're walking away from the investigation."

"You think I like this?" Kinnick asked. He scratched his forehead and patted down the gray hair that stretched across his skull from one big ear to the other. "Stoner's a friend of mine. But you're not making any headway."

"I need another three weeks. You said yourself, the mayor's hot on this one. If we don't have anything by then, I agree, it's a cold case. Guppo can take the lead. He's already got Kerry."

Kinnick shook his head and frowned. He sighed as if he were making an enormous concession. "Two weeks. And if we get anything else in here, I pull you early. Got it?"

Stride nodded. "I appreciate that. Thank you, sir."

The chief pushed himself out of the chair and wandered back to the elevator without saying anything more. The doors opened immediately and swallowed him up. The machinery hummed as it returned to the fourth floor.

Stride took a deep breath. He knew how it worked. K-2 hadn't come down here to pull him off the case. It was too soon for that. But he wanted Stride to know that the clock was ticking.

"What should I do?" Maggie asked. She stared down at three cards, adding up to twelve. The dealer's up card was a six.

Stride propped his cigarette in an ashtray, where its smoke curled up and merged into the gray cloud hovering over the blackjack tables. The haze clung to the low ceiling. When he inhaled, he tasted stale smoke. His eyes burned, partly from the unventilated air and partly because it was now after midnight, more than eighteen hours after his day began. He had stayed at city hall until Maggie called and threatened to haul him out by force.

"Stand," Stride said.

"But I'm only at twelve. I think I should take a card."

Stride shook his head. "Odds are the dealer's got a ten. He'll have to draw at sixteen, and he's likely to bust. Stand."

"Hit me," Maggie said. The dealer slapped a king of hearts on the table. "Shit."

Stride waved a hand over his cards, which showed fourteen. The dealer flipped his hole card, which was a jack, then dealt another card to his hand. It was a ten.

"Asshole," Maggie said.

Stride laughed as the dealer added two more chips to his stack.

The tiny casino reeked of sweat, collecting on the skin of a hundred people crammed into its claustrophobic quarters. Most were dressed in flannel for the winter night but sweltering in the heat generated by bodies and machines. It was close and loud. The slots pinged with electronic noises and the clatter of coins plinking into the trays. The room burbled with conversation and the occasional scream as a jackpot hit.

They had been playing for almost an hour, and he was up forty dollars. Maggie was down twenty. He took two chips and slid them into the betting area.

"You're winning," Maggie said. "Why not let it ride? If you bet more, you'll win more. You always bet two dollars every single time, even when you're on a streak." Maggie made a face, then clucked like a chicken. She took ten chips and dropped them on the table in front of her. "No guts, Stride."

"Big talk from a gal who's losing her shirt."

"Don't tempt me," she said, winking.

All day long they had reinterviewed people who knew Rachel. The late-night jaunt to the casino was a way to forget the case that had obsessed them for three weeks. But they couldn't escape. Bird Finch's interview showed up on the television suspended over the bar. They didn't need to hear the sound. It was bad enough to read Bird's angry body language.

"Maybe Bird is right," Maggie grudgingly acknowledged. "Maybe we have a serial."

Stride glanced at Maggie out of the corner

of his eye. Then he shook his head, not convinced. "The two just don't feel the same."

"Don't they? Or do you not want them to be the same? We've got two teenage girls who lived within a couple miles of each other, both disappearing without a trace."

"The method doesn't feel right," Stride said. "We both agree that Kerry was either a stranger perv or a hit-and-run, right?"

Maggie nodded. "Except I don't really buy the hit-and-run. They just run, they don't hide the body. I think someone grabbed her."

"Fair enough. That's what I think, too. But can you imagine the same guy stalking the inner streets of Duluth, where he can be seen from dozens of houses? It just doesn't feel right. A stranger's going to look for opportunities, a girl alone in the middle of nowhere. He's not going to drive up and down residential streets. The risk is too great."

The blackjack dealer, who sported long black hair and a wimpy mustache, assessed them nervously. He caught Stride's eye, then pasted a sober expression on his face and kept dealing cards.

"So it's just coincidence?" Maggie asked.

Stride shrugged. "We're not a small town

anymore. Shit like this happens. My bet is that whoever stalked Kerry isn't still in the state. And Rachel—the more I see of this case, the more I feel like the answer's at home."

"Emily and Graeme both passed the polygraphs," Maggie reminded him. "And the background checks came up clean."

"I don't care," Stride said. "There's something in that triangle that smells like trouble. You've got Emily and Rachel at each other's throats and Graeme walking into the middle of it. I want to know why—and what happened."

"We could get some heat about this," Maggie said. "If we push the family too hard without any evidence, what's K-2 going to say?"

"K-2 wants answers. Let's talk to the minister again. Dayton Tenby. Someone had to know what was going on inside that house."

"Okay. That's fair." Maggie pumped her hand as she landed another blackjack. She took a careful sip from her drink, avoiding the pineapple slice and frowning as the umbrella kept bumping her face.

"Hello, Detective."

Stride didn't know where the voice came from. It was suspended somewhere in the noise of the casino, yet close by, like a faint strain of music. He wheeled around to look behind him.

A woman stood there smiling at him. She wore a thigh-length black leather coat with a belt tied at the waist. Her blonde hair was wind-tossed. Her cheeks were flushed.

"It's Andrea," she said. "Remember me? From the school?"

"Sure," he said awkwardly, coming out of his trance. "I remember."

Maggie shifted in her chair and stared at both of them. She caught Stride's eye and cleared her throat conspicuously. Stride realized that he hadn't introduced her, and he saw, too, that Andrea suddenly realized that Maggie and Stride were together. She instinctively took a step backward, not wanting to intrude.

"I'm sorry," Stride said. "Andrea, this is my partner, Maggie Bei. We decided to play a few hands to unwind after pounding the pavement all day. Maggie, this is Andrea Jantzik. She teaches at Duluth High."

"Charmed," Maggie said slyly. "Why don't you join us? Take third base. Let Stride here teach you all he knows about blackjack, which is how to win and not have fun."

Andrea smiled and shook her head. "Oh, no, I don't want to intrude."

"You're not intruding at all." Maggie hesitated and concluded that subtlety wasn't working. "I'm just his partner in crime. That's all."

"Oh," Andrea said. She repeated, "Oh."

"In fact," Maggie said, "I think I'm going to try my hand at the slots. There's one here called the Big Pig, and it's supposed to oink when you hit the jackpot. I'd like to hear that. So why don't you take my place?"

"Are you sure?" Andrea asked.

Maggie was already out of her chair and guiding Andrea forcefully into it. She finished off her drink in two loud gulps, then took the umbrella and put it in her pocket. She waved at both of them. "Have fun, you two. I'll call you tomorrow, boss."

Stride nodded at her, smiling sarcastically. "Thanks, Mags."

Maggie gave him a broad wink while Andrea was settling into the chair next to Stride. Then, before she walked away, Maggie leaned over and whispered in his ear.

"She wants you, boss," Maggie said. "Don't blow it."

10

Andrea slipped her leather coat off her shoulders and draped it over the nearest stool. She was dressed to kill. Her black skirt strained to cover her thighs. Her legs were athletically curved and sleek under black stockings. She wore a pink satin blouse, which glinted under the casino lights. The top two buttons were undone, revealing a hint of bare skin that swelled as she breathed. Her makeup was impeccable and had obviously taken time to apply, from the pale gloss on her lips to the delicate streak of eyeliner above her long, light lashes. A thin gold chain graced her neck, and she wore sparkling sapphire earrings that accented her eyes.

It was a vampish look, full of invitation, but Stride realized that Andrea simply couldn't pull it off. She was uncomfortable. She tugged at her skirt, trying in vain to pull it farther over her legs. Her smile was shy and awkward, not at all confident. She played with her necklace, twisting it between her fingers, doing everything possible to avoid looking directly at him.

He realized she was nervous and didn't know what to say. Neither did he. It had been a long time since he had been on his own, dancing the delicate dance with the opposite sex. He tried to remember what it was like, but he had been with Cindy for so long that he couldn't remember anything that sounded clever. The last time he had dated was in high school, and he assumed that nothing he had said then would sound clever now.

Finally, the dealer coughed and gestured at the cards.

"Do you play?" Stride asked.

Andrea shook her head. "I'm afraid not."

"Do you prefer the slots?"

"Well, to be honest, I've never gambled," Andrea admitted. She turned and very briefly met his eyes. "Sometimes I'd come here or go to Black Bear with Robin, but I always watched him. I never played myself. This is my first real visit."

Stride saw the dealer sigh.

"Why did you come?" Stride asked.

Andrea nodded her head in the direction of the nearest row of slots. Stride turned and saw two women, pretending to play but obviously more interested in observing them at the blackjack table. The women were whispering and smiling. He recognized one as another teacher from the high school.

"My cheering section," Andrea explained. "They told me that it was Friday night, and as an eligible divorcée, I needed to strut my stuff in public. And I guess this is about as close as Duluth gets to a hot nightspot if you're over thirty."

"Well, I'm glad they did," Stride said.

"Yeah," Andrea said. "Yeah, I guess I am, too."

"Do you want to play?" Stride asked. "I'd be happy to help you lose some of your money."

Andrea shook her head. "The noise is giving me a headache."

"Would you like to go somewhere?" Stride

asked. "I know a place by the water that serves the best margaritas in town."

"What about your partner?"

Stride smiled. "Mags can take a cab."

Stride glanced at his watch. It was almost one-thirty in the morning. They drove down into Canal Park; the parking lots of the bars and restaurants were still jammed with cars. He steered onto the street that led across the canal bridge.

"I don't recall any good bars on the Point," she said.

Stride glanced at her, embarrassed. "Well, actually, I'm the one who makes the best margaritas," he said. "And my place is on the water."

"Oh," Andrea said. He sensed her sudden hesitation.

"I'm sorry, I guess I should have explained. Look, I don't have any intentions here. You said you hated noise, and my porch is quiet, except for the waves. But we can go somewhere else."

Andrea glanced out the window. "No, it's okay. I'm with a cop, right? If you get fresh, I can always call—well, you." She laughed, comfortable again.

"Are you sure?"

"I'm sure. But those margaritas better be good."

He reached his house a few blocks after the bridge and pulled into the strip of sand that counted as a driveway. When they got out, the street was still and dark. Andrea studied Stride's tiny house and the jumble of skeletal bushes out front with a puzzled smile.

"I can't believe you live on the Point," she said.

"I can't imagine living anywhere else. Why?"

"It's so rough out here. The storms must be brutal."

"They are," he admitted.

"You must get buried in snow."

"Sometimes the drifts go up to the roof."

"Doesn't it scare you? I think I'd feel like the lake was going to swallow me up."

He leaned across the roof of the car and stared at her thoughtfully. "I know it sounds crazy, but sometimes I think the storms are my favorite part. They're the reason I'm here."

"I don't understand," Andrea said, confused. She shivered as a gust of wind blew past them.

"Let's go inside."

He put an arm around her to warm her as they walked toward the door. She let her body drift against his, and it felt good. He could feel her shoulder through the sleeve of her leather coat and feel her hair brush against his face. He let go long enough to fumble for his key. Andrea wrapped her arms around herself.

He let them inside. The hallway was dark and warm. He heard the ticking of the grandfather clock. They lingered silently together after Stride closed the door. He realized now that Andrea was wearing perfume, something soft, like rosewater. It was strange to catch the aroma of a different woman's perfume inside his house.

"What did you mean about the storms, Jon?"

Stride took her coat and hung it inside the closet. In her skimpy outfit, she was obviously still cold. He hung his own coat up and closed the closet door. He rested his back against it. Andrea was watching him, although they were both barely more than shadows in the hallway.

"It's like time hangs there suspended," Stride said finally. "Like I can get sucked inside the storm and see anything or anyone. There are times, I swear, I've heard my father. Once I thought I could see him."

"Your father?"

"He worked on one of the ore ships. He was washed off the deck in a December storm when I was fourteen."

Andrea shook her head. "I'm so sorry."

Stride nodded quietly. "You still look cold."

"I guess this was a stupid outfit, huh?"

"It's beautiful," Stride said. He felt an urge to take her in his arms and kiss her, but he resisted.

"That's sweet. But yes, I'm cold."

"You want a sweatshirt and jeans to put on? I'm afraid that's the height of fashion in this house."

"Oh, I'll be okay. It's warm inside."

Stride smiled. "But I was going to suggest we sit on the porch."

"The porch?"

"It's enclosed, and I've got a couple good space heaters."

"I'm going to freeze my ass off, Jon," Andrea said.

"That would be a shame, because it's a very cute ass."

Even in the darkness, he felt her blush.

They walked into the kitchen. Both of them blinked as Stride turned on the light. He realized to his dismay that the last three weeks of the investigation had left his house in chaos, particularly the sink, which was stacked with dishes. The dinette hadn't been cleared in at least two days. In addition to dirty glasses and plates crusted over with the remains of spaghetti, stacks of research notes littered the table.

"Nice," Andrea said, smiling.

"Yeah, I'm sorry about this. I'm not used to having my house visitor friendly. Except for Maggie, who doesn't care. She lords it over me. I guess I should have thought of this before I asked you over here."

"Don't worry about it."

"The porch is clean, I promise. Let me grab you a blanket. You can warm your toes by the space heater, curl up under the blanket, and I'll get you plenty drunk with the strongest margarita you've ever had."

"Deal," Andrea said.

* * *

When the pitcher of margaritas was half empty, they barely noticed the cold anymore.

Andrea lay propped in a wicker chaise, her stocking feet poking out from under a multicolored Spanish blanket. A space heater glowed in front of the chaise, warming her toes. The blanket bunched at her waist. Above it, she wore only her silk blouse. From time to time, she rubbed the gooseflesh on her bare forearms. For the first hour, she had kept the blanket tucked under her chin, but eventually she let it slip down.

She held a bowl glass in her hand. Every minute or two, she extended her tongue to lick a trace of salt from the rim, then took a swallow of the green drink. Despite the dim light, Stride could see her do this, and something about the glimpse of her tongue on the glass was very arousing. He watched her from his own chaise a few inches away.

The porch was nearly dark. A faint glow from the house lights behind them cast shadows. Where the frost had not crept onto the glass, they could see through the tall windows to the inky darkness of the lake, illuminated only by a handful of stars and a half moon giving off a pale glow. For long minutes, they lay next to each other. It was late, but they were wide awake, keenly attuned to the sounds around them: the crash of waves, the hum of the space heater, the in and out of their breathing. Their conversation came in fits and spurts between stretches of silence.

"You're pretty calm about the divorce," Stride said. "Is that an act?"

She stared at him. "Yeah."

A few streaks of water appeared on the windows. Stride could see texture in the rain, a light mix of sleet and snow. They heard the patter increasing on the wooden roof above their heads and the whip of wind against the house. The frame rumbled. He reached for the pitcher of margaritas and refilled their glasses.

Andrea swirled the ice in her drink. A sad smile crossed her lips.

"I had to visit my sister in Miami. Denise had just had a baby. I got back, and there was a note. He needed some time alone, he said. To write. To 'find himself creatively' again. He never had the courage to call me. Not once. Just postcards. Goddamn postcards, for the whole world to see. Next thing I know, he's in Yellowstone. Then Seattle.

He's still writing great stuff. But somewhere along the way, he's realized that he just can't be himself around me anymore. That I'm stifling his genius. So maybe it's better if we call it quits."

"Shit," Stride murmured.

"It took five weeks and ten postcards for Robin to officially declare our marriage over and tell me he'd met someone else in San Francisco. On the back was a photo of the fucking Golden Gate Bridge."

"I'm sorry," Stride said.

"That's okay. I don't miss him so much as I hate being alone."

"It's the little things I miss," Stride murmured. "I'm cold in the mornings. Sometimes I wake up and try to roll over to get close to Cindy, like I used to. She'd always complain about my cold hands, but she was like a heater warming me up. But she's not there anymore. So I lie there freezing."

He heard his words die away. He was aware of the lingering silence. Without Andrea asking, he knew she wanted him to tell her more. Earlier, in a passing comment, he had mentioned Cindy's death, not going into detail, not wanting to cast her shadow over their evening. Andrea reacted with shock and grief, but like everyone else, she had no idea what to say or how to comfort him.

Even one little detail, a memory of warming up next to her in bed, made him want to tell all his stories. But he was stubbornly silent.

It was now actively snowing outside. The streaks of ice, slowly slipping down the window glass, obscured the view. Stride glanced at the Parsons table next to the chaise and realized the pitcher of margaritas was empty. He glanced at his watch but couldn't read the time in the shadows.

"You have succeeded," Andrea declared finally.

"At what?"

"I am now drunk. Thank you."

Stride nodded. "You're welcome."

Andrea looked over at him. Or he thought she did. He could barely see her.

"Tell me something," she said. "Do you want to fuck me?"

It was the kind of question that called for an immediate answer, although this was the first time since Cindy died that Stride had faced it. He knew what half a pitcher of margaritas and his stiffening crotch told him to do, but he still felt unfaithful. "Yes, I do."

"But?" she said, hearing it in his voice.

"But I'm drunk, and I don't know if I can, uh, rise to the occasion."

"You're a liar."

"Yeah."

"You haven't had sex since she died."

"Nope."

Andrea slid out of the wicker chair. She staggered to her feet. "Tough," she said.

Stride didn't move. He watched her hike up her skirt and yank down the black stockings and floral panties underneath. She peeled them off and tossed them aside. She was a real blonde, with a wispy patch of pubic hair nestling between her slim thighs. With clumsy fingers, she undid the buttons of her blouse, then unsnapped the bra inside. She pushed aside the fabric, exposing her small breasts with erect pink nipples.

Andrea bent over him and yanked down the zipper of his jeans. Her fingers squirmed inside his pants and found his erection.

"Looks like you rose to the occasion."

"Looks like it."

She extracted his penis with some difficulty. In one swift motion, she swung her leg over the chaise and straddled him. Using one hand to spread her vaginal lips, and the other to hold his cock, she lowered herself onto him. Stride felt his penis sinking into her wet folds, and he groaned.

"You like?"

"I like."

"Good."

He reached up to her breasts and caressed her nipples with his fingertips.

"Harder," she said.

He pinched them, then squeezed her whole breasts in his large hands. Andrea gave a loud shout of pleasure and sank forward, kissing him, forcing her tongue inside. Her buttocks rose and fell as she pumped up and down on top of him. Stride squeezed his hand onto her mound and found her clitoris and began to rub it in circles.

The porch creaked and whined. So did the chaise, complaining under the pounding of their combined weight.

Stride felt himself swelling. She was bringing him quickly to a marvelous, drunken orgasm. And it looked like she was having one, too. Her head rose back, and she had a wild smile on her face. Stride leaned forward and took her nipple in his mouth. She held his head tightly against her breast. He licked and tugged at the nipple, and the feel of her erect areola on his tongue sent him over the edge. Stride's hips rose up to meet her as he spasmed. He came with his mouth still closed over her breast. Strangely, Andrea started laughing.

"God," she murmured, half to herself. "And the bastard said I was cold in bed."

11

"Well?" Maggie asked.

She kicked the snow off her boots on the floor mat of Stride's truck, then folded her arms and stared at him expectantly.

"What?" Stride asked, smiling despite himself.

Maggie whooped. She punched Stride in the arm. "I know that smile," she said, beaming. "That's the smile of a man who got lucky last night. Did I tell you? Was I right?"

"Mags, give me a break."

"Come on, boss, details, details," Maggie insisted.

"All right, all right. We stayed up late, we

got drunk, we ended up in bed. It was great. Are you satisfied?"

"No, but you obviously are."

Stride shot her an irritated glance, then swung the truck out of the parking lot at Maggie's building. The tires slipped on the fresh snow. Only a couple of inches of heavy, wet snow had fallen overnight, enough to make the roads treacherous but not enough to get the snowplows out of the garage. Stride blinked. His eyes were red.

"So how do you feel?" Maggie asked.

Stride clenched the wheel a little tighter and fluttered the brake as he edged up to a stop sign. "Guilty as hell, if you must know."

"Look, you're not cheating on Cindy," Maggie said. "She'd have been pissed off that you waited this long."

"I know," Stride acknowledged. "That's what I've been telling myself. But my heart doesn't really believe it."

In fact, he had dreamed of Cindy, and then, when he had awakened and felt a warm presence next to him for the first time in a year, he had enjoyed a brief moment when he thought it really was Cindy beside him. In his drowsy state, he believed that the tragedy of the past year had been the real dream and that life was still sweet and normal. Then he saw Andrea, and he felt a twinge of sorrow. It wasn't fair. Andrea was pretty and sweet. Her naked body, half exposed above the blanket, was arousing to him. But he had to blink back tears.

"It was your first time," Maggie said. "You're back on the playing field. The more you date, the more comfortable you'll get."

"Maybe. Andrea and I are getting together again tomorrow night."

Maggie smiled slyly. "Oh, yes? I get it. Once you take the gun out of the holster, you can't stop firing, huh?"

Stride shot her a sideways glance. "You're crude, Mags. Who taught you to be so crude?"

"You did."

"Yeah, yeah," Stride said, chuckling.

"Just don't get carried away, okay?" Maggie said. "You're getting over Cindy's death, and she's getting over a divorce. You're both on the rebound."

"When did you become the expert on relationships?" Stride asked sourly, regretting the edge in his voice.

"Let's just say I know a little about taking a fall, all right?"

Stride said nothing. They drove on silently.

Their destination was on the south end of the city. They passed close to the harbor on their left and crossed a web of railroad tracks that led in and out of the docks. There was little development down here, other than a few windowless saloons, off-sale liquor stores, and gas stations. Another mile took them to the outer edge of town, where a large cluster of older houses clung to the land near the interstate. Most of the houses dated back before the 1940s, when they were modest but comfortable units serving ship workers. The houses were mostly ramshackle now, and the neighborhood was a magnet for the handful of drug dealers who called Duluth home.

"Marrying Graeme was quite a step up the social ladder for Emily," Maggie said. "You have to give her credit for landing him. I wonder how she did it."

"Well, the good reverend says she was quite a dish just a few years ago."

"He said that?"

"I'm paraphrasing. But Emily is obviously still close to Dayton, and it looks like he knows more about her and Rachel than just about anyone."

"But will he tell us anything?" Maggie asked.

"He agreed to see us. That's a start."

Stride navigated a series of snow-covered streets through the quiet neighborhood. The parked cars were lumps of little white hills to steer around on the narrow streets.

The church in which Dayton Tenby served as pastor was a beachhead from which the neighbors were battling back crime and vandalism. The churchyard was meticulously clean and landscaped with neatly trimmed bushes, sporting white snowcaps, carefully planted across the wide lawn. There was a large swing set and a cedar jungle gym for children. The church itself boasted a fresh coat of paint and bright red trim around the tall narrow windows.

They made the first set of tire tracks in the lot as they pulled in and parked. When they got out of the car, the air was crisp and cold. They kicked through the snow to the main door of the church. The wide lobby inside was chilly, with the heat vanishing into the high ceiling. They hugged themselves and looked around. Stride noticed a bulletin board crowded with notices about drug rehabilitation, abuse prevention, and counseling for divorce. In the middle of the board was a missing-person notice, with Rachel's photo prominently displayed.

"Hello?" Stride called.

He heard movement somewhere in the church, then a muffled voice. A few seconds later, appearing out of the shadows of a long hallway, Dayton Tenby joined them in the lobby.

Tenby wore a pair of dark dress slacks and a gray wool sweater with leather patches on the elbows. He greeted them with a nervous smile, and his handshake, as it had been when Stride first met him, was damp with sweat. His forehead, too, was lined with moisture. He had a yellow pad, crammed with spidery writing, under his arm and a pen wedged behind one ear.

"I'm sorry I wasn't here to greet you," Tenby said. "I was in the midst of writing tomorrow's sermon, so I'm a little distracted. Let's go in the back where it's warmer."

He guided them down the hall. Tenby's church apartment was boxy and small, furnished in dark wood, with a large oil painting of Christ hung above the mantel of a modest fireplace. A fire burned there, making the room pleasantly warm. Dayton seated him-

self in a green upholstered chair by the fire
and laid his yellow pad on the ornate end
table beside it. He gestured at an antique,
uncomfortable-looking sofa. Stride and Maggie sat down. Maggie fit perfectly, but Stride
wriggled to find a position that suited his tall
frame.

"When we first met, you told me you
thought Rachel had run away," Stride said.
"Do you still feel that way?"

Tenby pursed his lips. "This is a long time
to carry a joke, even for Rachel. I would
never say so to the Stoners, but I'm beginning to fear this may be more than a childish
game."

"But you have no idea what else it could
be?" Maggie asked him.

"No, I don't. Do you feel she was abducted?"

"We're not ruling anything out," Stride
said. "Right now, we're trying to find out
more about Rachel's relationships and her
past. We're trying to construct a picture of
her. Since you've known her and her family
for a long time, we thought you could help."

Tenby nodded. "I see."

"You sound reluctant," Maggie said.

He folded his hands in his lap. "It's not reluctance, Detective. I'm trying to decide what I can say and what I can't. There are things I've learned in my role as a religious advisor that naturally must remain confidential. I'm sure you can understand."

"You mean you counseled Rachel?" Stride asked.

"Briefly. A long time ago. I've worked with Emily much more. She and I have tried to work through the problems with Rachel for many years. Without a great deal of success, I'm afraid."

"Anything you can tell us would help," Maggie assured him.

"In fact, I did talk about your visit with Emily," Tenby said. "I had a suspicion this kind of topic might come up, you see. Emily was gracious and gave her permission for me to talk about our conversations freely. Naturally, I don't have Rachel's permission, but perhaps, under the circumstances, I would be doing a disservice to keep things hidden. Of course, I have to say that Rachel told me very little that shed much light on her soul."

"Maybe if you started at the beginning," Stride suggested.

"Yes, indeed. Well, you know that many of

the problems between Emily and Rachel
date back to her first marriage to Tommy
Deese. He drove a wedge between Rachel
and Emily, and the gap only widened after
Tommy's death. Of course, I only learned
about most of this in retrospect. I knew both
of them from church, but neither one made
an effort to confide in me."

"They lived near here?" Maggie asked.

"Oh, yes. Right down the street, in fact."

"Did Rachel have many friends?" Stride
asked.

Tenby drummed his fingers on the end
table. "She was never really close to anyone.
Except, perhaps, for Kevin. He always had
quite the crush on her, but it was a one-way
thing."

"This is the same Kevin who was with her
in Canal Park on that last night? Kevin
Lowry?" Maggie asked.

"Oh, yes. Kevin and his family still live
here. I expect he'll be a lawyer or vice president someday, a real success story. I'm
afraid his one weakness is Rachel. He always seemed to want to save her, but
Rachel didn't have much interest in being
saved. Well, that's all right, he's better off
with that girl Sally he's dating now. I'm sorry,

that sounds rather cold, doesn't it? It's not that I have any ill feelings toward Rachel, but she would never have been right for Kevin."

Maggie nodded. "I take it you don't believe Kevin could have had anything to do with Rachel's disappearance."

Tenby's face revealed real shock. "Kevin? Oh, no, no. Impossible."

"Let's talk about Emily and Graeme," Stride said. "Did Rachel resent Graeme? Did she resent Emily bringing a new man into their lives?"

"You'd think so, wouldn't you?" Tenby said. "But it didn't seem that way. They seemed to get along, at least for a while. I think Rachel thought she could use Graeme as a wedge against Emily, just the way Tommy did with her. Turn Graeme and Emily against each other, you see. And maybe it worked. It hasn't been a very happy marriage."

"How so?" Maggie asked. "Fights? Infidelity?"

Tenby held up one hand. "I'm afraid I'm getting thirsty. I need a glass of water. I can't afford to have a sore throat before my sermon! Can I get the two of you anything?"

Stride and Maggie both shook their heads. Tenby smiled and excused himself, disappearing into another room. They heard his footsteps tapping on a hard floor, then the bang of pipes as he turned on the water. He returned a few seconds later, sipping from a red plastic cup.

"I'm sorry," he said, sitting down again. He looked more relaxed. "Where were we?"

"Emily and Graeme," Maggie said.

"Yes, yes. Well, I don't think there's been any violence in the marriage. I think it's the opposite problem. No passion. There just doesn't seem to be much love between them."

"Then why did they get married in the first place?" Stride asked.

Tenby frowned. "Graeme is very successful. I think Emily may have been a little blinded by all those dollar signs on his paycheck. When you've struggled to make ends meet your whole life, it can be very tempting to imagine a world in which you've got considerably more leisure. She may have allowed some of her dreams to get in the way of reality."

"And Graeme?" Maggie asked. "No offense, but Emily doesn't seem to be much of a catch for a bank honcho."

Tenby studied Maggie with an unusual

smile, as if he found the question very amusing. "Well, who knows why anyone is attracted to anyone else? Emily is a lovely woman. Rachel didn't get her good looks exclusively from Tommy, despite what Emily might say. Plus, there are a lot of men who are attracted to women who need to be taken care of. That may have been the case with Graeme."

Stride didn't think that sounded like Graeme at all. "How did they meet?" he asked.

"Oh, it was rather sweet, as Emily tells it," Tenby said. His voice was suddenly louder, almost boisterous. It sounded forced. "Graeme had been at the bank for about a year, and I gather that most of the female staff considered him to be a very eligible bachelor. Good looks, a lot of self-confidence, and a high-paying position in the bank. What's not to like? But he didn't seem to take an interest in anyone. Emily mentioned him to me a couple of times, but she never dreamed he would look her way. She never even bothered trying to approach him. She was one of the few who didn't try. Maybe that worked in her favor. He may have seen her as the only one who was immune to his charms. In any event, one day, Graeme approached her in the parking lot after work. He asked if she'd like to have a drink. It seems he had been attracted to her for some time and hadn't had the courage to ask her out. Funny, isn't it? But you never know."

"I guess not," Stride said. He glanced at Maggie, who frowned.

"And not long after, they were married," Tenby continued. "It was a whirlwind romance."

Maggie shook her head. "And a few years later, there's no passion left?"

"It happens," Tenby said. "I see it all too often."

Stride nodded. "Forgive me, Reverend, but I'm still having trouble here. Even if Graeme asked Emily out, I find it hard to believe they found so much in common that he was ready to dive into marriage. This may sound callous, but did Emily lay a trap for him?"

Tenby bit his lip and looked uncomfortable. "I don't know what you mean."

Maggie smiled. "A trap. You know, women are awfully good at manipulating men to make them do whatever they want. Why,

Stride here will do anything I tell him to do. It's an art."

Tenby smiled nervously. "Well, I don't think Emily had any kind of strategy. She was too dazzled. As I say, the money may have caused her to overlook the fact that she really didn't feel much passion, but I don't believe she intentionally deceived him."

"Reverend, we really need to know the truth," Stride told him. "There's obviously something more."

Tenby nodded. "Yes, I know. It doesn't have anything to do with Rachel, though, so I don't see why anyone needs to bring up this kind of dirty laundry."

"If we don't have all the pieces, we can't solve the puzzle," Maggie said. "It's that simple."

"I suppose so." Tenby wiped his face, which was moist. "Well, you see, after they had been dating a few weeks, Emily found out she was pregnant. That was what really led to the marriage."

"I'm sure Graeme was thrilled," Stride murmured.

"Hardly," Tenby said. "He wanted her to have an abortion. She refused. I think he would have liked the whole thing to go away, but in a town like Duluth, in a position like his, you can't have a scandal coming out in public. So he married her."

"And the baby?" Maggie asked.

"Miscarriage at six months. Emily nearly died."

"Graeme didn't try to work out an amicable divorce?" Stride asked.

"No, he didn't," Tenby said. "He seemed to have resigned himself to the marriage. And I suppose he thought a divorce would have been extremely expensive. So he held up his end. But make no mistake, he didn't pretend to have his heart in it. It was simply a convenience to be married. For a while, that was okay for Emily, too. Love doesn't seem so important when you've struggled for years just to get by."

"For a while?" Maggie asked.

"Well, money is no cure for loneliness," Tenby said.

"So how do they deal with it now?" Stride asked.

"I think you'd better talk to each of them about that, Detective."

"Meanwhile, Rachel was in the middle of this happy scene?" Maggie asked.

Tenby sighed. "All three of them in that

house," he said. "And not very much happiness among them. It's a terrible thing. That's why I was so convinced that Rachel ran away. She had a lot to run away from."

"Did she ever talk to you about running away?" Stride asked.

"No, she never confided in me. I think she saw me as being on Emily's side, so that made me the enemy."

"And there's nothing else you can think of that might shed light on her disappearance? Anything you observed or overheard?"

"I'm afraid not," Tenby said. "I wish there was."

They all stood up. They shook hands awkwardly, and Stride felt that the minister was now anxious for them to be gone. He guided them back down the corridor into the cold lobby of the church. When the door closed behind them, Stride and Maggie paused on the porch, buttoning their coats and swinging scarves across their faces. The wind had blown away their footprints in the snow.

"What do you think?" Maggie said.

Stride squinted at the cold sun. "I think we could use a break."

12

Heather took a sip of tea from a chipped china cup and replaced it on the end table at a safe distance, where a spill would not be disastrous. Then she gingerly picked up the prints she had developed in the cold basement a few hours earlier.

First snowfall always made for beautiful work. She had found a giant, perfect spiderweb stretched between two trees in the woods behind the cottage. The snow crystals coated each diaphanous strand, just enough to make a patchwork, like lace. She had caught the image quickly, and even as she snapped the pictures, a puff of wind splintered the ice and sent the web fluttering away. One of the prints showed the web just as it separated, the snow gently tearing it apart.

Heather took off her half-glasses and laid them beside her. A Brahms concerto was in its final notes on the stereo. She closed her eyes, enjoying the lilt of the piano. As it faded away into silence, she realized how tired she was. She had spent most of the day tramping about in the cold and snow with her camera, until her feet were wet and her fingers were numb. Lissa had been with her the whole time, but the cold didn't bother the girl at all. Heather kept telling her to wrap her face up in her scarf, and Lissa kept pulling it off when Heather wasn't looking. They had taken a hot bath together when they got home, but Heather could still feel some of the coldness of the day inside her. She was ready to tuck her body into a long flannel nightgown and bury herself in a mound of blankets.

She clicked the lamp off and eased out of the recliner. She turned the overhead light off, and the house was dark, but the living room kept a reflected glow from the moon shining on a fresh white bed of snow outside. Heather tiptoed down the hallway, not wanting to awaken Lissa. As was her custom, she edged the girl's door open and peeked inside. Lissa always slept with a night-light. The room was filled with shadows. Her daughter was sleeping soundly on her stomach, her face lost in the pillow. She had thrashed out of the blankets, leaving half her body exposed.

Heather approached her, wanting to pull the blankets up around her again. The night was going to get even colder. She lingered at Lissa's bedside, studying the girl's tranquil face and smiling at the occasional murmurs she made in her sleep. Heather bent over and brushed her lips against her daughter's forehead.

She tugged the blanket up and fitted it around Lissa's shoulders. As she did, something tumbled out of bed and landed softly on the carpet. Heather looked down, seeing something glint in the shadows. She bent over, confused, and picked it up. It was a gold bracelet.

Heather hadn't purchased it for Lissa and didn't remember seeing it before. She wrinkled her brow, wondering where Lissa had found it and surprised that her daughter hadn't mentioned it. Knowing Lissa, that probably meant it had come from some illicit source.

She left the girl's room, taking the bracelet with her.

Heather continued to her own bedroom. She put the bracelet on top of a rickety five-drawer bureau and studied it thoughtfully for a moment. Then she shrugged and turned away. She unbuttoned her red plaid shirt and tossed it in the laundry basket. She wasn't wearing a bra. She yanked off her jeans, left her panties and socks on, and quickly pulled a nightgown over her head.

She tugged her six blankets down and crawled under them. She clicked on the radio, looking for music. Instead, the hourly headlines were winding down. She paid little attention to the stories, which were too depressing. A farmhouse south of town had burned, killing an elderly woman. The girl from Duluth, Rachel, was still missing. The Trojans had lost a big game.

Heather reviewed the wall of framed photographs beside her bed. She had just added one of the prints from her photo shoot at the barn. The waning sun that had lingered behind her on the edge of the treetops cast shadows in the barn's sagging crevices. Dead leaves scattered over the earth like a carpet. The sky on the horizon was steel gray. She had been aiming for an image filled with decay, and she had achieved it.

As Heather stared at the photograph, she finally remembered.

In her mind, she saw Lissa running around the corner of the barn toward her, shouting about something she had found. Heather had been distracted, concentrating on her camera, but she remembered Lissa showing her a gold bracelet, and she remembered telling the girl to put it right back where she found it. Now a few weeks later, here was Lissa with a secret gold bracelet hidden in her bed.

"That little sneak," Heather said aloud, peeved.

She got out of bed with a sigh and retrieved the bracelet from the bureau. It was not particularly heavy or expensive. She guessed that a high school girl had lost it in the middle of a tryst behind the barn.

Heather looked at the bracelet and saw letters inside.

T ♥ R

T loves R, she thought to herself. *Right.* She suspected R was a pretty sophomore, and T was a football player who figured jewelry was a great way to get into the girl's jeans. Heather laughed. She put the bracelet on her nightstand and clicked off the light.

In the darkness, she tried to sleep, but instead she tossed and turned. A few minutes ago, she had barely been able to keep her eyes open. Now she was awake. A jumble of thoughts flitted idly through her brain. High school. Pretty girls making out behind the barn. An old woman dying in a fire. Football games. Gifts of gold bracelets. Young love. Young lust.

Initials.

She saw them in her head again.

That was when Heather's eyes flew open, and she stared sightless into the black room. Under the blankets, a chill rippled through her flesh. She scratched blindly for the light, then blinked as it flooded the room.

She looked at the bracelet but didn't dare touch it.

T loves R, she thought again.

R.

13

Stride stood on the dirt road outside the search area near the barn. The snow had been matted down into a slippery gray streak by the coming and going of police cars throughout the day. He dug in his boots, stiffening his body against the swirling wind. The cold felt like knives on the sliver of his face where the wool scarf left his skin exposed. He had a red cap pulled low on his forehead and the hood of his parka pulled over his head and tied closed at his neck. His hands were buried inside leather gloves. The wind chill was ten degrees below zero.

Nature wasn't cooperating. Neither was Stride's luck.

They had been searching since noon, and five hours later, it was almost night. All they had to show so far for the painstaking, back-breaking work in the bitter cold was dozens of overlapping tire tracks, broken glass, used needles, and a dizzying range of common trash. All of it went into plastic bags, carefully labeled to reflect the exact square yard within the grid where each item had been found.

If the tip from Heather Hubble had come two days earlier, they would have been able to search the field surrounding the barn with relative ease. Instead, the evidence, if there was any, lay hidden beneath three inches of snow. As his men searched each square in the checkerboard, they had to carefully brush away the powdery snow into a section of the grid that had already been searched. With each gust of wind, the snow drifted back. It was slow, cold work, but they had no choice but to proceed inch by inch, looking for details as small as a hair trapped be-neath the white blanket, somewhere in the dirt and brush.

That wasn't what really bothered Stride,

though. The worse stuff lay ahead. More
snow was predicted by morning, a storm
that could dump another ten inches all over
the northern woods. If that happened, they
wouldn't see the ground again until April,
when there would be little evidence left to
find. They had to work quickly. He had ordered in portable overhead lights, which
were being set up now, so they could sift
through the search area throughout the
night. Even so, it wasn't much time to do a
thorough job.

Plus, of all places, it had to be the barn.

Anyplace else in the wilderness, they
would have found nothing but birch bark and
dead leaves. Here, they might as well have
been in the parking lot behind the high
school. He could only guess how many
teenage couples had left behind irrelevant
evidence that would have to be meticulously
analyzed, researched, typed, and ultimately
excluded. On the walkie-talkie, Guppo kept
up a litany of the bizarre items they had already found. They had started near where
the little girl, Lissa, thought she had found
the bracelet and begun working their way
outward. Along the way, they had already
found a pair of panties (four sizes too large

for Rachel), an orthodontic retainer, a cherry Life Saver, a king of spades with a naked blonde woman wearing a crown, and nine condoms.

He knew the odds of tying anything directly to Rachel were slim. Even so, Stride felt a sense of excitement. The Stoners had definitively identified the bracelet as belonging to Rachel. The initials cinched it: "Tommy loves Rachel." The bracelet had been a gift from her father years earlier.

Kevin Lowry had already reported in his original statement that Rachel was wearing the bracelet when he last saw her in Canal Park. Now it had been found here, near the barn, their first solid evidence of where Rachel had been after her disappearance. But he tempered his professional satisfaction with the grim reality of what the discovery meant.

Emily Stoner's face had gone white when she saw it. Stride understood. All along, she had still been harboring the hope that Rachel had gone off by herself, a runaway, part of a cruel practical joke. As Emily held the bracelet in her hand, that hope vanished.

"She would never have left it behind," Emily said simply. "Never. Tommy gave it to

her. She wore it everywhere. She wore it in
the shower. She never took it off." Then, with
her husband looking on, she disintegrated
into sobs. "Oh my God, she's dead," Emily
murmured. "She's really dead."

Stride didn't try to fill the moment with
empty hope. He could easily have told her
that finding the bracelet meant nothing in
and of itself, but the truth was clear to all of
them. For weeks, they had been searching
for a live girl, trying to unravel the mystery of
her life, hunting for answers to a riddle.

Now, they would begin a different search.
For Rachel's body.

Stride heard the slam of the van door and
the shuffling of footsteps in the snow behind
him. He glanced back. Maggie wore a black
winter bowler cap over a pair of furry ear-
muffs. A red wool coat draped to her ankles.
She trudged through the snow in her leather
boots with square two-inch heels. She didn't
wear a scarf, but her golden skin seemed
unaffected by the bitter assault of the wind.

Maggie stood next to Stride, reviewing the
work of a dozen policeman hunched over
with brooms, walkie-talkies, and evidence
bags.

"You must be freezing your balls off out

here," Maggie said. "Why don't you come back to the van?"

"Guppo's in the van, right? I'm safer out here."

Maggie wrinkled her nose. "I made sure he didn't have any raw vegetables, and I cracked the window so we've got fresh air when we need it."

"No, thanks. I've got to do the media circus soon anyway. It's almost evening news time."

Stride glanced down the dirt road. The police cars blocked travel about fifty yards away, sealing off the area. Beyond the roadblock, he could see the glow of media lights, where at least two dozen reporters waited for him, shivering, complaining, and shouting for attention. He couldn't hear much above the wind.

He glanced at his watch. Ten minutes before five o'clock. He had promised them a live interview to kick off the news.

"So, you ever come out here when you were a kid?" Maggie asked.

"What do you mean?"

Maggie grinned. "Well, the woman who found the bracelet, she said this has been a hot make-out spot for years."

Stride shrugged. "I took my girls to nice, safe dirt roads near the lake, thank you very much."

"Then who came out here?" Maggie asked.

"The easy ones."

"Is that a sexist remark I should be reporting as harassment?" she teased him.

"If you could convince a girl to take a romantic drive with you along the lake, well, maybe you stood a chance of getting to second base."

"Tell me again what second base means," Maggie said. She playfully caressed her teeth with her tongue. "We didn't play baseball in China. Is that breasts, nipples, what?"

Stride ignored her. "But if you suggested going to the barn, and the girl agreed, you knew exactly what you were going to get. On the other hand, you didn't suggest it unless you knew what kind of girl you were dealing with. Otherwise, you got your face slapped."

"And you?"

"I recall mentioning the barn in passing to Lori Peterson," Stride said. "She threw a Coke in my face."

"Good for her," Maggie said. "Does this mean Rachel was easy?"

Stride bit his lower lip. "That's what everyone tells us."

"Except we still haven't found a boy who admits sleeping with her," Maggie said.

"Yes, that's interesting, isn't it? Although who wants to step up to the plate and declare himself a suspect when the girl disappears?"

"So you think it was a date?" Maggie asked.

"Maybe," Stride said. "She left Kevin just before ten o'clock and told him she was tired. Rachel doesn't strike me as a girl who gets tired early on a Friday night."

"So maybe she was meeting someone else. Someone who picked her up at her house."

Stride nodded. "They go for a little romp at the barn. But something goes wrong. Something gets out of hand. And suddenly the boyfriend has a body on his hands."

"We're assuming she's dead?" Maggie said.

Stride sighed. "Aren't we?"

"So who is this mystery stranger? Another boy at school?"

"That's the first place to start, Mags. Time

to reinterview anyone who even smells like a boyfriend."

Maggie groaned. "A whole day interviewing high school jocks with overactive hormones who think they're God's gift to everyone with a pussy. You give me the nicest jobs, boss."

"Dress for the occasion, Mags. You'll get more out of them that way."

"Great," Maggie murmured. "It's not like I've got any cleavage to show off."

"You'll think of something."

Maggie punched him in the arm, then turned and stalked back toward the van. Stride smiled. He started walking toward the media crowd down the road, bringing up his walkie-talkie in his gloved hand and shoving it up under his hood.

"What have we got, Guppo?" Stride asked.

Guppo's voice boomed through the walkie-talkie. "What the hell is this place, Lieutenant?" he called. "Shit, we've got more crap in each grid box than I'd expect to find in a New York crack house. You had to pick this place as a crime scene?"

He heard something else, and then Maggie complained in the background. "Son of a bitch, Guppo, I'm back in the van for five seconds, and you have to do that."

Stride chuckled. "Tell her to quit whining, Guppo. Ask her what she's going to wear to work tomorrow."

He heard a voice crackle in the background. "Fuck you, Stride."

Stride transmitted again. "Look, Guppo, do we have anything that suggests a connection to Rachel?"

"Could be all sorts of things. Could be nothing. We won't know until this stuff is tested. There's plenty of evidence of sex, drugs, and rock and roll, but without fingerprints and blood work, it's all speculation."

"Nothing like a confession from a murderer tied around a rock?"

"Not yet. We're still looking." Guppo belched.

"Okay," Stride said. He shoved the walkie-talkie back in his coat pocket. He approached the police cars and talked briefly with the two officers who were entrusted with the thankless job of keeping the media and spectators out. On the other side of the yellow tape, it was a mob scene, much as it had been on the night Rachel disappeared. Stride squinted as a series of floodlights illuminated him. The hum of voices escalated into a roar.

Stride pointed at one of the television reporters he knew. "Can your crew do the lights?" When the reporter nodded, Stride continued. "Okay, we'll have one team light me up, and the rest of you, keep the flashbulbs off, all right? If I hear shouting, I'm out of here. You want to ask a question, you raise your hand, I call on you, you ask one question."

"When did you get elected president, Stride?" Bird Finch retorted from the front of the crowd.

Stride grinned. "Listen up, everybody. Bird has already asked his one question. Move him to the back of the crowd."

The reporters laughed derisively. A few of them tried to push in front of Bird and take his place at the edge of the tape, but the muscular ex-basketball player wasn't giving an inch. He shot Stride an icy smile.

Stride felt the heat of the television lights burning on his face. It was the first time that day he had felt relief from the cold. Only his feet, damp and in shadow, still felt chilled. "You guys ready?" he asked. "I'll make a brief statement, then take questions."

He saw red lights flash on a dozen hand-held television cameras. A few flashbulbs burst, blinding him, despite his prohibition.

"Let me tell you what we know right now," he said. "Early this morning, we received a call on our hotline from a woman who had in her possession a bracelet she believed might be connected to the disappearance of Rachel Deese. We retrieved the bracelet, and Rachel's mother positively identified it as belonging to her daughter. We believe that Rachel was wearing the bracelet on the night she disappeared. According to the witness who found the bracelet, it was behind the barn at this location. We are currently conducting a grid search of about one hundred square yards around the area where the bracelet was discovered. That's all I have at this time."

Three people shouted questions simultaneously, and Stride stared them down, not moving or answering. Bird Finch dramatically raised his hand. He was already a head taller than everyone else, and with his arm in the air, he looked like a black Statue of Liberty.

May as well get it over with, Stride thought. "Bird?" he said.

"Do you now believe Rachel is dead?" Bird asked. He put just enough of an edge on the word "now" to suggest that Stride had been delinquent in understanding what everyone else had known all along.

"I don't want to speculate on anything like that," Stride said.

Before anyone else could get a hand up, Bird injected a follow-up question into the silence. "But you are going to be searching for a body now, aren't you?"

"We are currently in the midst of a grid search for evidence. This is an intense, highly focused exercise that will take many more hours. Our next steps will be determined by what we find here, if anything. But the full analysis will take weeks."

Another hand went up. Bird had shown them the way, and the others followed. "When you complete this search, you'll also be searching the surrounding area, right? Are you hoping to find a body?"

"I'm hoping we don't find a body," Stride

snapped. "But we do plan to begin a search of the woods around this area for any other evidence we might find."

"They're predicting more snow. Will that slow things down?"

"Of course," Stride said. "This is Minnesota. That's going to make any search harder at this time of year."

"Are you looking for volunteers to help in the search?" one reporter asked.

"I'm sure we'll able to use any extra help that's offered to us. We'll be posting details on our Web site about how volunteers can help us and where they should go. What we don't want is people combing through the woods by themselves. All that will do is harm the investigation. If people want to help, they need to let us coordinate their efforts."

Hands shot up. "Have you found anything else to suggest Rachel was here?"

"Not yet," Stride said.

Another hand. "Do you have any suspects at all?"

"No," Stride said.

Bird Finch didn't wait to be called upon again. "You've been at this more than three weeks, and you have no suspects at all?"

"The evidence so far has not suggested any persons of interest."

"What about sex offenders?" asked a reporter from Minneapolis.

"We have interviewed all individuals with any history of sexual violence in the surrounding area. But I want to make it very clear again. We have no evidence linking any specific person to Rachel's disappearance."

Bird again. "Are you now more inclined to see a connection to Kerry McGrath's disappearance? A crime in which you also seem to have no suspects?"

"We have not established any connection between the two incidents. We're not ruling it out, but there's no evidence at this time to suggest the disappearances are related."

"Does this break in the case leave you more encouraged that you will find out what happened to Rachel?"

Stride couldn't even see the woman who asked the question, just her arm in the air. He hesitated, framing his words in his mind. "Yes, I am encouraged. We now have a link, a location, that may finally bring some answers. I also want to make an appeal to anyone who is watching: If you were anywhere near this area on the night of Rachel's disappearance, and you saw or heard anything, please call us. We know Rachel was here. We want to know how she got here. We want to know what happened."

He pointed at another raised hand.

"How long are you going to be out here?" a woman from the St. Paul newspaper asked.

"It could be all night," Stride said.

It was.

As the police finished each grid, the evidence bags came back to the van, and Stride and Maggie examined each one before filing them away in a series of banker's boxes. Stride didn't see anything that suggested a connection to Rachel, although he could have been looking right at it and never known. The lab would eventually tell them more.

Stride checked his watch, which told him it was nearly four in the morning. A pizza box lay on the floor of the van, empty except for two square crust pieces that remained uneaten. Stride didn't know how Guppo had missed them. Maggie sat opposite Stride, her head nodding as her eyes blinked shut. She propped her elbows on her knees and cupped her face in her hands.

Stride, frozen and tired, allowed his thoughts to drift to Andrea. She had understood when he called to cancel their date, although he was pleased to hear disappointment in her voice. He was disappointed, too. He wasn't sure if it was the sex or just the opportunity to be close to a woman's body again, but he was anxious to see her. Andrea was very attractive. It wasn't like it was with Cindy, of course, but nothing would be. Andrea was different, and he couldn't expect her to live up to a ghost.

Stride jumped as the speaker in the van crackled. He wondered if he had fallen asleep for a few seconds. "It's starting to snow," one of the officers outside reported.

"Well, that's just fucking great," Stride said.

He pushed himself to his feet in the cramped van. His muscles ached, and he felt a twinge in his back. Normally he did a series of stretching exercises each night to keep his back limber, but for several nights he had skipped it. Now he was paying the price. His arm hurt, too, where he had taken that bullet several years back. It was always worse in the cold.

He peered through the van's frosty rear window. In the glow of the lights they had erected for the search, he could see huge flakes floating peacefully to earth. Each one looked small and harmless, and together, he knew, they would soon bury his crime scene.

"How bad?" Maggie asked quietly.

"Bad enough," Stride said.

Stride stared at the shadows of the forest. He tried to imagine the scene again as it must have been that night. Rachel in the passenger seat. Someone pulling a car in behind the barn. Just the luck of the draw that no one else was there. How did the bracelet get outside? They wouldn't have had sex outside, not when it was a cold night. Maybe they simply went outside to stare at the woods, like he was doing. And then the boy tried to pull her back to the car, and the bracelet slipped off, and they struggled, and then—what?

Or maybe things started to get rough in the car, and she tried to run. He followed her. The bracelet came off in the struggle. He hit her. Strangled her. Then what would he do with the body? Take it deeper into the words? Take the car and go somewhere else to hide her?

Stride heard the speaker come to life again.

"Any of you guys remember what Rachel was wearing that night?" one of the officers radioed from outside.

Stride and Maggie looked at each other. Maggie recited from memory. "Black jeans, white turtleneck."

The speaker was silent. Then, a few seconds later: "You said a white turtleneck?"

Stride spoke up. "That's what we said."

Another pause, longer this time. "Okay, guys. We may have something."

The triangular piece of fabric was small and jagged, about six inches in length, with frayed edges. Despite the dirt caked over it, the fragment was obviously white. Along one side, where the cloth had torn from the rest of the garment, was a reddish-brown stain soaked into the fibers.

14

Emily believed she was going insane. Not since she had attacked Rachel on that one terrible night had she felt so out of control. She was drifting at sea, alone, without hope of rescue.

She paced frantically back and forth, wearing a path in the carpet. She grasped her forehead in her hand, fingers outstretched, squeezing it like a vise. Her dirty hair spilled over her face. Her eyes were wide, her breath loud. She was hyperventilating. The pain in her head throbbed, like a tumor growing inside her.

"I'd like to show you this bracelet," the detective had said. She took one look and screamed.

Emily never really believed the day would come. She knew what the other mother, Barbara McGrath, had told her during the broadcast. How she was afraid of that one day when the police would be at her door, somber expressions on their faces. But Emily didn't believe it. She believed Rachel was alive. One day, the phone would ring, and the familiar, mocking laughter would be on the other end.

She believed it right up until the second she saw the bracelet. Now she knew. Rachel was dead. Someone had killed her.

It was as if the police had pulled the ground from under Emily's feet. Hours later, she was still consumed by despair.

The quiet sounds of the porch thundered in her head. The furnace hummed, pumping warm air into the room. The wooden branches of the spirea plants outside made squeaking noises as they rubbed against the windows. The timbers in the house creaked, shifting under the weight of an unseen ghost.

And the worst sound of all, tap tap tap, was Graeme working on his laptop a few feet away, oblivious to her agony.

Tap, tap, tap.

She had never believed the two of them could sink so far. What was worse, she knew she had brought it all on herself.

"I'm pregnant," Emily said.

She tensed, waiting for his response. She was seated on the sofa in her tiny living room, her hands folded awkwardly in her lap. Graeme was in the upholstered chair opposite her. He held a drink in his hand. It was his second since dinner, and she had already plied him with champagne to go along with the prime rib she had roasted in the oven.

Now, with both of them relaxed, she had blurted it out.

"You said you were taking precautions," Graeme said.

Emily winced. This wasn't what she wanted to hear. Not love, not excitement. Just vague recriminations.

"I'm on the pill," Emily told him. "But nothing's foolproof. It was an accident. It was God's will."

"I'm not sure we're ready," he said.

"I'm not sure anyone's ever ready," Emily replied.

"I mean, I'm not sure we should keep it."

Emily felt tears welling inside her. Her breath was heavy. She spoke in a quavering voice. "I won't kill my baby."

Graeme said nothing.

"I won't do it, Graeme," Emily repeated. "How can you ask me to? This is your baby, too."

Emily got off the sofa. She went around the coffee table and knelt in front of him, taking his hands in hers.

"Don't you want to give our baby a home together?" she asked him.

He seemed stricken for a few interminable seconds, his eyes focused over her shoulder. Then he nodded, just the barest movement of his head.

Emily felt a huge grin of relief and joy spread across her face. She threw her arms around Graeme's neck and hugged him tightly. She kissed him all over his face. "Let's get married now," she said. "Right away. This weekend."

Graeme smiled. "All right. We'll drive up the coast this weekend and find some little small-town church. We can bring Rachel, too."

A cloud passed briefly across her

mind. She had almost forgotten her daughter in the excitement of the moment. Then it, too, passed. She felt strong and confident. This would be the right thing. For her. For Graeme. Even for Rachel. It might finally make them a family again. A family that would never have to worry about money.

"Yes, let's do it," Emily told him.

Emily leaned back and began unbuttoning her blouse, watching his eyes follow the movement of her fingers. As the flaps of fabric fell away, his hands reached inside, squeezing her breasts.

Graeme's pager beeped, a high-pitched whine filling the room. Both of them jumped. Emily fell back on her butt, her breasts spilling out of her shirt. Graeme reared out of the chair and grabbed for the pager. He plucked it off his belt and stared at it.

"I have to go."

Emily straightened herself, smoothing her hair and quickly attending to her open blouse. She shrugged and smiled at him. "That's all right."

She walked him to the door and stayed there, with the night air blowing in, while he backed his car out of the driveway. She watched the car until she couldn't see it anymore, and still she stayed there, enjoying the breeze on her face.

Emily closed the front door quietly. She headed for the kitchen, humming to herself.

"You looked pretty funny with your tits hanging out," she heard someone say.

Rachel was sitting on the top step of the short stairway to the second floor. Her long bare legs dangled over the stairs. She wore short shorts and a black halter top that fit snugly around her full breasts. Her black hair was wet, as if she'd just come out of the shower. Her skin glowed.

"You were spying on us?"

Rachel shrugged. "Graeme saw me. I didn't want to interrupt your big moment."

Emily didn't want to get sucked into Rachel's games tonight. She headed for the kitchen without another glance at her daughter.

Rachel called after her. "Up to your old tricks, huh?"

Emily stopped. "What does that mean?"

Rachel screwed up her face and mocked her mother's voice. "'I'm on the pill, darling. It was an accident. It was God's will.'"

"So?" Emily retorted.

"So what do you call these?" Rachel said. She held up a tiny pocket-purse, then flipped it open to reveal an un-opened wheel of small green pills. "They look like birth control pills to me. What happened, Mother? Did you fall a little be-hind?"

Emily's hands flew to her mouth. Her face went white. Then she steeled herself, her mind working furiously. "You don't understand."

Rachel jabbed a finger at her mother. "Don't I? You're the manipulative bitch I always thought you were. Just like Daddy said you were."

Emily said nothing. Rachel was right—she had deceived Graeme. But it was for a greater good, for both of them. To finally have a little security. To not have to work. She wasn't trying to trap him, only to make him realize he loved her.

"I suppose I should thank you," Rachel said. "Didn't you pull the same trick on

Daddy? Isn't that why I'm here? You knew you could never keep him on your own."

Emily bit her lip. She wanted to scream a denial. But the long pause was enough to convince Rachel of the truth.

"You're becoming predictable," Rachel said.

"Are you going to tell Graeme?" Emily asked. She knew the answer. Rachel wouldn't miss an opportunity to drive a knife into her mother's heart. All the carefully laid plans would unravel.

But Rachel surprised her.

"Why would I do that?" Rachel said. "It's the first time I ever thought we had something in common."

The girl turned and disappeared into her room.

Emily wished they would have let her keep the bracelet. She had only been able to catch a quick glimpse of it in the plastic bag, enough to see the inscription from Tommy. Then the detective had whisked it out of sight. Evidence, he said.

She'd get it back after the trial. If there ever was a trial. If they ever found out what really happened to her.

She continued pacing. The headache got even worse as she tried to squeeze it out of her head with her hands. The reality was too terrible to bear. She needed someone to hold her and tell her it was all right, or just let her cry endlessly into his arms. When she stopped and stared at her husband, she shook her head in mute rage. He worked on his computer as if she weren't even in the room. He ignored her moans, her cries, the sound of her feet shuffling back and forth on the carpet.

Tap, tap, tap. Fingers on the keyboard. Her daughter was dead, and he was playing with spreadsheets.

How did she miss it? How did she fool herself into thinking she loved him, or that he could ever love her?

Her eyes burned into his back. She asked herself again how they had come so far. Rachel was gone, and all she could think of was that her whole life was hollow, starting with her marriage. Everything was gone.

Her silence finally attracted his attention. He turned around, catching her eye as she stared fiercely back at him. Her eyes were wild. She didn't know how to deal with all the grief exploding out of her. The cork had come out of the bottle. She stood there, trembling.

"Emily, sit down," Graeme said. "Relax."

Funny how he always said the wrong thing. How she hated the sound of his voice now. The calm delivery, each word without emphasis. She couldn't handle it anymore.

"Relax?" she hissed. "You're telling me to fucking relax?"

They stared at each other. His eyes were dead, staring right through her. He was patient and pleasant. A stranger.

"I know how you feel," Graeme told her, as if he were speaking to a hysterical child.

Emily put both hands on her forehead. She closed her eyes, grimacing. Tears streamed down her face.

"You don't know how I feel, because you don't feel a goddamn thing! You just sit there in your chair, and you smile at me, and you pretend like we're this loving couple, and all the while I know you don't feel anything for me."

"You're just being irrational."

"Irrational?" She squeezed her fists open and shut. "God, why ever would that be? What would make me irrational?"

He didn't answer.

She shook her head, not believing it. "She's dead. Do you understand that? She's really dead."

"They found her bracelet. It doesn't necessarily mean anything."

"It means everything," Emily said. "I don't have Rachel. And I don't have you, either, do I? I never did."

"Emily, please."

"Please what, Graeme? Please go away? Please don't bother you with my petty problems?"

He didn't reply.

"Why did you marry me?" Emily whispered. "You could have given me money. I wouldn't have told anyone the baby was yours. I would have left town if you wanted. Why marry me if you felt nothing for me?"

Graeme shrugged his shoulders. "Did you give me a choice?"

Emily barely heard him. But he was right. Her fault. Her guilt.

"I guess I should have had the abortion," she said. That would have been so much easier, a simple procedure, vacuuming away the life inside her. Easier than losing the baby months later in a river of blood.

"That would have made it all right,

wouldn't it, Graeme? No need to marry me then. No need to marry anyone at all. You could be happy, playing with your little spreadsheets, dialing up your phone-sex girlfriends."

Graeme looked up sharply. This time she had struck a nerve. He was staring at her. He even looked a little afraid. *Good.*

"You didn't think I knew, did you? I followed you downstairs once. I saw you in here, on your knees, pumping your cock, panting into the phone. I heard you tell that girl how much you wanted to fuck her. That's better, isn't it? Better than having to pretend you enjoy fucking me."

Emily stared at the ceiling. "All of you would have been better off. You and Tommy and Rachel. I've done nothing but screw up all of your lives, haven't I? If only I'd had the abortion. If only I'd done it the first time, too."

She sank to her knees, then onto all fours on the plush white carpet. She pounded the floor over and over with her fist, then rolled over onto her back, pulling her knees to her chest, hugging them. "God knew what he was doing, didn't he? He didn't want me to have another baby. Look what a fucking mess I made of the first one."

She saw Graeme kneeling over her. He had pasted an expression of concern on his face. It was false, like everything else in their life.

"Don't touch me. Don't you touch me! Don't pretend, all right? Don't pretend!"

"Emily, why don't you go upstairs? Take a pill. It will help you sleep. This has been a terrible day, and you're out of your head."

Emily lay on the carpet. She had run out of fire and anger. She had run out of everything. They had won, all of them. Tommy, Rachel, and now Graeme. She had fought them all for so long, but it wasn't worth the pain and misery.

She could almost see them standing over her.

Tommy, next to Graeme.

Rachel, in the doorway, a child again.

Graeme, still kneeling near her. "Take a pill," he repeated. It wasn't a dream. He really said it.

Emily smiled. He was right, of course, because Graeme was always right, always exactly balanced. It was time to go upstairs, and she knew he wouldn't follow her. It was time to sleep. Asleep, she could forget all of it. All of them. She pushed herself to her feet and brushed by Graeme. In her imagination, Tommy and Rachel still lingered there. She could hear the echoes of their laughter.

"Okay," she said. "You win."

Take a pill, she thought. That's what she would do.

15

"You must be cold," the bartender said, casting an eye over the bar at Maggie's bare legs.

Maggie's black leather skirt extended to midthigh, and when she sat down, she kept her legs glued shut to avoid giving the world a glimpse of her bright pink panties. Her red wool coat was draped over the barstool next to her. She wore a sleeveless burgundy silk blouse.

Yes, she was cold.

"What'll you have? Cup of hot tea?" the bartender asked, smiling.

Maggie smiled back and ordered a tall mug of tap beer.

When the bartender returned, he laid the beer in front of her. Ice clung to the side of the glass and floated inside. "What are you, a model or something?" he asked.

Maggie laughed. "That's a good line. I like that one. In fact, I'm a cop."

"Yeah, right."

Maggie reached over and flipped the flap of her red coat on the bar stool. Her shield, pinned inside, gleamed up at the bartender. He raised his arms, surrendering. "Okay, you win. Isn't there something about cops not drinking on duty?"

"Who said I was on duty?" Maggie asked.

In fact, she was still on duty, but she needed a drink.

Maggie sipped the beer slowly. It was Monday night, and the bar was half empty. All day long, she had suffered under the leering stares of teenage boys. And it all resulted in nothing. Nada. Zip. She didn't find a single boy who would admit that he or anyone else had ever fucked Rachel behind the infamous barn. Each one of them had plenty to say when Maggie was casually crossing and uncrossing her legs, but they clammed up tight at Rachel's name. No one wanted to paint a target on his chest for the police.

She noticed a nervous teenager standing next to her.

"Are you Ms. Bei?" Kevin Lowry asked.

Maggie gave him a quick once-over. He was a solid kid, heavy and strong, with blond hair shaved almost down to his scalp. He wore the basic uniform of the restaurant's waiters, including black jeans and a red T-shirt that barely stretched around his barrel chest. Like all the other boys, Kevin let his eyes travel quickly up and down Maggie's body, taking note of her legs.

They chose a small table in the corner of the bar, away from the smoke and noise. Maggie brought her beer with her. She asked if Kevin wanted a soft drink, but he shook his head. Maggie relaxed, leaning close to Kevin with her elbows on the table. Kevin sat uncomfortably across from her.

"I don't bite," Maggie said with a warm smile.

Kevin responded with a smile that came and went quickly. "How's Mrs. Stoner?" he asked quietly.

"It was touch and go, but the latest word from the hospital is that she'll be fine."

"I feel bad. She's had a tough time."

"Because of Rachel?" Maggie asked.

Kevin shrugged. "Sometimes. Parents and kids always have some kind of problems."

"Seems like they had more than their share," Maggie said.

A ghost of a grin. "Maybe."

"Why do you think she took the pills?"

"I guess she couldn't take it anymore," Kevin said.

"Take what?" Maggie asked.

"All of it."

Maggie waited until Kevin looked up. "People tell me you're close to Rachel. They said Rachel would have been better off with you, but she never really appreciated you. That must be frustrating."

Kevin sighed. "Rachel has always been kind of a fantasy. I never really expected anything to come of it."

"So what about that last night?" Maggie asked sharply. "You told us that Rachel came on to you."

"That was nothing. She can be cruel that way."

"Could she have been meeting someone else that night? Another boy?"

"Maybe. Rachel dated a lot. We didn't talk about it."

Maggie nodded. "You know, it's funny. I talked to dozens of guys at the high school today. No one admitted going out with Rachel."

"Big surprise," Kevin said. "Everyone's scared. They know what you found at the barn."

"So they're lying."

"Sure," Kevin said. "I bet she dated all of them."

She could hear the bitterness in his voice.

"How about you?" Maggie asked.

"I already said no."

"Except for that night," Maggie said. "That's kind of weird, don't you think? She comes on to you, and that night, she disappears."

She saw anxiety instantly bloom in his eyes.

"What do you mean?"

"You said Rachel made a date with you for Saturday night. But when you arrived at her house, she was gone."

Kevin nodded.

"You're sure the date wasn't for Friday night? You didn't make plans to go to her house later?"

"No!" Kevin told her, his voice rising.

"You didn't go back?"

"No, I didn't. I went home. The police talked to my parents. You know that's what happened."

Maggie smiled. "I know a lot of kids who are pretty good at slipping out without their parents knowing. Look, if Rachel wanted to disappear, you would have helped her, wouldn't you? You would have done anything she asked."

Kevin bit his lower lip and said nothing. He looked around as if he were hunting for an escape.

"So did you? Did you help her run away?" Maggie said.

"No," Kevin insisted.

"Did you go back later anyway? Did she have another date? That would have pissed you off, right? I can understand, Kevin. You've loved her your whole life. She's your fantasy. And then she starts playing games with you. That must have made you mad."

Kevin shook his head fiercely.

"It didn't? You didn't go over and wait for

her? Try to convince her that she was wasting time with all those other guys? They weren't right for her. You were. But she rejected you."

Kevin was angry now. "I didn't see her. I didn't go to her house."

"You have to admit you've got a great motive."

"Cut it out," Kevin said.

"Maybe you two went out for a drive. Just to talk. And maybe you ended up at the barn. Maybe the talk didn't go so well."

Kevin clenched his fists. "That's a lie."

"We found blood and condoms at the crime scene, Kevin. What are we going to find when we do a DNA analysis?"

Kevin stood up. He was trembling with rage. "You'll find out it's not mine! Because I wasn't there!"

Maggie stood up, too. She touched his arm softly, but he yanked it away. She tried to coax him into looking at her. "Sit down, Kevin. I know you weren't there. But most of the time, I don't know—not until I push people. The guilty ones don't push back. Please. Sit down."

"Rachel's the last person in the world I would ever hurt," Kevin said.

"I know. But it looks like someone did hurt her. So, if you didn't go to Rachel's house, who did?"

Kevin shook his head. "Don't you think I'd have told you if I knew?"

"You don't remember anything Rachel said? You didn't hear any rumors at school? From what I understand, the barn was a popular place. It's hard to believe there weren't stories going around."

"Oh, sure, everyone knows about the barn. Lots of people talk about it. But who knows what's real and what's just locker room bullshit, you know?"

"But you're sure she went there," Maggie said.

"I don't know it for a fact. But I can't believe she didn't."

"Why?"

Kevin spread his arms in exasperation. "She talked about having sex all the time."

"Was it just talk?" Maggie asked. "Or did she really do it?"

"I don't know. She didn't mention names."

Out of the corner of her eye, Maggie saw a plump teenage girl with chestnut hair standing in the doorway of the bar. Hands firmly on her hips, the girl swiveled her head, studying each table like a velociraptor. When she spotted Kevin in the corner, her face lit up in a smile. Then she saw Maggie, assessed her outfit in a single glance, and frowned. She marched toward them.

"Hello, Kevin," the girl said loudly.

Kevin glanced up, surprised. "Sally!"

He leaped to his feet and planted a kiss on Sally's lips.

"I came in with my parents for dinner," Sally said. "Paula said you were in here. She was sort of pissed." Then she added bluntly, "Who's this?"

"This is Ms. Bei," Kevin said. "She's with the police."

"The police?" Sally said, her eyebrows raised.

Maggie stood up and extended her hand, which Sally shook limply.

"We've both talked to the police already," Sally said.

"I know. Kevin was just telling me he didn't really know any of Rachel's boyfriends," Maggie said. "We're thinking someone must have gone over to her house after she left the two of you. Can you think of anyone?"

"I don't think anyone was special to

Rachel," Sally said. "She used people up and threw them away."

"That sounds like a good way to get people pissed off," Maggie said. "Anyone sound like he was obsessed with Rachel? Did she ever complain about someone who wouldn't leave her alone?"

"Complain?" Sally said. "Not hardly."

"Okay, let's forget about Rachel for a while. What about other girls at school? They ever talk about boys who were giving them a hard time?"

Kevin scratched his chin. He looked at Sally. "What about Tom Nickel? Remember how Karin said he was always sending her those creepy notes? Real prick."

Sally shrugged. "Sure, but that was two years ago. He graduated last year."

"But he goes to UMD," Kevin said. "He's still in the area."

"I suppose."

Maggie wrote down the name in her book. "Anyone else?"

"Most of the guys in school are jerks," Sally said. "That's why I'm so lucky." She slung an arm around Kevin's waist, and he kissed her hair.

"How about girls who had a bad time at the barn?" Maggie asked.

There it was.

It lasted only a split second, but Maggie saw the look in Sally's eyes. Her whole demeanor changed, the cool arrogance replaced by fear. Then, just as quickly, the moment passed. Sally turned and kissed Kevin again, not looking at Maggie. When she turned back, she had pasted a mask on her face.

"I don't hang out with girls who go to the barn," she said.

Maggie nodded. "I understand."

"Kevin!" Someone shouted from the doorway to the bar. A fifty-something woman with a hassled scowl waved a stack of menus at them. "We're dying out here. I need you now, you hear me? Right now!"

Kevin turned to Maggie. "Was there anything else? I have to go."

Maggie shook her head. Kevin kissed Sally again and rushed out of the bar. Sally began to follow him, but Maggie tugged gently at her arm.

"Can you spare me another minute?" Maggie asked.

Frowning, Sally sat down where Kevin

had been. Maggie sipped her beer and kept her eyes on Sally. The girl watched her nervously. When Maggie put the mug down, she put a hand over Sally's on the table. Sally looked at her, confused and afraid. The feisty jealous glrl was gone.

"Do you want to tell me about it, Sally?" Maggie asked quietly.

Sally tried to act surprised. "I don't understand. Tell you what?"

"Come on," Maggie said. "Kevin's not here anymore. Your parents aren't around. It's just us girls. You can tell me."

"I don't know what you're talking about."

Maggie gripped her hand tightly now. "Something happened to you. I mentioned the barn, and you practically fainted. You've been there, haven't you? Look, I'm not judging you. But if you were out there and someone took advantage of you, I have to know."

Sally shook her head. "It wasn't like that."

"You don't need to make excuses for me. I'm a sister, okay? I know what men can be like."

"I don't want to get anyone in trouble," Sally said. "I never thought it was anything important. I mean, I'd pretty much forgotten about it. And even when they said Rachel's bracelet was found at the barn, well, I didn't think there could be any connection."

"Tell me what happened," Maggie urged her.

Sally sighed. "I never told Kevin. I never told anyone."

"That's okay. You can tell me. I can help, you know?"

She watched the tangled emotions in the girl's face. "Do you really think it could be important?" Sally asked. "It's just too crazy."

Maggie wanted to tear the words out of the girl's throat, but she patiently caressed Sally's hand and waited.

Sally's lower lip trembled. "About six months ago, I was biking out in the country-side north of town. I drive out there some-times and park, so I can bike on the back roads. It's always really deserted on Sunday mornings, so I thought it would be all right."

Maggie leaned forward. Oh, God, it wasn't a boyfriend. It was a psycho. Damn, damn, damn. She thought about Kerry McGrath, and she tried to let her eyes communicate the message. *That was stupid, girlie.*

"And?" Maggie said.

"My bike busted a chain. Someone picked me up."

"Someone?"

Sally nodded. "I mean, I knew him, so I wasn't scared."

"You went with him voluntarily?" Maggie asked.

"Yeah. I was miles from my car."

"Did he try something on you?"

Sally hesitated. "Sort of. Well, no, not really. But he stopped at the barn."

Bells began going off in Maggie's head. She could feel goose bumps rising on her skin, the way they always did just before a case blew wide open. Finally, finally, they were going to get answers.

"What happened, Sally?"

Sally swallowed hard. She stared down at her hands folded in her lap. Suddenly, she seemed very young. It was strange, Maggie thought, how these teenagers could pretend to be so adult and mature, and then when you scratched the surface, they became children again.

"We were just talking. He told me how nice I looked. He said it was a really hot outfit I was wearing, that I was obviously in great shape. He just seemed way too— serious, I guess. It started out harmless, but after a while it got creepy."

Maggie nodded. "Okay, what happened next?"

"Well, we were getting near the road that led to the barn. He asked me if I'd ever been there. I said no, I hadn't. He was teasing, saying we should check and see if anyone was making out there. And then he really turned. He started heading there. I was freaking out."

"Did you say anything?"

Sally shook her head. "I was too scared."

"So he drove you to the barn," Maggie said.

"Yeah. He pulled in behind it. I was ready to run. But he didn't try anything. He just kept talking, small talk, you know. It was like he was trying to decide if he was going to make a move on me."

"Were you afraid he was going to rape you?" Maggie asked.

"I don't know what I thought. I mean, it was really weird."

"But nothing actually happened."

Sally nodded. "Another car pulled in behind us. So he took off. It was like he didn't want to be recognized, you know? He hardly said a word to me the rest of the way, just took me back to my car and dropped me off. That was it."

"Nothing actually happened between you?"

Sally shook her head. "No. Like I said, I was sure he was going to try something. But after It was over, I began to think I was just being stupid."

Maggie took one of Sally's hands. "I really need you to tell me who it was."

"I know," Sally said. "I thought about coming forward before, but—I didn't really think it was important. I guess I had just convinced myself I was crazy, you know? He didn't really mean anything."

"Now you don't think so."

"I don't know. I really don't know."

"Okay," Maggie said. "Did anyone see the two of you together? Did you recognize the car that came in behind you?"

Sally shook her head. "We were out of there so quickly."

"Tell me, Sally. I won't let him hurt you. Who was it?"

Sally bent closer and whispered a name in Maggie's ear.

Maggie immediately pulled her cell phone out of her coat and dialed Stride's number.

16

Stride left city hall and stopped by the hospital on Monday night, but he discovered that Emily Stoner had been released an hour earlier, accompanied by Dayton Tenby. He wasn't surprised when he heard of her suicide attempt. He knew this was the most dangerous time, right after a parent or a spouse found out the truth, after weeks or months of fruitless longing for a miracle. The reality, hitting like a wrecking ball, sometimes was too much to bear.

He chose not to visit the Stoner household that night. There was nothing more he could tell them now, and he assumed the doctors would have ordered Emily straight to bed. He had already told Graeme by phone of the one significant discovery at the barn, a piece of bloody fabric that might be linked to Rachel.

He headed for home.

The roads were thick with slush. Snow had been falling all day, piling up on the streets and in the woods surrounding the city. The search at the barn continued, but at an agonizingly slow pace. His officers worked with ice hanging from their mustaches and cold seeping into the leather of their boots. They dug, scratched, and cursed the snow. They had begun another, more ominous search, too. Working with a cluster of volunteers from the surrounding area, they began fanning out into the woods around the barn, searching for Rachel's body. They penetrated the snow with ski poles and dug down whenever they found something unusual hidden below. Using walkie-talkies, they communicated their progress to Guppo in the police van. He mapped out a new search grid on a laptop.

Stride held out little hope they would find anything. The vastness of the northern woods worked to the benefit of murderers, who had thousands of square miles of forest in which to dispose of a body. Most of the time, the victims disappeared, and that was that. Like Kerry McGrath. They were out there somewhere, either buried or simply dumped far from the nearest road, easy targets for the animals that would come and desecrate their corpses. He shuddered to think of Rachel suffering the same fate. But the scope of the land and the crush of snow made him doubtful that they would ever find anything except that one scrap of white cloth to prove that Rachel was dead.

Stride pulled out his cellular phone. He noticed the battery was nearly gone. He had forgotten to take an extra battery from his desk, but he was almost home anyway. He punched in the number for his voice mail and listened to his messages.

The first one was from Maggie, at about two o'clock in the afternoon. It was short and sweet. "You suck, boss."

He laughed, imagining how her interviews at the high school had gone.

The second message was from the lab, about an hour earlier. They had confirmed the stain on the fabric was human blood, and they had matched it to type AB,

Rachel's blood type. The DNA tests were still to come.

The last message on his voice mail was at eight o'clock in the evening, only about five minutes ago. He expected it to be Maggie again, reporting in at the end of her day. But it wasn't.

"Hello, Jon," said a soft, nervous voice. "It's Andrea. I didn't really expect you to be there, but I guess I kind of wanted to hear your voice. That sounds silly, I suppose. And maybe it sounds a little silly to say I miss you. But the truth is, I do. Looks like you made quite an impression on me, huh? Anyway, the thing is, I'm still at work over at the school. I've got a pile of tests to grade, so I was working in the lab, but I was thinking a lot about us. And about Friday night. I know your time's not your own, but I hope we can see each other again soon. I'd really like that. Okay, fine, I've made a fool of myself, so what else is new? Well, give me a call sometime. Bye, Jon."

At the next intersection, Stride turned the truck around and headed back up the hill toward the high school.

He pulled into the lot, with the panorama of Duluth spread out on his left, and found a parking spot close to the building. Hurrying across the concrete, which had accumulated a couple more inches of snow since the plows had gone through, he jammed his hands in his coat pockets and blinked as the snow fell over his eyelids.

The school door was locked. Stride rapped his knuckles on the window, but no one was nearby to hear him. He swore. He pushed his face against the cold glass, peering inside. Nothing.

Stride took out his cell phone again, but he saw that his battery had gone completely dead. He swore again and trudged through the snowy grass around the side of the school. He was near the rear door when he saw Andrea emerge from a classroom door at the far end of the hallway. She was dressed in gray sweats that emphasized her long legs, athletic shoes, and a loose-fitting blue V-neck sweater. She didn't notice Stride, but instead made a beeline for a pop machine in the corridor. She fed in a bill, then retrieved a can of Diet Coke, popped it open, and took a long swig.

Stride banged on the door.

She stopped, turned around, and saw him. Her face lit up in a broad smile. She began jogging down the hall toward him, spilling her Coke and laughing as a geyser of brown liquid spurted onto the floor. She put the can on the floor, wiped her hands on her sweats, and hurried to the door. She opened it, grabbed Stride's hand, and pulled him inside. As the door crashed shut, blocking out the wind, she reached her sticky fingers around his neck and pulled him into a deep kiss. He was too surprised to respond at first, but then wrapped his arms tightly around her, and their lips explored each other.

"I'm glad you came," she said. "I don't have too much more to do. Why don't you come in and talk with me, and then we can go have a late dinner."

"That sounds perfect," Stride said.

Her arm went around his waist as they retraced her steps to the chemistry laboratory.

"It won't take me more than another half hour. These are multiple choice tests. I don't have to think, just grade."

"How are they doing?" Stride asked.

"Oh, I've seen better," Andrea said. "The attention span gets less and less each year. It's hard to keep it exciting for them."

"Well, science was never my strong suit either."

"Really? I would have thought a detective would enjoy all the forensic details, solving scientific mysteries, that kind of thing." Andrea scanned a test as she talked, wielding a red pen to mark errors.

"I let the lab technicians do the scientific analysis," Stride said. "I worry about figuring out the art of the possible."

"What do you mean?" Andrea asked.

"Most human acts leave some kind of trail. You have to get from place to place. You have to eat, buy gas, go to the bathroom, sleep. You leave behind skin, hair, fingerprints, fluids. All of those things can be tracked, assuming you can sift through the things that everyone else leaves behind and find the person you want."

Andrea smiled. "Like it or not, Jon, that sounds a lot like the scientific process. You couldn't have slept through all of your classes."

"I wouldn't have slept through yours," he said.

She blushed and looked down at her exams again. They were silent for a while. The only sound was the scritch-scritch of Andrea's marker on the page and the rustle of paper as she shuffled the tests. Stride let his eyes wander around the classroom, then found himself staring at Andrea, her head down, her narrow fingers nervously pushing her blonde hair back behind her ears. He could see smile lines at the edges of her mouth, like crescent moons. The sleeves of her sweater were pushed up, and he saw her bare, tapered forearms, slim but strong.

She felt his stare and looked up. They held each other with their eyes, but they didn't say anything.

He wondered what she saw when she looked at him. He knew, because Cindy had always told him so, that women found him attractive, although he never really understood it. He didn't have smooth, perfect features, but the look of a seaman who had squinted into too many storms. Like his father. Each time the barber cut his hair, he saw more gray littering the floor. He ached when he moved, and he felt the twinge of his bullet wound more intensely now than when he had been shot eight years ago. He was getting older, no doubt about that. But something about Andrea's honest stare peeled away the years from his mind.

She leaned back in her chair, covering her mouth with both hands, still staring at him.

"I'm a little embarrassed," she told him quietly.

Stride was puzzled. "Why?"

Andrea laughed and looked at him with a tiny smile. "I hope you don't think I go around picking up men in casinos and sleeping with them."

"Oh," Stride said. "I'm sorry. I shouldn't have let that happen. You were drunk. It wasn't fair."

"We were both drunk," Andrea said. "And we both wanted it. You don't have anything to feel guilty about. But the next day, I was scared. I thought I'd made a terrible mistake."

"You didn't," Stride said.

"Do you want to hear something terrible?" she said. "I resented it a little when you told me your wife died."

Stride looked at her strangely. "I don't understand."

"Cindy died, and there wasn't anything you could do about it. It wasn't about you. At least you can still feel good about yourself. That's what my husband took from me."

Stride shook his head. "That isn't your

fault. It's his. He sounds like a selfish son of a bitch."

"I know. But I still miss him. You must think I'm a fool."

"Join the club," Stride said. "Look, how about we go to dinner right now? I'm hungry as hell, and Briar Patch makes a one-inch steak that melts in your mouth. And the beer is ice cold."

Andrea nodded. "I'd like that. I think I've had enough for the day. Let me lock these in the department office, and then we can head out."

They walked out together into the empty hallway of the school. He heard distant sounds, like the thump of a basketball, but he didn't see anything or anyone around them. The lights seemed dim and shadowy, and the night outside yawned in at them through the windows like a giant black creature.

They climbed the stairs to the second floor of the school and found themselves in another dark, empty hallway. Andrea unlocked the door opposite the stairs and flicked on the light switch inside. The office was crowded with metal desks and filing cabinets and bookshelves lined with science textbooks. She chose the desk closest to the window, opened the bottom drawer, and dropped the stack of tests inside. He saw a photograph of a man on the wall beside her desk, and he assumed it was her ex-husband.

"All set," she said.

They turned off the lights, and Andrea locked the door behind them.

As they headed for the stairs, Stride saw a crack of light glowing from one of the offices at the far end of the hallway.

Andrea saw him hesitate. "What's up?"

"Probably nothing." But he suddenly felt a wave of anxiety. It came that way after a few years, a sixth sense that something wasn't right.

"Is that light coming from Nancy Carver's office?" he asked.

Andrea noticed the light in the hallway for the first time. "Looks like it."

Stride's eyes narrowed. "This sounds odd, Andrea, but just wait here, all right? I want to check something out."

"If you say so."

Andrea leaned against the wall, waiting. Stride took soft steps down the hallway, approaching the point where the office light shone into the corridor. As he got closer, he confirmed what he had suspected, that the door to Nancy Carver's office was ajar. He waited, listening, but heard no sounds from inside.

Stride coughed deliberately.

He expected to hear whoever was inside react. But the same silence pervaded the hallway.

He edged toward the doorway, close enough to peer inside and see part of the closet that served as her office. All he could see was a corner of her desk, enough to see a woman's shoulder and arm. She seemed to be sitting in her chair, not moving.

"Hello?" he called out.

He watched, but the woman didn't move. Stride gave the door a push. It swung open with a loud creak and thudded against the wall. He moved closer, filling the doorway.

Nancy Carver was inside, sitting motionless at her desk. As he entered, she looked up at him with hollow eyes, rimmed in red. The angry passion he had seen in her brown eyes was gone. Her cheeks were drawn. Her red hair was matted. She looked through him as if he didn't exist.

Stride was so taken aback by her appearance that he didn't notice for several seconds that she had a handgun lying in front of her on her desk, inches from her fingers.

"*What the hell is that?*" he said and leaped for the gun. He expected her to reach for it before he could get there, and point it either at herself or at him, but Nancy Carver didn't move. She just stared at him as he scooped it up in his hand and spilled the bullets on the floor, where they rolled crazily.

Stride leaned against the wall, breathing heavily. The gun dangled in his hand.

"Do you want to tell me what the hell is going on?" he asked.

He didn't add, *Do you want to tell me why two women in Rachel's life are trying to kill themselves?* Because he had no doubt that was what Nancy Carver was planning to do.

Carver shook her head vacantly. "I could have stopped him," she whispered.

Stride bent over the desk. "Stopped who?"

She looked up and met his eyes. "I thought she ran away," she said.

Stride said nothing.

Tears began creeping down her cheeks. "But instead, she's dead. And I could have stopped him. I knew all about it."

* * *

"I have to go," Stride told Andrea.

They were seated in his Bronco in back of the school, near her car. The radio was turned down low, playing a song by Patty Loveless.

"Will you get any sleep tonight?"

"Probably not."

"Why don't you spend the night at my house tomorrow? It doesn't matter what time you come. It felt so good sleeping beside you on Friday. I felt better just having you near me."

"It could be late. I don't know when I'll be done, and I probably won't be much company."

She smiled. "I'll leave a light on."

Andrea opened the truck door. As she got out, snow shook off the roof and dusted her blonde hair with flakes of white. She blew him a kiss, slammed the door shut, and ran to her own car. He watched her climb inside, then saw a match flare as she lit a cigarette. Her car started up on the first try. She waved as she pulled away.

Stride drove home, navigating the empty, slippery streets with less care than they demanded. Twice he lingered at a stoplight, motionless while it turned green, his eyes vacantly staring out of the streaked windows. The windshield wipers squeaked in a determined rhythm that hypnotized him.

I knew all about it.

He thought again about Nancy Carver and tried to quell his anger. She could have confirmed their suspicions weeks ago. Maybe there would have been something more they could have done. They would have been so much closer.

What if Emily Stoner had died, not knowing? Then again, he wondered if Emily had suspected all along.

There were times when it felt like a game, a puzzle they had to solve. And there were times when he hated knowing everything he did about the dark side of the human heart.

Stride crossed the bridge leading onto the Point. He drove two blocks to his home and pulled into the driveway. Maggie's car was parked on the street. He saw a light inside the house and guessed she was waiting for him. It saved him a phone call. He was going to need her tonight, and they had a long evening ahead of them at city hall.

He let himself into the house.

Maggie was in his kitchen, her feet propped up on a chair. She was eating a grilled cheese sandwich and reading the newspaper.

"You didn't answer your goddamn phone," she told him pleasantly.

"The battery's dead. Sorry about that."

"I've been waiting here for over an hour."

"Lucky for you I came home alone," he said. He wondered how he was going to break it to Maggie that she would need to be a little more cautious about using his house as a second home. He didn't think Andrea would understand their relationship.

He looked at her skirt, which was bunched up almost to her waist. "You look hot."

"I'm freezing," she said. "And it's your fault."

"Well, it was worth it if you got anything out of the boys."

Maggie smiled. "Nothing from the boys. But it turns out we were heading in the right direction all along. Family first."

Stride sat down opposite Maggie. "Graeme?"

She nodded. "Sally gave him up. Turns out Graeme took her on a little field trip to the barn last summer."

"Was she raped?"

"No, they were interrupted. But she thought that's where things were going."

"There's more," Stride told her. "How's this? Rachel told Nancy Carver she was sleeping with Graeme. She said it happened a few times, and then she cut it off, but Graeme wanted more."

Maggie's eyebrows shot skyward. "No shit? Do you think Emily suspects?"

"I'll bet she does, but she won't admit it to herself."

"Graeme's a cool customer," Maggie said. "Everything about him came up clean, right down to the polygraph. He's going to be hard to nail."

"Yeah, but him and Emily? No way. I think he was after Rachel from the beginning. And Rachel probably thought that fucking Graeme would be the perfect punishment for her mother. These two were made for each other."

"Except how do we prove it?" Maggie asked.

"We've got Carver's story. That's a start."

"It's hearsay," Maggie said. "We'll never get it in."

Stride nodded. "I know. But it'll get us a warrant."

17

Stride swore his team to silence as they prepared for the search, but it didn't help. As a battery of police cars pulled up outside the Stoner house, Bird Finch took to the airwaves, painting Graeme Stoner as a Jekyll-and-Hyde who had seduced his teenage stepdaughter and then killed her. Stride heard it on the radio and turned off the news in disgust.

Maggie, seated next to him, shook her head. "How the hell did he do that? No one knows about this."

Stride shrugged. "Let's go," he told her.

They headed up the long walkway to the

front door of the Stoner house with a swarm of uniformed officers. Stride gestured to one of the cops, pulling him closer.

"The word is out," he said. "You can expect the press to begin descending on this place in droves. I don't want them anywhere near here, okay? Tape it off, and keep them away. No curious neighbors, either."

The officer nodded and retreated to one of the squad cars, motioning for three other policemen to join him.

Stride whispered to Maggie. "Let's keep a close eye on the search, okay, Mags? I want everything by the book and witnessed. No screwups. If we end up charging this guy, he's already got Archie Gale in his corner, and you can bet everything we do is going to be second-guessed."

"Signed, sealed, and delivered," Maggie said. "Count on it, boss."

Stride didn't need to ring the doorbell. As he climbed the steps, Graeme Stoner swung the door open. Stride could see icy fury in the man's eyes.

"Hello, Lieutenant," Graeme said. "I see you've brought a few of your friends with you."

"Mr. Stoner, we have a valid warrant to

search these premises for any evidence related to the disappearance and possible murder of Rachel Deese."

"So I gathered. And is it ordinary police practice to engage in character assassination before you have any evidence? My phone is already starting to ring, thanks to Bird Finch's little report a few minutes ago. I called Kyle personally to complain."

Stride shrugged. Graeme's contacts at city hall weren't going to help him now. "I'll stay with you while my officers conduct the search."

Graeme turned on his heel and retreated through the living room without looking behind him. Stride followed him, and Maggie gathered the officers in the foyer, issuing instructions. Guppo would lead the team in the basement, she would handle the rooms upstairs, and they would do the first floor and the exterior and vehicles last.

"By the book," she told them, reiterating Stride's warning. "Stay in pairs at all times. Find it, photograph it, bag it, label it. You got all that?"

The sturdy police officers, all of them a foot and a half taller than the tiny Asian detective, nodded meekly and set about the search. Their footsteps sounded like thunder as they took different paths up and down the steps.

On the porch, Stride felt the chill in the room, emanating from the two people he found there. Emily Stoner sat where she had been when he first met her, in a recliner by the fireplace. She looked frail, her skin drained of color. Her body had shrunk, and her skin seemed to hang loosely on her frame. Her hair fell limply across her face. She was years older than she had been just a few weeks ago.

Emily didn't move and didn't say anything, but her eyes followed Graeme as he sat down in the recliner opposite her. Stride had always sensed tension between them, but this was different. Emily had heard the news along with everyone else. Stride knew what she was thinking—that the man sitting calmly a few inches away, who had shared her bed for five years, might be a monster.

It was Graeme's demeanor that surprised him.

Stride had dealt with criminals many times in the first moments after the truth came out. Most made angry protestations of innocence, denying the obvious. Others crumbled and confessed, releasing the burden of guilt that had been weighing on their souls. But he had never seen anyone look as calm and confident as Graeme Stoner. The man was furious but utterly controlled, and he still had a look of detached amusement, as if this whole process were nothing but a sideshow attraction.

Stride didn't know how to read him. He usually believed he could tell a man's guilt or innocence by watching for the truth written in his eyes and face. Graeme was a mask.

"You realize you've destroyed my reputation in this town," Graeme told him with a determined stare. "I hope the city can afford to pay the damages when I sue you."

Stride ignored him. He turned to Emily. "Please accept my apologies, Mrs. Stoner. If there had been any way of making this easier for you, I would have done it. I know what you've been through."

Emily nodded but said nothing. She kept staring at her husband, doing what Stride was trying to do—see the truth. Graeme's face revealed nothing.

"Mr. Stoner, I have to read you your rights," Stride said.

Graeme raised an eyebrow. "Are you arresting me?"

"No, but you are a suspect in this investigation. I want to make sure you understand your rights before we go any further." Stride rattled off the Miranda warnings, watching Graeme frown in disgust as he did so.

"Knowing that you don't have to say anything, are you willing to answer some questions, even though Mr. Gale is not present?"

Another shrug. "I have nothing to hide," Graeme said.

Stride was surprised—rich suspects *never* talked—but he wasn't about to question his good fortune.

"The leak regarding this situation was regrettable, Mr. Stoner. I apologize for that. I don't know how it happened." Stride didn't want to leap into the tough questions and have Graeme realize he was better off staying quiet. He wanted to worm his way slowly toward the ugly details.

"I suggest you find out how it happened, Lieutenant." Something in the man's eyes made Stride believe that Graeme was perfectly aware of the detective's strategy.

Stride nodded. "You can understand, however, that some of the details we have uncovered raise a lot of questions for us. We'd like to get your side of the story. That's why I'm here."

"I'm sure."

"Were you sleeping with Rachel?" Stride asked.

There was a heavy silence in the room. Emily seemed to hold her breath, waiting for Graeme's answer. Stride watched the man set his jaw and saw anger creep into his face. There was no hint of guilt in his expression, only contempt. His conviction made Stride wonder if they were making a mistake. Or was the man simply a consummate actor?

"What an offensive question. But the answer is no. Never. I would never have slept with my stepdaughter, Lieutenant. It did not happen."

"Rachel said it did," Stride said.

"I can't believe that," Graeme retorted. "The girl may not have had the best relations with either of us, but I cannot believe she would make up such an outrageous lie."

"She told a school counselor, Nancy Carver, that you started having sex with her shortly after you go married Emily."

Stride heard Emily wince and suck in her

breath. Graeme glanced at his wife, then back at Stride.

"Carver? No wonder. That interfering little bitch. Do you know she actually called and interrogated me? But she never came out and made any accusations like that. I think she's the one you should be investigating, Stride. It's obvious the woman is a lesbian. As I recall, I even called the school to complain."

Stride jotted a reminder in his notes. He wanted to check if there had really been a complaint lodged against Nancy Carver.

"Why would Rachel make up such a story?"

"I can't believe she did. Carver probably made up the whole thing."

"Rachel told someone else, too," Stride lied.

This time he caught a glimmer of hesitation in Graeme's eyes, but the moment quickly vanished. "I find that hard to believe. But if Rachel did that, all I can think is that she was having problems. Maybe the girl was having fantasies about me. Or maybe she was trying to drive a wedge between me and Emily. Who knows?"

"But you never slept with her?"

"I told you, no."

"You never touched her or had any kind of sexual contact with her?"

"Of course not," Graeme snapped.

"And she never touched you."

"I'm not Bill Clinton, Lieutenant. No sex means no sex."

Stride nodded. A definitive denial would help them in prosecution, if they could find any evidence to back up a relationship between Rachel and Graeme, but he knew that was a big if.

He doubted Stoner would be so adamant in his denial if there were any way of proving the two had been involved.

Or he was telling the truth.

"Do you know a friend of Rachel's named Sally Lindner?" Stride asked.

Graeme furrowed his brow. "I think so. She goes out with that boy Kevin, as I recall. Why?"

"Have you ever given her a ride in your van?"

"I really don't remember," Graeme said. "Maybe."

"Maybe?"

Graeme scratched his chin. "I may have given her a ride to her car one day. Her bike was broken. This was several months ago, and honestly, I can't even remember if it was her."

"Where did you pick her up?"

"Oh, somewhere north of town, as I recall. I had been visiting one of our branches."

"And where did you take her?" Stride asked.

"Like I said, back to her car."

"Did you stop anywhere?"

"Not that I recall," Graeme said.

"She says you took her to the barn."

"The barn? No, certainly not. I picked her up and dropped her off at her car. That's all, Lieutenant."

"It didn't happen?" Stride asked. "You never went there with her?"

"It didn't happen," Graeme told him firmly.

"Then why would Sally say it did?"

Graeme sighed. "How the hell would I know, Lieutenant? Maybe Rachel put her up to it."

"Rachel?" Stride said. "Why would Rachel do that?"

"She's a complicated girl," Graeme said.

Maggie pointed at a three-drawer oak filing cabinet. "You start there. I'll take the desk."

The other officer, a gangly twenty-five-year-old rookie who hadn't outgrown his pimples, nodded and chewed his gum loudly. His name was Pete, and he had been in private security for several years before joining the force a few months ago. Maggie liked his cocky confidence, but he had a lot to learn. Pete had made the mistake of blowing a bubble with his gum and popping it with his gloved finger. Maggie nearly took his head off, reading him the riot act about contaminating the scene. Besides, the noise really bugged her.

Pete stopped blowing bubbles, but he kept chewing the gum, just to annoy her. That was exactly the kind of thing she would have done, and she liked that.

They were in Graeme Stoner's upstairs office. He kept it impeccably organized. There was a monitor and keyboard on the big, custom-built oak desk, a small array of books arranged by subject, and two stacks of compact discs. Maggie glanced at them. One set of discs reflected Graeme's taste in music, which ran to loud Mahler symphonies. The other set included discs labeled as confidential and bearing the stamp of Graeme's bank.

"We'll have to get Guppo to look at all the discs and the hard drive," she said. "Make sure we label them and take them all with us."

Pete grunted. He dug his gloved hands into the first drawer of the file cabinet.

Maggie glanced around the room, absorbing Graeme Stoner's tastes. The walls were papered in a dark blue pattern, with a gold fleck that matched the rich gold color of the carpeting. Several original watercolors hung on the walls, mostly nature scenes, and to Maggie's untrained eye, they looked professional and expensive. The desk and its elaborate leather chair were the main furnishings, supplemented by the filing cabinet, a wall of built-in bookshelves lined with hardcovers, and an overstuffed chair with matching ottoman. A slender brass lamp with a globe light sat on the corner of the desk.

It was a rich, sterile room, full of money and devoid of character. The same had been true of the master bedroom—the kind of elegant space in which it was hard to believe people actually lived. She and Pete had spent nearly two hours in the bedroom and bathroom, sifting through drawers and searching for secrets. They found little. The rooms were as interesting for what they didn't find as for what they did. No birth control. No sex toys. No adult videos. She wondered when Graeme and Emily had last had sex.

It didn't really matter. The question was whether Graeme and *Rachel* had ever had sex. They had turned up nothing yet in either room to prove Nancy Carver's allegation, and Maggie knew from their original search of Rachel's room after the disappearance that she had left nothing behind as physical evidence of an incestuous affair.

Maggie shuddered. She tried to imagine Rachel alone with Graeme in this house. Was it in the bedroom? In her room? On the bathroom floor? Did he take her on top, or did he make her straddle him? Did he take her from behind? Did he force her to her knees and make her suck him off?

Evidence. That was the troublesome part. Graeme was safe in denying the affair, as long as Rachel never showed up, because little proof ever remained that two people had been having sex. All they had was what Rachel told people—which was worthless in court.

"What's in the filing cabinet, Pete?" Maggie asked.

The cop shrugged. "Tax records. Warranties. The guy saved everything."

"Check every file, and box up the tax records. We'll want to copy those."

Maggie focused on the desk. She took each book from the desk, flipped through the pages, and returned it. She opened the drawers one by one, examined them from front to back, then got down on her knees and checked the bottom of each drawer to make sure nothing was taped underneath.

She booted up the computer. She didn't have time to examine the hard disk byte by byte—that was Guppo's job—but she at least wanted to do a search for e-mails and review the pages Graeme had been visiting on the Internet. To avoid accidentally altering the evidence, she first printed out a full directory listing on the laser printer, noting the details of every file on the hard drive. Then she hooked up a jump drive to the machine's USB port and copied Graeme's hard disk. When she was done, she swapped the drive to the laptop she had brought with her and called up a mirror of Graeme's computer on her own machine.

When she called up Internet Explorer, she was surprised to find that the history of sites visited had been deleted and there was no listing at all in the Favorites box.

"This is interesting," Maggie said aloud. "Looks like Graeme has been cleaning up after himself."

"Huh?" Pete said.

"No Web sites at all. And yet the man is head of e-commerce at his bank. Does that make any sense? He doesn't want anyone to see where he's been surfing."

Maggie loaded Outlook. The e-mail software was equally clean, nothing in his inbox, nothing sent, nothing saved. It was as if the man had never sent an e-mail on the computer, although Maggie knew that was absurd.

Something felt wrong. She wondered if Graeme had a drop box stored on one of the public Web sites like Yahoo or Hotmail, where he could send and receive personal e-mails without leaving a trail on his computer. That was going to be a lot harder to find.

Her walkie-talkie crackled, and Maggie picked it up. "Yeah?"

It was Guppo. "We've covered the basement."

"Anything?"

"Clean as a whistle. Even the garden implements shine like brand-new. I don't think he spends a lot of time down here."

"Damn," Maggie said. She was hoping they might find evidence of the murder itself, even if they couldn't prove that Rachel and Graeme were having sex. Based on the evidence at the barn, though, she realized it was unlikely that he had killed her in the house. It was more logical that they had gone to the barn and that something had happened between them there—something that ended in Rachel's death.

"Okay, Guppo, you and Terry go after the minivan outside, and work it over. Check out every inch, pull up the carpet, run the UV search for blood residue. Hair. Fiber. Semen. Fingerprints. Anything. I want to know if Rachel was in that van."

"Gotcha."

The next voice that crackled over the walkie-talkie belonged to Terry. "Son of a bitch, Maggie, you want me locked up in a van with Guppo? It was bad enough being in the basement with him."

Maggie laughed. "Hey, I put up with it at the barn, Terry. You don't get any sympathy from me. Over and out." She hooked the walkie-talkie onto her belt again.

"I'm going to start on the bookshelves," Maggie said, eyeing the wall of hardcovers with distaste.

"The computer's clean?" Pete asked.

"At least on the basic stuff, yeah. Looks like Graeme kept it tidy. We'll have to have Guppo do a more thorough search."

"How about pictures?" Pete said. "You know, GIFs, JPEGs, that kind of stuff. Maybe he kept some dirty photos or other X-rated stuff around."

Maggie nodded. She did a search of the jump drive. First she typed in "Rachel" and did a global search for any file that might include the girl's name. That would have been too easy, she figured, and she was right. The search came up empty. She tried again with files starting with *R* but was overwhelmed by the results. She searched for "sex," then "fuck," then "porn," but found nothing.

Then she had another idea. She narrowed the search list to identify any file that had been created or edited in a two-week span surrounding Rachel's disappearance.

The search turned up only a handful of

files. She scrolled down slowly, ruling out the system files and checking out anything that looked like a word processing document or spreadsheet. Everything seemed work-related, full of details about online mutual fund transactions and branch profit-and-loss statements. She went through the files one by one, mentally crossing them off her list, doubting this search was going to be any more productive than the others. Graeme was too smart.

And then she saw it.

Fargo4qtr.gif. A picture file created two days before Rachel disappeared.

The name sounded like a business file, but it was in the wrong directory. And she hadn't seen any other GIFs among Graeme's work files. She moved the mouse over to highlight the file, and she hesitated before clicking on it. She held her breath. With a flutter of her fingertip, she clicked and watched the screen go blank. The picture seemed to take forever to load, although she knew that it was only a second or two as she heard the laptop's hard drive whirring. Then the screen refreshed, and a photo jumped onto the screen, filling it in full color.

Maggie gasped. "Oh my God."

She heard Pete turn curiously behind her. Then, seeing the screen over her shoulder, he exhaled, too. "Shit."

It was one of the most amazing pictures she had ever seen. Maggie considered herself a staunch heterosexual, but even she found herself wetting her lips with her tongue. Rachel's eyes drew hers like a magnet.

In the photo, Rachel was naked. She was in the wilderness somewhere, with trees out of focus behind her. The rain was falling, coating her bare skin, running in silver rivulets down her body. The photo captured drops of water on her breasts and little streams of water running into her damp crotch and slipping to the ground. Rachel's knees were bent. She had one hand between her legs, two fingers pushed out of sight into her slit. Her other hand cupped her right breast, reaching up to graze her nipple. Rachel's mouth had fallen open in pleasure, but her bright green eyes were open, staring into the camera.

Maggie realized Pete was beside her, practically panting. "God, I hope the girl's not dead," he said. "What I wouldn't give to fuck that."

"Shut up," Maggie said sourly. She fed the photo to the printer. It printed slowly, line by line, inking out the image of the teenager masturbating in the woods.

"That son of a bitch," she murmured.

The porch was silent. Emily and Graeme sat in dueling recliners. Emily stared vacantly into space, motionless, her hands folded in her lap. Graeme examined a file through his half-glasses, studiously ignoring Stride. When the detective had run out of questions, Graeme had simply gone back to work, as if he had nothing at all to be concerned about.

Stride knew that at least part of Graeme's calm demeanor was an act, because the insinuation alone would be enough to destroy his reputation. Like it or not, Graeme Stoner was finished in Duluth. And the man knew it. The only question was whether he would be free to go somewhere else or whether they would find what they needed to put him away for a long time.

The waiting game got old as the hours dragged by. Stride heard Guppo and Terry trudge back upstairs, then heard them disappear through the front door. He assumed Maggie had directed them to search the van, although he didn't hear the conversation. He had turned off his walkie-talkie rather than let the Stoners hear their dialogue.

He stared at Graeme, studying the man's face. He knew that Graeme could feel his stare even as he turned pages in the file, but the banker didn't flinch. It would be interesting to watch Dan Erickson do battle in court to put the man behind bars. Assuming they ever made it to court.

More time passed.

Stride heard Maggie's footsteps. She marched into the room, a piece of white paper flapping in her hand. This time, Graeme looked up with genuine curiosity and a faint nervousness.

Maggie whispered in Stride's ear. "Check this out."

Stride looked at the photo and blinked at the sight of the naked girl. He had to remind himself this was the teenager who was missing and presumed dead.

He looked up from the paper to find Graeme staring back at him. Stride suddenly felt he had an edge over the arrogant bastard.

"Tell me, Mr. Stoner, do you own a digital camera?" Stride asked.

Graeme nodded. "Of course."

"We'll need to take it with us," Stride said. "Do you recognize this photograph?"

He handed the paper to Graeme. Stoner's reserve cracked, and Stride saw his hand tremble as he tried to hold the paper steady. Emily saw what was on the page, and her hand covered her open mouth as she stifled a scream.

"Where did you find this?" Graeme said, trying to keep his voice even.

"On the computer in your office," Stride told him.

"I have no idea how it got there. I've never seen this before."

"Really?" Stride asked. "You didn't take the photo?"

"No, of course not. I told you, I had no idea it was on the computer. Rachel must have put it there. As a joke."

"A joke?" Stride asked, his eyebrows climbing. "Quite the joke."

"Who knows why she did it?" Graeme said.

Stride nodded. "You have no idea where or when this was taken?"

"None at all."

Maggie studied the man with cold eyes. "The file was added to your computer two days before Rachel disappeared."

"Two days?" Graeme asked.

"That's quite a coincidence," Stride added.

"Well, as I say, Rachel must have left it there. Maybe it was her way of saying a bizarre good-bye before she ran away."

Stride stepped closer to the man. "But she didn't run away, did she, Mr. Stoner? You and she went out to the barn that night. You went to have sex with her, like you had been doing for years. Did she say no this time? Did she try to run away? Did she threaten to tell your wife?"

"Graeme," Emily begged him in a weak voice. "Please tell me none of this is true."

He sighed and looked at her. "Of course not."

"We know Rachel was at the barn that night, Mr. Stoner. We know she made it back to your house, and that you were the only one here. Would you like to tell us what happened then?"

Graeme shook his head. "I never heard her come in. And I think that's all I have to say until Mr. Gale gets here."

He looked dazed. Stride was pleased to see that the man was capable of human error after all, that he could make mistakes, leave clues behind, and not know how to react when his lies were uncovered.

"Keep searching, Mags," Stride told her.

Maggie was about to return upstairs when her walkie-talkie squawked. Everyone in the room heard Guppo's voice.

"Maggie, Stride, we need you out here. There's residue of blood on the floor under the carpet in the back and on a knife he's got in a toolbox."

Maggie quickly switched off the handset, but it was too late.

Emily screamed.

Stride and Maggie both watched her, feeling the raw pain that sliced her voice.

She bolted up from the recliner, her face ashen. She turned and stared in horror at Graeme, who sat with a curious smirk frozen on his face, like a cat who had swallowed a canary. Emily sank to her knees.

Stride jumped forward, ready to catch her if she crumpled into a faint.

Instead, Emily moaned, then got down on all fours and vomited over the white carpet.

PART THREE

18

The Kitch, as the Kitchi Gammi club was known, was Duluth's attempt to emulate the elegance of New England city clubs. It was a four-story redbrick mansion with tidy, manicured gardens flowering in the warmth of springtime, wide gables, and a stately porch. The club boasted cozy upstairs libraries, with cherrywood antiques, elegant recliners, and all the day's news from Minneapolis and New York neatly placed on the lion's-paw coffee tables. This was where politicians and investors enjoyed snifters of brandy while they conducted the city's important business.

The doorman, a wizened Norwegian in his early eighties named Per who had worked at the Kitch longer than many of its members had been alive, drew to attention as a tall, stout man approached the steps of the club. The man was whistling a Sinatra song, as he had been doing for all of the thirty years Per had known him. He was in his late fifties, and nearly as wide as he was tall, but he had an energetic bounce in his step. He had gray curly hair neatly trimmed and receding well behind his forehead. His face was florid and wide, with razor-sharp blue eyes, tiny owlish glasses, and a peppery goatee. He wore a charcoal pinstripe three-piece suit. with a white shirt. Gold cufflinks peeked out from the ends of his coat sleeves. A flower was poked into the slit of his lapel. An aroma of cologne trailed him up the steps.

"Good evening, Mr. Gale," Per said, swinging open the door.

"Per, it is a pleasure to see you, as always," Archibald Gale replied in a booming voice. "What an astonishing spring day, isn't it?"

"Oh, that it is, Mr. Gale. I'm guessing you have another big case, then, don't you?"

"I do, Per, I do."

"Well, I always say there isn't anyone better than you."

"From your mouth to the jury's ears, Per," Gale replied.

He patted the old man affectionately on the shoulder and entered the dark foyer of the club. The door, with its heavy oak panels and stained glass, closed gently behind him. He checked his watch and noted that it was four forty-five, fifteen minutes before his appointment with Dan Erickson, the county attorney. Gale liked to arrive early, situate himself in one of the libraries with a single-malt scotch, and await his prey.

Although Gale was one of the state's most notable criminal trial lawyers, it was rumored that he won most of his cases at the Kitch, by demoralizing his opposing counsel over a cordial drink. His innocent hints and dark innuendos so thoroughly unnerved prosecutors that they began second-guessing their strategy and fumbling their presentations in court. Gale's reputation for psychological warfare had become so well known that prosecutors were now turning down his traditional offer of a chitchat at the Kitch on the night before a trial began.

But Daniel had too much ego to turn him

down. It was more fun that way. Gale had dealt with many ambitious, politically minded attorneys over the years, and he enjoyed poking holes in their arrogance. Daniel was more ruthless than most. Initially, when Trygg Stengard, the previous county attorney, had hired Daniel, Gale had given his old friend and adversary words of caution about his new number-two man. But Stengard, unlike Gale, was a politician with a soft spot for naked ambition.

"I expect you to soften the kid up, Archie," Stengard had told him. "Kick his ass a few times. It'll be good for him."

Gale had done just that. He was not surprised to find that Daniel was suave and effective in court and had done a good job as county attorney after Stengard died. Daniel had lost two big cases, though—both at the hands of Archibald Gale.

The trial of Graeme Stoner would be either Daniel's revenge or a humiliating strikeout.

Gale knew that Daniel was confident, and Gale was fully aware that the prosecutor had reason to be. Even without a body, the forensic evidence alone would be enough to sour a jury on a client who looked even more arrogant than the prosecutor, and if Daniel could make them believe that the man had truly been screwing his stepdaughter, Gale would have a difficult time keeping Stoner out of jail for the rest of his life.

But Gale enjoyed a challenge—and he had a few surprises of his own waiting.

Gale hopped into the ancient elevator and felt it sag under his weight. He usually took the stairs to stay in shape, but for his pretrial meetings, he didn't want to risk being winded. When the elevator finally creaked to a halt, he got out and headed down the hall to the large Ojibwe Library, with its three sets of chambered windows overlooking the lake. Margaret emerged from the kitchen, and he bent down merrily to give her a peck on the cheek. The old woman giggled and blushed.

"I've got your glass of Oban on the coffee table for you, Mr. Gale."

"Oh, Margaret, you're too good to me. Let's run away together, shall we?"

Margaret giggled again. "Do you know what Mr. Erickson will be drinking?"

"Make sure you have a Bombay gin with lots of ice waiting for him. Put it on my account. And I imagine he'll quickly want another."

Margaret smiled, as if they were sharing a little secret, and retreated back to the kitchen.

Gale made himself comfortable. He spent a moment or two reflecting as he stared out the windows, glanced at the headlines of the *Star Tribune,* which he had already read, and settled himself into a 1920s sofa, where he allowed his Oban to warm in his palm. He was calm. He was always that way before a trial. Other lawyers became energetic and restless. Gale became focused. He could feel his pulse slow down and feel his brain slowly bring itself to bear on the big picture of what lay ahead.

Five minutes later, Dan Erickson burst into the library, carrying a double shot of gin in a lowball glass, which he swirled in his hand, clinking the ice cubes. Drops of gin slurped over the edges and onto the carpeting.

"Hello, Daniel," Gale said. "My, my, you look nervous."

Dan stopped and smiled. "On the contrary. I can't wait to get started. Last time, you beat me, Archie."

"And the time before that, as I recall," Gale reminded him cheerily.

"Well, not this time."

Dan didn't sit down. He paced between the windows and the fireplace. He was dressed in a navy suit and polished black shoes. His blond hair was carefully sprayed in place. Although a short man, Dan was handsome and fit, and Gale suspected he had been going to a tanning booth for weeks to make an impression on the jury.

"Ah, but Judge Kassel already took my side regarding Nancy Carver," Gale said.

Dan shrugged. He picked up a small porcelain figurine from the fireplace mantel, passed it back and forth between his hands, and put it back. "Carver's testimony was hearsay. I knew we wouldn't get it in."

"So you say, but it makes it much harder to put Graeme and Rachel in bed together, doesn't it?"

"Oh, we have enough to do that," Dan said. "This is a very sick client you've got, Archie. You're not making yourself any friends in the community by taking the case."

Gale buried his nose inside his glass of scotch, then took an imperceptible sip. "Yes, I've already gotten the usual hate mail and death threats. It's ironic, don't you think, people saying they're going to kill me because I'm defending an alleged murderer."

"You're hardly on the side of the angels here," Dan said. He was at the window now, staring at the Monday afternoon traffic on London Road. Then he paced back to the center of the room.

"Sit down already, you're making me dizzy."

Dan smiled. He drummed his fingers on his pockets. "Just wait, Archie. Just wait."

"You do seem confident," Gale told him.

"That's because I've got Stoner nailed. I know it. You know it."

"Oh, if I were you, I'd look into a few of my witnesses a little more carefully. You might find they have other stories to tell."

A faint flicker of worry passed across Dan's face and then was quickly replaced by a broad grin. "Damn, you are an old fox. You lie almost as well as I do."

Gale chuckled. "High praise from you. But I'm not lying, Consider it a professional courtesy."

"Yeah, yeah. Look, you can wriggle and squirm, but you won't escape on this one. Your one chance was to get the case moved to another venue, and on that one, you lost. Hell, I don't need to worry about putting Nancy Carver on the stand to say that

Rachel told her she was boffing her daddy. The whole jury pool already knows. Not that I'll admit that outside this room."

"Yes," Gale acknowledged, sighing. "I was disappointed about the change of venue. I suspect the judge knows the case should have been transferred, but I really think she wanted it herself. She's a little like you."

Dan bent down, dipping his fingers into a crystal bowl and scooping out a handful of mixed nuts. He sifted through them, sorting out a white chunk of Brazil nut, which he popped into his mouth.

"You're right about that," he said, as the nut crunched between his teeth. "In fact, you should know that I slept with Catharine."

Gale's eyebrows arched in surprise. He reached over to the end table and retrieved his Oban. "You slept with the judge? Isn't that going a little far to win a case?"

"It was several years ago. She wasn't a judge, and I wasn't the county attorney then."

"But she *was* already married, as I recall," Gale said.

Dan shrugged and found a cashew from the pile in his hand. He ate it loudly without replying.

"I could ask for a different judge," Gale continued.

"You could, but you won't," Dan said.

"You're so sure?"

Dan nodded. "This won't be your last case in front of Catharine, and I don't imagine you want to be the one to air her dirty linen in public. Besides, you know you could do worse. Stoner will get fair treatment at her hands. More than he deserves."

"And from what I know of your reputation, Daniel, your affair with her may work to my advantage," Gale retorted dryly.

"Oh, I wouldn't go that far."

"Well, then, why tell me?" Gale asked innocently.

"You know perfectly well why, Archie. Now you can't claim to be ignorant. I've given you reason to remove her, and you've declined. If you had discovered the affair after Stoner was convicted, you'd have grounds for a retrial."

"True," Gale said. "Although Stoner will never be convicted."

"Come on, Archie. If I were you, I'd plead him. We've got Rachel's blood in his van, on his knife, and at the murder scene—a perfect DNA match. You'll never get the better of

Dr. Yee on the scientific evidence. No one ever does."

Gale shrugged. He had tangled with Yee many times. "Yes, if Dr. Unshakable says it's the girl's blood, then it's the girl's blood."

"Put the blood evidence together with the evidence of an incestuous affair," Dan added. "Plus, he has no alibi, and he's a rich, smug son of a bitch. The jury is going to loathe him."

Gale shook his head. He finished off his drink and pushed himself out of the chair with a groan. He smoothed his goatee. "Trust me, Daniel. You picked the wrong case to turn into a public circus."

"Meaning what?"

"Meaning you and Bird Finch and the rest of the media may already have declared my client guilty, but that verdict doesn't count. When I get done with the jury, they won't even need an hour to acquit him."

Dan flushed. "Because he's got the great Archibald Gale defending him?"

"Because you have no case," Gale said. "You don't even have a body. You know the odds of a successful murder conviction without one."

"It wasn't an impediment with the grand jury," Dan pointed out.

Gale snorted. "We're talking about the real jury now, Daniel."

"I'll take my chances," Dan said. "The jury's not going to reward Graeme Stoner because there are so many places up here to hide a body. You can blow smoke, Archie—God knows you do it well—but the jury will draw the right conclusion when I show them the kind of man Stoner is."

Gale approached Dan, towering over him, and put a fleshy hand on the younger man's shoulder. "Look, I don't want to humiliate you in the courtroom. Why don't we work this out now between the two of us? Drop the charges. Say there's not enough evidence right now, and you're waiting until you've got conclusive proof to make sure you don't have to worry about double jeopardy. Stoner will leave town. His life here is over regardless. And then everyone forgets about this."

Dan ate the last Brazil nut and dusted the salt off his hands. His eyes were cold and angry. He looked up at Gale and jabbed a finger in his face. "Don't think you can intimidate me. Stoner's life is over, all right. He's going to spend the rest of it in prison. He's a murderer, and I'm going to put him away."

"You're so sure he's guilty?"

Dan groaned. "Come on, Archie. This is just us boys. Don't tell me you think he's innocent?"

Gale shrugged and didn't reply.

"Well, I guess we have nothing else to say," Dan told him. "I'll see you in court."

"Yes, indeed," Gale said, still chuckling. "Don't say I didn't warn you."

19

Gale strolled southward along the back street, avoiding the early evening crowds on Superior. For a large man, he walked briskly and athletically. When he saw the circular Radisson a couple of blocks to his right, he turned up the street, keeping an eye on the people around him as he neared the hotel. He drifted casually into the lobby and headed for the elevators.

This was always the risky part. Gale was a recognizable figure, and he worried that reporters from the Duluth newspaper, whose offices were only a few blocks away, might be hanging out over drinks in the hotel bar.

He took the elevator to the seventh floor, got out, then retreated to the stairwell. He walked down three flights, took the elevator again, and this time got out on the eleventh floor. He glanced carefully down the corridor, then proceeded to the far end and knocked five times on the door of one of the hotel's suites.

He saw a shadow pass across the peephole.

Graeme Stoner opened the door.

"Counselor," Graeme said. "It's always a pleasure."

Graeme moved aside to let Gale in, then closed and locked the door behind him.

"Bird Finch is convinced you're still in Minneapolis," Gale told him.

"That's good. Otherwise, the hotel would be under siege."

Gale had succeeded in obtaining bail for Stoner, but he couldn't go home. The publicity surrounding his arrest put him in danger, and even if he had been safe, he was no longer welcome in his own house. Emily had filed for divorce. His bank had also fired him, although Gale had helped Graeme win a lucrative settlement in return for his walking quietly away without a legal challenge.

"What's the good word from Danny Erickson?" Graeme asked.

Gale chuckled. "As confident as ever. He wants to bury you, Graeme."

Graeme shrugged. "That's Danny boy. You know, we used to go out together now and then. I thought of him as a friend. But with Danny, friendship is important only as long as it is useful. Can I get you a drink?"

Gale shook his head.

"Well, I hope you don't mind if I indulge," Graeme said. He hunted under the bar and poured himself a glass of brandy, then situated himself in a comfortable chair by the window. The sky had turned to a deep blue twilight. Graeme was wearing a maroon golf shirt and pleated tan slacks. His laptop was glowing on a nearby desk. Gale asked him once what he did to pass the time, and Graeme told him he had increased his holdings in the stock market by 20 percent over the past five months. It was like a vacation for him.

Gale, still standing, studied his client. Even when Graeme called him on the day of the search, the man had been unemotional, calmly asserting his innocence and apologizing to Gale for talking to the police without his lawyer present. But, he claimed, he knew he was innocent and so had nothing to hide.

He wondered. It made no difference to the defense, of course, but morbid curiosity made Gale speculate on the truth. He had heard many liars in his day, and usually he could see through them immediately. Graeme was different. Either the man was sincere, or he was one of the most gifted liars Gale had encountered in his career. Unfortunately, he had always found that the better the liar, the more likely his client was guilty as charged.

Not that he couldn't make a jury believe otherwise.

But which was it?

Gale had to admit to himself that the prosecution had a compelling circumstantial case. The evidence in the truck and the barn pointed directly to Graeme, even though there was nothing specific to link him to either location. And though the prosecution had nothing (so far as he knew) to prove a sexual relationship between Graeme and Rachel, the hints were tantalizing, maybe enough to sway a jury of stolid Scandinavians who didn't approve of phone sex or promiscuous seventeen-year-olds. The truth? He simply didn't know. He could poke holes in the prosecution's case, and he had other suspects that the jury could readily believe were involved in Rachel's disappearance. None of that cleared Graeme in his own mind.

He just didn't know. It made him vaguely uncomfortable. He didn't mind defending guilty clients, and he enjoyed defending innocent ones. Being in the middle was a new experience for him.

Graeme was smiling at him. It was as if he could read his thoughts. "Do you feel like you're dancing with the devil, counselor?"

Gale took a chair opposite Graeme. "A totally different jury will have to decide who owns your soul, Graeme. Let's worry about the jury in court tomorrow."

"Touché," Graeme said. "Well, what did you learn from Danny? Did you psych the poor boy out?"

Gale shrugged. "He's got a pretty good case for a man without a body. And Daniel is good before a jury."

"But not as good as you," Graeme said.

"No," Gale admitted easily. "He's not."

"See, that's the confidence I'm paying for.

But tell me honestly, what's the outlook? Don't spare my feelings."

"All right," Gale said. "The physical evidence is the heart of the case. It's strong. And the publicity has been so vicious against you that much of the jury pool is likely to be tainted, regardless of what they say in voir dire. I'm afraid that most of them are going to walk in thinking you're a perverted son of a bitch."

"So what do we do?"

"Daniel knows the evidence only takes them to the edge of the cliff, and he wants the jury to stroll across the bridge to the other side. I want them to take a long look down and conclude the bridge isn't sturdy."

"A beautiful analogy," Graeme said. "I assume there's more."

Gale nodded. "Then there's the bogeyman theory."

"I've always liked that one."

"You should. It's not enough to plant doubt as to whether you did it. I have to make sure the jury realizes there are plausible alternatives. If you're the only game in town, they'll convict, even if the evidence is shaky."

Graeme finished his brandy and poured

himself another from the bottle. "But you assured me we do have alternatives."

Gale nodded. "I think so."

In fact, Gale was unusually suspicious that either of the persons he planned to paint as a culprit might actually be guilty. But there was something in Graeme's cool smile that disturbed him. He didn't like the man.

"You won't tell me what you've found, though," Graeme continued. "That doesn't seem fair."

"Sometimes the less you know, and the less you tell me, the better," Gale said.

"Well, then, give it to me straight. Do you think I'll be free to move to Colorado in a few weeks, or will I be checking into a less comfortable hotel for the rest of my life?"

Gale eyed his client. "I'm not a betting man, Graeme. I don't know if you're innocent or not, and I don't really care. But the fact is, it's hard to prove a murder without a body, and in this case, I don't think the circumstantial evidence will be enough. I think you'll walk."

"Even though the jury thinks I'm a perverted son of a bitch?" Graeme replied, smiling.

"We can get past that," Gale said.

Graeme nodded, satisfied. "I'm delighted to hear it. But I can think of at least one person who will be bitterly disappointed."

Gale could think of many people. "Who?"

"Rachel."

Gale stared at Graeme. "So you think she's alive."

"I'm sure of it."

"And the evidence in the van? The barn?"

"Planted," Graeme said.

"To frame you?"

"Exactly."

Gale's eyes narrowed. "And why would Rachel want to do that?"

"She's a complicated girl."

Gale realized again how much he disliked that smile. Every time he began to convince himself his client was really innocent, that smirk slid onto his face, and the evil twinkle came and went in his eyes. "Why are you so sure? Couldn't someone else have killed her and then framed you?"

"That sounds like reasonable doubt, so I'll say yes."

"But you don't think so," Gale said.

Graeme shook his head.

"This was all an elaborate plot by Rachel?" Gale asked. "She faked all this evidence?"

"That's what I think," Graeme said.

"You know, there's one thing that could sink our case and put you in prison."

"Oh? And what's that, counselor?"

"If Daniel can make the jury believe you were really fucking that girl."

"It's hard to prove something that never happened," Graeme said.

Graeme's face was darkened by the shadows in the hotel room. Gale could see only the man's eyes, not blinking. Graeme's voice conveyed the same smooth sincerity it always did, and his body language was perfect. There were no telltale signs of dishonesty, none of the usual symptoms the lawyer had learned to spot and exploit. But Gale realized that this time he didn't believe a word. Not any of it.

His client was guilty.

It was almost a relief. Now he could defend him.

"I hope that's true," Gale said. "If you had sex with her and Daniel can prove it, you're in big trouble."

Graeme smiled.

20

The port at Two Harbors was barely visible, just a long, narrow smudge that interrupted the line of trees. Behind them and overhead, the sky was blue and clear, but Stride could see dark clouds massing at the horizon, growing like a cancer in the sky and creeping closer to the boat. The wind whipped the lake into foamy white swells and tipped the boat from side to side like a bathtub toy. He pushed the throttle forward, and the engine churned against the waves, but the speed barely inched faster. The squall would reach them long before they made it home.

He felt like a fool, allowing them to be

trapped. The beautiful Sunday weather had been too tempting, and Guppo had offered him the use of his twenty-six-foot sport cruiser, a beauty he had inherited from his uncle. Stride had urged Andrea to join him. They usually did city things together, going to plays and concerts, or having dinner with teachers from the high school. Andrea liked to show Stride off to the women who had been so sympathetic when she divorced. They didn't do the quiet things closest to Stride's heart, like sailing on the lake. He wanted those things back in his life.

But the afternoon had been a disaster. Even under the warm spring sun, the lake was freezing, wind ripping through their middleweight coats. Stride had cast a line, only to have a gust of wind snap his pole. Andrea threw up, sickened by the endless up-and-down motion as they rode the troughs. They spent two hours down below in the cabin, huddled under blankets, barely talking except for Stride's occasional apology and Andrea's murmured response, accompanied by a weak smile. They had an unopened bottle of wine in the refrigerator and an elaborate picnic lunch, scarcely touched.

He offered to take her home. It was the

only time that day he saw enthusiasm brighten her face.

Now he was going to steer them right into a storm. It couldn't get much worse. He hoped she would stay below and not see the ugly blackness sliding toward them across the sky.

Stride tried to coax more speed out of the engine, but it was already doing its best to fight the lake. As it was, he would need to slow down soon simply to keep control. He angled the boat toward the waves and the wind, but the gusts kept shifting direction. He frowned as the clouds caught up with the sinking sun in the west, sending shadows across the blue water. The air seemed immediately colder. He wore gloves and a leather jacket and had a Twins baseball cap pulled down low on his brow, but his ears were raw, and his cheeks were pink and numb.

He felt hands slip around his waist and then felt Andrea's head lean against his back. She sidled up beside him, and he leaned down to kiss her. She smiled at him, but her skin was pale, and her lips were cold. When she looked toward land and saw the approaching storm, her eyes widened.

She glanced up at him, and he pretended everything was fine.

"How long until we make it back?"

He shrugged. "Maybe an hour."

Andrea cast a wary eye at the storm. "That doesn't look good," she said.

"Don't worry, we're just going to get a little wet. Why don't you wait below?"

Andrea didn't want the truth. She wanted comfort and reassurance. Cindy would have taken a look at his eyes and seen right through him, and then prodded him until he revealed what was in his heart.

The truth was, he *was* nervous. He had a coiled ball of worry lodged in his gut. He was worried about the storm, because he hadn't sailed in a year, and his skills were rusty. And he was anxious about the trial, which would begin tomorrow in earnest now that the jury had been impaneled after two weeks of extensive voir dire.

He was worried about Andrea, too.

He didn't know if they were groping their way toward love or just covering up each other's pain.

Their sex life had cooled. In the early weeks, they had been adventurous, working through months of pent-up passion. Andrea told him what a wonderful, caring lover he was, and how good he felt inside her. Now they made love only infrequently. Andrea let him take the lead, and she was strangely detached, kissing him, letting him love her, even reaching orgasm, but not letting herself go as she had before. Stride began to understand, although he would never breathe it out loud, why Robin had called her cold in bed. She seemed afraid to release herself. Or just afraid.

He kept asking himself if he was feeling the right things, if he was feeling the way he was supposed to feel. Stupid questions. What really mattered was that the hurt had now become something he could manage, and there was something much better in his life now. He liked the feel of Andrea's body next to him. He enjoyed how good she made him feel. He wanted to be with her.

He looked down at her, watching the nervousness in her eyes, but seeing, too, the emotional hunger she felt for him. It was there whenever she saw him. He wanted to wrap himself up in it.

"You're thinking about the trial, aren't you?" Andrea asked.

He wasn't, but it was convenient to say yes.

"What does Dan say about the jury?" she asked.

"It's as good as we can hope for," Stride said. "Dan likes his chances."

"You don't sound convinced."

Stride shrugged. "I wish we would have found more direct evidence. But Stoner is smart."

"I don't understand. You've got her blood in the van and at the murder scene. Won't that be enough?"

"With some lawyers, maybe, but I've crossed swords with Archie Gale before. He could make the jury believe I killed her." Stride laughed.

"Is he going to pull an O.J.? Try to say you planted evidence?"

Stride shook his head. "No, nothing like that. That wouldn't work here. I don't even think he'll challenge the DNA. Chuck Yee is too good for that. But we don't have a body, and we don't have anyone who saw Graeme and Rachel together on the night she disappeared. We also don't have anyone who can prove they were having sex, since Carver's testimony got thrown out."

"Are you sure he's guilty?" Andrea asked.

"I've been wrong before, but everything

points at Graeme. I'm just not sure we can prove it, and I hate to think of the bastard getting away with murder because he's smarter than we are and richer than we are. I've got a bad feeling. Like there's a piece of the puzzle we're missing. And if I think so, God knows Gale will think so. He just might find it, too."

"What are you missing?"

"I don't know," Stride said. "The case feels solid to me, but I can't help thinking there's part of the story we don't know."

He studied the sky. The clouds had almost reached them, and the blue sky had darkened around them until it was like night. The swells roared up and broke over the prow, dousing them in cold spray. The boat lurched, lifting out of the water and slapping down with a jolt. Andrea lost her balance and grabbed Stride's arm. He backed off the throttle until the boat was barely holding its own.

The storm swooped down on them with a fury, much worse than Stride had expected. Sheets of rain beat against them, driven horizontal by the wind, pelting their skin with such force that the pellets felt like thousands of bee stings. Stride was blinded. He tried to squint, but even through slitted eyes he saw nothing. The horizon had disappeared. Their only reality was the black mass engulfing them and the twisting blanket of rain.

He pushed the button on the control panel that unfurled the anchor somewhere below them. He wanted to make sure they didn't capsize. The lake tossed the boat in circles and made it dance on the tops of the waves. Even with the anchor down, the boat yawed so far left Stride thought they would overturn, and they had to grab the slippery brass handrail to avoid being thrown overboard. It righted itself but spun around crazily. He tried to keep it on an angle to the waves, but the effort was hopeless. He was more concerned now that they would be ditched into the water.

All Stride could think of was that if the boat went down, he hoped he drowned. Because otherwise, Guppo would kill him.

But they weren't going down.

He realized that the waves were smaller now. The rain lessened, allowing him to see a glimpse of the sky, which was lighter overhead. The boat still rocked and swayed in the deep troughs, but the engine was fighting back again, keeping them pointed in one direction. A few seconds later, the rain stopped completely. The clouds began to disassemble, leaving a patch of blue sky. The wind became calm, as if the storm had sucked all the energy out of the atmosphere.

He could see land again. He glanced at his watch and saw that only twenty minutes had passed since the storm hit.

"It's over," he said. "Come on, look."

Hesitantly, Andrea looked around, staring at the placid sky, then behind them at the storm disappearing out over the lake. She peeled her fingers away from his belt, then slipped, her knees buckling. Stride grabbed her.

"Why don't you go down below?" he suggested. "Lie down and rest. We'll be back home soon."

She gave him a wan smile. "You sure know how to show a girl a good time, Jon."

"We won't do this again," he said.

Andrea stretched, catlike, working out the kinks from her muscles. "I ache all over." She studied his face and reached up to caress his cheek. "Are you okay?"

"Yeah, I'm fine."

"You look like something's bothering you," Andrea said.

He shrugged. "It's just the trial. I always get this way."

Andrea didn't look convinced. "Is it me?"

He took his hands off the wheel and cupped her face. "You're the best thing that's entered my life in a long time."

That was the truth.

"I don't know, Jon. Can two wounded people make a go of it?"

"How else will we ever get better?" he said.

Andrea took his hand and stared at him intently. "I love you, Jon."

Stride waited several beats too long, but then told her, "I love you, too."

21

When they finally got back to Duluth, Stride stayed overnight at Andrea's house, which he now did several nights a week. They never stayed on the Point. He had to admit that Andrea's pillow-top mattress was more comfortable than the sunken twelve-year-old model he used at home and that her coffeemaker made coffee that could be sipped, not chewed. Still, there were times when he missed the rustic solitude of his own home. He sometimes yearned for the icy touch of the wood floors on his feet in the morning, rather than plush carpet. He missed hearing and smelling the lake, which was now just a great expanse in the distance, viewed from Andrea's bedroom window.

He fell asleep easily that night, with Andrea's head nestled on his shoulder. In the middle of the night, though, he had a bad dream, of being back on the boat, with Andrea still clinging to him. This time, he couldn't hold on to her, and she slipped away into the water. All he heard was her voice screaming to him before the lake swallowed her up. He woke up, panting, eyes wide. He was relieved to see Andrea still sleeping calmly beside him, but the dream was too intense for him to quickly get back to sleep.

Awake, he thought about the trial.

Dan was bursting with confidence, but Stride had seen Archibald Gale pull rabbits out of his hat for too many years. Besides, something still bothered him, as if he were overlooking something, missing a fact that would put his fears to rest. He wanted Graeme to be convicted. If something was out there, something that would seal the case, he wanted to find it.

The same feeling dogged him on many cases. He always wanted more. But as Maggie reminded him, there were only so many pieces left of the puzzle after the crime was done. They found as many as they could, and then they had to rely on the prosecutor and the jury to piece them together.

Dan was pleased with the jury. He had used a jury consultant, and they had ended up with what the consultant described as the ideal mix to be receptive to the circumstantial story of Graeme's guilt, including the hypothesis of his affair with Rachel. Eight women, four men. Four of the women were married, with children ranging from four years old to twenty. Two were divorced, and two were young and single. One man was a grandfather and widower, another single and gay, another married with no children, and the last a college student.

What they had successfully avoided, at the consultant's direction, was a middle-aged married man with teenage daughters—in other words, someone very much like Graeme.

When they completed the jury selection on Friday, Dan took Stride out for a celebratory beer. He spent two hours crowing about his victory over Gale, who had shown surprisingly little fight in the voir dire. The defense attorney's only victory had been convincing Judge Kassel to order the jury sequestered, to protect them from the barrage of press coverage that was bound to accompany the trial.

Stride drank along with Dan, but he was worried. If the jury was so good for the prosecution, why had Gale allowed it? Gale, who wasn't known for skimping, hadn't even employed a jury consultant.

Why?

Dan dismissed his concerns. "He's got you believing his mind games," Dan said. "Gale doesn't walk on water, Jon. He simply blew it. He thought he could handle the jury selection himself, and he got sandbagged. End of story."

Stride wasn't convinced.

He slipped out of bed, moving carefully so as not to awaken Andrea. Naked, he stood before the window. The city was illuminated by thousands of twinkling lights, with the blackness of the lake beyond. Silently, he cracked the window. Andrea didn't like sleeping with the windows open, and Stride, who did so well into the winter, had trouble adjusting.

The night air was cool and sweet.

He hadn't been honest with himself about

how much this case meant to him. That was why he wanted even more evidence—to be absolutely sure that Graeme would not slip through the fingers of justice. It was as if, having failed Cindy, having failed Kerry, he could not bear to fail Rachel, too. This time, one of the women in his life could rely on him to come through.

Stride stood there for almost half an hour, staring at the horizon and letting the gentle breeze swirl over his bare skin. Then, when he heard Andrea begin to stir, he closed the window and slipped back under the covers. He tossed and turned and finally drifted back to sleep.

The morning was stunning, as perfect a day as Duluth had ever enjoyed, with blinding sunshine, light blue skies, and a mild breeze floating in from the lake. Stride slipped sunglasses out of his pocket as he neared the courthouse. He put them on, hoping he could merge into the crowd and slip inside the building without being assaulted by the press.

The courthouse was just off First Avenue on a dead end called Priley Drive. A circular driveway led around a garden area, with the courthouse in the center, city hall on the right, and the federal court building on the left. It was normally a peaceful place to have lunch away from his basement office, on a bench near a bubbling fountain and a tulip garden, with the American flag snapping overhead atop a giant flagpole.

Not today.

The crowd filled the cobbled walkway and spilled into the street, which was clogged with television vans. Camera crews filmed reporters from different angles, all of them capturing the five-story brownstone court-house overrun with curiosity-seekers, demonstrators, and other reporters. Traffic had ground to a halt, backed up for blocks. Stride saw several of his officers at the top of the courthouse steps, struggling to hold back the crowd from entering the building. A cluster of reporters stood on the steps, thrusting microphones and cameras toward Dan Erickson, who was shouting answers to their questions.

The noise was overwhelming. Horns honked as drivers grew frustrated. Stride could hear radios and televisions booming. Several dozen women chanted loudly, carrying signs that protested pornography.

Graeme Stoner's taste for adult entertainment had been big news in the press, and the antiporn crowd had seen his affair with Rachel, and the subsequent violence, as a useful rallying cry.

Chaos. The Stoner trial was the biggest legal event to hit Duluth in years, and no one wanted to miss it.

Stride casually drifted into the crowd. He politely excused himself as he navigated through the milling people. When he saw reporters, he glanced away, just one more face among hundreds. Those who knew him rarely saw him in a business suit, so today he could well have been an executive on his way to pay a parking ticket. He left the crowd behind him and made it unscathed to the courthouse steps. He entered the foyer and took the marble steps two at a time. There was continual traffic up and down the stairs around him. He reached the fourth floor, slightly winded, and followed the hallway to the courtroom. He paused long enough to glance through the windows down at the seething mass below.

Archibald Gale was arriving. The media converged on him.

Two officers guarded the massive oak

doors of the courtroom. They recognized
Stride and let him pass. Everyone else had
either a courthouse pass or one of the coveted visitor passes that had been distrib-
uted by lottery. A handful of media members
had also been allowed inside, but without
cameras. Judge Kassel didn't want any
more of a circus in her courtroom than she
already had.

The courtroom itself was old-fashioned
and imposing, with long pews for spectators
and dark, intricately carved wood railings.
The visitor rows were largely filled. He saw
Emily Stoner, seated in the first row behind
the prosecutor's table. She stared at the
empty defense table, as if Graeme were already there. Her eyes were tearstained and
bitter.

Stride slid into the row beside her. Emily
looked down at her lap and didn't say anything.

Dan Erickson was directly in front of him,
whispering to his assistant prosecutor, an attractive blonde named Jodie. Stride assumed Dan was sleeping with her, although
Dan hadn't formally admitted it. He leaned
forward and tapped Dan on the shoulder.
The prosecutor paused, glanced back, and

gave Stride the thumbs-up sign. Stride saw Dan's fingers strumming like a nervous tic and his lower body quivering underneath the table. Dan was pumped.

"You look like you're in the zone, Dan," Stride told him.

Dan laughed. "I'm ready to rock."

He turned back to his conversation with Jodie. Stride watched Dan's right hand graze his assistant's shoulder. Then it briefly moved down and squeezed her thigh. Yes, he was sleeping with her.

Stride heard a whisper. "The man is a pig."

He realized that Maggie had slid silently into the row next to him. Maggie shot an icy stare at Dan's back. In the wake of her aborted pass at Stride the previous year, Maggie had wound up in a brief affair with Dan. It came to an ugly end when Dan turned out to be sleeping with two other women at the same time. Maggie's stare reflected zero forgiveness.

"He's cute, though," Stride said. He knew he was poking the bear, but he couldn't resist.

Maggie frowned. "You're a pig, too."

"Oink," Stride said.

"How's the teacher?"

"I almost killed both of us on a boat yesterday afternoon. Other than that, fine."

"She went on a boat with you voluntarily?" Maggie deadpanned.

"Funny. Don't tell Guppo. He almost lost his boss and his boat with one wave."

"The boss would be no big deal. He'd sue your estate over the boat."

A ripple of noise filled the courtroom. They noticed spectators craning their heads and turned to see Archibald Gale make his entrance with the panache of a movie star. Gale wore a navy three-piece suit, perfectly tailored as usual, with a neat triangle of handkerchief showing above his pocket. His small gold glasses glinted in the light.

Stride was always amazed at how light on his feet Gale seemed for such a large, imposing man. Gale almost seemed to glide. He stopped to shake several hands on his way to the bar, then roared through the swinging gate. He deposited his slim burgundy briefcase on the defendant's table, then interrupted Dan long enough to lean down and whisper something in his ear. Stride watched Gale's lips and could make out what the lawyer said.

"Don't say I didn't warn you, Daniel."

Seeing Gale, the bailiff opened a side door, and a guard escorted Graeme Stoner, dressed as impeccably as his attorney, into the courtroom. Graeme maintained the same even demeanor Stride had seen in him from the very beginning, cool, confident, with a slight amusement in his eyes. He didn't blink or flinch when he saw his wife, who was soon to be his ex-wife. Graeme simply smiled at her, then sat down and began a hushed conversation with Archibald Gale.

Emily, in contrast, could not take her eyes off Graeme. It was as if she had seen a ghost that she hated with all her soul.

At nine o'clock, the bailiff called for the crowd to rise. Judge Catharine Kassel, forty years old, with a black robe obscuring her slim figure, entered the courtroom. She had been appointed to the bench two years earlier, and soon afterward *Law & Politics* magazine named her the Sexiest Judge in Minnesota. With impeccably coiffed blonde hair and an elegant, tapered face, she lived up to the billing. Even so, most lawyers feared her. Her cool gray eyes could quickly turn to ice in the courtroom.

Seated, Judge Kassel cast a wary eye on the crowd.

"Let me remind all of you," she announced firmly, "that I want no demonstrations of any kind throughout the proceeding. Consider this a zero tolerance policy. Anyone who violates it will be escorted out immediately and will not return. I hope I am being very clear about that."

The courtroom was absolutely silent. Then Judge Kassel smiled, and she was radiant. "I'm glad we understand each other."

She motioned to the bailiff.

The jury was brought in and took their places uncomfortably, staring anxiously at the sea of faces in the courtroom. Judge Kassel welcomed them, adopting a more friendly tone to keep the jury at ease. They would spend the next several days separated from friends and family in the downtown Holiday Inn, and Stride could see in their faces that they were anxious for the trial to begin and end.

The judge gave the jury a minute to settle down and led the courtroom through the usual preliminaries.

Then she invited Dan Erickson to give his opening statement.

*   *   *

Dan took his time. He made eye contact with each juror.

He held up an enlarged school photograph of Rachel, a cryptic smile on her face. He looked at it, then held it delicately in his hands, facing the jury. He allowed her image to sink into all of their minds.

"This is Rachel Deese," he told them. "She's beautiful. A pretty seventeen-year-old girl with her whole life ahead of her. Unfortunately, a month after this photo was taken, Rachel disappeared. The evidence that was found in the subsequent weeks leads us to an unhappy conclusion. This beautiful girl was murdered."

Dan stared at his feet, shaking his head sadly.

"I wish I could make it easy for you. I wish someone had been there on that Friday night in October, other than Rachel and the man who killed her, to sit here in the witness stand and tell you how it all came about. But I think you know that most murders don't happen in public. Murder is an ugly, private business."

He turned and stared at Graeme Stoner, allowing the jury to follow his eyes. Then he continued.

"But if murderers keep their own secrets, how do we convict them? Often, as in this case, we use what is called circumstantial evidence. These are facts that, when taken together, lead you to an inescapable conclusion about a defendant's actions and his guilt. Let me give you an example. A man is found stabbed to death in his home. No one saw the crime. No one saw who killed him. There is no direct evidence at all. Nonetheless, we discover another man's fingerprints on the murder weapon. We discover that this man had a grudge against the victim. We discover that this man had no alibi for the night of the murder. We find traces of blood matching the victim's on his shoes. This is all circumstantial evidence that tells us the truth about the crime."

Dan waited, absorbing the looks on their faces, making sure they understood.

"And in this trial, you will see overwhelming circumstantial evidence about the murder of Rachel Deese. You will be convinced beyond any reasonable doubt that the man at the defendant's table, Graeme Stoner, killed this beautiful girl and disposed of her body.

"Who is this man?" Erickson demanded,

jabbing a bony finger at Stoner. "In this trial, we'll pull aside the mask that this man puts on for the world. We'll show you someone very different. Someone who keeps a naked photo of his stepdaughter on his computer. Someone who fantasizes about sex with teenage girls. Someone with a dark secret about his relationship with Rachel. He was having a sexual affair with her."

He paused, letting the jury reflect on this conclusion. He let them stare at Graeme and wonder what was behind his impassive expression. It didn't matter that Graeme was wearing a business suit, as he would for any workday at the bank. Dan wanted the jury to see his clothes as a facade for a dirty mind.

"And what of Rachel?" Dan asked. "I'm going to be honest with you. I don't know where Rachel's body is. There's only one person who does, and he's sitting over there at the defense table. You may wonder why we know a murder has been committed, if we can't show you a body. You'll hear the defense try to tell you that, because we have no body, it's possible for you to believe that Rachel is still alive."

Dan shook his head.

"Is it possible? Well, I suppose it's possible that Elvis is still alive. But you're not here to determine what's possible. You're here to determine the facts beyond a reasonable doubt. So remember this. When you see the physical evidence we have gathered, you'll realize that the only reasonable conclusion you can draw is that Rachel was murdered, and her body hidden somewhere in the vast wilderness of northern Minnesota. Sadly, no one may ever find her. It's a terrible, tragic reality. But not knowing where her murderer disposed of her body doesn't change the truth. Rachel is dead. You will be convinced of that.

"We're going to retrace her steps for you. We'll show you videotape of this girl driving home on a Friday night. She's safe. She's smiling. She's just made a date with a boy for the next night. And yet this same girl is never seen again. Instead, we find a fragment of a shirt she was wearing—a shirt she had purchased only a few days earlier—stained with her blood, in a wooded area a few miles north of town. We find a bracelet she treasured lying on the ground. That's the last we know of Rachel."

Erickson shot a withering look at Graeme Stoner, then turned sharply back to the jury.

"And what connects these two scenes? The girl in the car, alive and happy, and the bloody scrap of clothing found miles away? Well, Rachel was heading home that night, where Graeme Stoner was alone. Rachel's mother was out of town. And in the driveway of the house was Graeme Stoner's van, locked up tight. In that van, you'll find the evidence that links the scenes together. More of Rachel's blood. Rachel's bloody fingerprint on the blade of a knife. More fibers from the turtleneck she was wearing. And Graeme Stoner's fingerprints on the same knife.

"That's what I'm going to show you in this trial. Facts. Evidence. Blood and fibers that don't lie. My job is to lay out those facts for you, to show you what we found.

"Now, the defense has a different job in this case," Erickson told the jury. "They need you to overlook the facts, or to find wildly improbable explanations for them. Mr. Gale there, he's a showman, kind of like one of those magicians you see in Las Vegas. Magicians are talented people. They can dazzle an audience and pretend to levitate a beautiful girl right before your eyes. In fact, a good magician can be so convincing, you might even be tempted to believe that the girl really is hovering above the stage. But you know and I know it's nothing but a trick. An illusion."

He locked eyes with each juror, his face turning serious.

"Don't be fooled. Don't be tricked into giving up your common sense. Mr. Gale's going to try his magic out on you, but I want you to look at the physical evidence of this case. And you will see that the evidence leads you to one explanation only—that on that terrible night when Rachel disappeared, Graeme Stoner's obsessive relationship with his stepdaughter finally crossed the line into violence and murder. We may never know exactly what happened between them, or why. But an incestuous relationship is so ripe with evil that it can literally explode at any time. No one may have been there that night to see how the violence came about. But it happened. That's what the evidence will show you. It happened."

Archibald Gale stood up, taking off his glasses and depositing them carefully on the defense table. He looked down at Graeme Stoner, smiled, then turned his attention to the jurors. Gale wandered closer, patting all of his pockets, as if looking for something.

"You know, I was hoping to surprise you by pulling a rabbit out of my pocket, but I seem to have left all my magic tricks back at Caesar's Palace."

The crowd in the courtroom tittered, as did several of the jurors. Gale's eyes twinkled.

He rubbed his graying goatee, then slowly let his eyes travel around the courtroom. Gale had a flair for creating suspense. It didn't really matter what the facts were. What mattered was who told the most convincing story to the jury. With his commanding size and talent for drama, Gale was a natural.

"I have been in this courtroom many, many times over the past few decades," he began softly. "We have had some very newsworthy trials take place here. But I don't recall ever seeing such a crowd and such intense interest in a trial before today. Why do you suppose that is?"

He let the jurors think for a moment.

"Because what we have here is a mystery. Everyone wants to know how the last chapter ends. A girl has vanished. What happened to her? Did someone do violence to her, or did she run away, like tens of thousands of unhappy teenagers do each year? If something did happen to her, what was it? And why? Was it really the fault of her stepfather, as the prosecutor contends? Or did one of the other people in Rachel's life, who had reason to be angry and jealous of her, let their emotions become violent? Or did a brutal serial killer, who is still at large in our city, claim another victim?"

Gale nodded thoughtfully.

"I'd like to promise that when we're done here, you'll know what happened to Rachel. But you won't. Because we don't know. Graeme Stoner doesn't know. And neither does Mr. Erickson. All you'll end up with is questions and doubts. But that's all right. You may want to find the truth yourself, but it isn't your job in this courtroom to pick an ending to a mystery story."

He cocked his head. "Yes, I know what you may be thinking. There he goes again. The magician. Isn't that what the prosecutor told you to watch out for? That I'd be twisting his nice little facts and trying to make you go off on some improbable flight of fancy? Well, no, I'm not asking you to take my word. The difference is that Mr. Erickson plans to show you *some* of the facts, and I want to make sure you see *all* of the facts. When you do, you'll realize that Graeme Stoner is innocent of the crime of murder, and you'll send a message to the police that they need to go back and find out what really happened to this strange, unhappy girl."

Gale leaned over and grabbed the railing of the jury box. "Mr. Erickson says you should pay attention to the evidence. I agree. I want you to watch the evidence closely, so you can see what the prosecution isn't telling you.

"They're not telling you that Graeme was in his van with Rachel on the night she disappeared. Because they have no evidence that he was.

"They're not telling you that the Stoners' van was at the barn on the night Rachel disappeared. Because they have no evidence that it was.

"They're not telling you that they know Rachel is dead. Because they don't.

"They're not telling you that they can prove Graeme Stoner was having sex with his stepdaughter. Because they can't.

"Instead, they want you to make a leap.

They're going to give you little unrelated facts and stitch them together to try to make you believe what they can't prove. That's not evidence, circumstantial or otherwise. That's fiction. That's guesswork."

Stride felt his insides go soft. Bang bang bang, Gale was punching at the weaknesses in their case. Of course, he was right. They really couldn't prove any of those things. All they could do was lay out the pieces of the puzzle and hope the jury was smart enough to put it together.

"But there's more," Gale continued. "You'll also see that the prosecution, in its zeal to package a neat ending to the mystery, has ignored many other possible solutions. I'm afraid that Mr. Erickson is the kind of man who would find a lot of parts left over after he put his engine back together and conclude they must not be very important."

He winked at the jury, then grinned at Dan.

"Let's look at a few of those extra parts," Gale said. "Another teenage girl named Kerry McGrath, who lived within a couple miles of Rachel and who went to her school, disappeared the year before Rachel did. She, too, has never been found. The circumstances of her disappearance are remarkably similar to Rachel's. The police know that Graeme Stoner had nothing to do with Kerry McGrath's disappearance, and yet they ignore the grim possibility that a serial killer could be stalking the young girls of this city.

"Extra parts. On the night she disappeared, Rachel was behaving strangely. Why? Did she know something? Was she meeting someone? Was she planning to run away?

"Extra parts. Who else was with Rachel on the night she disappeared? Who else had reason to be happy if she vanished forever?

"Extra parts. What was the real source of Rachel's unhappiness? Was it her relationship with her stepfather? No. It was the miserable, bitter, *violent* relationship she had with her mother. Remember that word. Violent."

Stride glanced at Emily and saw a tear slip from her eye. She looked down at her lap, weeping silently.

Gale continued. "Questions and doubts. You'll have many at the end of the trial. But there will be no question, and no doubt in your minds, as to the right action for you to take. And that is to find my client not guilty of the crime of which he has been wrongfully accused."

Gale held the stares of the jurors for a few long seconds. Then he returned to the defense table and sat down.

Stride examined the jurors' faces. He figured it was a tie ball game heading into the first inning.

Batter up.

22

Stride took his place in the witness stand. He had done so hundreds of times before, so many that the chair felt familiar, as if he had worn an impression in it so it clung to his body. He made eye contact with the jurors.

Duluth jurors believed the police. He saw it in their eyes. This wasn't an urban jury pool, where the citizens felt the police were sometimes an enemy. He saw them studying his craggy features, the strands of gray in his dark hair and his sturdy physique, and concluding they could trust him.

Dan took him through introductions and allowed Stride to talk about his history on the force, his years of experience, his expertise on crimes and crime scenes. Only after the jury had gotten to know him did Dan begin to talk about Rachel. Stride explained how he had first been notified of the girl's disappearance and then, step by step, led the jury through a reconstruction of the evidence from Rachel's last night.

He described the bank video showing Rachel's car gliding by shortly after ten o'clock. Dan played the video for the jury. Then he held up a grainy, enlarged photograph, showing a girl's face behind the wheel. Despite the blurry image, everyone could see it was Rachel. She was smiling. She looked happy.

It was the last image, Dan reminded the jury, that anyone ever saw of Rachel Deese.

"Lieutenant, what is Rachel wearing in this photograph?"

"A white turtleneck," Stride said.

Dan returned to the prosecution's table and retrieved an exhibit—a receipt neatly packaged in a plastic bag. "Can you identify this item?"

Stride nodded. "It's a receipt found in a Gap bag found on the floor in Rachel's bedroom. We discovered it during our initial investigation."

"What is the receipt for?"

"It's for an item of clothing sold the Sunday prior to Rachel's disappearance. A white Gap-brand turtleneck."

"Did you find any white turtleneck during your search of Rachel's bedroom?"

"No, we did not."

Dan nodded thoughtfully. "Lieutenant, please tell us how you and your officers conducted a search for Rachel."

"We mounted an immediate and exhaustive statewide and region-wide search. My officers interviewed all neighbors within twelve blocks around the Stoner house. We checked the bus station, the airport, the train station, and all taxi companies in both Duluth and Superior. Throughout the state, police checked every service station and convenience store along the major highways, distributing Rachel's photograph and interviewing clerks. We posted a notice on our Web site and faxed information to police across the country. These efforts generated hundreds of leads, which were methodically researched by our officers and our fellow of-

ficers in other states. We had excellent photographs of Rachel to use with witnesses.
We conducted literally thousands of interviews. Nonetheless, we did not receive a
single verified sighting of Rachel after the
videotape at the bank. Not one. Not anywhere."

"What conclusion did you draw from this?"
Dan asked.

"We began to discount the possibility that
Rachel had run away. No one had seen her
alive since that Friday night. Plus, we were
doubtful from the beginning that Rachel
would have run away and left her car at
home. It seemed highly unusual to us that a
teenager with a car would leave her sole
means of transportation behind her. And as I
said, we covered all possible means of public transportation and found no evidence that
she had used any of them."

"Did you consider the possibility that she
had been abducted by a stranger?"

Stride nodded. "We interviewed all known
sex offenders within a hundred-mile radius
of the city. We investigated several who
could not provide definite alibis for Friday
night. There was no evidence that they were
anywhere near Duluth. No one recognized

their photographs or their vehicles in the area surrounding Rachel's house."

"Are there other elements of the crime that, in your experience, are inconsistent with a stranger abduction?" Dan asked.

"Yes. Virtually all stranger abductions occur in rural or isolated areas. Country roads, for example. It's highly unusual for a girl to be taken off a city street near her home. Most sexual predators don't want to risk identification by waiting in a populated area or abducting someone where their screams and resistance could attract attention from neighbors. Instead, they commit crimes of opportunity. A lonely road. An unfortunate victim. Since we know Rachel made it home that night—her car was parked outside—we know she was in a well-traveled neighborhood."

Dan returned to the prosecutor's table long enough to take a drink of water. He didn't want to rush the jury. Stride was presenting a complex scenario, and it was important that the jury follow the chain of evidence and conclusions.

"Eventually, did you find further evidence of what happened to Rachel?" he asked.

"We did."

Stride described the tip from Heather Hubble that led to the discovery of Rachel's bracelet and the search of the area near the barn where it had been found.

"As a result of that search, did you find other evidence that Rachel had been at this location?"

"Yes. We uncovered a scrap of white cloth with dark stains on it. The stains appeared to be blood."

Again Dan produced the evidence and introduced it. "Why was this discovery significant?" Dan asked.

"We believed that Rachel was wearing a white turtleneck that she had purchased the weekend before on the night she disappeared. The cloth matched the general characteristics of the turtleneck. We forwarded it to the Bureau of Criminal Apprehension in Minneapolis for analysis."

Dan didn't pursue any more questions about the turtleneck. Immediately after Stride, Charles Yee—Dr. Unshakable, as he was known in the Minnesota criminal court system—would take the stand to begin putting the forensics pieces in the puzzle. Yee had compared the cloth to another turtleneck from the same manufacturer and concluded that it was consistent with the brand and style of turtleneck Rachel was wearing, and the blood stains would be linked to her by DNA matching.

"At that point, Lieutenant, did the nature of your search change?" Dan asked

"Yes. We concluded that Rachel was dead and began searching for a body."

"But you didn't find a body, did you?"

Stride shook his head. "No, we searched miles and miles of forest surrounding the barn. We used both police and volunteers to go yard by yard through a precise grid. Unfortunately, there are simply too many places to hide a body up here."

"Nonetheless, are you firmly convinced that Rachel is dead?" Dan asked.

"Objection," Gale called. "The witness has no direct knowledge of whether this girl is dead or alive."

Dan shook his head. "I'm asking for a conclusion based on the lieutenant's extensive experience in homicide investigation. He's an expert."

Judge Kassel pursed her lips. "I'll allow it. The witness will answer."

"Yes, I believe Rachel is dead," Stride said. "It's the only reasonable explanation for the evidence."

"Let's backtrack for a minute, Lieutenant. In addition to the bloody piece of fabric, did you find any other evidence at the crime scene?"

Gale stood up again. "Your Honor, the prosecution has characterized the location as a crime scene without definitive evidence of a crime."

Judge Kassel nodded. "He's right, Mr. Erickson."

Dan was unperturbed. "Did you find anything else near where you found the piece of cloth?"

"We did," Stride said. "There were many overlapping footprints in the dirt area behind the barn, where cars usually park. We were unable to find anything useful there. But less than a yard from where the piece of fabric was discovered, we found several partial footprints of an athletic shoe, size twelve. We also found prints from a different athletic shoe, size eight."

Dan introduced photographs of the footprints, followed by reconstructions of the tread marks. "Were you able to identify the brand of shoe associated with the size twelve footprints?"

"Yes, the pattern is distinctive. There's a large red oval in the center of the heel. It comes from an Adidas shoe, model 954300. It's sold at three locations in the Duluth area."

Dan retrieved a paper from the prosecutor's table and again introduced it as evidence. He turned to Stride. "Will you tell us what this paper is, Lieutenant?"

"This is a copy of a check written by Graeme Stoner, dated four months prior to Rachel's disappearance. It's made out to a store called Sports Feet for a purchase of eighty-five dollars."

"How many locations of this store are there in Duluth?"

"One, in Miller Hill Mall."

"Does this store sell the model of Adidas shoe that matches the footprints?"

"It does. Their retail price at the time this check was written was eighty-five dollars."

Dan nodded grimly. "Tell me, Lieutenant, did you find a pair of Adidas shoes when you searched Mr. Stoner's residence?"

"No, we didn't."

"No athletic shoes at all?"

"We found a pair of Nikes that had been purchased recently. They had hardly been used."

Dan produced another copy of a check written by Graeme Stoner. "Tell us about this other check, please."

"This check is also made out to Sports Feet, this time for seventy-eight dollars. The check is dated the weekend after Rachel's disappearance. Seventy-eight dollars is the retail price for the model of Nikes we found in Mr. Stoner's bedroom."

"He bought another pair of athletic shoes only four months after he purchased the first pair?"

"That's right," Stride said.

"And what size were the Nikes you found?" Dan asked.

"Size twelve. Same as the footprints near the barn."

"One more question about feet, Lieutenant. Did you determine what size shoe Rachel wore?"

"Size eight. That matches the size of the other prints found near the barn."

Dan took a moment to stare at the jury and watch their eyes, making sure they were following the significance of everything

Stride had described. Stride saw the impact of his testimony in their eyes. They didn't like coincidences any more than he did.

"During the investigation, Lieutenant, did you obtain a search warrant for the Stoner residence?" Dan asked.

"We did," Stride said.

"Tell us what you found during this search."

"The first significant evidence was discovered on a computer hard drive in Mr. Stoner's personal office. It was a photograph of Rachel."

Dan retrieved an enlarged printout of the photograph. He introduced it as evidence, then showed the photograph to Stride without the jury seeing it.

"Is this the photograph?"

Stride nodded. "It is."

Dan approached the jury box. Slowly, he turned the photograph around so that all the members of the jury could see it. Several gasped. Stride could see that, involuntarily, the four men on the jury leaned forward. It was impossible not to react sexually to the image of the girl in the picture.

"In the course of your search, did you subsequently find any other evidence of a sexual nature?"

"We did. In a rear drawer of a filing cabinet, also in his office, we found several pornographic magazines. The magazines included titles like *Candy Girls, Jail Bait*, and *Lollypop Pussy*."

Still studying the jurors' faces, not looking at Stride, Dan asked, "What kind of magazines are these?"

"They include explicit photos of models made up to look like teenage girls."

Dan returned to the prosecution table, carrying the photo of Rachel. He and Stride had talked about whether to leave the photograph on display on an easel for the jury throughout the rest of his testimony, but both men concluded that the image would be too distracting for the men on the jury, and perhaps even for the women.

Dan brought out copies of the magazines discovered at Graeme's house and handed them one by one to the jurors. They flipped through them. Their faces twisted in disgust. Dan let them spend several minutes reviewing the highly explicit photographs, long enough to get a flavor for their perverted nature, but not long enough to become desensitized. He collected the magazines, then extracted another page from his stack of exhibits.

He handed it to Stride. "Can you tell us what this is?"

"It's a printout of phone calls from the Stoner household."

"What does it show?"

"There are regular calls to a number of phone sex services. They average two or three times a month for more than a year. The calls are all to services that emphasize teenage sexuality. Essentially, they allow callers to fantasize that they are having sex with young girls."

"Thank you, Lieutenant. Let's go back to your search of the Stoner household, shall we? Did your search include a minivan owned by Mr. Stoner?"

"Yes. The minivan was parked in the detached garage on the side of the house. The van was in the same location during each of our visits to the Stoner house."

"When you searched it, was the van locked?"

"Yes, Mr. Stoner provided us with a key."

"What did you discover in searching the van?"

"We analyzed the carpet carefully in the rear of the van. We found several small stains that appeared to be blood. We also found white fibers that were consistent with the fabric of Rachel's turtleneck. All of this material was sent to the BCA."

Dr. Yee would soon make the next connection for the jury: The fibers matched the brand of turtleneck Rachel was wearing on the night she disappeared, as well as the fabric found at the barn. The stains in the van and on the knife were also matched to Rachel's blood.

"You found the bloodstains and fiber evidence in the rear of Graeme Stoner's locked van?" Dan repeated.

"That's right," Stride said.

"Did you find anything else in the van?"

Stride nodded. "In a toolbox, we found a six-inch hunting knife."

Dan returned to the table and, when he turned back to Stride, brandished the knife in a menacing manner. "Is this the knife you found?"

"Yes."

Dan brought the knife closer to the jury, twisting and turning it in his hands, letting the overhead lights glint on the blade. "Did you find any evidence on the knife itself?" he asked.

"We found traces of blood on the blade of the knife. We also found two fingerprints on the knife that we matched to Rachel's thumb and middle finger."

"Were these fingerprints on the handle?"

"No, they were on the blade."

Dan looked back, seemingly confused. "On the blade?"

"Yes. Rachel's fingerprints were on the blade of the knife, facing upward, indicating a defensive posture."

"Objection," Gale snapped.

"Sustained," Judge Kassel ruled.

"Well, can you show us how the finger- prints and blood were laid out on the knife, Lieutenant?" Dan asked. He approached the witness stand and handed the knife to Stride. Carefully, the lieutenant turned the knife around so that the blade was facing his palm. He then curled his fingers onto the knife.

"Like this," Stride said.

He handed the knife back to Dan.

"I see," Dan said. "So let's say I came at you like this."

In an instant, Dan leaned over the witness

box, flashing the knife in Stride's face. Immediately, Stride reacted, trying to block the knife with his hand. His palm and fingers ended up in the same position he had demonstrated for the jury.

Gale stood up angrily. "This is rehearsed stagecraft, Your Honor. Rachel could just as easily have picked up the knife when it dropped on the ground. Mr. Erickson's little drama is misleading and irrelevant."

Judge Kassel nodded and gave Dan a severe glance. "Sustained. I'm instructing the jury to disregard this show by the prosecutor and the witness. And Mr. Erickson, no more of this kind of nonsense in my courtroom, is that clear?"

"Of course," Dan said.

But the message had been sent to the jury.

"All right, Lieutenant, one more thing. Did you find any other fingerprints on the knife?"

"Yes, we found fingerprints matching the defendant on the handle of the knife."

"And no other fingerprints?"

"None," Stride said.

"Thank you, Lieutenant. No more questions."

23

"Hello, Lieutenant," Gale began.

He pushed himself to his feet, standing behind the defense table. The lawyer studied Stride with sad eyes.

"I don't believe our paths have crossed since your wife passed away. I'm very sorry."

Stride said nothing at all. Gale had no shame. Hidden in a sympathetic comment was a message to the jury. Maybe the lieutenant's judgment was clouded by grief. Maybe he overlooked things.

"Rachel isn't the first teenage girl to disappear in this area, is she?" Gale asked.

"No," Stride said.

The defense lawyer took off his glasses and idly slid the frame between his lips. He squinted at Stride.

"Another teenager, a girl named Kerry McGrath, disappeared a little more than one year earlier than Rachel, is that right?"

"That's right," Stride said.

"She was the same age as Rachel," Gale said.

"Yes."

"Went to the same school?"

"Yes."

"She lived within a couple miles of Rachel?"

"Yes."

Gale shook his head. "That's remarkable, isn't it, Lieutenant? Do you call that a coincidence?"

He glanced at the jury in consternation as if to say, *Can you believe this guy? Is he blind?*

"We found no evidence that the two cases are related," Stride said.

"And yet you considered the cases similar enough that you tried to find evidence that might implicate Mr. Stoner in Kerry's disappearance. Isn't that true?"

Stride shrugged. "We typed all physical evidence we found against both Kerry and Rachel. It's standard procedure."

"And the fact is, you found absolutely no evidence whatsoever that might point to my client's involvement in Kerry's disappearance."

"That's right," Stride acknowledged.

Gale nodded. "No blood?"

"No."

"No fibers?"

"No."

"In fact, Kerry McGrath's disappearance is still unsolved, isn't it?" Gale asked.

"Yes."

Gale spread his arms wide, his glasses dangling between the fingers of his left hand. "So here we have two teenage girls missing in very similar circumstances. Isn't it just as likely, Lieutenant, that some deranged maniac, some stranger, one of the dozens of convicted sex offenders living in northern Minnesota, abducted both Kerry McGrath and Rachel Deese? That both these girls were the victim of a serial killer? Isn't that an equally plausible theory?"

Stride shook his head. "No. That's not what the evidence tells us."

"Ah, the evidence," Gale said, smiling at the jury. "Yes, we'll get to that in a moment. But let's look at this from a different angle, Lieutenant. You don't know for sure that Kerry McGrath is dead, do you?"

"No."

"And yet you're sure that Rachel is dead."

Stride nodded. "We found additional evidence in this case."

"A drop or two of blood. A scrap of cloth."

"It was Rachel's blood. Rachel's shirt."

Gale rubbed his goatee thoughtfully. "Was there enough blood found to suggest someone bled to death?"

"No."

"There wasn't even enough blood to prove any kind of crime took place, was there?"

Stride eyed Gale calmly. "I doubt Rachel cut herself shaving."

"But you don't really know, do you? She could have reached into the toolbox, cut herself on the knife, and bled on the carpet and on her clothes. Isn't that possible?"

"Only if you take the evidence out of context. We also found blood and fiber evidence at the barn."

"But still not enough evidence to suggest someone died, isn't that right?"

"On the contrary. I think that's precisely the conclusion this evidence suggests."

Gale raised a furry gray eyebrow. "So you say. Tell me, Lieutenant, do you know how many teenagers run away from home each year?"

"Thousands."

"Tens of thousands, in fact," Gale said. "Rachel wasn't happy at home, was she?"

"No."

"In fact, Rachel fits the classic profile of most runaways, doesn't she?" Gale asked.

"I'd have to say no. Runaways don't leave behind the kind of evidence we found. Her blood. Fibers from the shirt she was wearing that night."

"But what if she didn't want people to look for her?" Gale asked.

Stride hesitated, briefly losing his cool. "What?"

"Well, if she had taken her car, as you suggest, everyone would have known that she had run away, right? You'd be looking for her all over the country. But let's say Rachel wanted to disappear, and she didn't want the family she hates or the nosy police on her trail. Couldn't she have pricked her finger and left behind a hint of physical evidence that she met with a dark end?"

Stride shook his head. "That doesn't make sense. If she was faking her death, she would have made the evidence obvious. As it was, we did look for her all over the country. We did conduct an exhaustive search. Rachel had no way of knowing we ever would have stumbled on the evidence in the van—and certainly not at the barn."

"And yet here we are." Gale straightened, studying Stride, then the jury. "Let's talk about the barn, Lieutenant. This is a place where high school kids go to do all the things their parents don't want them to do at home, right?"

"Pretty much."

"Do you have any idea how many teenagers go there in any given week?" Gale asked.

"No."

"All right. Well, do you know how often the police were called about the barn in the last year?"

Stride shook his head. "I don't know."

"Would you be surprised if I told you it was thirty-seven times?"

"No, I wouldn't."

"And would you be surprised if I told you there were eight accusations of rape involving the barn in the past five years?" Gale asked. His smooth voice took on a hard edge. His eyes became hard azure points.

"That's possible."

"More than possible. It's true, Lieutenant. This is a dangerous place, isn't it?"

"It can be," Stride acknowledged.

"You've got teenagers raping teenagers, and the police don't seem to do anything about it."

"The barn is periodically raided," Stride said. "The kids keep coming back."

"That's right, Lieutenant. Kids. This is a place where kids do bad things. Doesn't the fact that evidence of Rachel was found at the barn suggest that another teenager may have been involved?"

"We investigated that possibility and discarded it," Stride said.

"In fact, it was your first thought, wasn't it? You sent people out to the high school to question teenage boys immediately after the bracelet was found. Didn't you, Lieutenant?"

"Yes, we did," Stride said.

Gale nodded. He chewed on his glasses again and then took a long swallow from a paper cup. He dabbed at his lips with the handkerchief from his pocket and wiped his brow.

"What size shoe do you wear, Lieutenant?" Gale asked.

The man was good, Stride thought to himself. He wondered how Gale had found out. "Twelve."

"I see. So it could have been you who left those footprints at the barn, right?"

"Objection," Dan Erickson snapped.

Judge Kassel shook her head. "Overruled."

"I don't own a pair of shoes that match the pattern of the tread found at the barn. Whereas Graeme Stoner bought such a pair only four months prior to Rachel's disappearance. And those shoes are now missing."

"But do you know how many of that brand of shoe, in size twelve, were sold in Minnesota in the past year?"

"I don't," Stride admitted.

"It's more than two hundred. Couldn't any of those people have left the footprints?"

"Yes. But none of them is Rachel's stepfather. And they don't own a van in which we found Rachel's blood."

"But apart from those footprints that could be from you or several hundred other men, you don't have any evidence to place my client at the barn on Friday night, do you?"

"No."

"In fact, you don't know *when* those footprints were made, do you?"

"No."

Gale paused to let the jury focus on this exchange.

"How about the van, Lieutenant? You make a big point of finding my client's fingerprints on the knife you found in the toolbox."

"That's right."

Gale shrugged. "But it's his van and his knife. Wouldn't you expect to find his fingerprints on it?"

"If someone else had handled the knife and wiped it clean, there would have been no fingerprints on it at all," Stride pointed out.

"Unless whoever handled it wore gloves," Gale said. "Isn't that true?"

"That's possible," Stride acknowledged.

"But doing so very likely would have smeared other fingerprints, which didn't happen."

"But couldn't Rachel have deliberately left the evidence on the knife herself, knowing that Graeme's fingerprints would be there, too?"

Stride shook his head. "There's no evidence at all that she did that."

"There's also no evidence that she didn't, is there? But let's stay on the van for a while longer. No witnesses saw Graeme Stoner driving the van that Friday night, did they?"

"No."

"So we don't know that the van went anywhere that night, do we?" Gale asked.

"I disagree. The fibers found in the van match the fibers found near the barn. Rachel's bracelet was also found at the barn. Rachel was wearing the bracelet and the white turtleneck on Friday night. Connect the dots, Mr. Gale."

Gale smiled. Stride saw a brief twinkle in the lawyer's eyes, like a nod of appreciation. Score one for the good guys.

But Gale wasn't finished.

"If someone did take Rachel in the van,

Lieutenant, how do you know it was Graeme Stoner?"

"It was his van. It was locked."

"Oh, it was locked. I see. No one else could have taken it."

Stride nodded. "Not without hotwiring the engine. Plus, if you suggest someone else took the van, that person would have had to use his own car to get to Rachel's house. It's ridiculous to think a murderer would park his own car on the street, kidnap a girl, steal a *different* car, drive to the barn, then come back to collect his own car again."

"Unless the killer walked," Gale said.

"Maybe he flew," Stride retorted. The jury laughed. Judge Kassel frowned and looked sharply at Stride.

Gale waited for the amusement to subside. "You took photographs at the Stoner house when Rachel disappeared, am I right?" he asked quietly.

"That's standard procedure," Stride said. He wondered where Gale was going.

Gale returned to the defense table and retrieved a photograph of his own. He put it on an easel near Stride, in full view of the jury.

"Is this an enlarged detail from one of those photographs?"

Stride studied the photo briefly. "Yes, it is."

"The enlargement shows a table in the hallway in the Stoner house, directly beside the front door, is that correct?"

"That's correct."

Gale reached inside his suit coat pocket. He extracted a gold Arrow pen and pointed to an object on the table. "Can you tell us what this is, Lieutenant?"

Stride recognized it. "It's a crystal ashtray."

He knew where Gale was going.

"And what's inside the ashtray, Lieutenant?"

"It's a set of keys."

"In fact, they are Mr. Stoner's car and house keys, isn't that right?"

"I believe so."

"The keys to the van. In an ashtray on a table right next to the front door."

"Yes," Stride said.

"So anyone who came to the door could have simply reached in and taken them. And taken the van. And taken Rachel."

Stride shook his head. "No, that's not a reasonable conclusion from the evidence. According to your scenario, the killer would have to be someone who knew Rachel was home, walked to the house, wore gloves, knew the keys would be there, and wore the same size and brand of shoes as Graeme Stoner. This sounds like part of your magic act, Mr. Gale."

"None of that, Lieutenant," Judge Kassel snapped.

Stride nodded and apologized. Still, he had temporarily derailed Gale's theories. He just hoped the jury wasn't getting confused in the web of outlandish possibilities the lawyer kept throwing in front of them.

Gale offered Judge Kassel a warm smile. Then, carefully patting his gray hair down on the top of his head, he turned back to Stride. "All right, Lieutenant, let's talk about this so-called affair Mr. Stoner was having with his stepdaughter. You don't have any physical evidence to support this wild notion, do you? No semen anywhere? No vaginal fluids?"

"I'm sure they did their laundry," Stride said.

"No witnesses?"

"It's not the kind of thing they were likely to do in public," Stride said with a slight smile.

Gale didn't smile back. "I'll take your answer for a no, Lieutenant. You also spend a

lot of time worrying about Mr. Stoner's fantasy life. He indulges in some rather taste-
less pornography." Gale sighed. "In other
words, he's a man. But none of the material
you found was illegal, was it?"

"No," Stride said.

"You can get those magazines on the
main street in Duluth, can't you?"

"I believe so."

Gale grabbed the phone records that Dan
had introduced as evidence and flapped
them in the air. "And as for these phone sex
calls—well, no offense, Lieutenant, but if a
man were really having sex with teenagers,
would he need to pay five dollars a minute to
simulate it on the phone?"

"It shows his taste for sex with minors,"
Stride said.

"These numbers Mr. Stoner called from
time to time, do you know how many other
men in Duluth have called the same numbers in the last six months?" Gale asked.

"No."

"I do. It's nearly two hundred. Including a
few men who I believe are on the police
force, Lieutenant. Did you investigate all of
them as suspects?"

"No, we didn't."

Gale nodded. "Of course not. Because you and I know that these calls are fantasies and have nothing to do with the reality of how a person behaves. Right?"

"That depends on the context. And the person."

"And yet you don't know the contexts of these people, do you?" Gale asked.

"No."

"No, you don't. In fact, when you get right down to it, the only physical evidence you have that suggests any kind of sexual relationship between Rachel Deese and my client is this amazing photograph you found on a computer in his home. Correct?"

"The photograph is extremely suggestive," Stride said.

"In more ways than one," Gale retorted. "But you don't have any evidence that Mr. Stoner ever saw this photograph, do you?"

"It was on his computer."

"Yes indeed, but Rachel herself had access to that computer, didn't she? She could have put the photograph on Mr. Stoner's hard drive at any time, couldn't she?"

"Again, we have no evidence to suggest she did that."

Gale waved his big hand dismissively.

"But you don't have any evidence that she didn't, isn't that right? Who knows what possesses teenage girls? She could have been playing a joke. She could have been trying to embarrass him. She could have been trying to cause a fight between her mother and her stepfather. You don't really know, do you?"

"No," Stride said.

"Tell me, Lieutenant, when was that photo loaded on Mr. Stoner's computer?"

"The file statistics indicate it was loaded two days before Rachel disappeared."

"And when was the photograph last accessed on that computer?" Gale demanded.

"That same time."

Gale reared back in disbelief. He stared at Stride, stunned. He knew perfectly well what date was on the file, since he had seen all the evidence in discovery. But for the jury, it was as if Gale learned this shocking news for the first time.

He retrieved the enlarged photo and displayed it for the jury again, letting it linger there so every one of them could drink in Rachel's erotic power. "The same time? You say this man was obsessed with his stepdaughter, Lieutenant. In the midst of a torrid illicit affair. And he loads this incredible photograph on his computer—and then *never looks at it?"*

Gale flapped his hand in front of his face as if he were trying to cool down.

"My God, Lieutenant, if this photo were on my computer, I don't think I'd get any work done."

Dan Erickson jumped to his feet. "Objection."

Gale raised his hands in surrender. "Withdrawn, withdrawn."

Then he smiled wickedly at Stride.

"Now, Lieutenant, let's be realistic. This breathtaking photo is loaded on Mr. Stoner's computer, and for weeks afterward, he never even bothers to open it up. Maybe he put it there. Maybe he had incredible willpower. But isn't the most logical explanation that he didn't know the photo was on his computer at all?"

24

Dan called Emily Stoner as the first witness on the second day of the trial.

Her dark hair was neatly styled in a short bob. Her skin, under heavy makeup, looked smooth and pink. She wore a pale shade of lipstick, a pearl necklace, and matching earrings. Her navy blue dress, with white trim on the collar, was obviously new and hugged her body. Watching her, Stride saw a glimmer of what Emily had been like a few years earlier. The only telltale sign of Emily's age today, like yesterday, was in her eyes, which couldn't hide her exhaustion and despair.

Emily squeezed into the aisle. Her heels

tapped on the marble floor as she approached the witness stand and was sworn in. She didn't look at Graeme, and Stride noticed that Graeme ignored her. Gale noticed, too, and Stride saw him discreetly jab his client with an elbow. Graeme had lost his wife over these false charges, and he had to display grief.

Emily settled into the chair. She took a quick glance at the jury, then looked away nervously. Her hands were folded in her lap. She was an attractive, sympathetic figure, but to Stride's eyes, she looked unstable. The events of the past few months had deepened the cracks in her soul. Stride began to wonder if the only reason she hadn't made another suicide attempt was to have this chance to testify against Graeme and see him put away. He hoped she got the chance.

"Mrs. Stoner, I know this is difficult for you," Dan began.

Emily swelled her chest with a deep breath and briefly closed her eyes. She straightened her back, steeling herself to tell her story. Her face was intense and determined. "I'm all right," she said.

"How did you meet Graeme Stoner?" Dan asked.

"I was a teller at the Range Bank. He joined the bank as an executive from New York. He was single, attractive, and wealthy, and all the women in the office were crazy about him. Me included."

"Did he show any interest in you?"

"No. Not at first. He would pass me without looking at me, like I didn't exist. It was the same with all the women. He ignored them."

"And then?" Dan asked.

"Well, one day, Rachel came to the bank. She was dressed in a tight halter and short shorts. I scolded her about it, and we got into an argument in the lobby. Graeme saw us together, but he didn't say anything. Later that day, though, he asked me out on a date."

Dan zeroed in on Emily's story, his voice rising. "The day that Graeme approached you was the day he saw Rachel with you in the bank?"

"Yes."

"After several months of ignoring you?"

"Yes."

"Had he seen Rachel with you before?" Dan asked.

"I don't see how. Rachel hardly ever came to the bank."

"Okay. So the two of you began dating. How did Rachel react to your having a man in your life again?"

"She was friendly to Graeme. She flirted with him."

"Eventually, you and Graeme were married. What did you observe about Rachel and Graeme's relationship after that?"

Emily took another deep breath. "They did things together, just the two of them. They went out on photography trips in the woods and were gone for hours. Graeme bought her gifts—clothes, compact discs, that kind of thing."

"How did you feel about this?"

"Initially, I thought it was fine. I was happy to have a family again. But I began to be concerned that Graeme was spending more and more time with Rachel and less and less time with me. He became very distant, very cold. It was like he was shutting down our relationship, and I didn't know why."

Dan took a long look at the jury, then said quietly, "Mrs. Stoner, did you ever have reason to believe that your husband was having sexual relations with your daughter?"

Emily's eyes flashed with anger. "The signs were there. I was blind to them. I didn't want to believe it. But looking back, I can point to things that should have set off warning bells in my head."

"Like what?"

"Well, one time, I was putting groceries in the back of the van. It was a Monday, and Graeme and Rachel had gone out hiking together the day before. I came across a pair of Rachel's panties in the van."

"What did you do?" Dan asked.

"I asked Graeme about it. He said Rachel had slipped while crossing a creek and fallen in. Her clothes got wet."

"Did you talk to Rachel, too?"

"No. I just washed them and put them away."

"What else did you observe?" Dan asked.

"Another time, I saw them kissing. I had already gone up to bed, and I heard Rachel and Graeme coming up the stairs. Rachel was giggling. The lights were on in the hallway, and I heard her say good night, and then I saw her put her arms around his neck and kiss him. On the lips. It wasn't a chaste kiss."

"Did you talk to Graeme or Rachel about it?"

"No. I pretended I was asleep. I couldn't face it."

Dan waited, letting Emily's story sink in. "Did this close relationship between Graeme and Rachel last?"

Emily shook her head. "No, something changed. Two summers ago, Rachel's relationship with Graeme soured. She became very cold and indifferent. I hadn't seen anything to precipitate it, no arguments, no fights. But she turned him off like a switch. Graeme tried to win her back. He was almost pathetic about it. He bought her a new car, but nothing changed. Rachel treated Graeme from that point very much the way she treated me. Like an enemy."

"Objection," Gale snapped.

"Sustained," Judge Kassel said.

"Mrs. Stoner, why didn't you tell any of this to the police when Rachel first disappeared?" Dan asked.

"I tried to tell myself it was impossible that Graeme could be involved. I was fooling myself, as if the things I had seen didn't mean anything. And I guess it was too humiliating to think that something so horrible was going on under my nose and I never saw any of it."

Gale objected again and was sustained again. But Dan had made his point. He was ready to wrap up.

"We know you had a difficult time with your daughter. After all that happened between you, did you still love her?"

Passion flowed into Emily's face. It was the first time that Stride could recall seeing any life at all in her tired eyes. "Of course! I loved her with my whole soul. I still do. I know how much pain she went through, and I would have done anything to reach her. I never could. It tore me up inside. It will always be the greatest regret of my life, that I couldn't find a way to mend the gap between us."

Dan smiled. "Thank you, Mrs. Stoner."

25

Stride assumed Gale would treat the mother of the victim with kid gloves. He was wrong. There wasn't a hint of sympathy in Gale's demeanor.

"The fact is, Mrs. Stoner, your relationship with your daughter was awful, wasn't it?" Gale began.

"It wasn't very good. That's what I said."

Gale snorted. "Not very good? Rachel regularly said she hated you, didn't she?"

"Well—she said that a few times."

"She regularly called you a bitch," Gale said.

"Sometimes."

"She would destroy things you owned, personal things, just for the hell of it."

"Sometimes."

"She would do despicable things for the sole purpose of hurting you?"

Emily nodded. "That's true." Then she lobbed an angry missile: "Like having sex with my husband."

"Or like running away and leaving your life and your marriage in ruins?" Gale demanded.

"She didn't do that."

Gale threw his beefy arms in the air. "How do you know? Wasn't she bright enough and devious enough to have staged all of this?"

"Objection," Dan said.

Gale shrugged. "I'll withdraw it. Mrs. Stoner, by your own admission, you didn't tell anyone about these so-called suspicions until after the police told you your husband was a suspect, is that right?"

"I was in denial," Emily said.

"Denial? The truth is, you really didn't think they were having an affair, did you?"

"Not then, no."

"And the only reason you think so now is because it seems to fit with Mr. Erickson's little mystery story, isn't that right?"

"No. That isn't true."

"Isn't it?" Gale asked, his voice dripping with disbelief. "Everything you've told us, it's all about you and Rachel, isn't it? Not about Graeme. It was about Rachel playing games with you. Tormenting you. Trying to hurt you."

"It was difficult," Emily said.

"So difficult you beat up your own daughter once, didn't you?"

Emily cringed. She began to withdraw, staring into her lap. "Yes," she murmured.

"Speak up! You were angry, and you beat the hell out of her, didn't you?"

"It was just once."

Gale shook his head. "Oh, so you only abused your daughter once. That's all right, is it?"

"No! I'm so sorry!"

"Your daughter pushed you until you viciously assaulted her, right?"

Dan stood up. "Mr. Gale is badgering the witness, Your Honor."

The judge nodded. "Back off, Mr. Gale."

Gale changed direction. "If she pushed you far enough, you'd do it again, wouldn't you?"

"No."

Gale lowered his voice and continued with

a wicked calm. "In fact, weren't you the one with the motive to kill Rachel?"

Emily's eyes flew open. "No!"

"No? After she humiliated you for years?"

"I would never hurt her."

"You just told us you did."

"That was a long time ago," Emily pleaded. "It happened once and never happened again."

"Didn't it?" Gale asked. "Didn't you finally have it out with Rachel once and for all on that last weekend?"

"No—no, of course not! I wasn't even there!"

Gale was patient. "Where were you?"

"With my sister in St. Louis."

"On Friday night?" Gale asked. "The night Rachel disappeared?"

"Yes."

Alarm bells began to go off in Stride's head.

"But not on Saturday," Gale said. "You weren't in St. Louis on Saturday night, were you?"

Emily shook her head. "No. I stayed at a hotel in the Cities. I was tired. I had been driving all day."

"Where did you stay?" Gale asked.

"I don't remember. Somewhere on the Bloomington strip."

"Could it have been the Airport Lakes Hotel?"

"Possibly. I really don't remember."

Gale retrieved a piece of paper from the counsel's table. "In fact, isn't this a copy of your receipt from the Airport Lakes Hotel in Bloomington for that weekend?"

Emily paled. "Yes."

"Well, then," Gale said, frowning. "We have a problem, don't we?"

Emily was silent.

Gale held up the paper. "Because this receipt shows you checking in on *Friday* night, not Saturday, doesn't it?"

Stride murmured, "Son of a bitch."

Maggie leaned over and whispered, "Goddamn it, the sister covered for her. She swore Emily was there on Friday night."

In the witness stand, Emily hadn't spoken. Gale spread his arms, the receipt held high in his left hand. "Well, Mrs. Stoner?"

"It must be a mistake," Emily said in a ghastly voice.

"A mistake?" Gale was scornful. "They

billed you for two nights, and you didn't notice? Shall we call the desk clerk who
checked you in?"

Emily's eyes darted frantically, looking for
cover. As Stride watched, she seemed to
look repeatedly in one place, at the man
seated a few feet down the row. At Dayton
Tenby.

Stride glanced at the minister and saw a
look of panic in Dayton's eyes, too.

Emily crumbled. "All right, yes, I was there
on Friday night. I did some shopping at the
Mall of America on Saturday. Graeme
wouldn't have liked it, and that's why I lied. It
didn't seem like a big thing."

"How convenient," Gale said. "But the fact
is, you could easily have driven to Duluth
and back on that Friday night, couldn't you?"

"I didn't do that," Emily insisted.

"You check in, you head north. You would
have arrived just after ten, right? Just when
Rachel was getting home?"

"No. That's not what happened."

Gale smiled. "No? Tell us, Mrs. Stoner,
what did Rachel do that night? What did she
say? Did she push one button too many?"

"No, no, no."

Dayton Tenby leaned forward, and Stride saw him whispering furiously to Dan.

"You knew about the barn, right?" Gale persisted.

Emily didn't answer.

"I need a yes or no. Did you know what the barn was and where it was?"

"Yes."

"You'd been there yourself, hadn't you?"

"Not in years."

"But you had been there? You knew all about it?"

"Yes." Her voice was a lifeless echo.

"You had the real motive and opportunity to kill Rachel, didn't you? You had a history of violence toward her. She treated you like dirt."

Emily stared at him. "I didn't kill my daughter."

"You lied to the police. You lied to your husband. You lied to the jury. How do we know you're not lying now?"

Tears rolled in streaks down Emily's face. "I'm not lying."

Gale shrugged.

"That's all, Mrs. Stoner. I have nothing further."

* * *

Dan stood up on redirect.

"Mrs. Stoner, tell us again what you were doing on Friday night, when you claimed you were at your sister's house."

"I was shopping," Emily repeated.

Dan caught Emily's reluctant eyes. His voice softened. "You can't hide it anymore. It's time for the truth to come out. Now please, tell us. Where were you on Friday night?"

Stride saw Emily stare, stricken, at Tenby. He saw the minister nod his head gently. Emily took a deep breath and turned to the jury. She seemed composed again.

"I was at the hotel in Bloomington, just like the receipt says. I was having an affair. I didn't want my husband or anyone in the community finding out."

Dan nodded. "Who were you seeing in Minneapolis?"

"It was—I mean, I was meeting—Dayton. Dayton Tenby. He's been my pastor for years." Her words galloped out of her mouth as she tried to explain. "We didn't meet with the intention of having an affair. He was in Minneapolis for a conference. I wanted to talk to him, so I came back early. We had dinner, and then, well, one thing just led to another. We ended up spending the weekend together. It was beautiful. But I felt guilty and ashamed, and I didn't want to endanger Dayton's career. Even though it was my fault, I knew he could be hurt."

"Were you with him the whole time?" Dan asked.

"Yes."

"Did you have any opportunity to sneak up to Duluth?"

Emily shook her head. "Of course not. That's ridiculous. There's only one person who was at home with Rachel that night. And that's Graeme."

26

"I watched the news tonight," Andrea said, taking a large swallow from a glass of Chardonnay, which they were gulping like cold beer. "You know how they are, all the experts handicapping who's winning and who's losing. But this time, they didn't sound like they knew. Even Bird wasn't ready to call the trial one way or another."

"Nice to know something can render Bird speechless," Stride said.

"What does Dan think?" Andrea asked.

"He thinks we're winning."

"What do you think Gale thinks?"

"I think he thinks he's winning."

"So who's winning?"

Stride laughed. "Us, I think. Then again, I'm an optimist."

Andrea, who was already more than a little drunk, shook her head. "An optimist? You? I don't think so."

"Even better. We must really be winning, then."

"Does Maggie think so, too?"

"Maggie?" Stride asked. "Maggie hates Dan so much, I think she would be content to have Stoner go free just to have Dan fall on his ass. However, she calls it a draw so far, and she's probably right."

Andrea was silent. Then she said, "I don't think Maggie likes me too much."

Stride shrugged. "I've told you about Maggie. I think she still cares about me and won't admit it. She's probably a little jealous. This is about her, not you."

"She doesn't think I'm right for you."

"Did she say that?"

"No," Andrea said. "Women just know these things."

"Well, let's leave us to worry about us, and Maggie can worry about Maggie. Okay?"

Andrea nodded. She finished her glass of wine and poured the dregs of the bottle into both of their glasses, spilling a few drops on the glass coffee table. She rubbed it off with her finger, then licked her fingertip.

Stride sat next to her in the living room. The picture window, opposite the sofa, exposed a view of the city below them and the lake, darkening in the twilight. He had changed into a short-sleeved green polo shirt and old jeans. Andrea reached over, touching the thick scar on his upper arm.

"You've never told me about the bullet, you know," she said.

"It was years ago."

"So tell me," Andrea urged him.

"It was a suicide attempt," he said. "I was a lousy shot."

"Jon-a-than," she said, drawing out the syllables in exasperation. "Don't you ever give your morbid humor a rest?"

He smiled. "Okay, it was a hunting accident."

"Oh?"

"Yes, I hunted something that hunted me back."

"You're impossible. Come on, I really want to know. Please tell me."

Stride sighed. It wasn't a part of his life he

enjoyed dredging up, because he had spent a year unliving it with Cindy and a therapist.

"A few years ago, I ended up in the middle of a domestic dispute. We used to own a cabin west of Ely, and the couple that owned the place near us—well, the husband basically flipped out. He was a very good friend of mine. We were close. But he was a fragile guy, a veteran, and he lost his job and his marbles all at once. His wife called me one evening, told me he was waving a gun around, threatening to kill her and kill the kids. I knew him, knew he was serious. But I didn't call for backup, because I thought that was a good way for a lot of people to end up dead, him included. Instead, I went to talk to him."

"What happened?"

"I got inside, and he pointed a revolver with a six-inch barrel at me. Biggest fucking gun you've ever seen, right in front of my face. Seems he didn't want to talk. Well, I talked anyway. I was getting through to him, too, or so I thought. I got him to let the kids go outside. A few minutes later, I got him to let his wife go outside, although she didn't want to go. So it was just him and me. I really thought I was home free. My only challenge was to make sure he didn't kill himself. But I guess I underestimated him. He pointed the gun at his head, and I shouted at him. I started forward, hands up, trying to make him stop, to put the gun down. Instead, he pointed the gun right at my chest and pulled the trigger, just like that, no warning. I was already diving. The bullet sliced through my shoulder, spun me around, threw me to the floor. And then, with that little interruption out of the way, he put the gun in his mouth and blew out the back of his head with me screaming at him."

Andrea caressed his face. "I don't know what to say."

"See what happens when you get me drunk?" Stride said. "You get me to say things that upset you."

"My fault. I pushed. But I'm glad you told me."

"Well, enough of that, okay? Do you want to open another bottle?"

Andrea shook her head. "I've got to go to school tomorrow, remember? I don't think the kids would appreciate me having a hangover."

"So how come we didn't date in high

school?" he asked. It was the kind of question driven by several glasses of wine.

"I think it's because you had already graduated by the time I was a freshman," Andrea said.

"Oh, yeah. Just as well. I bet you wouldn't have given me a second glance."

Andrea shook her head. "I would have given you a second glance and a third glance."

"No, I don't think so," Stride said. "I was one of those intense, brooding loners. And you—you were a cheerleader, I bet, and in all the clubs, and with lots of boyfriends."

Andrea grinned. "Cheerleader, yes. Science club, yes. Boyfriends, no."

"Come on."

"Seriously! I got asked out all the time, but it usually didn't go beyond a first date." She cupped her breasts. "Once they figured out they weren't going to get their hands on these, they lost interest."

"Well, it is kind of like blowing out the birthday candles and not eating the cake," Stride said.

"Oh, don't pull that typical guy crap on me. I'm sure you were a perfect gentleman in high school."

Stride laughed. "There's no such thing as a sixteen-year-old gentleman."

"Anyway, you were lucky in high school," Andrea said. "You found your soul mate. You met Cindy during your senior year, didn't you?"

"Yes."

"And that was that, wasn't it?" she asked.

Stride smiled wistfully. "Yes, that was that. I was hooked. Love at first sight. It really was that fast."

She snuggled closer to him on the sofa, clutching his arm. Her cat, who was sleeping on Stride's lap, looked up, offended by the interruption.

"What was it about Cindy?" Andrea asked softly.

Stride stared into the distance, where he could still picture Cindy in his mind. Over time, the picture had lost a little focus. It wasn't a close-up anymore. It was a portrait, getting farther away.

"She wouldn't let me be a loner," he said. "She teased me and poked holes in all my defenses. And she was the most spiritual person I ever met. Not so much religious, but spiritual. She helped me see the things I loved, the lake, the woods, in a new light.

Once I saw it through her, none of it was the same. It was better."

He looked down at the cat, which was sleeping again, unimpressed with his memories. He looked over at Andrea, still nestled against his shoulder.

She was crying.

The next morning, Dan called Kevin Lowry to the stand.

Kevin made a perfect witness, a strapping, clean-cut teenager, looking slightly uncomfortable in his white shirt and tie. He shifted and squirmed to fit his husky body into the witness stand. His eyes darted around the courtroom, nervously studying the jury and then making eye contact with Emily Stoner. He gave her a small smile of support, but Emily didn't react.

Dan quickly covered the early days of Kevin's relationship with Rachel and then moved on to Graeme.

"Kevin, we've heard testimony that Rachel's relationship with Graeme changed abruptly. They were close, and then they weren't. Is that what you observed?"

Kevin nodded. "Oh, yeah. Big time. About two years ago, Rachel did a turnaround. She wouldn't go near Mr. Stoner anymore. She told me she hated him."

"Did she say why?"

"No. I asked her about it once, and she said—well, she called him something pretty harsh."

"What did she call him, Kevin?"

Kevin looked uncomfortable. "She said he was a fucking pervert."

"Did you observe Mr. Stoner's behavior during this time?" Dan asked.

"When I saw them together, he was real nice to her. Same as always. Although, I don't know, it was like he was trying too hard. Like right around the start of the school year, Mr. Stoner bought Rachel a new car."

Stride frowned. Something about Rachel's car bothered him. He remembered feeling that way from the beginning. But they had searched it thoroughly and found nothing.

"Did that make Rachel happy?"

Kevin shook his head. "No. I mean, she liked the car okay. She always hated driving that old hand-me-down from her mother. But she was sort of sarcastic about the new car. She said Mr. Stoner had to buy it for her, he didn't have a choice."

"Did she say what that meant?"

"No."

"And was this the car she was driving on the last night you saw her?"

"Yes."

"Okay, Kevin, let's talk about that night. Tell us what happened."

Kevin described the events in Canal Park with Rachel and Sally the way he had originally told them to Stride.

"Please describe Rachel's emotional state. How did she seem to you?"

"Normal. Happy. Not upset or anything."

"Was it just an ordinary evening?"

"Sure."

"Okay, what about the next day, Kevin?" Dan asked.

"Well, Rachel asked if I wanted to go out on Saturday night. But when I showed up at her house, she had disappeared."

"Did you talk to the defendant?"

"Yes. I told him I had a date with Rachel. He said he didn't know where she was. He told me he hadn't seen her that day."

"And where was Rachel's car?"

"It was parked right outside. I couldn't understand where Rachel would be if she didn't have her car."

Dan nodded. "Did you tell Mr. Stoner this?"

"Sure. I said that was really strange. It wasn't like Rachel at all. I asked if we should call someone."

"What did he say?"

Kevin shot an angry look at Graeme. "He said no, there was no reason for concern. He said Rachel was probably just playing games with me like she did with everyone else."

"When Rachel made the date with you on Friday, did it feel like a game?"

"No, she was serious. We were planning to go out."

"When Rachel left you that night, what did she say?"

"She said she was going home. She was tired."

"Did she mention going anywhere else or meeting anyone else?"

"No."

"Did she seem upset, anxious, distraught?"

"No."

"So once again, as far as you were concerned, it was an ordinary night."

Kevin nodded. "That's right."

"Thank you, Kevin."

* * *

Gale stood up.

"Kevin, you called this an ordinary night. Is that right?" Gale asked, allowing a faint rumor of disbelief into his voice.

"Sure."

"Okay. Now let's see, you said when you first saw Rachel, she was standing on the railing of the bridge."

"Yes."

"It was windy and rainy."

Kevin nodded. "It was an awful night."

"So Rachel was standing on a narrow railing, with the icy water below her, and the wind blowing like crazy? Do I have the picture?"

"That's right."

"She could easily have been killed, couldn't she?"

"I guess."

Gale's eyebrows rose. "You guess? Kevin, you were terrified, weren't you? You ran to save her."

"Yes, I did."

"Had she ever climbed up on the bridge like that before, that you know of?" Gale asked.

"No."

"Why, on that night of all nights, would she have been risking death?"

"I don't know," Kevin said.

Gale continued. "You said Rachel made sexual advances toward you that night?"

"Yes."

"In front of your girlfriend?"

Kevin frowned. "Well, Sally was on the ground. We were up on the bridge."

"But she could see you, couldn't she?"

"I suppose."

"Had Rachel ever done something like this to you before?"

Kevin shook his head. "No."

"So, on this night of all nights, she makes a sexual advance on her oldest friend, someone she's known her whole life, for the first and only time?"

"Yes." Kevin's voice was almost inaudible.

"I see. Now, about the date. Was this the first time Rachel had asked you out?"

Kevin nodded. "Yes."

"The first time ever?"

"Yes."

"So again, on this night of all nights, Rachel decides for the first and only time to ask you out on a date."

"That's right."

Gale smiled. "So really, there wasn't anything *ordinary* about that night, was there?"

Kevin hesitated. "I guess not."

"Why was Rachel behaving so strangely?"

"I don't know."

"Okay, Kevin. Let's talk about something else. You knew Kerry McGrath, didn't you? The other girl who disappeared two years ago?"

"*Objection!*" Dan practically screamed. "Counsel's question is irrelevant and outside the scope of direct examination."

Judge Kassel slammed her gavel down, and Stride thought she enjoyed the opportunity to do so. She eyed Dan impatiently. "Settle down, Mr. Erickson."

Then the judge stared down at Gale. Her attractive jaw settled in a hard line, but her eyes were intrigued. "Now, Mr. Gale, please tell me you have a point to this question. Because, despite counsel's outburst, I'm inclined to sustain his objection."

Gale knew he had piqued her interest—and the jury's, too.

"I hope the court will indulge me a little while on this line, Your Honor. I want to explore some facts that will play a vital role in my defense. The prosecution's witnesses have testified that there is no link between

Kerry's and Rachel's disappearances. I wish to impeach those conclusions, and that is certainly relevant. What's more, Mr. Erickson opened the door by exploring the witness's personal relationship with Rachel. I'm entitled to explore whether he had a personal relationship with another girl who disappeared under similar circumstances."

Kassel's lips curled into an almost imperceptible smile. Stride couldn't tell whether she was enjoying the drama or savoring the possibility that Gale might have an ace up his sleeve with which to embarrass Dan.

"We'll indulge you briefly, Mr. Gale. Very briefly."

"Thank you, Your Honor," Gale said.

In the silence that followed, the whole courtroom focused its cold attention on Kevin, squirming in the witness stand. Gale repeated the question.

"Sure, I knew her. We were in the same class."

"Did the two of you ever go out on a date?"

"No," Kevin said.

"Did you ask her out, and she said no?"

"No." His voice was a whisper.

"Your Honor," Dan pleaded.

"Mr. Gale?" Judge Kassel demanded. "Our indulgence is running out."

Gale shot his next question in quickly. "Did she ever ask you out?"

Dan rose to object again, but before he could open his mouth, Kevin let out a giant sigh and said, "Yes."

Dan slowly sank back into his seat. The jury and the rest of the courtroom were transfixed. Judge Kassel put her gavel down and eased back into her chair.

"When did Kerry ask you out?" Gale asked.

"It was the week before she disappeared."

A murmur swept through the courtroom.

Stride glanced at Maggie. She looked back at him in confusion. They had worked the McGrath case inside and out, and Kevin's name had never come up. There was no evidence the two of them had ever been together. Then, a second later, they understood.

"Did you say yes?" Gale asked.

Kevin shook his head. "No. I told her I was already seeing Sally."

"So you never actually went out together?"

"No."

"How did Kerry take the rejection?" Gale asked.

"She was okay about it. She said maybe another time."

Gale nodded. "How about Sally? How did she like the idea of another girl asking you out? Just like Rachel did that night."

"She was kind of pissed off. I told her it was nothing. We didn't talk about it again."

"And a week later, Kerry disappeared, just like Rachel did."

Kevin swallowed. "Yes."

"You don't have very good luck with girls asking you out, do you, Kevin?"

Dan shouted another objection, and this time Kassel directed her anger at Gale, sustaining the objection and instructing the jury to ignore the question. Gale raised his arms in surrender.

"I don't have any more questions for you, Kevin," Gale said quietly.

Before Kevin could get up, Dan quickly got to his feet. "Redirect, Your Honor."

Judge Kassel nodded. "Go ahead."

"Kevin, please tell the court where you were on the night Kerry McGrath disappeared."

"I was in Florida. I was at Disney World with my parents."

"And on the night Rachel disappeared, what did you do after she left you in Canal Park?"

"I went home."

"Did you see your parents there?"

Kevin nodded. "We watched a movie on television in the living room until after midnight."

"Thank you, Kevin."

"What the fuck was all that about?" Dan demanded, taking a bite from a portobello sandwich. " 'A vital part of his defense?' "

Stride played with a paper clip, folding and unfolding it. "It's obvious, isn't it? He's going to try to paint Sally as a jealous serial killer. Anyone comes after my boyfriend, they disappear."

"But you told me that's a nonstarter," Dan said. "You said she's got an alibi."

Stride nodded. "She does. I don't know where he thinks he's going with this, but he obviously thinks he can make it play with the jury."

"Well, if I yank Sally off our list, we can't

put Graeme at the barn. Besides, Gale will just call her himself, which will make us look like we're trying to hide something. That means in half an hour she goes on the stand. So you tell me, could this girl have done it? Should I be concerned?"

Maggie shook her head. "No way. I've talked to the girl. She may be a jealous bitch when it comes to Kevin, but I don't see her taking girls off the street and killing them. And she wasn't making it up about Graeme and the barn. I talked to her. The girl was telling the truth."

"Then why the hell does Gale seem to think this is his Get Out of Jail Free card?" Dan asked. "Do we know where Sally was when Kerry disappeared?"

"No," Stride said. "Her name never came up."

"We know she wasn't with Kevin," Maggie pointed out slyly. "You made sure of that on redirect. He was in Florida."

Stride intervened before Dan could explode. "She didn't do it, Dan. But you can bet Gale has already checked, and Sally doesn't have an alibi for that night. Or she doesn't remember where she was. Hell, it was almost two years ago. It's still smoke and mirrors. A coincidence. Give the girl a chance. She convinced Maggie. She'll convince the jury, too."

Dan slammed his briefcase shut and gave Maggie a malevolent stare. "All right. We don't change our strategy. We ignore the Kerry McGrath issue. By my estimate, we're still ahead on points. If the jury went out now, they might think about it for a while, but they'd convict. But if Gale can muddle their brains with another false suspect, he might talk them into reasonable doubt. And let me make one thing very clear. If we lose this case, the two of you are going to be scraping bird shit off statues in public parks for the next ten years. So you better damn well hope you've given me enough to put this pervert behind bars."

Stride and Maggie exchanged glances. They were both thinking the same thing.

What was Gale up to?

Or worse, what had they missed?

27

Jerry Gull couldn't take it anymore. He had to go. Badly. And there was still a long stretch of empty road between him and Duluth.

He had guzzled coffee throughout the four-hour seminar in Hibbing, then rushed out of the hotel without using the bathroom. Jerry had a phobia about public bathrooms and generally didn't go anywhere except at home or at the office. Normally, he would have made it home from Hibbing in plenty of time, but he was delayed by another hour on his return trip because he had to pick up Brunswick.

Brunswick was his girlfriend Arlene's dog, a Newfoundland who weighed more than Jerry. Stretched out, he was probably taller than Jerry, too.

Arlene had been married for a short time. In the divorce, her ex-husband, who had a small hobby farm outside Hibbing, was awarded custody of the dog. Jerry had never met Brunswick, but he made the ultimate miscalculation of talking to Arlene about his seminar, and she, in turn, had cajoled him into a promise to stop at her ex-husband's farm and bring Brunswick to her for a long weekend at her sister's place just south of the city.

That was why, squeezed into the back-seat of his Toyota Corolla, was a black moose the size of Canada.

Almost immediately the coffee began to work its magic. Jerry tried not to think about it and instead just drove faster. It wouldn't have been hard to stop at a fast food restaurant along the way, but he wasn't ready to confront his phobia, and he wasn't sure he could get out of the car without Brunswick escaping.

By the time he began to dance in his seat, squirming to push his legs together, he was in the woods, a long way from any town. There was something about the dog, too, that made the urge to go even worse. He could smell him and feel him puffing, hot and foul, against his neck. The dog dispensed at least a gallon of drool, most of it down the shoulder of Jerry's blue suit. His slobbering face rubbed against Jerry's cheek affection-ately and refused to leave him alone.

There was simply not enough room in the car for him, his bladder, and Brunswick.

Jerry eyed the shoulder of the highway, and like a miracle, a quarter mile ahead, he saw exactly what he wanted, a dirt country road winding back into the forest in the mid-dle of nowhere. It looked like a road that got no traffic at all, except for an occasional farmer or hunter cutting over to a parallel highway.

He turned onto the dirt road, and the Corolla bounced and rocked. Brunswick's jowls swung in a peculiarly compelling rhythm, spraying the car with drool. Some of it slopped onto Jerry's glasses, and he rubbed them clean with his hand, groaning in disgust. Jerry drove more than a mile down the dirt road, finding a place where the forest was thick with birches and there wasn't a sign of humanity anywhere.

His body was bursting with streams, rivers, waterfalls, and every kind of torrential, rushing body of water. He wasn't sure he was going to make it.

Jerry swung open the driver's door and literally ran from the car. He hurried around to the right-side shoulder, ran down into the trees, and began clutching for his zipper. His clumsy fingers reached for his penis and missed, and his eyes rolled as he tried to free it from within his briefs. Finally, blissfully, he got it out, where it began flooding immediately onto the spongy ground. He didn't have to hold it or point it; it just doused the brush on its own like a fire hose.

The relief was so great his eyes teared up.

Then, when he was almost done, something huge and heavy hit him from behind, sending Jerry sprawling. He twisted and landed on his back on the wet ground— ground he had made wet—and meanwhile, his penis was still busily doing its work, spurting like a broken sprinkler over his pants, shirt, tie, and face. Jerry screamed, so caught up in the horror of the moment that he barely realized the culprit who had attacked him was Brunswick, shooting like a cannon deep into the forest.

"Brunswick!" Jerry bellowed, unleashing some of his anger.

He pushed himself off the ground, looking down at his sodden clothes. He couldn't believe it. It was a nightmare. The worst part was, he had probably lost the dog forever, and Arlene would never forgive him. He really thought about getting into the car, driving away, and never going home.

Woof!

He heard a deep bark somewhere in the distance. Brunswick wasn't gone for good, but he wasn't very close by. By the sound of it, he was at least a hundred yards deep in the forest. Jerry called the dog again, then waited, hoping to hear the thunder of paws (which were more like hooves) trampling the ground as the dog rushed back.

No such luck.

Woof!

Jerry sighed and started hiking. He kept calling for Brunswick, and the dog would periodically answer, helping Jerry to home in on him. Jerry was wet and dirty, and he smelled. The earth was soggy, and the tree branches scraped at his clothes and skin. His shoes were covered in mud. To add insult to injury, it was starting to rain.

"Brunswick!" Jerry called. He was losing patience.

Woof!

Jerry turned in the direction of the latest bark, squinting to see between the birch trees. This time, he caught a glimpse of a black beast, nose to the ground, paws digging frantically in the soft earth.

"Finally," he muttered.

He came up on the dog softly, not wanting to spook him and send him running away again, but Brunswick was intent on his work and didn't seem to notice Jerry at all. The dog had found something of great interest in a tiny clearing, and he was scooping out the ground with gusto. Every now and then, he would shove his whole huge head into the hole he had created.

Jerry reached down tentatively, taking the dog's collar in his hand.

"You are a bad dog," he said, stroking the matted black fur.

Brunswick, finally feeling Jerry beside

him, looked up happily, drool spilling from his jowls. The Newfoundland's broad mouth clutched something long and white.

"So what was worth all this trouble, Brunswick?" Jerry asked him.

He reached down to take the object from the dog's mouth, and Brunswick, after a slight tussle, released it.

It took Jerry a minute, looking at the thing in his hand, to figure out what it was.

Then, with growing fear, he looked in the hole to see what else the dog had found.

"Holy shit," he said.

28

Sally looked young on the witness stand. She was dressed demurely in a white cotton sweater with a round collar and a blue skirt. The sweater was loose enough to avoid drawing attention to her chest. Her full hair was pulled back and tied neatly behind her head. Her face was pink, but without makeup. She didn't wear any jewelry, just a plain gold watch.

Stride looked at her. Was he wrong? He allowed a shadow of doubt to pass over him, considering the crazy possibility that they had all misjudged the case. Sally was jealous and possessive. Could she have crossed over the line into murder?

Twice?

He simply didn't believe it.

"Sally, I'd like you to tell the jury about an incident that happened to you last summer. Can you describe it for us?"

Sally nodded. Her face was serious and composed. "It was a Sunday morning in July. I drove my car north of the city and turned off on one of the rural highways. I parked there and began biking."

"How long did you bike?" Dan asked.

"Maybe half an hour, I guess. I was listening to my iPod and not really paying attention to the time. But then the chain on my bike broke. I was probably ten or fifteen miles from my car. So I turned around and started pushing it back."

"Did you go all the way to your car?"

Sally shook her head. "No. A minivan passed me on the road. The driver stopped and honked at me. It was Rachel's stepfather. Graeme Stoner."

"How well did you know Mr. Stoner?"

Sally shrugged. "Oh, we knew each other enough to talk. I had been over to Rachel's house a few times with my boyfriend. Kevin."

"Go on, Sally."

"He offered to drive me and my bike to my car."

"Did you accept?"

"Yes. I was tired. It sounded great to have a ride back to the car. So I got in the van, but then we sat there for several minutes. He didn't make any effort to start the van. It was a little weird. He just asked me a lot of questions. Personal stuff."

"Tell us what he asked you."

Sally hesitated. "He said he saw me with Kevin a lot. He asked whether he was my boyfriend."

"What did you say?"

"I said yes, he was. Then he asked me whether Kevin and I were being careful. He was kind of grinning."

"What did you take that to mean?"

Gale stood up. "Objection, Your Honor. Assuming this conversation ever took place, the witness is not in a position to act as a mind reader."

"Sustained, but leave out the aside next time, Mr. Gale," Judge Kassel instructed him.

Gale, with a tiny smile, sat down.

"Were you uncomfortable?"

"Well, not at first. But it dragged on. We

must have been sitting there for five minutes or so, with him just firing all these questions at me. I started dropping hints, you know? I said we'd better go. I told him I needed to get back to the city. Finally, he started the engine, and we headed off. But I realized he was going very slowly. I looked over, and he was only doing forty. Most people usually do sixty or seventy on those roads."

"Did Mr. Stoner continue talking to you as he drove?"

"Yes. He told me that I was very pretty. That he liked my hair. That I had such nice skin. All the time, he was looking at me. But not really at my face, you know?"

"Tell us what he was looking at, Sally."

She glanced nervously at the jury. "He was staring at my breasts. He kept sneaking looks at them. I tried crossing my arms, but it looked funny. Instead, I kind of twisted my body so he didn't have much of a view."

"How did you feel?"

"It made me uncomfortable."

"Did you say anything?"

Sally shook her head. "No, I just wanted to get to my car and get out of there."

"What happened next?" Dan asked.

"He asked me if I had ever been to the barn."

A murmur rustled through the courtroom, and Judge Kassel tapped her gavel, restoring silence. Stride saw the faces of the jurors, intent on Sally's words.

"Go on, Sally," Dan said.

"He told me he had heard there was some real hot make-out spot nearby, and he wondered if I had been there with Kevin," she continued.

"What did you say?"

"I said no. He was really surprised. He thought I was kidding. But I really hadn't been there."

"Where were you at this point?"

"We were at a crossroads. I knew the barn was nearby. Everyone knows where it is. He stopped the van at the intersection."

Dan leaned forward. "Just to clarify, Sally, is this the same barn where evidence about Rachel—her bracelet, her blood—was discovered?"

"Yes. The same place."

"So what happened then?"

"He asked me if the barn was just down this road. I said yes, I thought so. He got this gleam in his eyes, like he was trying to flirt with me, and he asked if I thought anyone was there now, making out."

"What did you say?"

"I said I didn't know. I said we should really get going."

"Did he do what you asked?"

"No." Sally grimaced. "He said we should check it out. He was insistent. He turned and headed toward the barn. I was really scared."

"What did you think was going to happen?"

"Objection," Gale snapped. "Calls for speculation."

"I'm asking the witness for her own perception of the situation, Your Honor, not what was in the defendant's mind," Dan countered.

Judge Kassel paused. "I'll allow the question. You may answer."

"I don't really know what I thought. I was just so freaked out. The way he was talking, I guess I thought he was coming on to me. Like he was going to try something."

"Did he take you to the barn?"

Sally nodded. "Yes. He pulled in behind the barn and parked. I was getting ready to make a break for it, you know? I mean, he had me spooked. There was nobody around, and he kept looking at me and telling me I was really pretty."

"Did he touch you?"

"No. Well, he didn't have a chance to. We were hardly there a minute or two before another car pulled in behind us. I've never been so happy in my life."

"What did Mr. Stoner do?"

"He hauled ass out of there." Sally hesitated. "I'm sorry. But that was really what he did. As soon as that other car came up, he hit the accelerator, and we peeled out."

"Did he say anything further to you?"

Sally shook her head. "No, hardly a word. He just headed back to the main road, doing sixty this time. We reached my car in just a couple minutes. He dropped me off, and that was that. I was glad to get out of there."

"Did you tell anyone about this incident?" Dan asked.

"No. Not then, anyway. I was embarrassed, and I felt kind of stupid. I tried to tell myself I had just misinterpreted what had happened. But it all took place just like I told you."

"That's all I have, Sally. Thanks." Dan turned to Gale. "Your witness."

Now, thought Stride, *the fireworks start.*

He leaned over to whisper to Maggie. That was when he realized that Maggie was gone.

29

Gale removed his reading glasses, shoved them into the breast pocket of his suit coat, and gave Sally an avuncular smile.

"This won't take long, Sally," he told her. "I just have a few questions for you."

Bullshit, Stride thought.

"You were out biking on the country roads several miles from town, is that right?" Gale asked. "Weren't you scared?"

"No," Sally said. "I go out there at least once a month."

Gale frowned. "And yet only a few months earlier, another girl in your school was abducted while jogging on the back roads. Didn't that worry you?"

"Objection," Dan snapped. "What the witness was thinking about or not thinking about is irrelevant."

"Your Honor, if the jury is to decide whether this incident really took place, they deserve to hear the full context," Gale said.

Judge Kassel nodded. "Overruled. The witness will answer the question."

Sally shrugged. "I suppose it should have worried me, but I didn't really think about it."

"So you weren't concerned at all that whoever abducted Kerry might abduct you, too?"

"Objection, asked and answered," Dan interrupted.

"Sustained."

"All right, Sally, you claim that Mr. Stoner picked you up while you were pushing your bike back, is that right?" Gale asked.

"Yes."

"And the event was very traumatic for you."

"Yes."

Gale paused. "But you didn't tell anyone about it?"

"No, I didn't. Not then."

"You didn't tell anyone?" Gale asked. "Not your parents? Or Kevin? Or a teacher?"

"No. I was scared. And I thought maybe I overreacted."

"You overreacted. In other words, you began to realize you had leaped to the wrong conclusions, right?"

Sally hesitated. "I didn't know what to think. I mean, I was just glad it was over. I didn't want to get him into trouble."

"The first time you told anyone about this alleged incident was when the police were questioning you, right?"

"That's right."

"But it wasn't the first time you were questioned, was it?" Gale asked.

"No."

"In fact, the police talked to you several times before you suddenly blurted out this story. Isn't that correct?"

"I told you, I was scared," Sally said.

"Yes or no, Sally, please."

"Yes." She raced on before Gale could stop her. "It wasn't until I found out about the evidence the police found at the barn that I realized it was important."

"It never occurred to you to bring it up before then?"

"Not really, no."

Gale changed directions. "You're in love with our previous witness, Kevin Lowry, aren't you?"

Dan stood up. "This is irrelevant and outside the scope of direct examination, Your Honor."

Judge Kassel pursed her lips. "No, I'll allow it."

Sally was pleased to answer. "Yes, we're very close," she said firmly.

"He's a good-looking boy. I bet other girls go after him from time to time," Gale said.

"Kevin loves me."

"He never looks at other girls?"

"No."

"No? But other girls do check him out, right? Didn't Kerry McGrath do that?"

Dan was immediately on his feet again. "Same objection, Your Honor."

"Mr. Gale?" the judge inquired.

"Your Honor, this line of questioning goes to the credibility of the witness."

"Very well, overruled. But I expect to see relevance very quickly, Mr. Gale." Judge Kassel offered the defense attorney an impatient frown.

"Didn't Kerry ask Kevin out?" Gale repeated.

"Kevin said she did once, yes."

"Didn't that upset you?"

"Kevin told her no," Sally said. "If he had said yes, that would have upset me."

"You weren't mad at Kerry for poaching on your turf?" Gale asked, smiling.

"No."

"You weren't? You didn't talk to her about it?"

Sally hesitated. "No."

"You don't sound so sure, Sally."

"Well, I may have mentioned to her that Kevin was off-limits. It was no big deal."

"You mentioned it? Was this sort of a good-natured girl thing, or a 'stay away from my man or I'll rip your hair out' kind of thing?"

Sally's eyes widened. She was catching on now. Stride could almost see the message sinking into her brain. *He's trying to pin this on me.*

"Objection," Dan called. "Your Honor, I'm confused. Who is on trial here, and which crime is at issue?"

Judge Kassel sighed. "Mr. Gale, I'm confused, too. Would you care to explain the relevance? I've been more than patient."

Dan came around in front of the counsel table and spoke before Gale could open his mouth. "Your Honor, may we discuss this issue in chambers? With all due respect to defense counsel, I don't want him getting in through the back door what you disallow through the front door."

"Your Honor, that's offensive," Gale retorted.

The judge took a long look at both men. Then she nodded. "Ten minute recess. In my chambers, gentlemen."

Seated behind her neatly organized walnut desk, Judge Kassel leaned forward, resting her elbows on the wood. Gale was comfortably seated in front of her. Dan paced.

"Well, Archie?" the judge asked pleasantly. "Let's talk relevance."

Gale spread his arms, as if the explanation were obvious. "Your Honor, I'm trying to demonstrate that an alternate and reasonable theory of Rachel's disappearance exists, and this line of questioning will add to the credibility of that theory. In addition, it will give the jury reasonable cause to believe the witness invented the entire story of Mr. Stoner taking her to the barn. She has no independent corroboration, so all the jury can rely on is her word. I'm entitled to challenge it."

Dan responded angrily. "Your Honor, what this witness said or didn't say to Kerry McGrath has no bearing on her credibility. All Mr. Gale is trying to do is use innuendo to smear the witness and suggest the wild notion that she was involved in the previous girl's disappearance. He hasn't a shred of evidence to back it up, because none exists. He simply wants to confuse the jury. It's outrageous."

Gale shook his head. "I've already established a circumstantial connection between the two disappearances—namely, both girls asked out the same boy shortly before they vanished. And we have a jealous girlfriend in the middle. I'm entitled to explore this connection, because it contributes to reasonable doubt that my client was involved in the second disappearance and impeaches the witness's credibility."

"It impeaches nothing," Dan insisted. "The only way to imply that Sally had reason to lie about the incident at the barn is to suggest that she killed two girls. That's absurd. The so-called circumstantial connection is nothing but coincidence. How many other students and teachers at the same school had dealings with both girls shortly before they disappeared? Does Mr. Gale intend to question them all? The fact is, we have nothing whatsoever to link this witness to either Kerry's or Rachel's disappearance. Nothing. It's a smoke screen."

"Mr. Gale?" Judge Kassel asked coolly. "Do you have any evidence other than coincidences and wishful thinking?"

Gale nodded. "I believe I do, Your Honor, with respect to Rachel's disappearance."

The judge frowned, twisting a pen in her hand. "How nice for you, since this trial is about Rachel's disappearance. But what about Kerry McGrath?"

Gale hesitated. "Nothing direct, Your Honor."

Judge Kassel glowered at him. "Then your line of questioning in this regard is over. Move on to the real issue in this trial, Mr. Gale. I will instruct the jury to ignore all references to Kerry McGrath in your questioning of both witnesses today, and I don't expect to hear her name again. Is that clear? I don't appreciate having my courtroom taken on a fishing expedition."

"I don't believe it is, Your Honor."

"I've made my ruling, Mr. Gale. Now let's get going."

The time stewing in the courtroom had not been good for Sally. Her determined composure was gone, and in its place was the unease of a confused, scared teenager who didn't know what was going to hit her next. Stride wondered if that had been the whole point of Gale's gambit over Kerry McGrath—to soften Sally up for what came next.

Gale gave up his pleasant demeanor. His voice was sharp, like a razor. He zeroed in on Sally but waited for a few agonizing seconds before questioning her again.

Stride, watching this melodrama play out, was briefly distracted, seeing Maggie glide back into the row next to him. She sat down, their legs touching. Stride bent and cupped one hand near her ear.

"Anything going on?" he whispered.

Maggie nodded. She glanced behind her, making sure no one from the media was nearby. "Guppo paged me. He's chasing down something north of town. Could be important, he says."

From the defense counsel's table, Gale began again, his voice like ice.

"Sally, where do you live?"

Sally, surprised, gave him the address.

"Where is that in connection to Rachel's house?" Gale asked.

"About a mile, I guess."

"Within walking distance?"

"Sure."

"Have you ever walked from your house to Rachel's house?"

Sally nodded. "A couple times, yes."

"And you've been inside her house?"

"Yes, a couple times. With Kevin."

"What kind of car do your parents drive?" he asked.

Dan stood up. "Objection, relevance."

Judge Kassel sighed. "Overruled. But time is running out, Mr. Gale."

"Please answer," Gale told Sally.

"A Chevy minivan."

"Similar to what the Stoners own?" Gale asked.

"I guess."

"Have you ever driven your parents' minivan?"

Sally nodded. "Yes."

"So you're familiar with the controls?"

"Objection," Dan said. "Asked and answered."

"Sustained. Move on, Mr. Gale."

"All right, Sally, let's talk about the last night you and Kevin saw Rachel. The three of you were in Canal Park together?"

"That's right."

"Can you tell me what you were wearing that night?" Gale asked.

Sally hesitated. She glanced nervously at Dan, who leaned back and shot Stride a confused look. "What was I wearing? I don't remember."

Gale nodded. "Maybe I can refresh your memory." He found his glasses in his pocket and adjusted them at the end of his nose. He flipped through several pages of his notepad. "Could it have been a red plaid shirt, jeans, and a red parka? Does that sound right?"

"Maybe," Sally said. "I'm really not sure."

"But you do own such an outfit, don't you?"

Sally nodded. "Yes."

Gale crossed his arms, studying the girl. "Now, you didn't stay at Canal Park the entire time that Kevin and Rachel did, is that right?"

"No, I left about nine-thirty or so."

"What did you do then?" Gale asked.

"I drove home."

"Did you stop anywhere?"

Sally shook her head. "No, I went straight home."

Gale flipped through his notepad again. "Did you go out again after that?"

"No, I didn't."

Gale smiled coldly. "You're absolutely sure about that?"

"Yes," Sally said.

"All right, then. Tell me, Sally, why did you go home early? Why didn't you stay with Kevin? He's your boyfriend, isn't he?"

"Yes, he is."

"But you left him alone with Rachel?" Gale asked.

Sally smiled weakly. "I was tired."

"Oh, come on, Sally. You know what Kevin testified, don't you? He told us that Rachel made sexual advances to him on the bridge."

Sally said nothing. She bit her lower lip and avoided Gale's eyes.

"The fact is, you saw them together, didn't you? You saw what they were doing?"

"No, I didn't."

Gale arched his eyebrows. "You weren't watching? Your boyfriend was riding the bridge with a beautiful girl, and you paid no attention? You simply left?"

"I told you, I was tired," Sally repeated.

"Actually, you were furious, weren't you? Your boyfriend was cheating on you in front of your eyes. This girl was kissing him and fondling him right there so you could watch." Gale paused. "You stormed away, didn't you, Sally? You were enraged and humiliated. Isn't that right?"

Sally blinked. A tear slid down her cheek, and she wiped it away. "I was hurt," she said softly.

"So you did see them."

Sally nodded.

"You were angry at both of them," Gale said.

"No, not at Kevin," Sally blurted out.

"You were mad at Rachel," Gale said.

Sally frowned. "It was like she could cast a spell over him. She did that with all the guys. But she didn't care about any of them. She just used them."

"And that really upset you, didn't it?" Gale asked.

"She was cruel," Sally said. "I knew she was just toying with Kevin. I knew she wasn't really interested in him."

"But how did Kevin feel about Rachel? Doesn't he have a crush on her?"

Sally flushed. "It was nothing. Just a crush. He loves me."

"And yet, Sally, wouldn't he throw you over in a second for a chance to be with Rachel?"

"No!" Sally shouted.

"But isn't that what he did that night?"

"That's not what happened!"

"What did happen?" Gale asked. "What did Rachel do that night?"

Sally looked down. "She kissed him."

"What else?"

"I don't know."

"You don't? You already said you saw them. What did Rachel do to your boyfriend in front of your eyes?"

Sally hesitated. "She put her hand inside his pants."

"She's up there making out with your boyfriend, and you're left alone on the sidewalk?"

"Yes."

"And you think she was just playing

games with him? She wasn't serious?" Gale asked.

"Yes! That was how she was! She didn't care about him at all."

"But Kevin cared. He was always secretly in love with her, wasn't he? And you knew it. And now here was his fantasy girl coming on to him. You were afraid he was going to dump you, weren't you?"

"Kevin would never do that."

"We know he made a date with Rachel for the following night. He broke a date with you. Didn't he?"

Sally bit her lip. She looked like she wanted to escape. "He called and canceled our date."

"And all this was Rachel's fault?"

"Yes!"

"So, after seeing the two of them on the bridge, you went home?"

"That's right."

"That was it, you just went home?"

"Yes, I did. I was upset."

"Didn't you want to confront them?"

"Not then, no, I couldn't. I couldn't look at them."

"And what time was this again?"

"About nine-thirty."

Gale took off his glasses. He ruffled the pages of his notepad as he closed it. Sally's eyes followed him. She started to get up, as if she thought Gale was finished, but as she stood, Gale turned back. Sally swallowed and sat back down. Gale tugged at his goatee and studied the girl thoughtfully.

"What did you do when you got home?"

"I talked to my parents for a few minutes, then I went to bed."

Gale nodded. "Did you call Kevin?"

"No."

"Did you call Rachel?"

"No."

"It must have been hard to sleep, since you were so angry."

"I don't remember," Sally said. Her lower lip bulged from her mouth. She was getting belligerent.

"Is your bedroom on the first floor?" Gale asked.

"Yes."

"So if you wanted to, couldn't you sneak out without your parents knowing?"

"I didn't do that," Sally said.

"You didn't walk over to Rachel's house to confront her? To have it out with her?"

"Objection, asked and answered," Dan snapped.

"Sustained."

Gale tried a different approach. "All right, let's be very clear about this, Sally. Did you see Rachel that night after you went home?"

Before Dan could object, Sally's eyes flew wide open. "No!"

Several of the jurors inched forward in their seats. Dan watched Sally suspiciously, then turned to Stride with an inquisitive and hostile stare.

Stride leaned down and whispered to Maggie. "What the hell is this about? Where's he going?"

Maggie's honey skin looked several shades paler. "I think you're going to kill me, boss."

"Tell me," Stride said.

Maggie whispered, "Her clothes."

Gale waited until the courtroom was hushed. Then, in a quiet voice, he said, "Sally, explain this to us. If you didn't go confront Rachel—if you didn't leave your room that night—why were you seen on the street just a few blocks from Rachel's house at a few minutes after ten o'clock that night?"

Judge Kassel banged her gavel as another wave of noise rippled through the courtroom.

Sally seemed to wilt in front of their eyes. "That's impossible. I wasn't there."

Gale sighed. He extracted a white piece of paper from his notes and approached the witness stand. "This is a police report, Sally, from the night Rachel disappeared. It's an interview with a Mrs. Carla Duke, who lives four blocks from the Stoner house. Would you please read the passage that's highlighted, Sally?"

Sally took the paper as if it were on fire, holding it at the corners with her fingertips. Her voice was almost inaudible.

"'I did see a girl going by a little bit after ten. I saw her in the streetlight. But she didn't look anything like this girl you're trying to find. She had bushy brown hair and was wearing jeans and a red parka.'"

Gale retrieved the paper from her hands. "Sure sounds like you, Sally."

"It wasn't," she murmured. "It wasn't me."

Stride murmured, too. "Son of a bitch, how did we miss that?"

"We were looking for people who saw Rachel," Maggie said. "Not other girls."

Gale shook his head in disbelief. "Some- one wearing the same clothes as you, same hair as you, near Rachel's house on the night she disappeared, just a few minutes af- ter Rachel humiliated you in the park. But it wasn't you."

Sally was crumbling. "No."

"I say you're lying, Sally," Gale snapped.

"Objection!" Dan said.

Judge Kassel nodded. "Sustained."

Gale wasn't bothered. "If we bring in Mrs. Duke as a witness, do you think she'll iden- tify you?"

"Objection, calls for speculation."

"Sustained."

But the message was getting through.

"What did you say to Rachel?" Gale asked. "Did you warn her to stay away from Kevin?"

"I didn't see her."

"Did she answer the door? Were the keys to the van right there inside the door? Did the two of you go for a ride?"

"No!"

"You were seen, Sally. Kevin's going to know it was you. It's time you tell him and all of us the truth. Now, for the last time: Did you go to Rachel's house that night?"

"Objection," Dan repeated. "He's badgering the witness, Your Honor."

But Judge Kassel was staring at Sally, like everyone else. She shook her head slowly. "Overruled. Please answer the question, young lady."

Sally stared at the judge, then at Gale, then at the jury. She swallowed hard and nervously ran her hand back through her hair. She twisted a lock in her fingers. Tears began seeping down her face.

Then, with a sigh, she said it. "Yes, I did."

The courtroom erupted, and the judge tried in vain to quiet the crowd. Sally's next words were almost drowned out as she screamed, "But I didn't kill her! I didn't! I didn't!"

Gale waited until the chaos subsided. "You've been lying all day, Sally. Why should we believe you now?"

"Redirect, Your Honor."

Dan had no choice. He couldn't leave the jury wondering what happened next. He had to pry the truth out of her.

"Tell us what you did that night, Sally," Dan said calmly.

Sally seemed anxious to talk now. "I did

sneak out of my bedroom. I was so mad at Rachel. She was being cruel, playing with Kevin like that, when I knew she didn't care about him. So I walked over to her house. I wanted to tell her off, tell her that was a mean thing she was doing to him."

"Then what?" Dan asked.

"Her car was already there when I got to the house. So I figured she was home."

"What did you do?"

"I went up to the door. I wanted to talk with her."

"And did you?"

Sally shook her head. "No."

"Why not? Had she already disap- peared?"

"No, that's not it. I was about to ring the doorbell, but I didn't."

"Why not?"

Sally stared triumphantly at Archie Gale. "I heard voices inside. People shouting. I could hear Rachel screaming. She sounded really upset. And I could hear—I could hear Mr. Stoner, too. I recognized his voice. He was shouting at Rachel. They were having a huge fight. So I left."

Graeme Stoner leaned over to Gale and began whispering furiously.

Even Dan looked stunned. He stared at Sally and then simply said, "That's all, no more questions."

Stride shook his head. What a fucking mess.

Gale stood up again. If he was disturbed by Sally's sudden revelation, which was as good as a nail in Graeme Stoner's coffin if the jury believed her, he didn't show it.

"Sally, Sally, Sally," he murmured gently. "So many lies, what's one more?"

"Objection."

"Sustained."

Gale shrugged. "You ask us to believe you had information pivotal to this case and you chose not to reveal it at all? Not until now?"

"I was scared," Sally retorted.

"Of what, Sally?" Gale asked, looking bewildered.

"Of him. Of Mr. Stoner."

"Even after he was arrested?"

Sally stuttered, "Well, yes."

"And yet you weren't so scared that you held back on your little story about the barn. If you told that story to the police, why not the rest, Sally?"

"I wasn't sure they'd believe me."

"So you lied. Nice strategy."

"I didn't want my parents to know I went out again," Sally said. "Or Kevin. I was afraid of what they'd think."

"They'd think you killed Rachel."

"No!" Sally shouted. "That's not it at all."

"The fact is, you didn't tell anyone about this phantom argument between Rachel and Graeme because it never happened, right? You just made it up here and now."

"No, that's not true!"

"No? Come on, Sally. You now admit you went over to Rachel's house, after lying about this for months. What really happened there?"

"Objection, asked and answered," Dan interjected.

"Overruled," Judge Kassel said crisply.

It was a disaster. Even the judge didn't believe her.

"It happened just like I said," Sally insisted. "I heard them."

Gale sighed. "Really? What were they saying?"

"I couldn't make out the words," Sally said.

"I see. You just heard voices."

"Yes."

"And so, furious and humiliated, after

walking a mile to confront her, you just left without seeing her. Because you heard voices."

Sally nodded. "Yes, I did."

"And you never thought to mention this to anyone before? You supposedly have the crucial piece of evidence in a murder investigation, and you say nothing because you think your parents will ground you for sneaking out?"

"No, it wasn't—I mean, that wasn't it."

Gale was relentless. "Sally, can you give us *one single reason* why we should believe this story?"

Sally opened her mouth and closed it. She wet her lips with her tongue and didn't say a word.

"I'm finished, Your Honor," Gale said.

30

Stride didn't want to go outside. Neither did Maggie, but while they were milling in the tumult of the courtroom after Judge Kassel dismissed them for the day, Guppo paged her again, and she fought her way to the door. Stride and Dan stayed behind. He knew that the gauntlet of reporters would be waiting to feast on both of them. Gale was already outside, putting his spin on Sally's testimony, insisting it opened the door for an acquittal. But the reporters would want to see Dan and Stride, too, and hear their explanation.

Have you lost? Bird would ask.

They both knew. Yes, they had lost. It was as good as over.

Emily Stoner lingered in the courtroom behind them, looking confused and upset. She was alone. Dayton Tenby had been at her side all day, but he had left to pull his car around to the rear of the courthouse. The guards would spirit her out the back, away from the media horde.

She hadn't said a word yet, and Dan hadn't acknowledged her. But Stride knew she was the only reason Dan hadn't flown into an explosive rage.

"You told me she had an alibi," Dan said. His lips were stretched into a thin, cold line.

"She did."

"Yet a witness your *own men* talked to blew the alibi out of the water. And no one ever caught it."

Stride sighed heavily. "Look, Dan, what's the point of excuses? We fucked up. Pure and simple. We should have caught it, and we didn't."

"Humor me," Dan hissed. "Tell me why."

"We interviewed hundreds of witnesses in those first couple days. We were looking for people who had seen Rachel. Someone seeing a teenage girl on the street several blocks away, who didn't match Rachel's description, just wasn't going to be high on our list."

"Why the hell not?"

Stride shook his head. "Sally was never a suspect. Hell, she's still not a suspect. I don't believe for a second she had anything to do with Rachel's murder. There's no physical evidence at all to connect her to any of this."

"Maybe she's just too smart for you," Dan said.

"No way. If this was really a crime of passion, she would have left evidence all over the scene. Put me back on the stand tomorrow. I can point out that there were no unidentified fingerprints, no hair or fibers, nothing to put Sally in the van or at the barn. It wasn't her."

"You have no new evidence," Dan said. "I can't put you back to reiterate what you already told the jury."

Emily cleared her throat. The two men stopped, looking at her as if for the first time. Her face was white.

"I don't understand," Emily said. "You sound like this was a bad thing for the case. Shouldn't this be a good thing? I mean, she made the connection you needed. She heard Graeme and Rachel arguing that night. It puts them together."

Dan nodded. The anger drained away, and his eyes softened. "I'm afraid it's more complicated than that."

"But why?" Emily asked. "This should guarantee a conviction."

Dan took one of her hands in his. He met her eyes. "The question is, will the jury believe her? Mr. Gale raised doubts about Sally's credibility. We know she told one lie, about not going to see Rachel that night. The jury is likely to think she's telling another lie, to cover up something."

"Is that what you think?"

Dan sighed. "I really don't know, Emily. I'd like to believe her. It makes sense, given all the other evidence. If Sally had come forward with this immediately, we'd have a conviction now, no doubt about it. Under these circumstances, I'm afraid it makes it worse, not better."

"But why?" Her voice was plaintive.

"Well, it may open up reasonable doubt in the jury's mind. They may be sufficiently concerned about Sally's testimony that they feel they can no longer be absolutely certain that Graeme is guilty."

"He is guilty," Emily said passionately. "He did this. I know it."

"Many of the jurors may think so, too. The question is, are they sufficiently convinced to convict him?"

The reality seemed to dawn on her. "Are you telling me the son of a bitch could be *acquitted?* He could walk out of here?"

"I'm afraid that's possible," Dan said. His voice was hoarse and angry, as if that reality were only now dawning on him, too.

Stride looked up, hearing the thud of the courtroom door. Maggie was inside again, hurrying down the aisle, beckoning to him. He saw urgency written in her face. Without a word, Stride left Dan and Emily, pushed through the swinging gate, and met Maggie in the middle of the aisle.

"We found a body," Maggie said breathlessly. "Guppo's on the scene."

"Rachel?"

"No way to tell. It's just skeletal remains. The son of a bitch tried to burn her. Could be Rachel. Could be Kerry. Could be someone else."

Stride closed his eyes. A month ago, this would have been tremendous news. Three months ago, even better. One of Gale's best theories, that Rachel was really still alive, might have been stripped away.

"Where was she found?" Stride asked.

"Just a few miles north of the barn. If our search radius had gone another mile, we might have found her."

"Does Guppo have the scene sealed off?"

"Yeah. The medical examiner is up there, too."

"What's he say about it?" Stride asked.

"For now, not much. All he'll say is that the skeletal structure is consistent with that of a teenage girl. Otherwise, we'll either have to wait for the DNA or dental records or hope something turns up in a search of the surrounding area."

"Not a word to the press yet," Stride said. "Play it cool. I'll tell Dan, and then you and I can go up there."

Stride looked back at Dan and Emily and wondered how you break news like this in front of the girl's mother. He took a deep breath and told Maggie to wait for him. Returning to the front of the courtroom, he saw Dan and Emily watching him. There was no gentle way to say it.

"We've located a body in the woods north of the city," he told them.

Emily's eyes widened, and her hand flew to her open mouth. "Oh, no!"

Dan said, "Shit." He repeated it several times.

Emily crumpled into a seat. She sat there silently, like a piece of broken eggshell, then finally looked at Stride with bloodshot eyes. "Is it—is it her? Rachel?"

"We don't know yet," Stride said. "I'm very sorry. We only have skeletal remains, so it's going to take time to identify them."

"How long?" Dan asked.

"We'll probably have to wait for DNA tests, unless we can do something with dental records. Either way, it's likely to be a few weeks."

Dan shook his head. "We don't have a few weeks. We don't even have a few days."

Stride nodded. "I know."

"What do you mean?" Emily asked.

"The trial is almost over," Dan told her. "Without positive identification, we can't raise the issue in front of the jury. Our suspicions aren't evidence."

"But we have her body now," Emily pleaded. "You can't let that man continue to pretend to the jury that she may be alive."

"Unfortunately, we don't know yet that it is her body," Stride reminded her gently.

"This is insane," Emily said, shaking her head. "I can't believe this. My God, they can't just let him walk away now. They have to postpone the rest of the trial. They have to give you time to prove it's Rachel."

Dan sighed, and Stride knew what he was thinking. It was too little, too late.

"That's up to the judge," Dan said.

31

"A continuance?" Judge Kassel's eyebrows twitched, and her voice climbed an octave. "Mr. Erickson, please tell me this is an example of your charming sense of humor."

Dan spread his hands plaintively. "I realize this is unusual, Your Honor."

"Unusual?" Gale snorted. "Try outrageous."

The two men leaned closer to the judge's bench. Behind them, the courtroom was packed again, with hushed conversation buzzing through the crowd. Judge Kassel banged her gavel, but it did little to quiet them. Graeme Stoner sat alone at the defense table, his face stoic. Today, Emily sat immediately behind him, as if she wanted Graeme to feel her presence. Her eyes burned into her husband's neck. Graeme, after noticing her there when he first sat down, hadn't looked back once, but it was obvious that he could feel her there, close enough for her scent to reach him.

The jury was absent, secluded in the jury room while Dan pleaded for more time. They were the only people in the state of Minnesota who had not awakened to the headline splashed across the newspaper:

RACHEL'S BODY?

"No one could have anticipated something like this," Dan said. "But in the interests of justice, we simply must take the time to analyze the remains."

"He wasn't concerned about a body before, Your Honor," Gale said.

Judge Kassel stared down her nose at Dan. "That's true."

"He felt confident enough to make his case without any proof that the girl was dead," Gale continued. "He's had his chance."

"I haven't rested my case," Dan pointed out.

"Yes, but he has nothing more to add, Your Honor. I don't see any evidence. I don't see any witnesses."

Dan shook his head. "Much of Mr. Gale's defense was predicated on leaving the jury with the impression that Rachel might still be alive. He used that implication to try to establish reasonable doubt. If we can prove conclusively that Mr. Gale's insinuations were false, the jury deserves to know that."

The judge crossed her arms and leaned back. "Mr. Gale?"

"The whole situation is prejudicial," Gale argued. "The jury has heard all the evidence. It's fresh in their minds. Giving the prosecutor time to let the jury's memory fade is both unfair and unreasonable. The body could well turn out to be unrelated to this case, and it will be too late to repair the damage. Besides, we have no idea how long it will take them to make a conclusive identification, assuming they can do so at all."

"Archie, you should want the delay," Dan said. "Your Honor, even sequestered, the jury may very well know about the body. It's too easy for news to seep through one way or another. They'll conclude it's Rachel. It will influence their decision. We should allow them to decide on facts, not innuendo."

Judge Kassel offered a faint smile. "That's very charitable of you, Mr. Erickson. But the fact is, the jurors will not hear anything about any body if there's no delay. As soon as you called me last night, I shut down all phone calls in and out. That was before Mr. Finch's little broadcast, thank God. There are no televisions and radios in the rooms. Their transport this morning was closely moni-tored. They don't know now, and they won't know when they start deliberating in a day or so if we take appropriate precautions. I'll clear the courtroom if I have to."

"You could declare a mistrial," Dan sug-gested. "We could start over."

Gale opened his mouth, but Kassel waved him to silence. "I'm way ahead of you, Mr. Gale. No mistrial, Mr. Erickson. There's nothing wrong with this one."

"Your Honor, the people shouldn't be pe-nalized because the defendant did such a good job of hiding his crime that we didn't find the body until now."

Gale corrected him. "They found *a* body, not necessarily *the* body. And even if it is

Rachel, they have no additional evidence to tie Mr. Stoner to the body or the scene. It adds nothing of value to the record."

"We don't know that yet," Dan said heatedly. "We haven't fully analyzed the crime scene."

"Yes, let's not get carried away, Mr. Gale," Judge Kassel said. "Mr. Erickson is right. You got a lot of mileage out of the people's failure to produce a body. You can't argue that it's meaningless now that they've got one."

"They chose to proceed without a body," Gale repeated. "If this discovery had been made a week from now, Mr. Stoner would already have been acquitted."

"That's irrelevant, Your Honor," Dan said.

"Perhaps, but you did seem pretty anxious to get Mr. Stoner in front of a jury. Now you seem less anxious to have them decide his fate." Judge Kassel pursed her lips and again held up her hand before the lawyers could continue. "I'd like to find out more about this discovery and how long it might take to get some answers."

Her eyes found Jonathan Stride in the third row of the courtroom, and she crooked her finger, beckoning him to the bench.

* * *

Standing up, Stride felt all the eyes of the courtroom on him. He wasn't prepared. He hadn't slept, and his clothes were stained with mud. From early evening until two hours ago, when he sped back to the city, he had tramped through the mushy ground, under the glare of searchlights, hunting along with twenty other officers for additional clues. He knew it was a doomed effort, although they would sift through the dirt for days to come. After six months of rain, snow, and ice, there was nothing left to tie Graeme Stoner to the scene, no footprints, no fibers, no blood, nothing except a body that was no more than a jumble of bones.

But they had a body. The question was, whose?

Stride pushed through the swinging door at the bar and joined Dan and Gale in front of Judge Kassel. She eyed his clothes and the bags under his eyes.

"You've had a long night, I gather, Lieutenant."

"Very long, Your Honor," Stride said.

"I assume you can keep your eyes open long enough to answer a few questions."

Stride smiled. "I'll do my best."

"Thank you. Now, first of all, who told Mr. Finch and the rest of his friends in the media about this body?" Judge Kassel demanded. "It's bad enough to have this in the middle of trial, but worse to have it blared all over the state. We're lucky the jurors didn't hear about any of this."

"I'm very sorry about that, Your Honor," Stride said. "I wish I could tell you how Bird gets his information. I have no idea."

"All right, well, I guess that's his job. Now tell me exactly what you found. These are definitely human remains?" Judge Kassel asked.

"Yes. We confirmed it with the medical examiner."

"Sex?"

"The ME says female," Stride said.

The judge nodded. "And no ready means of identification? It could be Rachel or Kerry or some other girl?"

"There was nothing left to identify. No clothes, no personal effects. The body was partially burned. We'll be running DNA tests on the surviving bone."

"How long will all of this take?"

Stride shook his head. "I wish I could give you a clear answer, Your Honor. It could be a couple days, and it could be a few weeks."

"And you found no other evidence of note near the body?"

"No. We'll continue searching, but I'm not optimistic, given the amount of time that has passed."

Dan interrupted. "But the real key is the identity of the body, Your Honor. If this turns out to be Rachel, it has an enormous bearing on the trial."

"If, if, if," Gale said. "If this, maybe that. No evidence, but we'll continue searching. Maybe a few days, maybe a few weeks, maybe never. Mr. Stoner should not have to sit around while the police and the prosecution stall us with vague promises of evidence yet to come. Neither should the jury. There is really nothing here, Your Honor, except smoke."

Judge Kassel sighed. "I'm inclined to agree."

Dan grabbed the bench with both hands. "Your Honor, just a few days. Give us until the end of the week to confirm the identification. If we don't have anything by then, we'll wrap up the trial."

"And meanwhile the witnesses will be a distant memory," Gale said scathingly. "It's now or never."

"They can have any testimony they like read back to them," Dan said.

"Oh, please," Gale said.

Kassel cut them both off. "That's enough, gentlemen. Mr. Erickson, I'm sympathetic to your situation. I'm loath to proceed with the tantalizing possibility of new and crucial evidence so close. But right now, you have nothing but hopes and theories. You went into this case without a body, convinced you could get a conviction. You're going to have to abide by that decision."

The judge reached down, clicking on her microphone, and banged her gavel again to quiet the courtroom. She directed her announcement to the court.

"The motion for continuance is denied. We will proceed with the trial."

"Your Honor, I renew my motion that hearsay evidence of a sexual relationship between the defendant and Rachel Deese, as cited in deposition by Dr. Nancy Carver, be admitted, on the grounds that the declarant is unavailable as a witness."

"Denied. Anything more, Mr. Erickson?"

Dan clenched his fists in frustration. "No, Your Honor."

"Fine. Bailiff, please bring in the jury."

Stride turned away from the bench. He saw fury in Dan's eyes, a coldness, directed at him, he had never felt in his life. It was as if Dan's future had been buried in the shallow hole where they had dug up the body, and he could find only one person to blame.

Dan whispered, "You fucked this whole case up for me from day one."

Stride didn't reply. He didn't have time.

Something was wrong.

The buzz in the crowd had changed. The noise and whispering that followed the judge's decision turned into something else. People were confused, pointing, standing. Someone was shouting. It was Maggie, in the third row, calling Stride's name and scrambling across people to get to the aisle.

Close by, others began screaming.

Stride saw Graeme Stoner jerk up out of his chair at the defense table, as if an electric current were bolting through his skin. Graeme steadied himself with his hands flat on the table. His eyes were wide, filled with puzzlement.

Graeme's mouth fell open, as if he were about to laugh. Then his chest heaved, and instead, a trickle of blood dribbled from his lips. Graeme blinked. He looked down at the drips splashing on his white shirt like cherries in the snow.

He smiled.

Then his chest heaved again, and the trickle became a river.

Bright red blood streamed from Graeme's mouth, then his nose. The river poured over his suit, bathing his shoulders and chest, then spilled onto the table, soaking the raft of papers scattered there. It cascaded like crimson fountains into puddles on the floor.

Graeme's eyes turned gray and glassy and rolled up into his head. For another few seconds, he remained standing at attention. Then his body seemed to shrivel. His shoulders caved inward, and he collapsed in a pile on the table, his face dangling over the edge, still spouting a geyser of blood that now squirted over the courtroom floor in a growing lake. There was no way to turn off the spigot, and even Dan Erickson and Archibald Gale shouted and reared back as the red flood pooled around their shoes.

All the while, Graeme lay face down, draining the last few beats of his heart.

Stride tried to run, but he slipped in the blood. He regained his balance and dove forward. Maggie arrived first. She battled past the last few people who stood in her way, transfixed by the horror in front of them. She leaped over those who had thrown themselves to the floor, screaming, in an effort to escape.

Emily Stoner stood in the front row, as frozen as those around her, staring at the blood-soaked body of her husband immediately in front of her. Her right arm was held high. Maggie's tiny hands clenched Emily's outstretched arm in an iron grip, holding it in the air, but it was as if Emily didn't notice. She didn't move. She didn't let go.

Then Stride arrived, leaning past Graeme Stoner's dilapidated corpse to strip the red-stained butcher knife from Emily's hand.

Bedlam.

32

The chambered windows in the upper-floor library of the Kitch were closed, buffeted by a morning thunderstorm. Gale sipped coffee from a china cup as he leaned against the window frame. He glanced over at Dan Erickson, who sat on the sofa with a plate of eggs and sausage and a tall orange juice in front of him.

"You know, they would have acquitted him," Gale told Dan. His lips curled upward in a smile, and his eyes twinkled.

Dan's fork and knife clinked on the plate as he cut up his eggs, yolks oozing out.

"Don't be so sure. You heard the interviews Bird did with the jurors. They didn't believe Sally was involved. They thought Graeme did it."

"I believe they said 'probably,' and that would be reasonable doubt if we were in a courtroom. Besides, they all had the opportunity to watch your press conference last week. Angry prosecutor denouncing the unfounded allegations against an innocent girl. No evidence except what points to Mr. Stoner." Gale's face was illuminated by a flash of lightning. "Forget the fact that you couldn't prove it in court."

"Says you," Dan replied pleasantly.

Gale shook his head. "I can't believe Emily got in there with the knife."

"We had metal detectors, but the media was hounding her. She asked to be brought in through the rear door. Who knew she was going to go off the deep end?"

"You're saying it was a surprise? Please. I half think you wanted something like this to happen, Daniel." Gale sipped more coffee. "Did you work out a deal with her?"

"Manslaughter two. Three years, minimum security."

"A slap on the wrist," Gale said.

"Oh, come on. The man killed her daughter. Archie, we're not in court anymore. You don't really believe Graeme was innocent, do you?"

"I don't know if he was innocent. I don't know if he was guilty. Neither do you."

Dan dabbed at his lips with a napkin and stood up, smoothing his suit. He took the pot of coffee and poured himself a cup. "Well, it was brilliant putting Sally at Rachel's house. What tipped you off?"

"It's obvious you've never raised teenagers," Gale said, laughing. "She watches another girl come on to her boyfriend, and she just goes home to bed? Not a chance. That was a catfight in the making."

"And the Kerry McGrath thing?"

"I went looking for connections once I knew Sally had gone to see Rachel that night. When Kevin admitted Kerry had asked him out, it was almost too good to be true."

Dan shrugged. "Sally's father went back and checked his calendar. The whole family was in the Cities that weekend for a play. *Les Miz.* We confirmed the purchase."

"That's the kind of evidence a father can produce when his daughter's in trouble," Gale said.

"She didn't do it, Archie."

"Have it your way. But there's more to this story than came out in court."

The room rattled as a thunderclap shook the club. Gale studied the dark sky thoughtfully.

"With Graeme dead, we may never know," Dan said.

Gale stroked his goatee. "Oh, I wonder. Perhaps Rachel will come back and tell us the secrets herself. Like a ghost."

Stride listened to the violent rapping of the downpour on the windows and saw a glow behind his eyelids with each stroke of lightning. The oak timbers of the porch groaned under the gusts of wind. He could smell the sweet fresh air, soured by a hint of mildew in the wood.

When the thunder awakened him at four in the morning, he had taken his blankets to the porch, clicked on the space heater, and drifted in and out of a light sleep as the storm rolled overhead in waves from the west. In his bedroom, his alarm had gone off two hours ago. He didn't care. The sky outside was dark enough that it still looked like night.

The investigation and trial lingered in his mind. Stride felt no closure. He refused to believe that Stoner was innocent. That hadn't changed. But maybe he was lying to himself, trying to convince his brain that he hadn't been wrong from the beginning. He would swat his doubts away, but a few minutes later they'd be back, like mosquitoes, buzzing at his ear. Each time louder than before.

He thought about the postcard. It had been waiting in his mailbox when he came home last night. He kept looking at it every few minutes. And hearing the mosquitoes.

The floor groaned under the weight of footsteps. Stride's eyes snapped open. He craned his neck and saw Maggie standing in the doorway of the porch. Her black hair was soaked. Water dripped from her face and sleeves. She looked tiny and vulnerable.

"I see you're selling your house," she said.

The sign had gone up a few days ago. He closed his eyes again and shook his head, angry at himself. "I was going to tell you. Really, Mags."

"You're getting married, aren't you? You and the teacher?"

Stride nodded.

It had happened a week ago over dinner. He wasn't even sure, looking back on it, who had asked whom. They had started out sober and depressed and ended up, several hours later, drunk and engaged. Andrea clung to him, not wanting to let go. It was a good feeling.

"I'm sorry, Mags," he said.

She took one hand out of her pocket and pointed her index finger at him like a gun. "Are you out of your mind, boss? You're making a terrible mistake."

"I know you're upset," he said.

"Damn right I'm upset! I'm watching a friend fuck up his life. I told you not to get too serious, didn't I? Both of you rebounding from disasters. Cindy always told me you were the densest person on the planet emotionally, and I guess she was right."

"Leave Cindy out of this," Stride snapped.

"What? Like she's not in this up to your eyeballs? I'm going to say it again, boss. You're making a mistake. Don't do it."

Stride shook his head. "You and I, that would have been impossible. It would never have worked. You told me that yourself."

"You think this is about me?" Maggie

asked. She stared at the ceiling, as if pleading for divine guidance. "Unbelievable."

There was an awkward silence between
them. The only sounds were the roar of the
storm outside and the dripping of Maggie's
coat on the floor of the porch.

"Is it so wrong for two people who need
each other to get together?" Stride asked.

"Yes," Maggie said. "That's wrong. It
should be two people who love each other."

"Oh, come on, you're just playing word
games with me."

"No, I'm not. You're in love, or you're not.
You belong together forever, or you have no
business getting married."

"I thought maybe you'd be happy for me,"
Stride said.

"You want me to smile and pat you on the
back and tell you how great it is?" Maggie's
voice grew shrill with anger. "Fuck you. I'm
not going to do that. I can't believe you'd
ask."

Stride didn't say anything. He listened to
her harsh breathing.

Maggie shook her head and sighed,
gathering up her emotions like marbles
spilled on the floor. "Look, if this is what you

have to do, then you go and do it. But I couldn't live with myself if I didn't say my piece."

He nodded. "Okay, Mags. You've said it."

They stared at each other for a long while, which was like saying good-bye without words. Not good-bye forever, just to their relationship as it was.

"I came to tell you, it wasn't Rachel's body," Maggie said, slipping back into her cop voice, all business again. "We got the DNA tests back. It was Kerry."

Stride cursed under his breath. He thought about that sweet, innocent girl— about losing her, about losing Cindy. He was angry all over again. Angry that a killer had gotten away with murder.

And then he thought, *It wasn't Rachel*. He heard the mosquitoes at his ear again. Buzzing.

"I got something in the mail last night," Stride said quietly.

He inclined his head toward the picture postcard lying on the coffee table. Maggie glanced down at the photograph on the card, which showed a strangely proportioned, long-eared gray animal in the desert.

"What the hell is that?"

"A jackalope," Stride said. "Part jackrabbit, part antelope."

Maggie screwed up her face. "Huh?"

"It's a joke," Stride said. "A myth. It doesn't exist. People send postcards of jackalopes to see how gullible you are."

Maggie reached down to pick up the card.

"Edges only, please," Stride told her.

Maggie stopped, her hand frozen in the air, and gave Stride a curious look, as if she had sensed something horrible. Then she carefully picked up the postcard by the edges and turned it over. She read the message, which was scrawled in red ink, its letters dripping into streaks where rain had spattered the postcard:

He deserved to die.

"Son of a bitch," Maggie blurted out. She stared at Stride and shook her head fiercely. "This can't be from her. This can't be from Rachel. The girl is dead."

"I don't know, Mags. Just how gullible are we?"

Maggie eyed the postmark. "Las Vegas."

Stride nodded. "The city of lost souls," he said.

PART FOUR

THREE YEARS LATER

33

Jerky Bob lived in a trailer moored off a minor road a few miles south of Las Vegas. He had arrived, as so many vagabonds in the Las Vegas valley do, out of nowhere. About a year ago, the trailer appeared, dragged perilously by a truck that waited barely long enough to unhitch it before disappearing back into the city. A day after the trailer took up permanent residence off the dusty road, a hand-scrawled sign on a wooden stake appeared near the California highway. It read:

Jerky Bob

And then below it:

New Age Gifts
Psychic Poetry
Beef Jerky

Bob curtained off one end of the trailer, where the rear entrance was, put up a rickety table and cash box, and opened for business. He hung dozens of stained glass wind chimes, stuck pyramid magnets to a metal plate nailed to the wall, filled shelves with incense burners and sandalwood candles, and handwrote epic poetry that he copied on an ancient duplicating machine and tied up in scrolls with purple ribbons.

His repeat customers didn't come back for the wind chimes or the poetry, though. They came for the dried meats: beef jerky, chicken jerky, and turkey jerky, sold in flavors like teriyaki and Cajun from shoe boxes inside an old refrigerator. Most of the people who stopped were truckers. It only took a couple of them, stopping out of curiosity, to start a buzz that made its way through the trucker network of the Southwest. Word got passed. *Going to Vegas? Stop at Jerky Bob*. They came twenty-four hours a day, seven days a week, which were his regular hours. If they came while he was sleeping, they simply woke him up, and he sold them jerky. He made enough money each month that, if it had stayed in his pocket, he could have moved back to the city and opened a real shop, complying with health codes and paying taxes instead of flying under the government radar.

But money didn't last long with Bob. Half of it ended up down the gullet of slot machines. Half ended up in empty gin bottles, tossed from the back of his trailer into the desert, where they glistened like a field of diamonds.

He had committed suicide a year ago, but his body hadn't figured it out yet.

The truckers talked about it. Bob looked normal enough, a year ago, for a man marooned in the desert. From that point, month by month, he got older. He never shaved, other than cutting tangles out of his long, graying beard. His hair dangled in messy strands below his shoulders. His skin was shriveled and gray, and his eyes receded into his skull. He ate little but jerky himself, getting thinner and thinner until he was barely a hundred and twenty pounds. He never washed his clothes, which usually consisted of jeans and a Las Vegas T-shirt hanging on his skinny frame. The stench got so bad that some of his trucker customers refused to come inside, and they told him that even the jerky was beginning to smell. Bob just opened a window, letting dry, dusty air blow through the trailer.

He couldn't go into the casinos anymore. They turned him away at the door. Instead, he spent time every few days at a bar a half mile up the highway from his trailer, where he played video poker until the bartender got sick of the smell. Then he'd buy another bottle of gin and go home, drink, and pass out. In the morning, or whenever a trucker pounded loudly enough to wake him up, he would throw the bottle out back.

Last night had been a two-bottle night. Or maybe it had been two nights ago, or even three. He didn't know.

He didn't remember much. On the television it said Wednesday, but he couldn't remember when he had started his binge. His last visitor had arrived in the afternoon, and that night, whichever night it was, he had begun pouring glass after glass of gin. And now it was Wednesday.

Bob sighed. He had to piss.

He stood up, propping himself against the wall for balance. The trailer spun in his head for a few seconds before righting itself. He stepped down off the mattress onto the floor and watched a few bugs skitter away from him. The two gin bottles lay empty a few feet away. He crouched, picking them up and staring inside. There was a small puddle of gin in each one, clinging to the glass, enough to wet his tongue when he turned the bottles upside down over his mouth. His body was sufficiently poisoned that the taste caused his stomach to heave, and he had to swallow hard to avoid retching.

Bob held the two bottles by their necks. He looked around for his sandals, saw them under a chair, and stuck his feet into them. The sandals flapped as he padded to the center door of the trailer. The latch had long since broken. With his knee, he nudged the door open, and daylight roared in. Still naked, Bob shuffled down the rusty steps into the desert behind his trailer.

The sun was ferocious, like a yellow fire burning out of control above the hills. His eyes squinted, barely able to open, and his skin tightened, starting to cook. As he sucked in each labored breath, a furnace of air seared his lungs.

His penis twitched, ready to release. He began pissing a virtually clear stream of urine onto the ground. The liquid raised a cloud of dust, then gathered into a small pool in an indentation in the earth. He kept pissing into the center, causing droplets to splatter onto his toes. He watched the flow intently, as if it were his life's blood leaking out of him. The urine was frothy and reeked of gin. In a few seconds, the pool would be gone, baked away by the sun.

The stream dissipated to a trickle.

Underhanded, he heaved one of the gin bottles into the air, watching it glint in the sun in a shallow arc before crashing back to earth. He heard the glass shatter and saw shards burst in every direction. Carefully, he repeated the ritual with the second bottle, enjoying the noise as it whooshed in the air and then smashed on the ground.

There were dozens of bottles in pieces out there. It was his private little minefield. Most of the shards quickly gathered dust, but the recent ones shined, reflecting the sunlight like laser beams.

He squinted, staring at the desert. He had

only been outside a few minutes, but it was already time to go inside, where there was no relief from the heat but where at least his body didn't shrivel from the direct sun. His wizened skin had burned so often that he had small sores that oozed and never healed. He could feel them now, stinging as the sun burned them.

Even so, Bob lingered.

He didn't know what it was, but something caught his eye. He saw the tough little windswept creosote bushes and the yuccas that looked like dwarf palm trees. They were right where they should be. And the hills in the distance were the same. And the broken bottles glinted like they always did. Like diamonds.

Except—no, that wasn't true.

Something was out of place. He saw the sun shining, glinting, but not in the minefield where he always tossed the bottles. The reflections catching his eye were farther away, and off to the side, nowhere near any of the other shards he could see. But they shimmered in the hot sun, little diamonds winking at him from under one of the creosote bushes.

What were they?

Bob frowned. He didn't know why, but he found himself shuffling across the desert, wanting to know what it was he saw. The closer he got, the faster he walked, until he was almost running. He was out of shape and out of breath, but he jogged naked across the last twenty yards until he was right over the spot where the diamonds lay hidden. Then he stopped and stared down at his feet.

The glinting diamonds were really the shine of glitter sprinkled on skin, sparkling on a woman's body in the dirt.

It lay, face up, partially obscured by the overhanging bush. The body was as naked as he was, but utterly lifeless and ageless, a shrunken corpse whose cooked skin had collapsed in on itself, whose eyes were wide open but shrunk to tiny marbles, whose blonde hair was grayed with dust, whose mouth was open in a silent scream as desert beetles led a parade to eat her flesh from inside. It was almost unrecognizable as anything that had once been human and beautiful.

Bob sank to his knees.

She was staring at him. And her lips, which had no color at all, were curled into a smile. He tentatively reached a hand out to touch her skin, as if he was afraid she would suddenly awaken and grab him. But she didn't move. Her skin felt like sandpaper under his touch.

Then he saw her face twitch. It was like a nightmare. She couldn't be alive!

Bob stared in horror as a fat roach squeezed its way out of the corpse's nose and wiggled its antennae at him. He stumbled backward, then ran. He didn't head back to his trailer, just turned and sprinted clumsily for the road. His sandals fell away. The rocky floor of the desert scratched and cut his feet until he left blood trails with each footfall. He ran anyway, not slowing down or looking behind him, as if the girl's ghost were on his heels.

34

Serena Dial of the Las Vegas Metropolitan Police Department pushed her sunglasses to the tip of her nose and stared down at the body.

"Nice."

She said it to no one in particular. In fact, the scene wasn't nice at all. She hated desert corpses. They all looked about a hundred years old, and sometimes, if you got there after the birds and animals did, they were chewed up, with missing eyeballs, flesh eaten away, the kind of thing that flashed back in a nightmare. She mostly saw dead people with knives in their backs or gunshot wounds, which, when you got past the blood, were not really so hard to stomach. At least the body still looked like a body. Not like this.

Definitely a woman. That was easy enough to determine. The sun did terrible things to people who had the bad fortune to lie deceased in a desert, but it wasn't known to make cocks disappear. Breasts, on the other hand, flattened out into nothing. Except, she realized, this corpse still had a pretty good set. That was interesting. The body also seemed to glint in the sun, twinkling at her. That was interesting, too.

Serena got on her hands and knees, getting close to the body, staring at it from an inch or two away without touching it. She started at the girl's feet, moved up her legs, spent more time than she wanted to at her crotch, then her stomach, her breasts, and finally her face and lips, which looked ready to give her a macabre kiss.

Serena stood up, slid a digital tape recorder from her pocket, and dictated a few notes.

The wind tousled her hair, which was lush and black, shoulder length. She was as statuesque as a showgirl, which was what most strangers in Las Vegas mistook her for when they met her. She had taken to wearing her shield on the outside, which tended to cut down on the unwelcome advances from drunk convention rats. Serena was nearly six feet tall, lithe and well proportioned. She wore a sleeveless white tank top, tucked into snug, faded jeans. She was muscled and strong, from an intense workout routine. Her skin was tanned golden brown from days spent mostly in the sun.

Serena was in her midthirties. Her eyes, normally hidden behind the apricot lenses of her sunglasses, were emerald green. Her mouth was small, with pale lips and a soft curve forming her chin. She didn't look young, not girlish young, and she never had. She had looked the way she looked now, adult and beautiful, since she was a teenager. It was only recently that her age had begun to catch up to the image she had sported all her life. At idle moments, she wondered what she would look like as the years began to get ahead of her.

Probably the girl at her feet had wondered the same thing, but she wasn't going to find out. And it was just as well that this girl couldn't see herself now.

"Age," Serena said into her tape recorder. "Have to wait for the ME on that, but I'm thinking early twenties at most. Cause of death looks like blunt trauma to the head. There's matted blood in the hair toward the back of the skull, and without moving the body, it looks like the skull may be caved in back there. Hair originally black, dyed blonde."

Serena studied the desert floor where the body lay.

"She wasn't murdered here. Not enough blood on the ground. Whoever did it hauled the body and dumped her here. The body is nude, but no immediate sign of sexual assault, no bruising in the pelvic area, no broken fingernails, scratches, or other wounds. We'll run the rape kit. Time of death, no way to tell? I wonder if the ME will even be able to peg this one. At least a couple days, I guess. Rigor is long gone. We're just lucky the vultures didn't get her."

A thought occurred to her. She gingerly poked the dead girl's wrinkled breast with one finger. "Naturally," she said to herself, standing up again.

Serena continued taking notes. "Pierced ears, but no earrings in them. No watch. No rings. Fingernails and toenails are painted red. Evidence of heavy makeup on the face. Glitter on most of the skin."

She heard footsteps approaching and then a voice calling to her. *"Hola."*

"Watch where you walk, Cordy," Serena said without turning around. Not that it mattered. She had run searches in the desert before, and it rarely offered up any clues. Little wonder the gangsters of old Vegas liked to leave their targets to rot in the Mojave.

Cordy feigned offense. "And what am I? A rookie?"

Cordero Elias Angel was her partner of the last six months. Serena, who had earned a reputation with her lieutenant for being difficult to work with, went through partners quickly, but Cordy seemed to have staying power. He gave as good as he got, he did what he was told, and he hadn't once made a pass at her. Cordy preferred girls small, blonde, and young, and Serena was none of the three. He was also six inches shorter than Serena and six years younger. There was nothing romantic between them.

Looking like she did, Serena got plenty of offers, but when she lowered her guard and succumbed to a date, it usually ended early.

Her blunt style scared them away. She hadn't had sex in years. She told herself she didn't miss it.

Cordy, in contrast, had an active social life. In the short time they had been together, she had seen him with six different women, ranging from twenty to twenty-three years old. None of them lasted beyond the first calisthenics in bed. For at least two of them, it really was their first time in bed, or so Cordy claimed. Serena found it disgusting and told him so. Cordy just grinned, and she dropped it, rather than digging up old ghosts.

He was an attractive, if compact, package. He always dressed impeccably. Today, he wore a floral Tommy Bahama shirt and black silk pants. Cordy had jet black hair, greased straight back over his head. His skin had a dark cast, the color of virgin olive oil. His teeth looked noticeably white against it, and he had predatory brown eyes.

Serena jerked a thumb at the trailer. "So what's his story?"

"Ah, he's a pathetic old man. Not so old, but going downhill fast, you know? Spends each night drowning in a gin bottle. You see all the broken glass out here? He just tosses them out back when he's done."

Serena took note of the broad swath of glass shards behind the trailer. "Make sure the forensics team studies the glass pieces carefully. If our delivery man cut himself hauling the body in, maybe we'll get some blood."

"Uh-huh," Cordy said.

"We'll probably find Jerky Bob decomposing in the trailer in a few months," Serena said. "Did he call it in?"

Cordy shook his head. "He found the body and freaked. Started running naked down the road. A motorist spotted him from the highway and reported it. When the unis got to him, he was babbling about a corpse that was alive."

"Does he know the girl?"

Cordy shook his head. "Nah, he says he's never seen her before. Just saw the body when he came outside to take a piss. Surprise."

"How about timing? He have any idea when our little package may have been dropped off? Did he hear or see anything?"

"Man, he didn't hear nothing. *Nada*. Guy's been blacked out at least two days, maybe three. So it could have been anytime."

Serena sighed. "Great."

"So we don't got a lot to go on here, is what I'm thinking."

"I assume you scoped out the trailer for blood," she said.

"Uh-huh. His feet were bleeding from his run, but not enough to account for bashing in someone's head. And believe me, the place has not been cleaned up. Unless she was asphyxiated by the smell, the deceased was not inside. You should check out the jerky, though. He gave me a piece. Cajun turkey, I think it was. Good stuff, if you can stand the smell."

"If you have to pull off the road and take a dump in the desert on the way back to the city, you'll wish you hadn't tried it."

"I'm Mexican. Stomach of iron. Chiles, mama." Cordy thumped his chest.

Serena shook her head. "Salmonella, sweetie. It's not just for gringos."

"You forget. I wanted to see if he was hiding anything in his refrigerator, and I had no warrant. So now, one piece of jerky later, I know there is nothing in those shoe boxes but dried meat."

"Now you impress me, sweetie. You really do."

Serena took another look at the body,

wishing she could cover it up and give the girl a little dignity. Las Vegas had its share of bizarre crimes, and she was long past surprise at anything they found in the city. She had been involved in the strip search of a female suspect, only to discover, after baring her impressive breasts, that the girl was actually a she-male with oversized equipment. She had investigated the murder of a midget who had been put on a homemade rack by two thrill-seeking teenagers and stretched to death. She had arrested a man for walking downtown, naked, with two goats in tow. Weird, sick, stupid, she had been there, done that. Once in a great long while, though, she came across a case where her instincts told her she had stumbled into something deep, interesting, and dark. Which was exactly what her sixth sense was telling her now.

There was more, too. She felt a special pain when she worked on a case involving the murder of a young woman. It was too easy to remember her own teenage years in Phoenix and to realize that, if one turn or another had gone a different way, she could have been the body lying naked in the desert.

"What's your name, honey?" Serena murmured under her breath, staring at the girl's body.

"Looks like the cavalry is here," Cordy said. He pointed at the road, where a stream of police and medical vehicles had begun to arrive. "Tell me we're not going to stay out here and roast for five hours while they poke around the rocks."

Serena shook her head. "We'll get the scene sealed and transfer control to Neuss. An afternoon in the sun will do him good. We'll talk to the ME and see if he notices anything about the body that I missed. Then you and I are going to see if we can identify this girl."

"You want to tell me how you plan on identifying a body that no one's going to recognize?"

"Well, first you're going to have the department fax us local reports of missing persons, white, female, thirteen to thirty, in the last two weeks."

"Uh-huh. You want that bound or on CD-ROM?"

"I said two weeks, Cordy, not two years. I'll be surprised if we find her in there, anyway."

"Why?"

"I suspect she ran in circles where going missing isn't a big deal," Serena said.

"Uh-huh. So then what do we do?"

"Then we visit some strip clubs."

Cordy howled. "My kind of day, mama. You think the chick was a stripper? I hope she looked better than that. See that thing stripping off, and you'd be back home with the wife forever, you know?"

"Shut up, Cordy."

"Okay, so what am I missing? You find a stripper's union card or something? Why are you so sure she did the occasional lap dance?"

Serena shrugged. "She's got breast implants. That's why they didn't cave. Her pubic area is neatly shaved so that only a vertical strip of hair remains. There's remnants of sparkle on her breasts and thighs. She has a small tattoo of a heart on her left breast. Put it all together, and I say the girl's been twirling around a brass pole."

"Uh-huh. That only narrows it down to about four hundred joints. Not to mention all the on-call services."

"I said stripper, not hooker. Hookers don't bother with sparkle, sweetie. Or implants. Them's for show. We'll start with the big-name places and hope the girl was good enough at the bump and grind to break in there."

Cordy smiled. "You're the boss. If I have to spend my day talking to women who like to get naked in clubs, so be it."

35

Serena's eyes adjusted slowly to the darkness inside the club. The air was smoky and vaguely perfumed. Rock music blared from hidden speakers, with a thumping beat they could feel vibrating under the floor. The walls of the cramped foyer were covered with a dark wood paneling. A red upholstered door separated them from the interior of the club, and beside the door was a podium, with an erotic Chinese painting hung on the wall behind it. As they entered, a hulking man in a gray business suit slipped through the red door and confronted them with a smile. He had curly blonde hair and a bushy mustache.

He glanced at Cordy without interest, then his eyes lingered on Serena, drinking her in from head to toe.

"It's free for you, sweetheart. For Dudley Moore here, it's $24.95 cover."

The gorilla grinned at Cordy, and Serena thought she could see actual smoke coming out of her partner's ears.

"We're not customers," Serena said, flashing her shield. "We're from Metro. We're investigating a murder."

The smile vanished, replaced by cool indifference. "Whose?" the man asked, shrugging his broad shoulders.

"That's what we're trying to find out. It's a Jane Doe, found in the desert, back of her head bashed in. We think she may have worked one of the clubs."

Cordy slid a Polaroid from inside his jacket and presented it to Superman. "Recognize this girl?"

Serena watched the man's reaction, noticing his skin grow a shade paler and an involuntary grimace tighten his face.

"When was she in the business, 1940?"

"If you lie out in the desert for a few days, be sure to use sunblock," Serena said. "Do you recognize her?"

"No."

"Any of your girls gone missing in the last few days?"

The man laughed. It came out as a booming guffaw. "Are you kidding? Girls come and go every week, every day. This ain't exactly career work, you know?"

"We're just talking about the last few days," Serena said. She hated guys like this. Users. They gobbled up young flesh and then spit it back in the street when its value was gone.

"The answer is no."

"How about tattoos? You got a girl with a heart tattoo on her left breast?"

"Tattoos? We got dragons, kittens, boyfriends, barbed wire, sunflowers, and Dwight Yoakam. No hearts."

"You're sure?" Serena asked.

The man grinned. "I've seen them all."

"I'm sure you won't mind if we talk to the girls ourselves," Cordy said.

"You got a warrant?"

"We don't need a warrant to talk," Serena said. "On the other hand, if you want us to get a warrant, and we happen to find any drugs around here, well, that's going to take a bite out of business, isn't it?"

"Make it quick," the man replied, scowling. "And hey, some of the girls may look young, but they're all over eighteen, all right? I checked their IDs."

"Sure," Serena said. Her fake ID at sixteen had gotten her into clubs easily enough. Back in the bad days.

They pushed through the red door and entered the club. It looked and sounded identical to the seven others they had already visited today. The music, loud enough in the foyer, was deafening inside. A large, elevated runway, interrupted by shiny brass poles that reached to the ceiling, jutted out into the center of the club. Narrow schoolroom tables surrounded the runway, with squat stools squeezed side by side along the tables. Most of the action was on the runway, but there were also three low stages, with circular benches fitted around them, scattered across the club floor. Velvet-lined booths hugged the walls. The rest of the place was crammed with dinner tables and cocktail tables.

The club reeked of beer and pheromones.

A hazy cloud clung near the ceiling, where the smoke from the cigarettes gathered.

Serena counted about thirty men, ranging from horny college kids in T-shirts to old men in suits, with a mixture of freaks and drunks thrown in. Some of them got into it, hooting and hollering, trying to get as close to groping the girls as they could without getting bounced. Others sat in awe, their jaws hanging open, silly grins on their faces. Others sat and sipped their drinks and watched through slitted eyes. Those were the scary ones, who didn't show any emotion at all.

Serena felt the same claustrophobic sensation she had felt in all the other clubs. Involuntarily, she looked down, expecting to see her own body exposed, wondering what it would feel like to trade places with the girls up there. She was the only woman in the club, except for a couple of cocktail waitresses, who was wearing more than panties. Not surprisingly, she didn't attract much attention, except from a few men who didn't expect to see any women here at all who weren't naked. Those that looked at her gave her the same appraising glance they gave the girls onstage. Serena felt sick.

She studied the faces of the girls parading

down the runway, looking past the plastic smiles. You could see their age in their faces. The more makeup they wore, the more they were trying to cover up. In the smoky, dark environs of the club, it usually worked, because most of the men didn't bother looking at faces. Serena could tell, though. She could look in their eyes and see their secrets. This was a higher-paying joint, where the girls were younger, not yet ravaged by alcohol or drug abuse. A girl here could still fool herself that she would wind up rich, like another Jenna Jameson. But Serena had seen too many wasted faces over the years, perched atop taut bodies. Eventually their bodies sagged, too, and the downward spiral began.

She remembered arriving in town at sixteen, just her and a girlfriend, both of them escaping from their lives in Phoenix. Serena got a job at one of the casinos. Her girlfriend wound up here, at one of the clubs, doing lap dances. She tried to talk Serena into doing it, too. The money was better. It was tempting, but Serena had already seen enough of men that she couldn't imagine parading herself in front of them. Lucky for her. Her friend moved up to a nicer apartment, did some low-budget porn films, and eventually wound up with AIDS. She died a hideous death at age twenty-two.

The girl in the desert was dead. Her friend was dead. Sometimes Serena felt guilty that she had survived.

A cheer arose from one of the satellite stages. Serena and Cordy edged closer, watching a hole appear in the center of the small stage. Slowly, rising out of the well, they saw two black arms, sensually twisting to the music. The girl emerged inch by inch as the elevator platform rose from beneath the floor. Her long arms went on forever, and then Serena saw dark hair and a sculpted ebony face. This girl was perfect, barely eighteen and stunning. A newcomer—Serena could see it in her eyes. The girl was still aroused by the hypnotic spell she could cast and the throaty bellows of the men. She was enjoying herself, and the men knew it. There was nothing more exciting than a girl who was truly trying to turn them on and not playing a weary game. The men knew the difference, and this girl was it.

Someone shouted, "Lavender!"

The girl turned to the man who had called her name and gave him a thick-lipped smile and a wink. All the while, she kept dancing, as more of her body rose into view. She wore a spaghetti-strap teddy that was ruby red against her coal skin. Her breasts were ready to burst out of the lace. The flaps of the fabric left her taut stomach bare, and below, she wore a thong panty. Her legs, trim and smooth, stretched down to blood-red pumps with three-inch heels.

"Put your tongue back in your mouth," Serena told Cordy.

"It's hard, mama, it's hard," he whispered.

"Is that a weather report from down south?" Serena asked, grinning.

Cordy didn't reply. He was transfixed, watching Lavender pop the buttons one by one, letting her cleavage spill out.

"What gives, Cordy? I thought you liked your girls short and blonde."

"A good salsa is made up of many chiles," Cordy said.

"What is that, a Mexican proverb?"

"Nah, it's my new philosophy of life."

Serena watched as Lavender finally revealed her giant nipples, as hard as bullets. The girl cupped her full breasts in her hands as the crowd screamed.

"Come on, Don Juan, let's go backstage."

Serena dragged Cordy, craning his neck to keep an eye on Lavender, to the back of the club, where another upholstered door was labeled PERFORMERS ONLY. It was manned by a beefy black guard who wore a don't-fuck-with-me scowl. Serena explained that they needed to talk to the girls, and he scrutinized their shields before grudgingly standing aside.

Cordy smiled sweetly as he passed the guard. "Will the girls be self-conscious with a man down there?"

Serena laughed. The guard didn't.

They went down a flight of stairs, then entered the dressing room, which was a beehive of activity, filled with at least ten girls in different stages of nudity. Some were adjusting their breasts inside skimpy costumes, ready to go onstage. Others patiently sat before lighted mirrors and applied their makeup. Three girls who had completed their shifts were changing into their street clothes. They paid little attention to Cordy and Serena, although a couple of the girls gave Cordy an inviting smile. He smiled back.

Serena started with the girls who were getting ready to leave the club. One was already dressed; the second wore a black bra and jeans; the third, a natural redhead, was stark naked. She was reaching for a camisole on a hanger inside her locker.

"We'd like to ask you girls a few questions," Serena said.

The girls, who were chatting and laughing loudly together, clammed up. One of them shrugged indifferently. The redhead, seeing Cordy, twisted so her nude body was on display, right down to the trimmed auburn mound between her legs. She looked him right in the eyes and grinned, daring him to look down. Cordy resisted, although Serena knew it was killing him.

Serena explained why they were there and described the dead girl in general terms, mentioning the heart tattoo on her breast. When they heard about the murder, the girls' attitude changed. They were in a business that attracted more than a few sick freaks, and when one of their own got killed, they all immediately wondered who did it and whether they might be next on a killer's hit list.

"What about it?" Serena asked. "Do you know her?"

The girls glanced at each other.

"Girls come and go," the redhead said, idly stroking one of her breasts. "I mean, that description could fit a hundred girls who work in various clubs."

"How about the tattoo?" Cordy asked.

They all shook their heads.

It had been the same story all day. Girls come and go. Who notices if they're here one day and gone the next? And so many of them are young and half-blonde.

They quickly interviewed the other girls in the dressing area and got the same response from each one. They were about to leave and head for the next club on their list when Cordy pointed at the stage lift, which was now revolving slowly back to the floor, with Lavender on it, carefully balancing so she didn't tumble off. The black stripper stepped off onto the floor, and the lift returned upward to the circular stage.

She was naked except for a tiny G-string, fringed with cash stuffed inside. Her breasts jiggled as she crossed the tile floor, her high heels clicking. She stopped in front of a Coke machine and extracted a dollar from her waist. She bought herself a diet soda, popped it, and took a long swig. Then her eyes settled on Serena and Cordy.

"What do the two of you want?" Lavender demanded.

"They're police," the redhead called out helpfully. She was now dressed in the camisole and leather pants. "Looking for a missing girl."

"We're all missing," Lavender said.

Cordy made no pretense of keeping his eyes off this girl's body. He made eye contact, then slowly let his gaze drop down her long expanse of nude skin, pausing in all of the interesting places. Lavender had an amused smile on her face.

"Guys pay good money to see that," she said. "What makes you think cops get it for free?"

"If we go to dinner, that wouldn't be free," Cordy said. "What do you say?"

Serena rolled her eyes.

Lavender laughed. "Is your dick as big as your balls?"

"Only one way to find out," Cordy said.

Lavender glanced at Serena. "I take it you and he are not an item? I don't get into this three-way stuff."

"We're barely partners," Serena said, giving Cordy a sharp elbow to the side. "After today, maybe not at all."

"What's your name?" Lavender asked, looking at Cordy again. Serena knew the girl was interested. It was strange, watching Cordy's magnetism at work. She herself didn't feel it, but a lot of girls did.

"You can call me Cordy."

"I've got a few inches on you, Cordy. I wouldn't want to hurt you accidentally." Her lips twitched into a grin.

"You can't hurt anyone when you're tied up," Cordy teased her.

"Okay, that's enough, boys and girls," Serena said. "*No más,* Cordy, you hear me?"

"Friday night?" Cordy continued, smiling at Lavender.

Lavender shrugged, but it was an acquiescence. "Okay, slick. You got it. Pick me up here at eight o'clock. We'll have six hours until my next shift."

Serena sighed. "That's great. Real romantic. Meanwhile, we've got a dead girl, and we're trying to find out who she is."

"Girls come and go around here," Lavender said.

"I know. This one came and went. Five-foot-seven, black hair dyed blonde, somewhere between seventeen and twenty-five,

or that's what we're guessing. She's probably been missing at least two or three days."

"Could be anybody," Lavender said.

Cordy reached out and brushed his index
finger below Lavender's left nipple. "She had
a heart tattoo right about here."

Damn, the guy was good. Sometimes
Serena felt like a robot, watching all the sex
in this town and feeling no emotion about
any of it.

She knew what the other cops called her.
Barb. Not for Barbara—it was short for
Barbed Wire. The girl with the high fence and
the NO TRESPASSING sign. That was her own
fault. Even when she liked a man, she usually found a way to leave him bleeding on the
other side, instead of letting him in. Sometimes she envied Cordy that he could make
it look so easy.

"A heart?" Lavender said slowly.

Serena saw it in Lavender's eyes. For the
first time that day, she felt her pulse quicken.

"You knew her?" Serena asked.

Lavender bit her lower lip. "Maybe. There
was a girl at the last club where I worked,
had a tattoo like that, matched that description."

"What was her name?"

"Christi. Christi Katt. I mean, I figure it was a fake name, okay? Like I'm not really Lavender, and if I ever tell you my real name, I know you too well."

"What was the club?" Cordy asked.

"The Thrill Palace. On the Boulder Strip."

Serena knew it. "You know where this girl lived?"

"She had a dump of an apartment over near the airport. Oh, shit, what was the place called again? Vagabond, I think. Yeah, the Vagabond Apartments. Fits, huh? Most of the rentals there are weekly, I bet. Maybe daily."

"You remember much about her?"

"Not a lot. She wasn't a talker. Came in, did her thing. Most of the girls, we pal around, but she didn't do that."

"When did you last see her?" Serena asked.

"When I left the club," Lavender said. "About a month ago."

Cordy reluctantly slid the photo out of his coat pocket. "Could this be her?"

Lavender glanced at the photo and immediately shut her eyes, looking away. She opened them again and took another quick look. "Shit. That really sucks. No one deserves to look like that, I mean no one."

"Could that be her?"

Lavender squinted. "Could be. I don't know. Who can tell from that? Christi was really pretty, not like that thing. Hell, she was almost as sexy as I am. If that's her—well, shit."

She shook her head and handed the photo back upside down.

"Thanks, Lavender," Serena told her. "You've been a big help."

Cordy winked. *"Gracias.* See you Friday."

"Hey, you've already seen me, slick," Lavender said. "Friday I get to see you."

36

They got off I-15 at Tropicana Avenue and waited impatiently at the light at Las Vegas Boulevard. On their right was the fake Arthurian castle of the Excalibur hotel and, on their left, the fake Manhattan skyline of New York New York. Fountains sprayed from miniature fire boats surrounding a fake Statue of Liberty.

Some of the spray blew out in the street, and Serena felt dampness on her cheek. The cool water felt good. She glanced at the hordes of tourists milling outside in the stale early evening air, taking a break from losing their money inside. They looked hot, wiping their brows and tugging at their shirt collars. Even with the sun hidden behind the mountains, it was still ninety degrees.

The light changed. They headed past the MGM Grand and turned left at Koval Lane. Serena turned right again, and almost immediately, they exited the glitzy world of the Strip and found themselves in a seedy neighborhood, populated with two-bedroom houses with bars on the windows. The Vegas melting pot lived here, blacks, Mexicans, Indians, and immigrants from a dozen other countries who held down low-paying jobs in the service sectors of the casinos. It wasn't a high-crime area, not compared to the Naked City near the Stratosphere, where most of the city's murders took place. Old women still walked alone on the streets, pushing carts with groceries back to their homes. Children played in the yards, poking scorpions with sticks.

Half a mile down, they found the Vagabond Apartments, a two-level building with cracked white stucco, laid out like a motel. The ground-floor apartments opened onto the parking lot, and one flight up, the second-story units opened onto a narrow corridor with a rusty railing. All of the windows had thick curtains pulled shut, and the peeling navy doors had dead-bolt locks.

For a moment, staring at the building, Serena was a teenager again, back in the apartment in Phoenix. She felt a chill break through the stifling heat. Images popped like flashbulbs. Her mother's dead eyes, watching her. The tattoo of a lizard on the man's chest, wiggling its pink tongue at her. Afterward, brown water dripping from the shower head.

Serena took a labored breath and pushed the past away.

"I don't know," she said. "I pictured this girl for a higher-class kind of joint. You'd think she could have afforded better than this, working at the Thrill Palace." *Unless she was an alcoholic,* Serena thought. *Or an addict.*

"Maybe she was hiding out," Cordy said.

Serena shrugged. "Let's find the manager."

The nearest apartment on the ground floor had an open door that led into a small foyer filled with mailboxes. They passed a short, balding man of about fifty, wearing shorts and no shirt, flipping through his mail as he strolled out of the office. He didn't look up. Serena noticed him thumbing through a copy of *Penthouse* in the stack. They entered the apartment office, which was compact, with the mailboxes on one wall and vending machines for soda and snacks on the other.

At the rear of the office was a counter with a buzzer on it, and behind the counter was a closed door decorated with a nudie calendar. Several sections of the morning newspaper lay on the counter, one section open to the want ads, another to the comics. A paper plate with a few doughnut crumbs sat on top of the paper, gathering flies. Cordy pushed the call button, and they heard the muffled buzzer sounding behind the wall. No one came to greet them. Cordy pushed the button again, holding it down, until they heard footsteps inside.

The door flew open. A kid of about twenty, with earrings in both ears, long mousy hair, and sideburns, stared at them. He was tall and thin, with a narrow pimply face and protruding chin. Like the tenant they had passed, he was wearing shorts and no shirt.

"Yeah?"

He didn't sound happy to be interrupted. Serena could hear noises inside the apartment and figured the kid wasn't alone.

"We want an apartment, *muchacho*," Cordy said. "How about you show us the hot tub and the tennis courts?"

"What the fuck?" the kid said.

Serena smiled. "Are you the manager?"

"Yeah, so what?"

"We're cops. Does a woman named Christi Katt live here?"

"Yeah, so what?" he repeated.

"So you're going to lose the attitude and give us her key. Okay?"

Cordy grinned. "You can show us the pool later."

The kid shook his head. "Fucking cops, you guys are really something. Yeah, okay, apartment 204. She's been here about a year. Hot number, you get me? She's a lot nicer than the other trash we get around here."

He looked nervously over his shoulder, obviously wondering if his guest had heard him.

"When's the last time you saw her?" Serena asked.

"Don't know," the kid said. "A few days ago, I guess."

"But not in the last couple days."

"No, it's been a while, okay?"

Cordy wandered over to the wall of mailboxes and found the box labeled 204. "There's a lot of mail in here."

"Ain't that what I said? Maybe she's shacking up somewhere else."

"You see her around with anyone lately? Boyfriend, girlfriend, anybody like that?" Serena watched his eyes, trying to see a flicker of a lie.

"She kept to herself," the kid said.

"Nobody asking about her?" Serena asked.

"Just you."

"What kind of car does she drive?"

"It's an old beater. Red Chevy Cavalier."

Serena glanced at Cordy, who took a few steps out of the office. He came back a moment later and nodded. "It's in the lot."

"Have you noticed if the car has come and gone lately?" Serena asked.

"Who knows? I don't pay attention."

"Okay, let's have the key."

The kid hesitated. "Don't you need a warrant or something like that? Christi's going to be mad if I just let you in there."

Christi won't be mad at anyone anymore, Serena thought. She smiled at the young manager. "Just give me the key."

He shrugged and disappeared back inside his apartment. Serena heard a whiny female voice, and then the kid hissed, "Shut up." He reappeared a few seconds later with a key tied with a rubber band to a paint-stirring stick.

"You'll make sure I get this back, right?" The kid scowled at them, then retreated inside his apartment and slammed the door.

"Let's take a look at the car," Serena said.

They returned outside and wandered past the ground-floor apartments toward the end of the parking lot. The red Cavalier was parked on the street side of the lot. They walked over to it and peered inside, cupping their hands next to their eyes to block the glare. The car was locked and empty. Serena looked in the front and back seats for papers or trash, but if Christi Katt was the owner, she kept a clean car.

Serena noticed an Indian girl, about eight years old, walking toward the office with her hands folded behind her back. She wore a plain white dress with blue fringe on the collar. The dress fell to her calves. She wore sandals that clip-clopped on the pavement. Her straight black hair fell below her shoulders.

Serena beckoned her over.

"Hi," Serena said. "You know who owns this car?"

The girl's head bobbed. "Oh, yes. Very pretty lady. She lives upstairs."

Cordy smiled at the girl. "Have you seen the pretty lady around here lately?"

"I saw her on Sunday. She leaves for work. Since then, no."

It was Wednesday evening.

"Was she with anyone when you saw her?"

The girl thought about it, then shook her head.

"You didn't see her come back?"

"No," the girl said. "But I go outside at night to see stars, and her car is parked right there."

"What time was that?"

The girl shrugged her shoulders. "Late."

"Has the car been here ever since?" Serena asked.

The girl nodded. "Yes, parked right there."

"Thanks, sweetheart."

Serena and Cordy headed for the stairs, dodging crumpled fast food bags and candy wrappers littering the ground. They jogged to the second floor. Cordy rapped his knuckles sharply on the door to room 204, not expecting an answer. He didn't get one. They looked up and down the corridor to see if they had attracted any other attention, but the place was deserted.

"Gloves," Serena said.

Cordy nodded. He extracted a slim box from his suit pocket, and they both slipped on fresh pairs of white latex gloves, which clung to their hands like a second skin.

"Some people die from these things," Cordy said.

"Gloves?"

"Latex allergy. Like peanuts. People go into convulsions."

"Maybe it's the salt," Serena said.

"On the gloves?"

"No, the peanuts. Open the damn door, Cordy."

Cordy inserted the master key in the lower lock. Delicately, using two fingertips, he turned the door handle. The latch clicked, and he was able to push the door open. A crack of light streamed in, but the rest of the apartment was dark. Cordy took two steps inside, found the light switch, and carefully flipped it up with the point of the key.

In the light, he took a quick survey of the apartment and said, "Bull's-eye, mama."

Serena followed him in. Her eyes fell immediately on a dried reddish-brown stain, about two feet in diameter, in the middle of the carpet. The air in the apartment was stale, but the mineral smell of blood lingered.

"I'll call for a forensics team," Cordy said, sliding his cell phone out of his pocket.

Serena nodded. "And get some uniforms to start knocking on doors. We need to know when this girl was last seen, whether anyone was with her, who she hung out with, that sort of thing. Once we're done here, we can check out the Thrill Palace. Oh, and have someone run Christi Katt through the system. See what comes up."

"Uh-huh," Cordy said.

While Cordy connected with the station, Serena wandered around the apartment. It was a small unit, with a living area in which the murder had occurred, a matchbox kitchen, and a bedroom visible through a doorway on the rear wall. Christi's furnishings were sparse and cheap, including what looked like a garage-sale sofa and loveseat, discount-store shelving for a small television and boom box, and a few mismatched tables and chairs. The carpet was worn and gray.

Serena clicked on her recorder. "The

apartment looks sterile—nothing personal. No photographs. No posters on the wall. No knickknacks or collectibles that might suggest who this girl was or what was in her head. There's no history here."

Serena entered the kitchen and began gingerly exploring.

"No magnets on the refrigerator. Virtually no food in the fridge and nothing more than a few cereal boxes, dried pasta, and canned soup in the cabinets. We're not talking about Julia Child here. It looks like she just moved in, but the manager said she's been here about a year."

She glanced in the sink and found a heavy glass vase there, washed and left on its side. Serena retreated to the living room and began examining the shelves propped against the wall not far from the bloodstain.

"Find something?" Cordy asked.

"Maybe. There's a vase in the sink. I'm betting it's the murder weapon. Look here, on the shelf. There's a lighter ring in the dust. It's the right size and shape to match the bottom of the vase. Christi and the killer are standing here, okay? She turns her back, the killer grabs the vase and wham, splits her skull open."

"Uh-huh," Cordy said. "No sign of forced entry or struggle, either. I am guessing that, one, she knew her killer, and, two, the murder was an unplanned spontaneous act of passion. Anger. Jealousy. I would not rule out jealousy with this girl."

"And you base this on what?"

Cordy put a finger on the side of his nose. "It just smells right."

Serena laughed. "Sure. Well, smell your way into the bedroom. Let's see if this girl left any clues behind."

The bedroom was a twelve-by-twelve box, with a closet and bathroom on the right wall. Christi had a full-sized bed, a nightstand, and a small dresser. As in the rest of the apartment, the walls were bare.

"No blanket on the bed," Serena said.

"Maybe she was hot."

"Or maybe the killer used it to transport the body."

Serena went into the bathroom, which included a toilet, a pedestal sink, and a shower with a pink plastic curtain. She checked for traces of blood in the sink and shower and found nothing visible. The forensics team would check it with luminol. In the medicine cabinet, she found a sparse array of toiletries. To her surprise, she found no evidence of any kind of birth control. Either Christi's men brought the condoms or her sex life was about as exciting as Serena's.

She returned to the bedroom, where Cordy was examining the top drawer of Christi's nightstand. "Anything?"

Cordy shook his head. "Not much. Matchbooks from two other strip clubs. Those might be prior employers, so we can check them out. Otherwise, no letters, no postcards, no love notes, no bills, no receipts, no credit card statements. This girl was one private *señorita.*"

"My dresser drawers are a mess," Serena said. "Ten years' worth of shit. You could write my biography by going through it."

"Not Christi Katt. Or whoever she was."

"Well, keep looking. Any condoms in there, by the way?"

"Why, you running low?"

Serena sighed. "How are you feeling, Cordy? You're looking pale. It could be a latex allergy. Now tell me before you go into convulsions."

"No condoms," Cordy said, chuckling.

Serena explored the girl's closet, which didn't take long. There were a few pairs of high heels on the floor, several blouses, skirts, and dresses on hangers, and two small stacks of T-shirts and jeans on a wire shelf. She rifled through the pockets of the jeans and found only a small quantity of loose change and a few sticks of gum.

She emerged, shaking her head. "This girl is quite a little mystery. How about a wallet or keys? Find anything like that?"

"*Nada*," Cordy said.

"That's interesting. Where are they?"

"Maybe the killer took them."

Serena reflected. "Maybe so. Let's say Christi's at home, keys and wallet in her pockets. The killer comes to the door. For some reason, she lets him in. Either she knows him or she doesn't feel threatened. Big mistake. They talk, maybe argue, she turns her back, and it's lights out. The killer, a fastidious type, cleans the vase, wipes off prints—unless we're really lucky—and wraps the body in a blanket from the bed. No tracking blood outside that way. He waits until it's dark and deserted outside, hauls the body to his car, drives off, and dumps her body in the desert."

"Uh-huh," Cordy said. "Except the body was naked. I could see the guy taking the wallet and keys. But why leave her in the buff? Who knows, maybe a little horizontal tango with the corpse? This could be one sick dude."

"No shortage of those," Serena said. "Forensics can tell us whether there was sexual activity. But stripping the body down does make it seem like there's a sex angle. Unless she had a boyfriend with her and was already naked."

"But no condoms, right?"

"Right. So we've got virtually no trace of this girl's life, and yet she had someone angry enough to kill her. Nice. I hope she made some friends at the Thrill Palace. Or at one of those other clubs."

"Don't take bets on that, mama," Cordy said.

"I'm not. Look, check out the dresser, and make sure we haven't missed anything. I want to eyeball the living room again before all the guys with big feet get here."

She left Cordy in the bedroom. Slowly, she traversed the apartment for a second time, looking at every surface, studying the floor and the walls. In the kitchen, she checked for the garbage under the sink and found coffee grounds, orange peels, and an outdated *TV Guide.*

Back in the living room, she checked out a handful of compact discs near the boom box, opening each case carefully, but found nothing else inside. She found it mildly interesting that Christi liked jazz. Serena, too, had wallowed in jazz during her low periods as a teenager in the first few years in Vegas, before she grew up and went country. Jazz was for trouble. Country was for living.

She heard Cordy whistle, long and loud.

"What?" she called.

Cordy was silent.

Curious, Serena returned to the bedroom. She found Cordy sitting cross-legged on the floor. The full-sized mattress had been shoved half off the bed. Next to Cordy was a small stack of newspapers. Cordy had one of the sections unfolded, and he was reading it, transfixed.

"Her secret stash?" Serena asked.

Cordy nodded.

"You should have waited for the search team before touching this stuff," Serena told him. Then she gave in to her own curiosity. "What's in them?"

Cordy put down the paper. "So how long you figure that body's been lying in the desert?"

Serena shrugged. "A few days. Why?"

"Well, in that case, we got a problem, mama."

37

Stride heard Andrea slip out of bed at six o'clock on Thursday morning to get ready for work. He opened his eyes without moving in bed and saw her, in the darkness of their bedroom, as she slid her white nightgown over her head and peeled down her panties. Her naked body had become softer and fleshier in three years but was still attractive.

"Hi," he said softly.

Andrea didn't look at him. "Hi yourself."

"What was your name again?"

She shook her head. "Not funny, Jon."

"I know. I'm sorry." Last night, he and Maggie had interrogated a suspect in a gang-related Asian drug ring until past one in the morning. There had been a string of late nights for several months.

"A phone call would sure be nice once in a while," Andrea said. "This is three nights in a row, and I haven't known when I'll see you. You're not there for me. You're never there."

"This case—" Stride began.

"I don't care about the case," she said. "If it's not this one, it would be another one."

Stride nodded and didn't reply. She was right. And it was getting worse. He realized he was taking on parts of the investigations that should really be delegated down the line. Even K-2 had noticed it and asked him bluntly if he was looking for excuses to avoid going home. He said no, but deep down, he wasn't sure.

"How's Denise?" he asked. "I feel like I haven't seen you since then."

"That's because you haven't. You haven't asked me anything about it. Do you care? You don't know anything about me any-more."

Andrea waited, with her hands on her hips. When he didn't say anything more, she turned and stalked into the bathroom, shutting the door with a sharp click. He heard the shower running.

The problems had begun a year ago. They had spent two years in relative peace, avoiding conflicts by not talking about them, but recently the troubles between them had come into the open. It started with the issue of kids, which Andrea wanted desperately and Stride didn't. He was too old by now. He would be over sixty by the time the kids left home.

Andrea persisted. Eighteen months after their marriage, with his reluctant acceptance, she went off the pill. They made love at every time of the day, to the point where there was no longer anything romantic about it. For all the trying, nothing happened. He tried to look disappointed that they couldn't conceive, but he was afraid that his real relief showed in his face. He knew what Andrea believed, that if she had had a baby with her first husband, then he never would have left her, and her life would still be perfect. She was afraid that, if she failed again, she would end up losing Stride, too—so she had to get pregnant.

But it was not to be.

He told her over and over that it didn't matter to him, but misery gradually took over her face, and in the year since then, it had never really left. They were well on the road to becoming strangers.

He heard the shower shut off.

The door opened, and Andrea stood naked in the doorway, watching him. He could see beads of water on her bare skin, dripping on the carpet. She was biting her lower lip, and he could make out her face well enough in the shadows to see she had been crying. They stared at each other for a long while, silently.

It was as if she had read his thoughts, and they scared her.

"We need to talk," she said.

He heard it in her tone. He knew it was coming. Divorce. The only question was which one of them would say the word first.

"I'm sorry," she said in a hushed voice.

"I'm the one who should be sorry," Stride told her.

He spread his arms wide, and she came to him. He folded up her wet body in his grasp. He saw anxiety in her bloodshot blue eyes. He put his hands up to her face, cupping her cheeks, and they both smiled weakly, trying to make the pain go away. He was conscious of her naked body on top of his, and he responded automatically. He shifted, wanting to enter her, but she let go and rolled off him onto her back, tugging gently on his shoulder. He followed her, sliding on top. His hands slid behind her neck. He went to kiss her, but she turned her face away. He felt her legs spreading for him, her knees bending and coming up. She didn't move; she just held onto him as he slid into her. The sex was quick and unsatisfying. Eventually, he eased down on top of her, and they lay like that for several minutes. When he felt gentle pressure from her hands, he knew to roll off her. She kissed him, a brush of her lips, then got out of bed quickly before he could touch her.

He heard her clean herself up in the bathroom and watched her as she hurried to put clothes on. She didn't say a word. When she was dressed, she hesitated in the doorway. She looked at him with an empty expression on her face, then turned and left, leaving him alone.

He was in the midst of uneasy dreams when the phone rang, startling him awake. He noticed the clock and groaned as he fumbled for the receiver. It was nine-thirty, an hour past his morning meeting.

"I'm late," he growled into the phone. "Sue me."

Stride expected a sarcastic barb from Maggie. Instead, after a pause, he heard a low, teasing laugh that was new to him.

"Is that Lieutenant Stride? You sound like you just woke up."

He lay back in bed and closed his eyes. "I did just wake up. And I won't admit to being Stride until I make a pot of coffee. So how about we call this a wrong number?"

"That's too bad. Someone named Maggie told me you give great phone sex."

Stride laughed, confused now, but also intrigued. "Not that Maggie would know. Who the hell is this?"

"My name is Serena Dial. I'm with the Las Vegas Metro Police. Unfortunately, I have news about an old case that you're not going to like, Lieutenant."

Las Vegas. Stride was immediately awake. It didn't matter that three years had passed—he knew why Serena was calling. Rachel. He heard the girl's name in his head and saw her body again in that amazing photograph.

The silence stretched out on the phone. Finally, Stride said, "I'm guessing you have her in custody."

"No. In the morgue."

"Rachel's dead?"

He didn't understand. In his idle fantasies, when someone from Las Vegas called him, Rachel was still alive. Sometimes he imagined Rachel herself would call.

"Dead. Murdered. Dumped in the desert. I know this causes problems for you."

Stride wondered if he was dreaming. "When?"

"Last few days, as near as we can tell," Serena told him.

She really was alive, Stride thought. *Until now.* "Do you know what happened? Who killed her?"

"Not yet," Serena said. "But if you can pick me up at the airport this evening, maybe we can work it together."

"You're coming here?"

"That's where the trail leads, Lieutenant. To Duluth."

38

Maggie readily confessed to everyone who drove with her that her body wasn't made for driving a truck. She sat on a phone book to make sure she could see over the steering wheel, and the accelerator and brake pedals had blocks to allow her feet to reach them. Before she married Eric Sorenson two years ago, she owned a miniature Geo Metro. But Eric, an ex-Olympic swimmer, didn't fit in her small car, and so their first purchase together was a much larger vehicle, in which Eric could ride without hugging his knees on his chest.

Stride didn't like driving with Maggie. She

wasn't the greatest driver to begin with, and the jury-rigged modifications to make her body SUV-compatible didn't help. He also suspected she drove more recklessly with him, purely out of spite. He tried not to jam his foot into an imaginary brake or to wince audibly at the many close calls.

It was early evening on Thursday. Serena Dial's plane from Las Vegas, via Minneapolis, was expected in half an hour. As they climbed farther from the lakeshore, heading up Miller Hill toward the Duluth airport, the air roaring between the open windows got warmer.

Maggie shook her head. The light ahead of them turned red, and she honked her horn as she sped through the intersection, not slowing down.

"She was alive the whole damn time," Maggie said. "Archie Gale's going to love this."

Stride nodded wearily. "Dan won't be happy to learn that he prosecuted a man for murdering a girl who wasn't dead. I don't think it's going to give his campaign a boost."

"Have you told him yet?" Maggie asked.

"Not yet. I asked K-2 if I could hold off until tomorrow. The detective from Vegas agreed to keep it under wraps until we could tell Emily."

Maggie frowned. "I hope Emily doesn't fall to pieces. Imagine killing your husband for killing your daughter and then finding out he was innocent."

Stride shrugged. "Innocent of murder, maybe. I still think Graeme was sleeping with Rachel."

"The question is, what the hell really happened to her?"

"She had to have help disappearing," Stride said. "No way she left town on her own. We would have picked up some trace of her. Maybe she got someone to drive her to Minneapolis. She disguised herself and hopped a bus from there. The friend drove back to Duluth and kept quiet."

"And the evidence we found at the barn? The bracelet, the blood, the footprints?"

"I know, that's the problem. We know Rachel was at the barn that Friday night." Stride rubbed his lower lip and stared out the window at the fast food restaurants and liquor stores passing by. "Okay, what about this? Rachel gets home that night. Graeme wants a rendezvous, since Emily's out of town. He and Rachel drive to the barn, climb in the back of the van, and start steaming up the windows."

Maggie frowned. "Why go to the barn? No one's home, why not just do it in the bedroom?"

"Who knows? Maybe the barn was their place. Maybe Graeme didn't tell her what he had in mind. One way or another, he gets her out there. But something goes wrong. Maybe Rachel says no this time, and that's not what Graeme wants to hear. Or maybe they're playing a kinky game with the knife that starts to go too far. Rachel manages to get out of the van, and he chases her. They struggle, she loses her bracelet, her shirt is torn. He wrestles her back to the van."

"And then what?" Maggie asked. "Remember, he didn't kill her."

"I know. Graeme suddenly comes to his senses. He's never gone this far before, and it scares him, like a cold shower. Or maybe it's just like what happened with Sally. He hears another car coming and hightails it out of there. He pretends it was all a mistake, drives Rachel home, and tells her to forget the whole thing."

Maggie jammed on the brakes as a car turned in front of them. She squealed into the left lane and roared around the other car, shooting a dirty look through the window.

"But when they get home, Rachel is scared shitless," Maggie speculated.

"Me, too," Stride said.

"Big baby. You taught me to drive like this, you know. So what happens next? Rachel is scared. She's fed up."

"Right. She calls a friend and says, 'Get me out of here.' And she's gone."

"Okay," Maggie acknowledged. "Then why not take her own car? Why not pack some clothes to take with her?"

Stride bit his lip, thinking. "Panic, maybe. She doesn't want to be found, and the car is easy to trace. She doesn't want to stick around another minute, even to pack. Maybe she thinks Graeme is going to try again, so she doesn't even go in the house with him."

Maggie turned off the main road and onto the lonelier highway leading to the airport. She immediately accelerated to seventy-five miles an hour, and the dashboard began to vibrate. "If we're right, that means someone knew that Rachel was alive. And whoever it was didn't come forward, even with an innocent man on trial for murder."

Stride nodded. "If Rachel told him what

happened at the barn, maybe he thought Graeme was getting what he deserved."

"And why didn't Graeme explain what happened?"

"Graeme? Tell the truth?" Stride laughed. "Forget it. If he admitted having sex with the girl, he was toast. I'm sure Gale told him that. No one would believe his story. He was better off saying none of it happened."

"Okay, take your theory one more step. Who's the mysterious friend?"

"I don't know," Stride said. "It never seemed to me that Rachel had any friends. At least no one she would really trust."

"Except Kevin."

Stride nodded. "Yeah. Except Kevin. But can you picture him staying quiet? He doesn't seem like a smooth enough liar to have pulled it off on the witness stand."

"Well, how about Sally? We know she was hiding something. Hell, we know she went to Rachel's house that night. And I don't imagine she would have been unhappy to see Rachel go away forever, where she couldn't bother Kevin anymore."

Stride put the pieces together in his head. "That's an interesting theory."

"You think we should talk to her?"

"Definitely," Stride said. "Rachel won't be coming back to seduce Kevin, and Stoner's out of the picture. Maybe she'll tell the truth this time."

Maggie turned left onto the entrance road into the Duluth airport and continued along the curving road that led up to the terminal building. The terminal was barely a football field in length, built in the shape of a triangle and dominated by a steep chocolate brown roof. Maggie pulled up to the far end of the terminal and parked, leaving her police placard on the dashboard. They proceeded through the giant revolving doors into the lower level of the terminal, which was almost empty, and took the escalator up to the second level. Country music played softly on the speakers overhead. Stride recognized Vince Gill's gentle croon.

They still had a long wait before the plane arrived. He dropped a quarter in a pinball machine, a two-level model decorated with a huge-busted girl in a micro-mini pointing a gun at his face and squealing, "Hit me." He had been pretty good at pinball in his high school days, but unlike riding a bicycle, it didn't come right back to him. He lost the first ball straight down the middle. The second danced around at the top, winning him a few thousand points, before slipping around the graveyard corridor on the left. By the third ball, he had some of his rhythm back, swiveling his hips as he banged the flippers with the heels of his hands. Maggie went and got a Coke from a vending machine and drank it as she watched him play.

"Does this cop from Vegas think someone from Duluth killed her?"

Stride shrugged without taking his eyes off the machine. "She didn't say. She just said the trail leads here."

"Serena Dial," Maggie said. "She sounded sharp on the phone. I bet she's a looker."

"Why's that?"

"She's from Vegas. All the girls in Vegas are gorgeous."

"I've never been there," Stride said.

"You need to get out more, boss."

"Well, my idea of a vacation is being alone in the woods, not surrounded by thousands of people in Coney Island." He got distracted and almost lost the last ball, but rescued it with a nifty flip at the last second.

"Alone?" Maggie asked.

"You know what I mean."

The building quivered as loud thunder

rumbled around them, a jet engine bellowing as a plane landed on the runway outside. Stride noticed a ticket agent, chewing gum, emerge from the escalator and head toward Gate 1. He took his eyes from the machine long enough to let the silver ball slip past the flipper, ending the game.

He and Maggie headed for the gate area.

"How will we recognize her?" Maggie asked.

"We'll wing it."

Recognizing Serena wasn't a problem. All of the passengers on the jet were typical Minnesotans, dressed in quiet clothes, blending into their surroundings, not attracting attention. Except for Serena Dial. She stuck out from the other passengers as loudly as a piece of crystal amid a row of Burger King plastic cups. She was dressed in baby blue leather pants that clung to her long legs like a second skin. A silver chain belt looped around her waist, with the ties dangling between her legs. She wore an undersized white T-shirt that didn't reach far enough to cover the last inch of skin on her flat stomach. Her black leather raincoat draped almost to her ankles. She had glossy black hair, loose and luscious.

"Wow," Maggie said.

Stride couldn't remember when he had seen a more attractive woman in his life. It occurred to him that, had Rachel grown up, she might have looked just like her.

Serena stopped at the end of the gate area and studied the people from behind her honey-colored sunglasses. She picked out Stride and Maggie immediately, and with a hint of a smile, she glided over to them. Everyone nearby followed her every move, but she didn't seem to notice.

"You Stride?" she asked. With her heels on, she was as tall as Stride, and she looked right at him.

"That's right." He found himself holding eye contact with her. Flirting. "This is my partner, Maggie Bei, who spreads lies about me on the phone."

"It's Sorenson," Maggie said. "He forgets I'm married." She took note of the way Stride and Serena were looking at each other and smirked. "Apparently, he forgets that he is, too."

Stride shot Maggie an evil glance, and she quickly stuck out her tongue at him.

"I love your uniform," Maggie added. "Do all the chick cops in Vegas get to wear that?"

Serena stripped off her sunglasses and studied Maggie from head to toe. Her smile curled into something more wicked. "Only the chick cops with tits, sweetie."

Maggie laughed out loud. She turned to Stride. "I like her."

Stride took another glance at Serena's body and didn't try to hide his interest. He felt something electric when she looked back. "You're in Minnesota now," Stride told Serena. "There's a dress code."

"You mean boring?"

"Exactly."

"Well, you guys don't seem so boring," Serena said.

Maggie laughed. "Wait until you get to know us."

They headed out of the gate area. Heads continued to rotate in Serena's direction as she passed by. Maggie and Stride lingered a few steps behind, and Maggie, laughing, leaned closer and whispered, "Do you two want to be alone?"

"Oh, shut up," Stride retorted.

On the lower level, they retrieved a hard-sided blue Samsonite suitcase that matched Serena's leather pants. Stride lifted the case off the carousel and gasped under the weight.

"Holy shit, did you bring the body with you?"

Serena laughed. "Oh, sorry, would that not be correct procedure here?"

They returned through the revolving doors. The air was still warm, but a breeze rolled in across the hills. Serena put on her sunglasses again and took a deep breath. "God, that's great. Fresh air. Feels like winter."

"Well, it's a little cooler in winter," Stride said.

"Like a hundred degrees cooler," Maggie said.

Serena nodded. "Yeah, I looked up Minnesota on the Web, and it pretty much sounded like the icebox of the nation. But this is nice. It's a buck twenty back home. Hot. Preheat your oven sometime, then stick your face inside. That's Vegas."

"I was married in Reno," Maggie told her.

"Yeah? I like Reno. I love the mountains. I keep telling myself someday I'll get the hell out of the desert."

"You married?" Maggie asked her.

Serena shook her head. "No."

They reached Maggie's SUV. Serena clambered into the backseat and leaned casually over the front seat to talk with Stride as they got inside. Stride felt her elbow grazing his neck and could smell a hint of perfume. Her breath was sweet. He was uncomfortably aware of everything about her.

"You're absolutely sure the body you found in the desert is Rachel Deese?" Maggie asked her.

Serena nodded. "I'm sure. Prints matched what you put in the system. Plus, a witness identified her photo from a news clipping. Sorry about that. I know it puts you guys in an awkward position."

"We're used to that," Maggie said, chuckling.

"Does anyone else out here know about this yet?" Serena asked.

Stride shook his head. "Just us and the chief. I didn't want it leaking out. I thought we could break the news to her mother first. It'll hit the papers and television as soon as we start talking to people."

"Yeah, I imagine this will be big news around here. I read the newspaper report. Bizarre case. If I were you, I would have thought she was dead, too."

"Thanks," Stride said.

"Anyway, after we tell the mother, I guess we should open up the case files and start investigating the girl's friends and anyone else who knew her."

Stride twisted around in his seat. Their faces were only a couple of inches apart. "How's that going to help solve a murder in Vegas?"

Serena took off her sunglasses again, and Stride looked into her jade-green eyes. Originally, when he saw her walk off the plane, he thought she was younger than she was, but close up, he could see the maturity in her face. Her smile lines were deep. She must have been in her midthirties, which to Stride was still young, but her face was etched with an older, wiser sensibility. Her smile came often and easily, and her eyes joked with him, but there was also a distance, a lack of trust, that hovered between them like a thin film. He wondered if it was because she sensed the same sexual chemistry between them that he did.

He realized she hadn't answered his question.

"Well, Serena?" Maggie asked, giving them both a sideways glance.

"I take it you guys are familiar with the Range Bank," Serena said.

"Sure," Stride said. "I bank there, along with half the city. What difference does that make?"

Serena leaned even closer. "CSI found part of an ATM receipt from the Range Bank in Rachel's apartment. So either she was back here recently or someone from home paid her a visit."

39

Stride picked up Serena at the motel on Friday morning just after nine o'clock. He knocked on her door, and when she answered, her black hair was damp from a recent shower, and her skin glowed. She had toned down her wardrobe, wearing a faded pair of blue jeans, a snug navy T-shirt, and cowboy boots. She flashed a welcoming smile.

"Hey, Stride," she said. "Come on in. I'm almost ready."

Her shower had left the tiny room humid and fragrant. The mirror beside the television was steamed over. He saw her suitcase

open on the bureau, her clothes folded inside. A queen-sized bed was squeezed between the walls.

"Sorry about the room," he said. "Summer's the busy season here."

Serena shrugged. "That's all right."

She sat on the edge of the bed and began
to put on tiny silver earrings. Her fingertips
seemed to caress her earlobes. Stride found
he couldn't take his eyes off her. Serena
looked up and noticed and, after a long moment, glanced nervously away.

"I called Rachel's mother on the cell
phone on the way over," he said, feeling awkward. "I finally got through to her. We can
stop there first."

"Did you break the news?"

Stride shook his head. "No, I just said I
wanted to talk to her. She probably suspects."

Serena stood up. They were close enough
to kiss, and Stride felt a wild desire to do just
that.

"We better go," he said.

Outside, they climbed into Stride's truck.
The seats were coming apart, and he had
covered the dashboard with Post-it notes related to various investigations. A day-old

mug of coffee was lodged in the cup holder, and part of the Duluth newspaper was strewn on the floor.

Serena saw his embarrassment and smiled. "Don't worry. I like a truck with that lived-in look. How old's the coffee?"

"Old."

"You guys got a Starbucks near here?"

"Sure. But I usually go to McDonald's. It's hot and cheap. Want to drive through?"

"Okay," she said. "But I may hit you up for some real coffee later."

They got two steaming cups of coffee, and Stride threw out the old one. He also ordered some hash browns and munched them as they drove. Serena dangled her arm outside the truck. The breeze whipped in and mussed her newly brushed hair. She sipped her coffee. Stride stole glances at her, and once or twice, she looked back his way. They didn't say much.

A few islands of fog lingered on the road. He switched on his headlights as he drove in and out of the patches of mist. At the crest of the hill, overlooking the rest of the city, he saw Serena lean forward, staring down at the hints of lake visible through the haze.

"This is amazing," she murmured. "When

you live in the desert for a long time, you forget about water and trees."

"I've never been to the desert," Stride said.

"Never? You should go. It's beautiful in its own way."

"Are you from Las Vegas originally?" Stride asked.

"No, Phoenix." He watched her green eyes grow distant, and he guessed that he had stumbled onto sensitive ground. "I moved to Vegas with a girlfriend when I was sixteen," she added.

"Young," he said, wondering what she had been running away from. Serena didn't explain.

Stride followed the curving road down to the freeway and headed south, which was the fastest route toward the neighborhood in which Emily and Dayton Tenby lived. They had gotten married while Emily was still in prison, and she had been paroled six months ago.

"I'm freezing," Serena said, rubbing her arms.

"I've got a sweater in the trunk. You want to borrow it?"

Serena nodded. She wrinkled her nose. "I smell cigarettes. Do you smoke?"

"I used to," Stride admitted. "I finally quit about a year ago. The smell lingers in here."

"Was it tough to quit?"

Stride nodded. "But I saw another guy on the force die of cancer last year. He was only about ten years older. That scared me."

"Good for you," Serena said.

Stride found Dayton and Emily's house without difficulty. It was only two blocks from the church that he and Maggie had visited in the snow more than three years earlier. He parked on the street and retrieved a rust-colored wool pullover sweater from his trunk. Serena shrugged it over her shoulders as they walked up the driveway. She pushed the sleeves up to bare her forearms.

"You're a lifesaver," she told him and squeezed his arm.

Emily answered the bell at once. He expected that prison would have aged her, but if anything, she looked younger than she had during the dark days of the trial. Her makeup was neat, her lipstick smoothed and red. Her blue eyes, once sullen and dead, were bright again, and her dark hair was cut in a cute bob. She wore a pair of brown slacks and a loose-fitting white cotton blouse.

"Hello, Lieutenant," she said. "It's been a long time."

"Yes, it has. You're looking well, Mrs. Tenby."

"Please, call me Emily," she said pleasantly.

"Of course. And this is Serena Dial. She's with the police in Las Vegas, Nevada."

Emily's eyebrows rose. "Las Vegas?"

Serena nodded. Emily's lips pursed in concern. She pulled the door open farther, inviting them in.

"Dayton is in the living room. I'm sorry you weren't able to reach us last night. We got your message, but we got home very late. Our flight into the Cities was delayed by two hours, and then we still had to drive north."

"Were you on vacation?" Serena asked.

"Partly, and partly work for Dayton. There was a national church convention in San Antonio, down by the River Walk. We added on a few extra days to make a week out of it."

She guided them into the living room. Dayton Tenby was seated on the sofa, and he immediately got up and extended his hand to both of them. Dayton's hair was now completely gray, although there was little of it left, except around the crown of his narrow skull. He had put on a few pounds, enough to make him look less gaunt than he had when Stride first met him. He wore gray dress pants, a starched white shirt, and a black acrylic vest.

Emily and Dayton sat down next to each other on a love seat and held hands. Stride and Serena sat opposite them on the sofa. Stride could see that marriage had agreed with both of them. Despite more than ten years' difference in age between them, they seemed to be happy.

"I want you to know, Lieutenant, that I still don't regret what I did," Emily said. "I don't mind paying my debt to society, but if I had it to do over again, I would do the same thing."

Stride hesitated. "I understand."

Dayton looked at them. "We don't expect that this is a social call. You must have some news for us."

"Yes, we do," Stride said. "I want you to understand that this could be very upsetting."

"You found her," Emily said.

"Yes, we did. But not in the circumstances you might expect. Earlier this week, Ms. Dial was called to a location in the desert just outside of Las Vegas. A young girl's body was found there. I'm afraid it was Rachel." He paused and went on. "She had only been dead for a short time. Just a few days. It appears that Rachel was actually alive these past three years."

"Alive?" Emily whispered, her eyes widening. "All this time?"

He saw Emily squeeze Dayton's hand tightly. She closed her eyes and leaned her head slowly against his shoulder.

"How did she die?" Dayton asked.

"I'm sorry," Serena told them softly. "She was murdered."

Dayton shook his head. "Oh, no."

Emily straightened up, rubbing her eyes. She pulled a tissue from a box on the coffee table and sniffled into it. She blinked and tried to compose herself. "You're telling me that Graeme didn't kill my daughter?"

"That's right," Stride said.

"Oh my God." She turned to Dayton. "I killed him. And he didn't do it! She was alive!"

"He may not have killed her, but that doesn't mean he was innocent," Dayton told her.

"I know, I know. But she must have been laughing wherever she was. She tricked me into killing him!"

"Do you have any idea what happened?" Dayton asked Serena. "Who killed her?"

"We're still investigating," Serena said. "I know this is a difficult time for you, but I do have to ask. Did you have any reason to believe that your daughter might still be alive? Did she ever try to contact you?"

Dayton and Emily looked at Stride.

"Just the postcard you showed us," Dayton said.

Stride explained to Serena about the postcard he had received shortly after the trial, with the Las Vegas postmark.

"Did you pursue it?" Serena asked.

"As far as we could. There were no prints on the card and no DNA on the stamp. I alerted the Vegas police and asked if they could scout around for me, but they didn't seem too keen on using their resources to hunt for an eighteen-year-old runaway who might or might not be dead and who might or might not be in Las Vegas."

"I'm not sure I would have done anything differently in their shoes," Serena admitted.

Stride nodded.

"I did investigate, Ms. Dial," Dayton announced.

Stride and Serena both looked at him in surprise. Dayton paused, asking permission from Emily with his eyes. She nodded at him.

"To me, the postcard—well, it seemed exactly like the kind of game Rachel would play. To taunt us. It convinced me she was alive. Emily was in prison, of course, and I didn't want the trail to grow cold, as it were. So I went to find her."

"You went to Las Vegas?" Stride asked.

"Yes, for a week. When you told me the police there weren't being helpful, I decided to look into it myself. For Emily. She deserved to know the truth."

"How did you go about it—the search, I mean?" Serena asked.

"Well, I know I sound like one of the Hardy Boys," Dayton said. "I took a photograph of Rachel with me. I just went to all the casinos and showed the photograph around at the security desks. You know, to see if anyone had seen her. They keep close tabs on people there, if you believe the television shows. I just assumed if she was there, she'd be working at a casino. It seems like everyone does. So I went up and down the Strip, and then downtown, and then to the outlying areas."

"And did you find her?" Stride asked.

Dayton shook his head sadly. "Not a trace. No one had seen her. After a week, I began to believe that it was all a mistake, that the postcard wasn't from Rachel."

"Have you been back to Vegas since then?" Serena asked.

"No, I haven't."

"Have you had any other reason since then to believe Rachel might be alive?" Stride asked, making eye contact with both of them. "Any other odd communications? Phone calls?"

"Nothing at all," Emily said. "Frankly, I never believed it, like Dayton did. I never thought she was alive."

"Oh? Why?" Serena asked.

An ironic smile flitted across Emily's lips. "I was in prison. If she were alive, I was sure Rachel would have found a way to throw that in my face."

Stride nodded. "We've taken up enough of your time," he said. He stood up, and Serena followed his lead.

"How do we arrange to have Rachel's body sent back?" Dayton asked.

"I'll have someone call you," Serena said. "We'll release her just as soon as we can. It's a criminal investigation, you understand. But one word of advice, if you don't mind. You may not want to view the body when it's returned. She was found in the desert, and, well, the desert isn't very kind to human remains."

Emily swallowed hard. "I understand."

They shook hands, and Dayton escorted them to the door. Serena offered the minister a small smile.

"Once again, I'm very sorry. I hope at least the two of you had a nice vacation before this."

Dayton hesitated. "Oh. Yes, we did. Thank you."

"I love the River Walk in San Antonio," Serena continued. "Where did you stay?"

"The convention was at the Hyatt."

"Did you get a chance to get out of the city?"

"Not really. We visited the Alamo, that kind of thing."

"Of course," Serena said.

Dayton touched her shoulder as they turned to leave. "May I ask you something?"

Serena nodded.

"I was wondering if you knew what Rachel was doing. Where she worked. I was just thinking, if I had searched a little bit harder—"

"She was working in a strip club," Serena told him without sugarcoating.

Dayton wet his lips with his tongue. "Ah. Well. I didn't look there."

40

"Do you believe him?" Stride asked as they headed back to the city. He glanced out his window and saw charcoal clouds massing in the southwest corner of the sky. A summer storm was bearing down.

"If he's lying, he's good at it," Serena said. "But I'm a cynic when it comes to men and teenage girls."

"You think a preacher who sounds too good to be true probably is?" Stride asked.

"It's more than that, Jonny."

She didn't explain. He couldn't help but wonder about her secrets. The fact that she called him Jonny also rolled around in his head. It flowed from her casually, without thought—he wondered if she even knew she had done it—but there was a familiarity in how she said it that was intimate.

He didn't think Andrea's voice had ever carried such weight in calling his name, and he remembered that a similar intimacy had been there from the beginning with Cindy. Those were scary, unwelcome thoughts. He realized that he had avoided thinking about Andrea since Serena arrived. His attraction to her was so sudden and intriguing that it seemed to push aside his other emotions. He was not the kind of man to have an affair, but right now, he wanted one. Badly.

"Have you really been to the River Walk?" he asked.

"Never," Serena said, with a sly smile.

Stride laughed. "You're beautiful."

He wanted her to feel the double meaning in his voice. He wasn't sure, but he thought she actually blushed.

"I'll have Maggie check it out," he continued. "We'll look into this church conference and make sure they were really there."

"Even if they checked in, they could have gone to and from Vegas in a day. In and out. No one would know."

"We'll check the airlines, too. And credit card records."

Before he could reply, Stride heard the chirping of his cell phone. He slid it out of his pocket and pressed it to his ear.

"We need to talk," a man's voice said. Stride recognized Dan Erickson.

"Yes, we do," Stride said. "You got my message?"

"You're goddamned right I did. Are you sure about this?"

"Yeah, we're sure."

"Shit," Dan hissed. There was a silence, and Stride could almost hear the calculations grinding in Dan's mind. "This is unbelievable. I don't want to do this over the phone."

"You want me to swing by your office?"

"Hell, no. I don't want you anywhere near my office. Meet me in the parking lot of the high school in an hour."

"Won't we need some kind of secret code to identify ourselves?" Stride asked.

"Funny. Real fucking funny. Just be there."

Stride clicked the phone off.

Serena raised her eyebrows. She could make out most of the call.

"Dan   Erickson   prosecuted   Graeme

Stoner for Rachel's murder," Stride said. "He isn't too pleased with the news."

"Why the cloak-and-dagger?"

"Dan's the county attorney, but he's going after the Democratic nomination for state attorney general. I think trying someone for murdering a girl who wasn't dead is likely to be a 'negative spin event' for his campaign."

Serena frowned. "Watch your ass, Jonny. A politician like that would have you fired if it meant deflecting blame from himself."

"Yeah, that would be Dan's style," Stride said. He heard "Jonny" on her lips again.

"You don't care?"

Stride stared through the windshield as the first drops of rain began to fall. "It's funny. I'm not sure I do."

By the time Stride dropped Serena at the station and reached the hillside road that led to the school parking lot, his windshield wipers were screeching in protest as they pounded back and forth, sluicing aside gallons of water. Stride leaned over the steering wheel, squinting to catch a glimpse of the pavement through his headlights. Somewhere in the summer sky, the sun was high, but it might as well have been night, with the swath of black clouds overhead.

Stride drove to the far side of the lot before he spotted Dan Erickson's Lexus, parked off by itself. He pulled around and parked next to it. The Lexus was navy blue with smoked windows. Dan had left the lights on and the motor running.

The rain beat down on Stride's truck. When he pushed open the door, the rain flooded over him, stinging his skin like tiny pinpricks. He slammed the door and yanked on the passenger door of the Lexus. It was locked. Already soaked, Stride pounded on the window. He heard a low click, and he piled inside the car, bringing a smattering of rain with him.

"Good to see you, too, Dan," Stride muttered, flicking droplets of water around the car as he shook his sleeves.

"These are leather seats," Dan said, scowling.

The interior of the car smelled like Dan's wife, which meant it smelled like money. Stride knew the Lexus and everything else belonged to Lauren, not Dan, but Dan wore the trappings well. On his left hand, Stride saw a fat wedding ring with a ruby stone, and on his wrist, a gold Rolex. His navy suit looked custom-tailored, and it bent in easy folds without wrinkling.

The local public radio station was on in the background. Dan reached over and turned it off. They sat silently for a moment while the rain thumped on the roof.

"It's not on the news yet," Dan said. "Let's keep it that way."

Stride shook his head. "That's impossible. This will be big news, you know that. The most we can hope is to keep it bottled up for a couple more days, but even that's optimistic. It only takes one leak."

"Who knows about this?"

"The Vegas cops and several members of the force here in Duluth. Plus Emily and her husband, Dayton Tenby."

"You should have talked to me before informing them."

"Christ, Dan, she's the girl's mother," Stride protested.

Dan sighed. "Tell me exactly what happened."

Stride explained about the discovery of Rachel's body in the Las Vegas desert and the possible Duluth connection in the murder.

"But we don't know yet what happened in

Vegas," Stride continued. "We also don't know what really happened when she disappeared the first time. Obviously, Stoner didn't kill her."

"Do you have any leads?"

"Not so far, no. We're reviewing the files from the original investigation, and we're going to start tracking down the people who were involved back then."

Dan frowned. "The more people you talk to, the more likely this will all come out."

"I'm aware of that. But this isn't just ancient history. This is an active murder investigation. Someone killed Rachel less than a week ago, and I want to know who. The only reason we're not holding a press conference is I want the element of surprise when I talk to these people."

"Great," Dan said. "Just great. The Republicans are going to love this."

"I have faith in you, Dan. You'll talk your way out of it."

Dan looked at Stride sharply. "Is that a crack? Look, Stride, I put the responsibility for the original failure squarely on the investigating team."

Two points, Serena.

Stride nodded. "We made some mistakes,

no question about it. But it was your decision to go to trial without a body, Dan."

"I recall your telling me that Stoner was the guy. He did it."

"That's what I thought. That's what we all thought. But our evidence was weak. I told you so from day one."

Dan shook his head. "We're not getting in a public shooting match over this. I expect you to take full responsibility. Am I clear? I want you to stand up and tell the world this was a police screwup. I was acting in good faith based on misinformation from the police. You guys already let one killer get away—the guy who did Kerry McGrath. And you were so desperate to solve Rachel's disappearance that you cut corners."

There were elements of truth in what Dan said. Stride could hardly deny the obsession he felt back then to find Rachel or to bring her killer to justice. He might have sacrificed some of his objectivity, because he was convinced that Stoner was guilty.

But it was Dan, personally, who chose to go to trial for murder, without a body, despite the long odds.

"I'll take my share of the blame," Stride said. "But that's not the whole story."

"It is now."

"That sounds like an ultimatum," Stride said.

Dan shrugged. "Take it however you like, but you can bet there will be consequences if you try to wriggle out of this. I won't give K-2 any choice."

"Well, I guess I'll have to give it some thought. You got any other helpful words of advice for me?"

Dan was silent.

Stride shoved open the door and clambered out. He held it open, letting the rain roar in, soaking the passenger seat and spraying Dan's nice suit. Finally, he slammed the door shut and waited in the downpour as Dan sped away.

41

Serena sat alone in the basement conference room in city hall, her eyes blurring as
she made her way through a mountain of
yellowing paperwork. Page by page, the records from the investigation told her the story
of Rachel's disappearance. The girl was becoming real to her. They all did eventually,
but this time, it was like looking in a mirror,
right down to the raven hair and emerald
eyes. Rachel might as well have been her
twin.

That made Serena think of her mother.
She's my little evil twin, her mother used to

say about Serena when she was a child, because they looked so much alike.

But her mother was the evil one. Selling herself to the devil for a few grams of white powder—and her little girl, too.

She understood the venom in Rachel's heart. She didn't have to read far to know what kind of man Graeme was and what kind of game the two of them were playing. It could have been her. She had felt the same choking desire for revenge. The only difference was, she had escaped, although she knew in her soul what a very close escape it was.

Serena checked her watch, feeling lonely and distraught. The memories did that. They made her long for a drink, too, and that was dangerous. It was after six o'clock. Maggie had gone out into the rain a half hour ago to get dinner for the two of them. Stride was missing in action. He had called in the early afternoon to say he was on the scene of a bank robbery across town, playing gopher for the Feebs.

She wanted him back, and she wanted him to stay away.

Even so, her heart raced when she heard

footsteps in the hall. She made a special effort to look calm and disinterested. Which was a lie.

But it wasn't Stride. Maggie breezed into the conference room in a damp raincoat, balancing a pizza box in one hand and two liters of Diet Coke in the other. The tiny Chinese cop grinned at her.

"Special delivery. And it's sausage, so don't give me any shit about vegetarian pizza or whatever it is you eat out west."

Serena laughed and opened the box, letting the aroma of mozzarella and seasoned pork waft into the room. Maggie filled two plastic cups with pop, then grabbed a slice and sat down, leaning her chair back until it was propped against the wall. Her feet dangled above the floor.

"Got the case solved?" she asked.

"I still think Graeme did it," Serena said, smiling.

"Yeah, it was a lot easier that way. Any word from Stride? Guppo called and said the boss was heading back here."

"No, nothing from Jonny." Serena took a slice of pizza and put it down without biting into it.

Maggie took a long swallow of Coke and then, watching Serena, her eyes narrowed with concern. "You okay?"

"Sure, why?"

Maggie tugged on her eyelid. "Glassy eyes. Tears. What's up?"

"Oh, that," Serena said. She shook her head. "It's nothing. Thinking about the bad old days. Something about this case, it gets to me."

"That happens to all of us."

"Even a hard-ass like you?" Serena asked, teasing her.

"Me, no, I'm a rock," Maggie said. "Come on, try the pizza, it's delicious."

Serena picked up the slice again and took a tentative bite. She realized she was hungry, and she began to take larger bites, finishing the first piece and reaching for another. She washed it down with a drink, belched long and loud, and began giggling uncontrollably.

"Nice," Maggie said, straight-faced. "Do you take requests?"

Serena started laughing again and was afraid the Coke would wind up coming out her nose. Maggie lost it, too, and the two of them spent five minutes cracking up before they ran out of breath. Serena wound up hot and sweaty. She wiped her brow and used a napkin to blow her nose.

"You are too much," she told Maggie.

"Thank you," Maggie said, in her best Elvis voice. "Thank you very much."

"Oh, God, don't get me started again." Serena pushed her hair out of her face. She closed her eyes and propped her chair against the wall, like Maggie's.

"Tell me something," Maggie said.

Serena was mellow now, her defenses down. "Sure."

"Was that real smoke I saw coming off you and Stride in the airport?"

Serena flopped her chair back on the floor with a bang and opened her eyes. Maggie had a broad grin spread across her golden face. "What?"

"Oh, don't play innocent with me, girl. You know he wants you. Stride couldn't hide it if he tried. And it seems to me you want him, too."

"Maggie, he's married. And we just met."

Maggie took another piece of pizza. "Call it marriage if you want, but it's long gone and dead. The Big D is around the corner. Thank God. And don't get hung up on time, kiddo. I mean, is there a right time? A week? A month? It only took me about a day to fall in love with Stride."

"You?"

Maggie nodded. "Oh, yeah. I had it bad for years."

"What happened?"

"Nothing happened. He was in a real love match back then. When she died, I took my chance. But we were made to be friends, not lovers. Fortunately, I met Eric eventually, and he managed to break through all my cynical wisecracks, the little shit. And I think it made Stride kind of jealous, which was a nice bonus."

Serena gave her a small smile. "I admit, I'm very attracted to him."

"So go for it."

"Yeah, right. Not so simple. They don't call me Barbed Wire back home for nothing. I've got skeletons in the closet. Big, ugly ones."

"You won't scare him off," Maggie said.

"Watch me."

"Do you want to sleep with him?"

"Sure I do, but I'm not going to."

"I thought everyone in Vegas had a great sex life," Maggie said.

"I've got a terrific sex life, but I'm usually alone."

Maggie laughed again, long and hard. "Hey, whatever works. But I can attest that with the right guy, there's no substitute."

Serena scrunched up her face. She wasn't convinced. "I just met him," she repeated.

"Fight it all you want, girl," Maggie said, sighing. "But it pisses me off, you know, that I tried to turn him on for years, and all you had to do was walk off the fucking plane. Your breasts ain't that great."

"Like hell they're not," Serena replied.

When he returned to city hall, Stride didn't know how to read the chemistry in the conference room, except to realize that Maggie and Serena had become fast friends during the course of the afternoon. He draped his wet coat over the back of a chair. With a tired groan, he sat down and put his feet up on the scratched wood of the tabletop.

"FBI," he announced. "Full of Bullshit Ideas."

"It's enough to bask in the reflected glow of their presence," Maggie told him.

Stride nodded. "I'm glad you feel that way. I told K-2 that you could babysit the Feebs next time."

"Thanks a lot," Maggie said.

"What happened with Dan Erickson?" Serena asked.

Stride groaned again and gave them a run-down of Dan's threats.

"I told you he was an asshole," Maggie said.

"And you were right," Stride admitted. He explained to Serena. "Maggie and Dan had a brief fling a few years ago. It ended badly. Something about her burning down Dan's house."

"That's a gross exaggeration," Maggie said. "It was an accidental cigarette burn on a Burberry coat."

"Yes, but you don't smoke," Stride reminded her.

Serena chuckled. "I love you two."

"Did you come up with anything while I was gone?" Stride asked.

"We made some breakthroughs, but on a different case," Maggie said, winking at Serena. Stride noticed that Serena gave Maggie a withering stare, then turned beet red and grabbed a manila folder from the desk and began reading. He noted that the folder was upside down.

"What case?" Stride asked.

"A head case, actually. The twisted mind of Jonathan Stride."

Stride smiled. "Do you charge by the hour?"

"You can't afford us."

"Lucky me. In between, did you get any actual police work done while I was arranging lattes for the FBI?"

Serena put the folder down, composed again. "Nothing that gets us any answers. But at least I know the case now."

"All right, let's get back to Rachel's original disappearance," Stride said. "I'm betting if we knew what really happened then, we'd know why she was killed."

"Except we were all wrong three years ago," Maggie said.

"Yes, but we know something now that you didn't know then," Serena pointed out.

"Such as?" Stride asked.

"We know Rachel was really alive."

Stride nodded. He stood up and poured a cup of lukewarm coffee. An air-conditioning vent hummed loudly, blowing cold air on his head. "That's true. All right, what else do we know?"

"We know Rachel was at the barn that night," Maggie said.

"Do we?" Serena asked. "Could the evidence have been planted?"

"What, you think a mysterious stranger came by with an eye dropper and left her blood?" Maggie shook her head. "Rachel was there—and she was in the back of Graeme's van, too. The fibers from her shirt matched."

"It wasn't just Rachel," Stride reminded her. "We've got Graeme's footprints at the barn, too—don't forget that. Remember the shoes he bought and then couldn't produce? To me, that says they were both there. Whatever happened between them, it was enough to spook Rachel and make her run."

"But we know Graeme didn't kill her," Serena said.

Stride proceeded to explain to Serena his alternate theory about what might have happened between Rachel and Graeme that night at the barn, and how Rachel might have turned to a friend to help her escape.

Serena stared at the ceiling, nodding

thoughtfully. She brushed her hair out of her eyes and drank from a can of Diet Coke. "That's not bad. But it leaves us with no obvious motive for anyone from Duluth to kill her three years later."

"Except for Dan," Maggie said, smirking.

"If Rachel ran, who helped her?" Serena asked. "Dayton Tenby? I'm still suspicious of him hunting up and down the Strip for little lost Rachel."

Stride shook his head. "Dayton and Emily were in Minneapolis that Friday night, having an affair."

"Unless Rachel called her mother," Serena said.

"I think Emily is the last person Rachel would have called," Stride said.

Maggie pursed her lips. "This all comes back to Sally. We know she saw Rachel the night she left town. She lied about it from the start. And she would have been very unhappy if Rachel came back to Duluth after all these years to say hi to Kevin."

Stride pulled out his cell phone. "Sally and Kevin are shacking up in an apartment near the university. I tried to call them earlier, but there was no answer."

He dialed again. After five rings, he was

ready to hang up, but then he heard a female voice on the line.

"Hello? Sally?" Stride frowned and listened. "Do you know where she is? I'm a friend, and I need to reach her right away."

He waited for the reply and then hung up with a brief good-bye.

"It seems Kevin and Sally are due back later tonight. That was the neighbor who's taking care of their cat. They've been on a cross-country driving trip for the last two weeks. To the Grand Canyon."

"Well, well," Maggie said.

"I-40," Serena added. "Five hours to Vegas."

42

Cordy enjoyed the envious stares as he and Lavender promenaded through the lobby of the Bellagio, underneath the giant, multicolored glass flowers that decorated the ceiling. As a couple, they were cool and attractive, a perfect fit for the upscale surroundings. Cordy wore a black collarless silk shirt, a gold chain, and a crisply pressed tan linen suit. His shoes were polished to a reflective glow, and a waft of fragrance oozed from his slicked hair. Lavender wore a formfitting red bodysuit, with ovals strategically cut away to reveal generous patches of ebony skin and to confirm for everyone who stared that she wore neither a bra nor panties. She couldn't have attracted more attention if she were naked.

As they entered the Bellagio's elegant Japanese restaurant, he saw the eyes of a dozen Asian businessmen lock onto Lavender through a cloud of cigarette smoke. She flirted with them as she sat down, confidently staring back.

"What's it like?" Cordy asked.

He didn't say what he meant, but Lavender understood. The attention. The stares. *What's it like to trail men's eyes wherever you go?*

"I love it," Lavender said. She had a sly smile and a breathy voice, with a hint of the street lingering in her twang. "I'm the queen, baby. I've got the power."

She licked her broad lips with her tongue, and Cordy felt her shoeless foot stroking his ankle under the table. The waiter came over, a wizened, expressionless Japanese man in a starched tuxedo, and Lavender began ordering things he didn't recognize, like *ika, maguro,* and *uni.*

"What are we getting?" Cordy asked when the waiter left.

"Tuna. Yellowtail. Squid. Sea urchin. Things like that."

"Sea urchin? I'm going to throw up."

"Trust me," Lavender said.

Cordy jerked his thumb at the Asian businessmen at the other tables. "No offense, Lav, but why work where you do? I mean, shouldn't you be living on an island with one of those guys?"

"You got a problem with what I do? If so, tell me now, okay? Don't waste my time."

"No, no," Cordy protested.

Lavender jabbed a finger at him. "The only people who humiliate themselves are the guys drooling in the audience every night. I'm in control. They worship me. There's nothing wrong with that. You ask why I do it. Simple. For the m-o-n-e-y."

"Sorry," Cordy said.

"Don't be. Everyone asks. But you have to get over it, baby, or we've got a short evening ahead."

The waiter brought a black lacquer tray, elegantly arrayed with gold-flecked rolls and slivers of fish, each tied to a sticky mound of rice with a black belt of seaweed. It turned out that Cordy liked sushi a lot, particularly the way Lavender balanced each piece on the chopsticks and fed him bites. She herself ate in a big way, stuffing a roll into her mouth and grinning at him as she wolfed it down. He didn't recall ever being so turned on simply by eating dinner.

When they were done, Lavender ordered sake, and Cordy was surprised to find the liquor both hot and intoxicating, given how little fit into each glass and how smoothly it slid down his throat. They went through two miniature carafes before Cordy called for the check and paid it with a slight grimace of pain.

They left the restaurant, and Cordy discovered to his delight that they were now holding hands. Her hips swished against his side as they strolled through the casino. Her fingers rubbed the inside of his palm, and he realized that even that small touch aroused him. The stares of other patrons continued to follow them.

"So how come you're not dating your hottie partner?" Lavender asked.

"Who, Serena? She's a friend, and that's that. Not my type."

Lavender poked him in the side. "Yeah, right. She may have a few years on you, but she's still a looker. You never made a play for her?"

Cordy shrugged. "She set me straight from day one. No hanky-panky. And everybody already knows her reputation. Guys ask her out, she cuts off their balls. She's got barbed wire around her."

"Why is that?" Lavender asked.

Cordy shook his head. "She hasn't told me." He let his hand slide down her back and come to rest on the curve of her buttocks. He rubbed her skin through one of the oval slits in her dress. "So you want to play for a while?"

"You mean gambling or fucking?"

"Isn't it the same thing? I get screwed either way."

Lavender threw her head back and laughed. "I like you, baby. Yeah, I like you."

"I like you, too. Listen, I got a five-hundred-dollar bill in my wallet. Let me play until I lose it or double it, and then we'll go to your place."

Lavender tugged on his chin and planted her luscious lips on his mouth, pressing her tongue inside. "Just make it quick."

Cordy steered her to the high-limit slots area. He normally played five-dollar blackjack at the tables at Sam's Town, but he didn't feel like sitting at a table and getting into the rhythm of the game. Besides, it felt like penny ante tonight. His luck was high, and he wanted to ride Lavender like a good luck charm. He chose a five-dollar Triple Play video poker machine that took up to five coins per hand, which meant the maximum bet on each pull was seventy-five dollars. Win or lose, it would be quick, and then they could get to the real business of the evening.

Over the next ten minutes, he shot ahead three hundred dollars, before sinking back after a quick series of losing hands. Then he hit a straight on two out of three hands and was well ahead again, although he hadn't quite doubled his money. He felt the usual fever overtaking him, and the only thing that kept him from losing himself in the game was the sensation of Lavender's fingers creeping closer to his crotch. Between the blips of the machine and the aching of his erection, his mind was flying.

He barely heard Lavender when she asked, "So did you and the hottie figure out what happened to Christi?"

"Damn!" He had a pair of aces, but he

couldn't pull a third ace on the draw. "What did you say?"

"Christi. The girl who got killed. Did you find out who did it?"

Cordy watched another seventy-five bucks come and go on the next series of hands. "Huh? Oh, not yet. Serena's in Minnesota now."

"Minnesota?"

Cordy nodded. "Yeah, the girl, Christi, came from some town up north in Minnesota. Looks like someone from home paid her a visit."

Cordy bet the max again and held his breath. He pumped his fist when he saw four-fifths of a spade flush flip up on the original deal. "Come on, mama, give me a spade."

Lavender wasn't watching the screen. She let one finger slip between his legs, where she traced the swelling there. "Is that from me or the game?"

Cordy didn't answer. He carefully held four cards, then punched the draw button and held his breath. "Fuck!"

Lavender sighed and removed her hand. She began studying her painted nails. "I see why I don't gamble."

"Huh?" Cordy said idly.

"Nothing. I'm surprised whoever killed Christi was from out of town. I would have thought it was that creepy boyfriend of hers."

"Yes!" Cordy shrieked as the machine dealt him three kings. "Come on, four of a kind, four of a kind!"

He fluttered his fingers over the button, then pushed it with a silent prayer. The remaining cards popped up: three, ace, seven, nine, queen, king.

"Yes!" Cordy screamed, watching the fourth king fill out the third hand. *"Yes!"* He grabbed Lavender, wrapped her tightly in his arms, and planted a long, extended kiss on her lips, to which she responded with enthusiasm. When he disentangled himself and looked back, he saw he had doubled his money. More than five hundred bucks!

Cordy cashed out, relishing the loud clanking of five-dollar coins banging into the tray. He filled two plastic buckets with the coins and stacked them on top of each other as he peered around for the nearest change booth. With the buckets under one arm and Lavender hanging on his other side, he strutted through the casino as if he were on top of the world. At the booth, he handed the buckets to the attendant and watched her pile them into the counting machine, then licked his lips as the numbers shot over a thousand dollars.

It was only then that his brain caught up with the whirl of thoughts in his head. Cordy felt his blood turn to ice, and he swung around on Lavender, his face tense and his fantasies of sex and money leeching away.

"Boyfriend?"

43

Stride and Serena sat in the dark in his truck, underneath a broken streetlight, parked opposite Kevin and Sally's university apartment building. The truck windows were open, letting the cool evening air blow through with a few lingering raindrops. They had staked out the building for an hour. He knew they could have waited until morning to talk to them, but he wanted the element of surprise, before Kevin and Sally had time to rehearse their reactions.

It also gave him a reason not to go home, which was the last place he wanted to be. That was the ugly truth. He was intensely attracted to Serena, and he wanted to be with her. Not with Andrea. Not with his own wife.

She was a silhouette seated next to him, but he knew that she could feel him studying her. Broadcasting his feelings. Shouting them silently.

"Tell me about Phoenix," he said. "About your past."

She shook her head. "I don't talk about that."

"I know. But tell me anyway."

"Why do you care about my past?" Serena asked. "You don't know me."

"That's why. I want to know you."

Serena was silent. He heard her breathing, which was fast and nervous.

"What is it you really want, Jonny?" she asked. "To sleep with me?"

Stride didn't know what to say. "How do I answer that?" he said finally. "If I say no, you know I'm lying. If I say yes, then I'm another shallow cop looking for an affair."

"You wouldn't be the first."

"I know that. And all I can say is, I know where I should be. Home. Not here with you. This is not me, not the man I am. But here I am anyway."

"You tell me something," Serena said,

turning to him in the dark. "Maggie says your marriage is over. That it was over three years ago. Is that true?"

He was tired of pretending. "It's true."

"Don't you lie to me, Jonny," Serena insisted. "I'm nobody's fling, understand? You don't know how rare it is for me to talk to a man like this. Particularly someone I just met."

"I think I do. And I'm not lying."

"Tell me why. Why it's over."

He struggled to find the right words. "We've both got ghosts rattling around in our attic. Her first husband ran off. I couldn't fill the void."

"And what about you? What's your ghost's name?"

Stride smiled. "Cindy."

"Did she break your heart?"

Enough time had passed that Cindy was a dull ache in his soul, not the sharp wound she once was. He told Serena about losing her, and it was a faraway tragedy, as if it had happened to someone else. Serena listened silently, then reached over and laced her fingers with his.

For a few still moments, the truck was a bubble, a little universe of its own.

"You really want my story?" Serena asked.

"I do."

He could see her wrestling with her fear and mistrust.

"When I was fifteen in Phoenix, my mom got into drugs," she began quietly. "She became addicted. She ran through our money. We lost our house. My dad left us. Left me."

Her voice sounded flat, not like Serena at all, as if she had drained the emotions out of her words. He sensed that something profound was happening between them, that she had invited him into a world that was previously just for her.

"We moved in with her dealer. I guess you could say I was part of my mother's payment plan. He did whatever he wanted with me. My mother would watch, stoned out of her mind."

Stride felt his emotions stir. He was angry for her. Protective.

"I got pregnant," Serena continued. "I went to a clinic by myself and had an abortion. And then I never went home again. If I went home, I knew I'd kill them both. I mean that. I spent time thinking about how I would kill them. But I wasn't going to give up my own life because of what they'd done to me. So I hooked up with a girlfriend, and we took the bus to Vegas. Sixteen years old, alone on the Strip. I took shit jobs in the casinos. I went to school at night. Became a cop."

"Most girls with that background would have wound up dead."

"I know. Like Rachel."

"You're amazing," he told her.

Serena shook her head. "I'm no angel. I can be a bitch. Most guys would tell you that I am. I've spent most of my life fending off men."

"Why aren't you fending me off?" he asked. "Or is that what you're trying to do?"

"Sure I am, Jonny. For your sake."

He didn't say anything. When a lamp went on in the nearest apartment, it cast a faint light on their faces. He found his eyes drawn to her pale lips. She was conscious of his desire, and she let her lips barely part. Hesitating, uncertain, she leaned toward him, her long hair tumbling forward.

The light went off again, as quickly as it came. They were invisible as they kissed. Then Serena pulled away, and they were silent for the next hour, without any need to talk.

* * *

The strawberry Malibu pulled up around midnight.

They watched Kevin and Sally shrug backpacks onto their shoulders and tramp wearily up the steps of the apartment building. When they were inside, Stride touched Serena's shoulder, and they followed across the street.

Stride knocked on the third-floor apartment door, and Kevin answered immediately, his eyes bloodshot. Kevin assessed him suspiciously, then realized who he was. The recognition dawned, and Kevin, quick as lightning, knew why he was there.

"It's Rachel, isn't it?" he asked.

Stride nodded. "Sorry to surprise you like this, Kevin. And yes, it's about Rachel. We've found her body."

Kevin backed up from the door, his eyes growing moist with tears. He was maturing into a handsome man, with wavy blond hair and sunburned skin.

Stride introduced Serena as they entered the apartment, not mentioning that she was from Las Vegas. He took a quick look around at the garage-sale furniture and immediately realized that something was missing.

Their backpacks weren't there.

"Where's Sally?" he asked.

Kevin looked up blankly. "What? Oh, doing the laundry."

"The laundry!" Serena said. She turned and ran from the apartment, and Stride followed on her heels, leaving Kevin standing in the doorway. They found the stairs and took them two at a time down to the basement, where they emerged into a darkened corridor that hummed with machinery. Stride stopped and listened. He heard the familiar chug-chug of a washing machine across the hall.

They burst into the laundry room.

Sally sat on the end of a ratty sofa. She was reading a copy of *People* magazine. Her eyes widened with surprise and fright as the door swung open and banged into the wall.

Stride saw the two backpacks lying empty on the floor and two washing machines rinsing away any evidence. He cursed softly and switched them both off.

"What the hell is going on?" Sally demanded, her voice quavering.

Stride took a long look at Sally. She had lost weight, and it looked good on her. She wore a pink tank top, white short shorts, and one sandal that she dangled on her left foot. The other sandal was on the yellowing linoleum floor in front of the sofa.

"Do you remember me?" Stride asked.

Sally studied his face, and her eyes narrowed. She relaxed a little. "Yes, I do. And I still want to know what the hell is going on."

"Who gets home at midnight from a long drive and does laundry?" Serena asked.

"I do," Sally said. "I don't want smelly laundry in my apartment, thank you very much. Now what do you two want?"

"Rachel's dead," Stride told her bluntly.

He saw what he wanted to see: confusion flitting across Sally's face. That was the first telltale sign of the truth of what had happened when Rachel disappeared. Sally was *surprised* to hear that Rachel was dead. And that meant, when Rachel vanished, *Sally knew she was still alive.*

It also meant she hadn't killed her.

As the reality dawned on Sally, he saw something else, too. The girl could barely keep a smile from her lips, and a look of vast relief and satisfaction crept onto her face. "Where did you find her?"

"Las Vegas," Stride said. "This is Serena Dial from the police department in Nevada. Rachel was murdered there last weekend."

"Murdered?"

"That's right," Serena said. "How did you like the Grand Canyon?"

Sally nodded slowly, understanding. "Oh, I get it. You think we went to Vegas. You think we saw her."

"Did you?" Stride asked.

"Like I'd let Kevin get anywhere near Rachel," Sally snapped. She looked Serena up and down. "And I don't approve of gambling or any of the other things that go on in that city. We didn't go there."

"She's telling the truth," a male voice announced. Stride saw Kevin in the doorway. He had been listening outside. "I can't believe Rachel was alive all this time."

"It's a hell of a coincidence, Kevin," Stride told him. "You and Sally were just a few hours from Las Vegas when she was killed."

"We didn't go there," Sally repeated.

Kevin nodded. "That's right."

Stride and Serena exchanged quick looks, and they came to the same conclusion. These two were telling the truth.

"We're still going to need to check your clothes and your car," Stride said. "I'm sorry."

"All you'll find is dust and bugs," Sally said.

"I'm going to assume you two are telling the truth," Stride said. "But we're trying to find out if there's a connection between Rachel's murder and her original disappearance. It means it's more important than ever to know what really happened back then."

Sally's face clouded over, and she looked away.

Stride realized he wasn't going to get anywhere while Kevin was in the room. "Kevin, can you give us a couple minutes to talk to Sally?"

Sally's eyes widened. She didn't want to be left alone. But Kevin's mind was far away, under Rachel's spell again. Like a robot, he slouched from the room without looking back at Sally.

Serena closed the door, and Stride leaned against an empty dryer and stared down at Sally on the sofa. Sally glared at both of them and folded her arms defiantly.

"She's dead, Sally," Stride said. "You don't have to keep her secrets now."

Sally resumed a lotus position on the sofa and closed her eyes.

"It's just us now," he said. "No judge, no jury. No Kevin, either."

"I don't know what you're talking about."

"Sure you do. You lied in court. You never heard Rachel and Graeme fighting that night. You made that up. It doesn't matter now, Sally. No one's going to arrest you for perjury. You're in no danger. But we do need to know the truth."

"Rachel's dead, and we want to know why," Serena said.

Sally shrugged. "You thought she was dead then. What's changed?"

"We know you were at her house that night. You were seen on the street."

"So what?" Sally asked. "I walked over, I didn't see her, I walked home. End of story."

"If that's true, then why lie about Rachel fighting with Graeme?"

Sally hesitated. "I panicked. That lawyer was trying to make it look like I was involved, which was crazy. And I really thought Graeme was guilty. Hell, they fought all the time. It wasn't such a big lie."

"The trouble is, you're lying again, Sally,"

Serena said. "You can't bullshit another woman."

Stride knelt by the sofa. He was level with Sally's face, only a few inches away. "You knew Rachel was alive."

"That's ridiculous," Sally said. But her voice trembled.

"You helped her escape," Serena said.

"I *didn't*."

"Then tell us what happened that night, Sally." Stride reached out and laid a hand gently on her shoulder. "Look, I know what Rachel was like. I know how she could manipulate people."

Sally stared back at him. "No, you don't," she whispered.

Inside her coat, Sally balled her hands into tight fists. Her elbows were squeezed against her side, and her feet stamped on the sidewalk, causing her curls to bounce. All she could think about, all she could see in her head, over and over, was Rachel and Kevin on the bridge.

Rachel kissing Kevin.

Rachel's hand slipping over Kevin's crotch.

And, worst of all, the sly little smile as Rachel's head turned to make sure Sally was below them, watching. It wasn't enough to steal him away. Rachel needed to humiliate her, too.

She couldn't compete, not with Rachel. Her only salvation all along had been that Rachel had never taken the slightest real interest in Kevin. She toyed with him. Teased him. Flirted with him. And that was all.

Until tonight.

In her room, Sally's rage boiled over. She couldn't get the ugly image out of her head. A part of her wanted to say "Fuck you" to both of them and let Kevin see how happy he was in the arms of that sleazy whore. If that was what he wanted, fine. Let her destroy him. Let him see what life would be like under her thumb.

But she couldn't do it. This wasn't Kevin's fault. He was helpless, a fly caught in Rachel's web.

She decided to have it out with Rachel once and for all—and give her an ultimatum: Stay away from Kevin.

So she climbed out of her first-floor window silently and hurried down the street, her entire body coiled tightly like a spring. She barely noticed the blocks passing, or the cold that turned her rapid breath to steam. In her mind, she went over all the things she was going to say. She rehearsed a big speech, muttering it under her breath, going over and over the words until it was just perfect. But when she found herself on the sidewalk out-side Rachel's house, all of the words she had carefully practiced vanished from her mind. Her tongue felt swollen and useless, and her insides turned to jelly. Her courage evaporated. She was frozen.

Rachel was home. Sally had thought Rachel might still be with Kevin and she would have to wait. That would have made it easier. Catch her as she's getting out of the car, when she isn't expecting anyone to confront her. But Rachel's car was parked in the driveway. All Sally had to do was march up to the door and ring the bell. She tried to screw up her courage by remembering yet again the sight of the two figures on the bridge. Rachel and Kevin. The kiss. The seduc-tion. The smile.

Bitch.

Ring the bell, and Rachel would answer. And then Sally would unleash all the pent-up fury she had been carrying inside. Scream at her. Slap her. Show her that, for once, a girl was going to fight back.

But Sally was paralyzed. Her mind willed her forward, and her feet remained planted on the street. She didn't know if she could face Rachel, no matter how angry she was, no matter how much Kevin meant to her.

Inside Rachel's house, the downstairs light went off. The house went dark.

That's it, **Sally thought.** She's going to bed. I'm too late.

Then she heard a clicking inside, like the turning of a dead bolt, and she realized that someone was opening the front door of Rachel's house. Sally's courage fled completely, and she ducked off the sidewalk and pressed herself into a row of tall hedges. She could still see the house in the pale glow of the streetlight.

In the shadows, she recognized Rachel, dressed as she was before, slipping from her house. Rachel furtively studied the street for almost a full minute, waiting, not moving, holding back in the protective darkness of the porch. Then she hurried down the driveway. She clutched a large plastic bag in her hand.

Sally realized Rachel was heading her way. Rachel was bound to see her. Sally wanted to curl up in the hedges and hope she would walk right by, but she knew this was her one chance. It was now or never. Sally swallowed hard, then stepped out onto the sidewalk right in front of Rachel.

"We need to talk," Sally said. Her stomach flip-flopped, and she cursed herself as she heard the quivering in her voice. She sounded like a frightened child.

Rachel saw her and stopped dead. Shock filled her eyes, replaced in an instant by cold hatred and contempt.

"Oh, shit," Rachel hissed. "What the fuck are you doing here?"

Sally coughed. "I want to talk about Kevin," she said weakly.

Rachel glanced up and down the street. They were alone, just the two of them. She pushed her face practically to Sally's nose. "You have no idea what you're meddling with," Rachel said. "You're going to ruin everything."

Sally was confused. She had never seen Rachel like this. "What? What do you mean?"

Rachel grabbed Sally's wrist and twisted it until she grimaced in pain. "Look, this is none of your business. Do you get me? You never saw me here tonight."

"I don't understand," Sally said. "You're hurting me."

None of this was going as Sally had planned. She had no idea what Rachel was talking about, but she was scared of the look in her eyes.

"I'll do more than that if you don't shut up and listen," Rachel said. "You may be a fool, Sally, but I think you're smart enough to know two things. First, I don't have any interest in Kevvy. He's all yours, God help him. And second, you know damn well that I could take him away from you any time I want to."

"That's not true," Sally said.

Rachel laughed. "He'd do anything for me. And that's after a little hand job on the bridge, Sally. Did you enjoy the show? Did you like watching me make your boyfriend come?"

"Stop it," Sally pleaded. "Don't."

"Good. I'm glad we understand each other. So let's be clear about this. You're going to go back home, and you're going to forget all about this little conversation. It never took place. You never saw me. Because I'll make you a promise, Sally. If you ever tell anyone about this, I'll come back and make sure Kevvy never looks at you again. I don't care if you marry him tomorrow, I'll sleep with him the day after that, and believe me, he'll never spend another day with you."

Sally said nothing. She didn't know what to do.

Rachel sidled closer to her. She stroked Sally's hair, and Sally tried to pull away. Rachel held her. "Do you under-stand me, Sally?"

"I don't understand any of this."

"Then just tell me you believe me. You believe me, don't you? You know I'd take Kevvy away from you in a second."

Sally nodded.

"Good," Rachel said. She grinned. With her other hand, she let a finger run along

Sally's cheek. Then she leaned closer and, with sweet breath, kissed Sally softly on the lips. The kiss lingered, and Sally felt sick.

"Don't forget," Rachel told her. "Not a word."

Stride listened to Sally's story with growing horror. He shook his head slowly.

"Do you realize the hell you could have saved everyone if you'd told us what happened?" he asked her.

Sally shrugged, completely unrepentant. "You didn't know Rachel, Mr. Stride. She meant what she said. If I had told anyone about seeing her, she would have made it her life's mission to take Kevin away from me. I knew what she was capable of. Back then, it seemed like I was the only one who did."

"You were willing to let Graeme Stoner go to prison? When you knew he was innocent?"

Sally's eyes flashed with anger. "Innocent? Like hell. I told the truth about him hijacking me in his car. If he hadn't been scared off at the barn, he would have raped me. And I'll bet I wasn't the only one. You already knew he was fucking Rachel."

"But why lie on the stand?" Stride asked.

"I had to think fast," Sally said. "I figured I was sending Rachel a message, wherever she was: I'm keeping my end of the bargain. You keep yours."

Serena stared into Sally's determined eyes. "You wouldn't have liked it if Rachel came back, would you?"

Sally didn't blink. "No, I wouldn't have liked that at all. She was dead. I wanted her to stay that way. But if you're still thinking we went to Vegas and I finished the job, you're wrong. Rachel kept her end of the bargain. She never came back."

"You never heard from her?"

"Never. I think you're looking in the wrong place. You should be in Vegas, seeing whose lives she was destroying there. A bitch like that never changes. You can bet she was up to the same old tricks."

"Do you know what was in the plastic bag she was carrying?" Stride asked.

Sally shook her head. "I couldn't see."

"And she didn't have anything else with her?"

"Nothing. Just the clothes on her back. Same clothes she was wearing down in Canal Park that night."

"The white turtleneck?" Stride asked.

"Yes."

"Was it ripped in any way?"

"I didn't notice," Sally said.

"How about the bracelet?" Stride asked. "Was she still wearing it?"

Sally closed her eyes and reflected. "I think so. Yeah, I'm sure she was. I can still see it dangling on her wrist."

Stride nodded, his mind working through the possibilities. "Did she say how she was getting out of town? Was she meeting someone?"

Sally shook her head. "I don't know. I really don't. She didn't say anything about going away."

But she had to be leaving town, Stride thought. Did something else happen that changed her plans—something at the barn? Because she *was* at the barn that night. The bracelet put her there. Sally saw her outside her home, and somehow, later that night, she ended up at the barn, leaving behind evidence that pointed the finger at Graeme Stoner. Then she was gone.

"You must have thought about it later," Stride said. "What did you think?"

"I was as puzzled as everyone else. I figured she either hitched a ride with a guy and seduced him to keep him quiet, or she conned one of the guys at school to drive her to the Cities."

"But you didn't help her? You don't know anything more?"

"No, I don't. And I'd like to get back to Kevin now."

Stride nodded. "All right, Sally."

The girl pushed herself off the sofa and brushed past him, leaving Stride and Serena alone in the laundry room.

"What do you think, Jonny?" Serena asked.

Stride stared at the washing machines and wondered how much Guppo was going to love getting out of bed in the middle of the night to pack up a giant bag of wet dirty laundry.

"I think Rachel's dead, and she's still playing games with us."

44

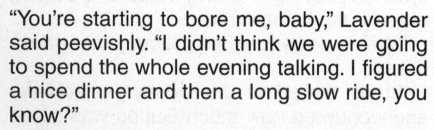

"You're starting to bore me, baby," Lavender said peevishly. "I didn't think we were going to spend the whole evening talking. I figured a nice dinner and then a long slow ride, you know?"

Cordy took her face in his hands and kissed her. He dropped one hand to her right breast and caressed it softly, slipping his thumb inside one of the open patches. "Me too, mama. But I need to know, okay?"

She put her hand over his and tightened it on her breast. "Just so you know what you're missing," she said.

Cordy groaned. "Just a few more questions."

Lavender sighed and let go.

They sat in his car in the Bellagio parking lot. Cordy drove the black PT Cruiser he had won on the slots of Sam's Town two years earlier—the biggest jackpot he had ever scored. He pampered the car like a baby and always parked it in a far corner, safe from dings and dents. The leather interior smelled of salsa and cigars, his two biggest weaknesses after sex and gambling.

He tried to concentrate, which wasn't easy, staring at the tight fabric on Lavender's chest.

"Tell me again about the boyfriend," he murmured.

"I only saw him once, Cordy," Lavender said. "I've told you that three times."

"And each time you remember a little more, mama. That's the way it works."

Lavender rolled her eyes. "It was a really hot night, just like this one. We were at the club. Christi and I both danced there, same shift. She was good, you know? She didn't like it, not like I do, but she was real good. Anyway, that night, about a year ago, this guy came backstage at the club after she was done with her act and hung out with us for a while. No name or anything like that. But I remember Christi calling him an old boyfriend. That was funny."

"Why?"

Lavender giggled. "'Cause he was so old. You know, old boyfriend. Get it?"

"How old?" Cordy asked.

"I don't know. Forty. Fifty. You know, old."

"What did he look like?"

"Oh, I don't remember. Average."

"Dark or light hair?"

"Uh, dark, I think. Graying, maybe. I don't know."

"Height?"

"Kinda tall," Lavender said.

Cordy realized he was getting nowhere. "And you had never seen him before? Christi never mentioned him?"

Lavender shook her head. "Nope."

"What about after? Did you see him after that?"

"Nope," she said again.

Cordy took a new tack. "You called him creepy before. What was creepy about him?"

Lavender frowned. "He didn't talk much. Christi was kind of ignoring him, and he didn't like it. It looked like he really wanted to get her alone, and she obviously didn't want that. Looked like two people in the middle of a fight, you know? Plus, he had this look in his eyes. Real intense. You know—creepy. If he wasn't a boyfriend, I would have figured him for a stalker. We get a lot of that kind. But he had it bad for her."

"How do you know?"

"Well, hey, this was the dressing room, you know? Half the girls were naked. Beautiful girls. Hell, I was naked, right in front of this guy. He didn't react at all. Didn't even see us. He didn't see anyone but Christi."

Cordy tried to imagine anyone not noticing Lavender naked. It was impossible.

"Do you remember what they talked about?"

"No. He sat off by himself, and every now and then, he would whisper something to her. But she mostly talked to the rest of us girls, not him. She was teasing him a little, I think. Trying to piss him off by ignoring him."

"Did Christi ever have other boyfriends meet her at the club?"

"Never. That was the only time. I don't think I would have remembered otherwise. Christi was a loner, a real cold fish."

"How so?"

"Well, like I said, she was talking to us that night, not him. And that was rare. She didn't talk much to the other girls. She came in, did her dance, and left, you know? Some of the girls thought she was a stuck-up bitch. Others thought she was ashamed."

"What did you think?" Cordy asked.

"That girl wasn't ashamed. You can't be as good as she was and be ashamed. I think we were all just nonpeople to her. Didn't exist at all. Hell, when I talked to her about my idea, she barely let me finish before slamming the door on me."

"What idea?"

Lavender poked him. "A Web site. Online sex shows. Christi would have been perfect, and it would have made her a lot of money. But she said there was no way she was going to be seen on the Internet. That was funny, because guys could see all they wanted live and in person every night. That didn't matter, though."

"She say why?"

"No, just that she wasn't interested. Period."

"Uh-huh. Look, Lav, I've got to find this boyfriend. This Christi, she's a puzzle, see?

There's nothing personal in her apartment. The way you describe her, she barely had a life. This boyfriend is the only clue we've got."

Lavender shrugged. "I've told you everything I remember, baby. I don't see how you're going to find him. I mean, you could talk to the other girls who were there. A few of them might still be in town. They might remember something."

Cordy nodded, knowing it was a long shot. "Okay, I'll have you write down their names."

"And maybe some of the other people at the club saw him. Bouncers, bartenders, waitresses. I left the club not too long after that, so he might have come back when I wasn't there."

"Yeah, that's a start. I'll run 'em all down tomorrow."

"Sorry, baby," Lavender said. "You look disappointed."

"I am. This could have been a big break, but I'm afraid it looks more like a dead end."

Lavender smirked. "I know how to make it up to you."

She slid her tongue out between her lips and reached for his zipper. Effortlessly, she pulled it down. "You want some head, baby?"

Cordy was immediately hard. "Oh, yeah." Her fingers skillfully reached inside.

"Mmm, dessert," she whispered.

Lavender's upper body sank forward, and her hair tumbled over his lap. Cordy closed his eyes, waiting for the delicious warmth of her mouth closing over him. It never came. With a start, Lavender straightened up, and Cordy opened his eyes, enormously disappointed.

"What's wrong, mama?" he pleaded.

She stared at him with bright eyes. "I may, I just may, have a picture of him."

"Who?"

"The mystery man. The boyfriend."

Cordy felt his erection wither, but his mind was excited. "A picture? Get out of here."

"Yeah, yeah. We were clowning around with my Polaroid that night, making faces, shooting our tits and asses. I remember because Christi wouldn't let me take her picture. Kept turning her back. But it's possible creepy-face ended up in the background of one of the shots."

"You still have the pictures?" Cordy asked.

"I think so. In my apartment. I have a drawer where I dump all of them."

Cordy turned the key in the ignition, and

the engine of the Cruiser fired into action. He clutched the wheel with tight fists. "Where's your apartment?" he asked.

Lavender told him, and before she was even finished, Cordy rocketed the car toward the ramp that led out of the parking lot. The tires squealed, and the rear of the car threatened to fishtail.

"Don't speed," Lavender said, grinning.

"Why not?"

Laughing, Lavender pointed between his legs, where Cordy's penis still dangled out of his pants. "Well, if another cop pulls you over, how are you going to explain that?"

45

Stride still didn't want to go home.

When he came to the intersection that led back to Serena's motel, he turned toward the lake instead, following by habit a route that had long ago become ingrained in his head, even though he hadn't driven it in a long time. He didn't ask himself where he was going. He just knew, because his heart pulled him there.

"Let's go down to the water," he suggested to Serena.

"Fine by me."

He guided them through Canal Park and across the bridge to the Point. There were no ships to delay them tonight. The steel buzzed under his tires, and a few seconds later, he was back where he had once felt more at home than anywhere else. Even at night, he could see the passage of time by the glow of the streetlights. Some trees were larger, and some were gone. New homes had been put up and others torn down. He had stopped coming here, but life had gone on without him.

He slowed as he drove past his old house. Glancing in the mirror, seeing no one behind them, he stopped in the street and rolled down his window.

"That was our place," he told her. "Me and Cindy."

"I'd love a place like that," Serena said.

The house looked good. The new owners had gone with yellow paint this season, which brightened it up considerably, and they obviously had a green thumb, judging from the flower gardens decorating the lawn. The grass and bushes were neatly trimmed. The driveway was paved now. They had put in a swing set for their kids.

All the lights were off. They were gone, or asleep, or lying in bed listening to the waves, as he and Cindy used to do.

Stride continued through the rest of the Point, which was dark and deserted. He followed the road all the way to the park at the very end and got out of the truck. Serena joined him. They held hands as they followed a sandy trail through the trees to the lake. When they emerged, the sky opened up, drowning them in stars, and the water loomed ahead, loud and black. The soft wind teased the trees behind them. Waves tumbled in, whooshing onto the shore. The strip of beach was lonely and dark as far as they could see.

He saw Serena smile with delight. She tugged on his hand, pulling him toward the water. They went to the edge of the wet sand where the incoming waves glided almost to their feet. Every few seconds, they had to dance back to stay dry.

Serena spun in a circle, soaking up the sights around her. She pointed at the thin line of houses stretching toward the city.

"You lived here?" she asked. "Why move?"

"Andrea didn't like it," he explained. "Plus, there were too many memories."

"Does it hurt being here now?"

He shook his head. "Not at all."

Serena retreated from the water and

looked for a flat stretch of sand. "Sit with me for a while, Jonny."

He leaned down and scooped a handful between his fingers. "The sand's still damp from the storm."

"That's all right."

He saw it in her eyes. A leap of faith for her. An act of trust. For him, there was no turning back, and he knew only that he didn't want to stop it, not for anything.

Serena kicked off her shoes. She unbuttoned her jeans, slipped them down her slim, long legs, and stepped out of them. She stretched her arms up to the sky, revealing a stretch of bare stomach and, below, white bikini panties. With both hands, she peeled up the bulky sweater of Stride's that she was wearing and the navy T-shirt beneath it. Her breasts strained at the fabric of her bra. She knelt in the sand and held her hand out to him.

"You'll freeze," he told her.

"Keep me warm."

He took off his own shoes. He left his shirt on but removed his pants and tossed them aside. He sat down next to her, their legs touching, and the sand beneath him didn't feel cold at all. Her arms came around him, her hands digging under his shirt, clutching his back, pressing into his skin. They kissed hungrily. Their bodies sank until they were prone in the sand.

He kissed her neck and slid a bra strap off her shoulder, pulling it down until her breast spilled into his hand. His mouth covered her nipple, sucking on it. He heard a soft rumble of pleasure in her throat. He exposed her other breast and kissed it. Her fingers found the slit in his boxers and slipped inside to stroke his erection with her nails. She pulled aside the flap of fabric, and he felt cool air as his penis slid out.

"Quickly," she whispered.

He reached for her panties and pushed his thumbs inside. She rose up from the beach, and he slid them off and tossed them away. Her hands grabbed for him and pulled him over her. He licked her breasts, but she took his face in her palms and brought him up to kiss her. He kissed her lips. Her cheeks. Her eyes.

Her legs spread and wrapped around him. He felt his penis brushing against her mound and sinking lower.

"We're not—" he murmured. *Not safe. Not protected.*

"Yes, we are," she told him, and there was a sadness in her voice, and he wondered if he had killed the moment.

But his penis found its way inside her in the next second, and she was wet and waiting. He gasped with pleasure. She did, too, and her legs held him tightly, and her fingers rippled against his neck. He began to thrust inside her, so deep they could have been one person. The stars watched them. The waves roared in his ears.

She watched him make love to her with her eyes wide open. He had never felt more naked, or connected, than having her see him like that. She kept them open until, finally, her head tilted back, and a smile and a cry escaped from her mouth at the same moment, and her body quivered in his hands. And he closed his own eyes and let himself go.

She had put her T-shirt back on, but she was nude below, and he stroked her legs and her mound gently as they lay on the beach. Sand streaked her skin. She was propped on both elbows, watching the sky.

"Feel guilty?" she asked.

"I should, but I don't."

"Good."

"Can I ask you something?" he said.

He watched her lips draw into a tighter line. She already knew the question. "The abortion," she explained. "I waited too long. It didn't go well. I can't have kids."

"Does that bother you?" he asked, thinking of Andrea.

"You go through phases. At that age, with what I'd been through, I couldn't imagine why anyone would want kids. Then there was a point in my twenties where I felt very sorry for myself, and I cried a lot, and I drank a lot. I almost drank my way off the force. Like mother, like daughter, you know? Addictive personalities. But I found a good shrink, and she helped me through it. Today, it comes and goes. But I haven't lived my life like I missed something by not having kids."

"Same here," he said.

"Tell me something," Serena said. "I know this sounds weird. Was I good?"

"What?"

"Making love. Was I good? In the past, it wasn't like this, and I knew it was because of me. All my baggage. It got in the way."

"You don't really need me to answer that, do you?" Stride asked.

She smiled, laughing at herself, but she looked relieved. "No, I guess not."

His caresses on her upper thighs became more directed, and he let his hand slip between her legs. Her hips thrust against his fingers. "Make me come again," she told him.

But he had hardly begun when muffled electronic music began playing in Serena's discarded jeans. She groaned, and they both laughed. Stride found her cell phone in a rear pocket and handed it to her.

"This is Serena." Then, a moment later, "Cordy, your timing sucks."

He heard a voice on the phone talking at a rapid clip.

"Slow down, Cordy," Serena said. "What the hell are you saying?"

Although he couldn't make out the words, he saw Serena's eyes, as she listened, light up with intense interest.

"Are you *sure* it's him?" Serena said into the phone. "If you're wrong, we're going to look like fools."

Stride heard the pitch of her partner's voice rise. Cordy was sure.

"I'll be damned," Serena said. "All right, get someone to watch the place, but don't roust him. See what he does. I'll fly back tomorrow."

Stride felt his breath leave his chest, leaving only a tight ache behind.

"Good work, Cordy," Serena said. "I'm sure you and Lavender will find a way to celebrate."

Serena flipped down the phone.

"We may have been searching in the wrong city after all," she said.

"What do you mean?"

"It turns out that Christi—Rachel—had a boyfriend. Cordy found a photograph from the club where she worked. The guy was in the background. He recognized him."

"How?"

"We know the guy," Serena explained. "Except now he looks more like Howard Hughes. It's the same old drunk desert rat who owns the trailer where Christi's body was found. And that sure puts a new spin on the ball."

"He kills her and simply dumps the body behind his own place?" Stride asked.

"This guy doesn't exactly have all his cereal in one bowl, at least when he's been drinking. If he was dating Christi, and she dumped him, it could have sent him over the edge."

"So he goes to her apartment to try to

convince her to take him back," Stride speculated. "She tells him to take a hike, and he
drops a vase on her head. He brings the
body home, dumps it, and then ties one on."

"It's possible," Serena said.

Stride shook his head. "But what about
the ATM receipt? The connection to Duluth?"

"Maybe I was wrong," Serena said, trying
to put the pieces together. "Maybe Duluth is
a red herring."

"You weren't wrong," Stride insisted.
"There's something else going on."

Serena leaned over and kissed him with
cool lips. "Come with me."

"What?"

"You were in at the beginning, Jonny. You
deserve to be there when it all ends. Even if
it turns out this guy didn't kill her, he must
know something. Let's go see him together."

Stride got up out of the sand and began
gathering their clothes. "All right," he said.
"But there's something I have to do first."

She knew. "Talk to your wife?"

He nodded.

"I feel responsible," Serena said.

"You're not. I am."

He didn't dread the idea of divorce the
way he had for so long. Andrea had already

opened the door. Now he would walk through.

"We may find the answer tomorrow," Serena said.

Stride wasn't so sure. He knew there was a mystery in Las Vegas, but he didn't believe for a minute he would find the truth there. The truth would still be here in Duluth. Waiting for him to come back and find it.

46

During the three years of their marriage, Stride and Andrea had carved out Saturday mornings for themselves. They had remained faithful to that except for the few weekends a year when Andrea visited her sister, Denise, in Miami. Even when he was in the middle of an investigation, Stride tried to keep Saturday morning free. Usually, they drove to Canal Park for breakfast overlooking the lake and brought along the paper to read over coffee. Or they jogged a few times around the high school track and rewarded themselves with pastries at the Scandinavian bakery. Those times, more than any other, he felt like they were husband and wife.

But here he was, on Saturday morning, packing for a flight to Minneapolis and then on to Las Vegas. It was like broadcasting an alarm. Andrea got the message. She stood in a corner of the bedroom, her arms folded, her jaw set in a pinched, unhappy line. Much of the anger she had first sent his way, upon learning of his trip, had dissolved already into bitterness and hurt. She didn't want to hear his explanations, and he had few to offer.

"Don't do this," she murmured, not for the first time. "Don't walk away from me, Jon."

Stride shoved a few pairs of socks into the end pocket of his duffel bag. "I have to do this."

"Oh, come on," she snapped. "This isn't your problem anymore. Why can't you just let it go?"

What could he say? He owed it to Rachel to uncover the truth. She had haunted him for years, and he wanted to unravel her mystery once and for all. But there was no denying to himself that he had another motive left unspoken. He also needed to know where his relationship with Serena was going. Because his marriage was over.

She seemed to read his mind. "You're leaving me. I've been there before. I know what it looks like."

He stopped packing. "Okay. Maybe I am."

"That's how you deal with this?" Andrea demanded. "By running away? For months, we've been like strangers. For days, you've hardly come home, never called. Where the hell were you last night?"

"Don't go there," he said.

"Why not? You think I don't know about you and Maggie?"

"There's nothing between me and Maggie. I've told you that before. I'm not talking about this."

"If we talked, we could work it out," Andrea insisted. "Goddamn it, all you can do is shut me out. I'm telling you not to go. I need you to stay here."

In his mind, he could hear Maggie warning him years ago. "I know. But you don't love me. You never did."

"That's a lie!"

"Don't pretend," he told her. "I'm done with pretending."

Andrea was defiant. "I'm asking you to stay here and work this out."

He heard the implicit message: *You're my*

husband. Do this for me. He wanted to make her happy, but he had been trying and failing for years.

"I'm sorry. This is something I have to do."

Andrea gasped, putting a hand over her mouth. "You want a divorce, don't you?"

He closed his eyes. "Don't you?"

"No!" she insisted. "No, I don't want that. I would never want that!"

"But you're not happy," Stride said. "I'm not happy. There's only one answer here."

"We can fix this if you'll just stay and work with me, but all you can talk about is going away."

He took her hands in his and shook his head. "We can't fix this, Andrea. It's going to be better for both of us if we make new lives. And I think you feel that way, too."

She whirled away from him in anger, her blonde hair falling across her face. She squeezed her hands against her head, her eyes wild. From her dresser, she grabbed a bottle of perfume and threw it against the wall, where it shattered, filling the room with a sickly sweet scent. Andrea stared at the glass sprinkling the floor. It seemed to transport her. She seemed to be somewhere else entirely.

Stride put an arm around her shoulder. She shrugged it off.

"Just go," she told him.

"I'm sorry."

Her eyes were fierce. "No, you're not. You've already decided what's important to you. If it matters so much to you, then just get the hell out, and go. I hope you get what you want. And when you find it, I hope you ask yourself why you wanted it so damn bad."

47

Stride was on the highway by the edge of the wilderness. It was the chase dream again, where he was running after a girl he couldn't find, but this time, after pursuing her along the trail and hearing her laughter luring him on, he did find her. He found Rachel in the middle of a clearing, dead in a ruby pool of her own blood. Surrounding her, looking down at the body, were Cindy, Andrea, and Serena. All of their hands were stained in red.

"Who did this?" he shouted.

Each of the women, in turn, raised a finger and pointed at him.

He started awake.

Serena was next to him, reading the airline magazine. She looked at him. "Bad dream?"

"Sort of. How did you know?"

"You called out Rachel's name."

Stride laughed. He rubbed his hands over his face and through his hair, trying to escape the fuzzy feeling of waking up. "Did I really?"

"No. I'm teasing. You just looked like you were somewhere you didn't want to be."

He leaned over and kissed her. "I'm exactly where I want to be."

Stride could feel the plane descending. He craned his neck to look out the window, but their seats didn't allow a view of the city. He saw only a bright glow suggesting an enormous source of light somewhere nearby. As they touched down, he could see little in the darkness but the guiding lights of the taxiways. When the plane turned toward the terminal, however, he caught a glimpse of a shimmering gold tower, angled toward him like a boomerang.

"That's Mandalay Bay," Serena said. "Amazing, huh?"

As they exited the plane and made their

way inside the gate, Stride stopped, assaulted by the flood of color and neon that flashed everywhere. He couldn't help but smile, thinking of Serena in the quiet Duluth airport, comparing the terminal to the spectacle here in Vegas. It was another world.

In the baggage claim area, he noticed a man detach from the crowd and approach them. Serena gave the man a quick hug.

"Jonathan Stride, this is Cordy Angel, my partner."

Stride shook his hand. "That was a terrific break, making the connection between the body and the boyfriend."

"I am an extraordinary detective," Cordy said, winking.

"A lucky bastard is more like it," Serena said.

Cordy turned to Serena. "We've got trailer-man staked out. He left earlier this afternoon and drove to the liquor store. Got himself stocked with more gin. Then he went home, hasn't moved since."

Serena scowled. "Shit, that means he'll probably be incoherent tomorrow. I wanted him to have at least one foot in the real world."

"I don't think he spends a lot of time there."

"Well, we can always sober him up at the station," Serena said. "How about the warrant? You got that?"

Cordy nodded. "We can go in and tear the place apart. But I've been there. It ain't going to be me going through that pit of a trailer."

Stride interrupted them. "Did you find out any more about this guy's background with Rachel? Or Christi, I guess I should say."

Cordy smoothed down his slick black hair. *"Nada.* His so-called shop is unlicensed. Lavender only saw him once and said Christi never talked about him. He's one of those Vegas drifters, came from nowhere, going nowhere."

"Well, he had to come from somewhere to land a girl like Christi," Serena said. "We'll head out with a team first thing in the morning. Can you drop us off at my place?"

Cordy raised an eyebrow. "Whatever you want."

Stride deliberately didn't meet Cordy's stare, which was probably an admission of guilt as far as the other cop was concerned.

"You ever been to Vegas?" Cordy asked.

Stride shook his head. "First time."

"A Vegas virgin," Cordy said, chuckling.

Stride sat in the back seat of Cordy's PT Cruiser, staring out the window agog at the parade of mammoth casinos on either side of Las Vegas Boulevard. Cordy didn't want to take the Strip, but Serena insisted, to give Stride a view of the city. They were stalled in bumper-to-bumper Saturday night traffic, crawling between Tropicana and Flamingo. On his left, Serena pointed out, was the Monte Carlo. On the right was the Aladdin. Up ahead was Paris, then the Bellagio, then Bally's. The size of each property overwhelmed him.

He couldn't believe the heat. When they stepped out of the airport, it hit him in the face like a fire, sucking oxygen from his lungs. It was night, but the temperature still hovered near ninety. He could taste desert grit in his mouth with each breath. Fortunately, Cordy had the air conditioner at full power, and it was now cold enough inside the car to make him shiver.

"Greatest city in the world," Cordy said proudly. "Who'd want to live anywhere else? This is the tops, man."

"People live here?" Stride asked, only half seriously.

"Now, now, Jonny," Serena murmured. She glanced back over the front seat and winked at him.

"You know what makes this town tick?" Cordy asked, as he pounded the horn at a limousine cutting in front of him.

"Oh, shit, not the breast thing," Serena said.

As if he hadn't heard her, Cordy explained, "Las Vegas is all about breasts, man."

Stride laughed. "What?"

"Breasts! It's true. You see more breasts in this city than anywhere else on earth, okay? That's what makes it special. That's what gives Vegas its character. It's not gambling, it's not drinking, it's not eighty million hotel rooms. It's walking down the street and having all these breasts quivering like Jell-O in front of you. All shapes. All sizes. Spilling out of everything they wear. Cotton, Lycra, nylon, bikini, tankini, halter, I don't care what, you know? Just so long as it's tight or see-through or shows lots of skin or lets you see their nipples, they'll wear it. Women come here so they can show off their breasts, and all the men walk around so horny they can't see straight."

"Cordy's something of a sociologist of tits," Serena explained dryly.

"Am I wrong? You tell me if I'm wrong."

Serena didn't have a chance to reply. Three women in their twenties, two blondes and a brunette, ran through the stalled traffic in front of them. The brunette passed closest to Cordy's cruiser, and Stride's eyes were drawn instinctively to her chest. She wore a low-cut T-shirt, from which her breasts overflowed. Cordy honked the horn and gave her a thumbs-up. The girl stuck out her tongue at him and wagged it lasciviously.

Serena sighed. "I didn't say you were wrong."

"Uh-huh. Good thing, mama. The only reason this town can put so many strippers through college is that all of the men are so wired from watching the rest of the girls, they'll pay anything to see what's underneath."

Serena just shook her head.

When they passed Flamingo, traffic loosened slightly. Serena pointed out the next wave of megaresorts, stretching from Caesar's at the southern end to the Stardust in the north. As they passed the Mirage, the resort's street-side volcano exploded into action, cascading columns of water, steam, and fire into the air before a crowd of gawkers. He had never seen a city that pulsed with life the way Vegas did. The sensation was electric, watching the streams of people flowing in and out of the casinos and jostling to cross the street. Cordy was right: There were loose, jiggling breasts everywhere, plus the smell of sex, cigarettes, and money.

Even so, Stride noticed that the glitzy aura of the Strip faded quickly the farther north they went. Instead of expensive casinos catering to high rollers, he noticed porn shops and massage parlors, bars with nickel video poker signs, and motels with burned-out neon signs. The crowds of tourists on the sidewalks thinned; most of them were smart enough not to explore these neighborhoods. He saw hookers on every corner, grinning at them from behind garish lipstick and dyed hair. Several homeless people slept in doorways.

"No volcanoes here," he murmured.

Serena shook her head. "We call this the Naked City. And that's not a breast joke. You've got the Stratosphere tower, but all around it, there's more drugs and murder here than anywhere else in the city."

After another mile, they turned off the Strip on Charleston, leaving both the casinos and the Naked City behind them as they headed west. Out here the town looked like any other inner-ring suburb, with strip malls, discount stores, and chain restaurants. They reached Serena's town house complex in less than ten minutes. The gated community was a beehive of bone white, two-story stucco buildings with bright red roofs. Serena waved at the guard, who opened the electronic gate and let Cordy's Cruiser slide in. Cordy, who was obviously familiar with the grounds, navigated a bewildering maze of intersecting roads and driveways, pulling up to a unit at the far back of the complex.

"Home sweet home, mama," he announced.

Stride and Serena recovered their luggage from the trunk. Heat radiated from the pavement. The stiff, dry breeze out of the mountains offered no relief. Stride felt the urge to wipe his brow, but he realized the arid landscape was too dry even for sweat.

"Let's meet here at nine o'clock tomorrow

morning," Serena told Cordy. "Alert the search team to meet us at the site at ten."

Cordy winked at Stride. "You sure you want to stay here? We could hit some clubs I know."

"Good night, Cordy," Serena said.

"But hell, mama, how can you let him stay in your boring town house? It's his first time in the city. The man deserves to have some fun."

"He'll have fun," Serena told him.

48

Morning sun streamed in through the vertical blinds in Serena's bedroom. Stride, long since awake, watched Serena sleep.

She lay on her stomach. Her hair fell loosely across her face. Her arms were tucked under the pillow, leaving the swell of her right breast visible where it pressed against the mattress. Her back sloped downward to the valley at the base of her spine, then rose again at her buttocks. She had one leg under the sheet and one leg above it.

Serena rolled over, and he was treated to the sight of her naked breasts and soft brown nipples. Her eyes blinked slowly, then opened to narrow, unhappy slits, unwilling to face the daylight. She brushed her long hair from her face. "What time is it?" she asked sleepily.

"Late. Almost eight-fifteen."

Serena groaned. "Shit. Cordy will be coming soon."

He moved to touch her breasts, but Serena nimbly slapped his hand. "None of that, Lieutenant. We only have five minutes to shower."

"I can do five minutes," he said.

"Hush." She scrambled out of bed, and his eyes followed her as she retreated into the bathroom. He heard her shout, "Make coffee, okay?"

"Okay."

Naked, he made his way downstairs. He hunted through cabinets and found a mason jar filled with ground coffee. With some difficulty, he figured out how to use her Scandinavian coffeemaker and started it perking, then returned upstairs. Serena was back on the bed, rubbing her damp hair with a towel. Beads of moisture glistened on her bare skin.

"I know what you're thinking, and don't think it," she told him casually.

"How do you know what I'm thinking?"

Her eyes traveled southward, and he looked down. "Oh."

"Yeah, oh. Now get in the shower. I suggest cold water."

When he emerged from the shower, he smelled the aroma of coffee. He didn't see Serena, but a few seconds later, she came back into the bedroom with two steaming cups on saucers in her hands. She was half dressed, wearing bikini panties and a white V-neck tee.

"We better get moving, Jonny. Cordy's always on time."

"So if we're going to do something, we better move fast."

"What you're going to do is get dressed," Serena told him. Then he saw her eyes slide down his body again. She cocked her head. "Can you really do five minutes?"

Stride sat in the backseat of Cordy's Cruiser as they headed south on I-15, leaving the Strip behind and heading into the wasteland. He felt a rush of anticipation. Somewhere ahead of them, on the fringe of a desert road, was a man who knew Rachel after her disappearance. Someone who had seen her in her life after death. Someone who might be able to give him answers to four-year-old questions.

They were also about to meet a man who might have bashed in the back of a young woman's skull and dumped her body in the desert. Serena had retrieved her 9 mm SIG-Sauer pistol from the locked glove compartment of her own car and lodged it securely in a shoulder holster under her loose, waist-length blue jacket. Stride's own Ruger was similarly holstered inside his charcoal sport coat.

Cordy turned off the main highway and kicked up a trail of dust on a frontage road. He pointed down the road a quarter mile, where Stride saw a ramshackle trailer just off the north side. "Down the road, that's him."

"This is where she was found?" Stride asked.

"This is it," Serena said.

Cordy parked the car directly in front of the trailer, leaving the engine running. Serena turned to Cordy and said, "Give us a few minutes with him, okay?"

Stride and Serena both got out. Stride studied the surroundings. The trailer was gray, permanently encrusted with dirt and grit blown from the expanse of desert around it. There was no sidewalk, only a worn path where visitors went to and from the door. He pricked up his ears, listening to a strange cacophony that rose and fell on the wind. It was a grotesque tune, without any rhythm, just a tinkling noise like a thousand children playing with toy bells.

"What the hell is that?" he asked.

"Wind chimes," Serena said. "A lot of them."

Serena led them up the trailer steps, which sagged under their weight. At the screen door, she stopped, banging on the aluminum siding of the trailer. There was no answer, just the singing of the chimes.

On the door, someone had painted the words ALWAYS OPEN. Serena glanced back at Stride, shrugged, and pulled the door open carefully. She stepped inside, with Stride immediately behind her. The noise inside the trailer was deafening. A window in front of them was open, creating a cross breeze that made several dozen stained glass wind chimes spiral and clang against each other in a wild, multicolored dance. They both put their hands over their ears. Serena took two steps and banged the window shut. The breeze died, and slowly the chimes settled down, tinkling softly like a formless music in the background.

Then they heard a voice.

"So you figured it out."

They both spun around. Bob sat at a card table six feet away, in front of a lopsided curtain that separated the shop from the rest of the trailer. A metal cash box sat on the table next to him, its lid open. Bob's T-shirt hung on his skinny frame, and his shorts were several sizes too large. He wore ratty old sneakers.

He had manic eyes, fierce and tiny, like two black holes. He studied them both in turn, first Serena, then Stride. His eyes lingered on Stride, and he squinted as if he saw something in Stride's face that was strange and unexpected. The longer Bob stared at him, the more Stride felt like an insect pinned to a collector's board. The eerie sensation went deeper, because when he stared back, his brain flashed a message. *I know you.*

But the man was a stranger to him.

"What's your name?" Stride asked.

Bob shrugged. "It's on the sign."

"It won't be difficult for us to find out," Serena said.

"No?" Bob asked. "Well, I have no records, I file no taxes, and I've never been fingerprinted. So you tell me how you plan to find out anything about me."

"You sound pretty smart," Serena told Bob. "I expected an old drunk."

Bob scowled and thrust a thumb toward the rear of the trailer. "The gin's in back. It's there in case I chicken out."

"Chicken out?" Serena asked.

Bob rubbed his long beard and pulled at the tangles. He put a finger to his head like a gun and pulled the trigger.

"You're planning to kill yourself?" Serena asked. "Why?"

Bob turned to Stride and smiled darkly, as if sharing a secret joke. "*You* know."

"How would I know?"

"You're a man. Why does a man do anything?"

"A woman," Stride said.

Serena leaned closer to Bob. "Are you talking about Christi?"

Bob's anger subsided, and he looked wistful. His voice cracked as he stared at Serena. "You look a little bit like her. She had green eyes, like you. But hers were cold. She destroyed me. I mean, just look around. Look at my life. But if I could get her back, I'd go through this hell all over again."

Serena's eyes narrowed. "You wanted her that much? She was that good?"

"Not good. She was never *good*. She was evil."

"What was it?" Serena asked. "Did she reject you?"

Bob laughed wildly. "If only it were that fucking simple! It's like having the keys to the palace, okay? And then one day they change the locks. And you look back and realize you gave up everything, destroyed everyone around you, for a *fantasy*."

"When did you see her last?" Serena asked.

Bob waved his hand impatiently. "Don't waste my time. You want to ask me? Ask me."

Stride knew the question he meant. "Did you kill Rachel?"

"Someone had to," Bob said.

"But did *you* do it?" Stride asked again.

"Isn't that what you want me to say? Won't that make it easier for you?"

"We just want to know what happened," Stride said.

Bob flicked a cockroach off the table. It skittered away toward the rear of the trailer. "No, you don't. You already know all you need to know."

"We don't know why," Stride said.

Bob laughed. "It was a game to her. She destroyed people. When you do that, sometimes people destroy you back."

"I think we ought to continue this conversation somewhere else," Serena told him cautiously, reaching for her cuffs. "Why don't you come down to the station with us? We can clean you up, get you a decent meal."

Bob's eyes snapped open with the gleam of a predator. "You don't get off so easy," he snarled at them.

His speed caught them off guard. Bob's left hand dove into the cash box, and with a shout, he leaped to his feet, the chair toppling backward onto the trailer floor behind him. Bob's left hand swung upward out of the cash box, his whole arm a blur of motion. He pointed his arm straight up, almost grazing the roof of the trailer. Stride saw the object clutched in Bob's fingers—a Smith and Wesson revolver with a four-inch barrel.

"Gun!"

Stride and Serena jumped backward,

tumbling into a maze of wind chimes that clattered and then fell around them, shattering on the floor. Stride twisted to his right and slammed his body to the ground. Broken glass cut his hand as his palm scraped the trailer floor. He snaked his bleeding hand inside his jacket and slid the Ruger into his slippery palm. In a single motion, he flipped off the safety and rose to one knee, taking aim at Bob's chest.

Three feet away, Serena did the same. She came up on both knees and steadied her automatic with both hands.

Bob didn't move. He stared them down with a bizarre grin of triumph, his eyes darting between the two detectives like a Ping-Pong ball. The revolver quivered in his hands.

"What are you waiting for?" Bob demanded.

"We don't want to hurt you," Serena told him, her voice steady. "Put down the gun."

"I'm getting out," Bob said. "And you're going to help me."

Stride saw Bob's fingers tighten on the grip of the revolver. Bob lowered his gun arm.

"I'm going to take the shot," Serena called.

"No!" Stride insisted. "Wait! Wait!" He saw his one window on the truth sliding closed.

Bob hadn't cocked the hammer. He wasn't ready to fire. But he was now pointing the black hole of the barrel directly at Stride's head. Stride stared back along the path of Bob's outstretched arms, sighting down the barrel of his pistol. The revolver gaped back at him. Stride's arm twinged where his friend in Ely had shot him. He could hear the sound of that gun in his memory and feel the flesh ripping apart in his shoulder.

"Bob, you're not going to shoot me," Stride told him. "Put it down, and this time you win. You can beat her."

Bob shook his head. "She always wins."

Stride clicked the safety back into place on his Ruger. His fingers loosened, and the gun slipped upside down in his hand. He bent down slowly, laying it on the ground.

"Jonny, what the hell are you doing?" Serena hissed.

"I'm just not going to do it," Stride told Bob.

Bob was silent, hesitating.

Ting-a-ling, ting, ting, went the wind chimes.

"It's not me doing this," Bob said. "It's her. It was always her."

Stride shook his head. "You can't blame

her anymore. She's dead. This time, it's all you. Is that what you want?"

Bob's hand trembled. He exhaled a long, mournful breath, and his muscles seemed to cave in as the air went out of his body. His gun arm sagged, the revolver going limp in his hand.

"Now just lay it on the table. Real easy. Real slow. Okay?"

Stride felt a wave of relief wash over him.

Then Bob's face contorted in panic and fear. His eyes widened as if he were a frightened child. His mouth dropped open, and he took a horrified step backward. He was fixated on something just behind Stride.

"There she is!" Bob wailed.

"Jonny, he's losing it," Serena warned.

Stride knew she was right. Bob was disintegrating.

"There's no one here," Stride told him firmly.

"YOU'RE DEAD!" Bob bellowed.

He swung the revolver up in a single motion, its barrel quivering. His jaw clenched, and he bared his teeth. Bob's thumb flicked to the hammer of the gun.

"Stop!" Serena screamed.

Stride tensed, waiting for Bob to fire, expecting to feel the air sucked out of his chest.

Serena's bullet blew Bob backward onto the floor. The gun spilled harmlessly from his hand. He landed hard, his eyes wide open and terrified. He gurgled, unable to breathe, and foam and blood sputtered from his lips. His whole body twitched, his limbs rocked by spasms.

Serena scrambled from her knees and ran to him.

Bob had enough strength to lift his head off the floor and contemplate the wreckage of his chest and smile. Blood was filling his lungs. He tried to speak, but the words died in a rattle, and his jaw went slack. His eyes flitted between them, his pupils giant and black.

"Cordy!" Serena shouted as the trailer door burst open. "Get an ambulance!"

But they both knew Bob would be gone before they heard the sirens.

Stride realized he was watching the mystery die with him.

He sat in the backseat of Cordy's car, the rear door open, his legs outside. For the first

time in months, he felt the craving for a cigarette, and he rubbed his fingers together as
if one were lit in his hands. He felt a trickle of
sweat on his neck, dripping to the back of his
spine.

Twenty yards away, two internal affairs detectives, looking cool as snakes even under
the relentless sun, grilled Serena about the
shooting. Her beautiful face was stoic—void
of emotion, no hurricane churning inside
her. Stride knew better. He had seen the delayed reaction among cops in Duluth, even
tough veterans who had seen plenty of bodies, all killed by someone else. Firing your
weapon, taking a life, watching someone die
at your hands, was devastating. It sent cops
into therapy. Some left the force.

Then came the second-guessing. People
who weren't there, who hadn't experienced
those terrible moments, felt entitled to question your judgment.

All Stride could do was sit tight and wait
his turn, then tell them what it was. A good
shooting. Unavoidable.

The ambulance had arrived too late to do
anything but attend to the corpse. He
watched as two orderlies maneuvered a
stretcher through the doorway of the trailer.

Bob's body lay beneath a white sheet, with a bloom of red in the center where the blood seeped into the fabric. A dusty breeze erupted from the desert floor, picking up a corner of the death sheet and fluttering it in the air like a flag of surrender.

Stride found himself staring at Bob's bony, lifeless leg and at the old sneaker that clung to his foot. The heel of the shoe winked at him like a bloodshot eye, oval and pink.

In that moment, Stride felt the world grinding to a halt, all the noise and motion winding down like a music box, until he could hear only the raging sound of his breath and feel each beat of his heart thumping like it could break through his chest.

Stride half expected the body to bolt upward from the gurney. He expected Bob to point a skeletal finger at him and cackle like a magician who has seen his audience gape at his latest trick.

But this was no trick. There was no mistaking the sole and the red oval in the center of the heel, worn pale from four years of use. Bob was wearing *Graeme's shoes.*

The shoes that left Graeme's footprints at the barn. The shoes that went missing when Rachel disappeared.

Stride stood frozen, his brain trying frantically to catch up with the reality in front of his eyes.

A moment later, he knew.

It had been a frame-up all along. Rachel stole Graeme's shoes. They were in the plastic bag she carried from the house. And that man—the dead man under the sheet—wore them. He had been there that night in Duluth.

Stride leaped up, running across the crusted ground, startling the attendants with the stretcher. He ripped the sheet down, revealing Bob's face, his dead eyes still wide open.

"Hey, what the hell!" the orderly complained.

Stride felt the man grab his shoulder, and he wrenched away. He bent down, inches from Bob's face. The odor of death, blood, and waste wormed into his nostrils. He stared at Bob, hunting for the truth. *I know you.*

He whirled around, seeing Serena out of the corner of his eye. He could feel her reading his thoughts, seeing his fear. Thank God, she didn't say anything, didn't react. She pulled her eyes away before the other cops turned his way.

Right behind him, a voice said, "You okay, man?"

"Cordy!" Stride hissed. He dragged the young detective away and got in his face. "You said there was an old photograph. Before he looked like this. Do you have it?"

"What, of the dead guy? Sure, sure, man. Lavender gave it to me. Figured we could sweat him with it."

"Let me see it."

Cordy dug a plastic evidence bag out of his loose pants pocket, and Stride grabbed it out of his hand. The glare of the sun blinded him. He squinted and couldn't see through the plastic. Not hesitating, Stride tore it open and threw the bag away.

"Fuck it, you can't—" Cordy began, but stopped when he saw Stride's face.

Stride held the photo as if it were on fire.

"No, no, no, no," he murmured, not believing what he saw, feeling his mind spin out of control, and wishing the dry cracks in the desert earth would split apart and swallow him up.

49

Stride took a sip of cold coffee from a Styrofoam cup. His impatience was growing.

He stared through the floor-length windows and watched tourists wilting in the heat as they scurried between rows of rental cars. The thunder of another plane landing at McCarran rumbled overhead, rattling the walls. He saw the early evening shadows lengthening minute by minute.

The glass door banged. One of the rental agents waddled in, sweating, from the huge parking lot. Her thick fingers clutched a plastic clipboard.

"How long?" Stride called.

The agent stopped and propped her hands on her hips. Her bare ebony midriff ballooned from between powder blue sweatpants and a white concert T-shirt. "Do I look psychic to you? I told you, they were due in two hours ago."

"Do the guys outside know to hold it?" Stride asked. "I don't want them cleaning the car before we get to it."

"Tan Cavalier, Texas plates." She rattled off the license number. "Soon as it comes in, you get first crack at it, honey. So sit tight."

She disappeared into the back office behind the counter.

Serena sat nearby on a metal chair, her elbows propped on her knees. Her black hair fell messily across her face. She pushed herself up wearily and came up behind Stride, kneading the knotted muscles in his neck.

She leaned forward and whispered, "We don't have to do this."

"I do. I need to know."

Serena sighed. "Whatever you want."

Stride knew she was right. It was better to walk away. He knew what they would find when the car came in, and when he had the truth, he would wish he had left the mystery back in the desert to die with Bob.

But he couldn't stop. The photograph had led him here. From the desert to the airport to the rental agency, following the trail that had been left for him. It was so obvious that he wondered if it had all been laid out that way for him to find.

Serena borrowed his cup of coffee, took a drink, and made a face. "Oh, man. Two words for you, Jonny. Star. Bucks."

Stride couldn't help but smile.

"That's better," she said.

"Look, you don't need to worry about me," Stride told her. "I'll be fine. You've got your own shit to deal with."

"You mean, because I killed a guy? Because I just spent six hours reliving it five hundred times with IA? Just a day in the life."

"Ha."

Serena shrugged. "They'll make me talk to a shrink. It'll be like old times. I'll cry later." She looked down at her shoes, which were still dirty with dust and blood. "You want the truth, Jonny? It was easy. Too easy."

Stride didn't need to say anything.

The plus-sized agent emerged from the

office with a walkie-talkie at her ear. "Your car just came in, honey. One of my boys is driving it over here."

Stride felt his insides seize with tension. "What's the routine when a car comes back? Vacuum the interior? Wash the mats?"

"You got it," she said.

"Trunk, too?"

She shrugged. "If someone barfs in it. Which happens, honey."

"And you're sure this is the first rental since it came back last weekend? No one else had it in between?"

"Nobody."

An attendant parked the Cavalier near the rental building a few minutes later, leaving the driver's door open and the engine running. Stride and Serena both put on gloves and went outside. He carried a halogen flashlight from Serena's car, which he directed into the backseat of the Cavalier.

It was clean, no trash, no stray papers. Stride got down on his knees and shined the flashlight carefully under both seats, examining the floor. Then he and Serena spent half an hour studying the fabric on the rear seats, going square inch by square inch, finding nothing.

Stride straightened up. "Let's do the trunk."

"She was probably wrapped in a blanket," Serena reminded him. "It was missing from the bed."

"Blankets leave tracks," Stride said.

It didn't take them long. When they popped the trunk, Stride lit up the interior, and almost immediately he zeroed in on a dime-sized brownish stain on the carpeted fringe. He kept the light on the stain while Serena leaned in and took a closer look.

"Could be blood," she said quietly. Then she added, "I've got something more here."

He watched her reach into a pocket and slide out a tweezers. She extracted something trapped in the metal edge of the trunk, then backed out and held the tweezers in the beam of the flashlight. Stride leaned closer and saw a wispy strand of blonde hair that spiraled down to a jet black root.

"It might be nothing," Serena said. "Lots of dye jobs in this town."

But they both knew what it meant.

"I have to go back," Stride said.

The rental agent waved her clipboard at them from the doorway. "Hey, officers, what's the word? Am I getting my tan Cav back?

Otherwise, I need to find another car, or someone's going to be walking, know what I mean?"

Stride and Serena exchanged a long, sober look. It was her call, but Stride knew there was only one decision she could make. Impound it, call for forensics, bag the evidence, and bring his whole world crashing down.

Serena tore her eyes away. She slammed the trunk and waved at the agent.

"Take it," she said.

50

He found Andrea secluded in her office on the second floor, grading papers amid the tomblike silence of the school. Her door was open. She had her head down, deep in concentration, not having heard his footsteps on the stairs.

He couldn't help but think of the first time he had met her here. They had both been so wounded then, two people suddenly alone after they had envisioned a lifetime with someone else. He had really believed then that he could wash away her hurt, but her bitterness never seemed to fade, no matter how much time they spent together, even after they stumbled into marriage. They had made a mistake. He never imagined how costly that mistake would prove to be.

"Hello, Andrea," he said.

She looked up from the papers on her desk. He wasn't sure what he expected to see in her eyes: fear maybe, or anger, or sadness. Instead, he saw almost nothing, as if in this short time she had become a stranger to him.

"Welcome back," Andrea said evenly. "I didn't expect to see you so soon."

She looked older, although it may have been the lack of makeup on her face. She wore a gray college sweatshirt she had owned for years. Her blonde hair was pinned back away from her face, and she wore half-glasses, pushed down her nose.

"Did you find out?" Andrea asked, a cold edge rising in her voice. "Was it worth it?"

Stride could feel the blame spitting out of her, as if it were his own fault.

He entered the office and sat down heavily in the wooden chair opposite her desk. He hated to tell her.

"He's dead, Andrea."

She sucked in her breath and pushed back sharply from the desk. She stripped off her glasses, and he could see her terrified eyes.

She was waiting for him to say it.

Stride nodded. "Robin."

He almost wanted her to lie, to paste a look of shock on her face at the idea that Robin, her ex-husband, was Rachel's lover.

But there was no surprise. Andrea closed her eyes. "That stupid bastard," she whispered. "How did it happen?"

Stride explained briefly what happened in the trailer. Andrea didn't break down, but a single tear worked its way out of her eye and slid in a streak down her face. He let her grieve in silence for a few seconds before his anger caught up with him. "You knew," he said. "Goddamn it, you knew, and you didn't tell me. You let me go down there, knowing what I'd find."

"I told you not to do it," Andrea retorted, wiping her cheek. "You were the one who couldn't let it go."

"Because that's my job!" Stride said. He got up, pacing, and slammed the office door. He confronted her again. "How long? How long have you known? Did you know back then? We were running around in circles, and you knew Robin had run off with Rachel."

"No, I didn't know!" Andrea insisted. "He left me months before Rachel disappeared. Don't you see? That was how she wanted it. No connection. It was all her, all part of her plan. She told him to come back for her in the fall."

"Then when did you find out? How?"

Andrea stared down at her desk. "He sent me a letter last month."

"And he told you about Rachel?"

"Are you kidding?" Her mouth twitched as if she had bitten into something vile. "Everything was Rachel, Rachel, Rachel. How she seduced him. How she dumped him. The pathetic shit was obsessed with her."

"Where's the letter?"

Andrea hesitated. "I burned it."

"Why?" Stride asked. "Why would you do that?" He suspected he could open her desk drawer and find it there.

"I don't know why, I just did it. I wanted to erase him. I wanted to forget what he did to me."

Stride shook his head. "Now you're lying. Don't lie to me. Robin was obsessed? My God, what about you? He threw you away for a seventeen-year-old, and you still love him."

She didn't deny it. He saw her jaw jutting out in defiance.

"Explain it to me, Andrea," Stride insisted. "He writes you a letter and grinds his affair into you like broken glass. And what do you do? You run to him. You go crawling to him in Vegas and try to get him back."

Now he saw fear.

"I didn't—" she began.

Stride cut her off. "Don't insult me. Do you think I'm stupid? First you beg me not to go, and when I do go, I find your ex-husband drinking himself to death in a trailer. What's my first thought, Andrea? You. I went to the airport. I called the credit card company. I know you flew from your sister's in Miami to Las Vegas last weekend."

"It's not what you think," Andrea told him. "I didn't want him back. But I was scared. His letter talked about suicide. I couldn't sit here and do nothing. That's why I went—to talk to him."

"I don't care about that," he interrupted. "This isn't about you and Robin."

The sudden silence between them was pregnant with anxiety.

"I want to know what happened between you and Rachel," Stride said.

He studied her as if she were a suspect, watching for every flicker of a muscle in her face. He saw what he expected to see.

Guilt.

"I want to know why you killed her."

Andrea was calm. "Do I need a lawyer?"

"You think I'm going to turn you in? You don't know me at all. As far as the police in Las Vegas are concerned, a drifter named Jerky Bob killed Rachel. Case closed."

"How do you know it didn't happen that way?"

Stride exhaled in disgust. "Please, no games, Andrea. Robin would have killed himself before he killed Rachel. We both know that. And you left a trail a mile wide. I tracked down the car you rented. There was blood and hair in the trunk from when you drove Rachel's body out to the desert."

"I wanted him to see her," she said bitterly. "He wanted her so badly. Let him have her."

"Tell me about it," Stride said. "I need the truth."

Andrea nodded. She nervously tucked a

stray hair behind her ear and bit her lip. "I didn't mean for this to happen."

She stood up and came out from behind the desk. She stood close to Stride but didn't look at him. Instead, she stared at photos on the wall. Of her and Stride. Of her and Robin. She kept them up even now.

He smelled tobacco. She was smoking again.

"The letter almost destroyed me, Jon," she said. "I knew you and I were in trouble. I was already dealing with that. Or not dealing with it. And then to hear from Robin and find out what really happened—I just had to see him. I didn't go there to see *her,* for God's sake. That never even crossed my mind. I went to see him."

She turned back to Stride. "You were there. You saw what he was like. I couldn't believe it. I couldn't believe what she'd done to him."

"He did it to himself," Stride said.

"No, this wasn't his fault. Robin was always weak. I knew that about him. And Rachel saw it, too. She used him. He told me how she read his poetry and told him he was such a genius. How she made him believe they were meant for each other. But it was just another lie, and he swallowed all of it. Once Graeme was dead, she threw him out. She just cut him out of her life. She didn't need him anymore. It was like she was ripping his heart out. He started drinking, sliding downhill. He didn't have anything left to live for."

"Tell me about Rachel," he persisted.

"Yes, all right. The crazy thing is, I never planned to see her. Robin told me where she worked, but I didn't care. I wasn't there for her. Robin and I talked for a couple of hours, if you can call it talking. He was too far gone. I couldn't take it anymore."

"So you went to confront Rachel."

"No, it wasn't like that. I was heading back to the airport, coming home. But more and more, I kept thinking about Rachel and what she did to us. To me. It's not like I consciously decided I was going there, but somewhere along the way, I realized I wasn't driving to the airport. I wound up at the club. I just wanted to see her, see what she looked like. Look into her eyes. When she came out onstage, it took me a minute, but I knew. I knew it was her. And she was everything that Robin said she was. Beautiful. And cold as ice.

"That was when I realized it wasn't enough just to see her. I needed her to look at me and admit what she'd done. So I waited in the parking lot and followed her. When I got to her apartment, I almost couldn't go through with it. What do you say to someone you've never met who ruined your whole life? But I thought about Robin wasting away in that trailer, and what our lives had been like, and I got angry all over again."

"Did she recognize you?" Stride asked.

"Oh, yeah. Right away. She laughed. She said If I'd come to take Robin back, I could have him now. And she knew all about the investigation. About me and you. She thought it was funny. 'I caught a husband for you and a murderer for him.' That was what she said. That we should thank her."

Andrea began crumbling.

"I don't know what—I mean, none of it was going the way I wanted. She had no regrets, no shame. She stared at me with those horrible green eyes like I was an insect. Something to play with and then swat away."

Stride saw Andrea's hands trembling. He wasn't sure how far he could push her before she lost control entirely. "What else did she say?" he asked.

"She lied," Andrea retorted, balling her fists. "All she did was lie."

"Lie about what?"

"About everything! I told her she had no right to break us up. Robin loved me." Her eyes narrowed to slits, almost reptilian. "And do you know what she said? She said Robin was going to divorce me anyway. He was so fucking easy to seduce because he could barely keep it up in bed with me. Making love to me was like humping a corpse. I couldn't get pregnant, because there was nothing alive between my legs."

"Son of a bitch," Stride murmured.

"That's when I knew. She wasn't lying. It was all true. I'd been the one lying to myself all along. About Robin. About myself. So I stood there, with this rage bubbling over like nothing I'd ever felt before, and all she could do was smirk at me. Like my life was a joke to her. Like everything she'd taken from me meant nothing."

"What did you do?" Stride asked quietly.

"There was a vase on the bookshelf. I

grabbed it, swung it. I wanted it to shatter. I wanted glass flying all over the apartment. But I didn't let go. I hung on to it, and it hit something. My eyes were closed. I didn't even know what I'd done. But I hit something, and then there was this heavy sound, of something falling . . ."

Stride had heard these stories too many times, from people he had arrested, from defendants pleading for mercy. He had hardened his heart to them. But not this time.

"She was dead. I couldn't believe it, but she was dead. I had killed her."

"Rachel's been dead a long time," he murmured.

Andrea stared at him, her eyes pleading. "I never expected you to be pulled back into this, Jon. You have to believe that. I never thought anyone would make the connection to Rachel."

Stride knew there was no gray area here. If they were in court, she would be guilty. But it occurred to him that Andrea wasn't entirely responsible. Neither was Robin. He, too, had to bear some of the blame. Maybe that was why he knew he could never give up the secret. Who would it satisfy?

"What now?" Andrea asked.

Yes, what now? he asked himself.

"Now we both have to live with it."

"I know what a difficult thing this is for you to do," she whispered. "To walk away."

"The truth is, it isn't difficult at all. I guess that should tell me something."

He was anxious to go now, to say good-bye, to be alone with his own guilt. But he knew he needed to tell her something, to give her something to hang on to. So that the past wasn't entirely a lie.

"Robin knew you killed Rachel," he told her, as he turned to leave. "He took the fall. He wanted us to blame him. That was for you, Andrea. He did it for you."

Stride realized he had nowhere to go. He was homeless in his own hometown.

He wound up on the bridge over the canal, standing where Rachel had stood on her last night in the city. Before she went home and planted evidence in Graeme's van. Before she stole Graeme's shoes. Before she met Robin waiting for her on a back street and lured him to the barn to play their little game.

Chase her into the meadow. Cut her clothes. Cut her skin. Blood. Fabric. Clues.

I played right into their hands, he thought.

Stride stared into the dark water, which barely stirred tonight under the cool lake breeze. He took hold of the railing with both hands and imagined Rachel balancing there. If a gust of wind had pitched her into the frigid canal that night, his life would be very different today. Better or worse, he didn't know.

At least he knew Rachel's secrets. Except for one. He still didn't know why.

Why the game. Why the bitter war between Graeme and Rachel. It surprised him that Rachel hadn't left a clue, when she had dropped a trail of bread crumbs for everything else. Unless the cryptic postcard was her message to him. *He deserved to die.*

Stride turned and leaned against the railing, watching the cars come and go between the city and the Point. He reconstructed the timeline in his head, now that he knew Robin was the missing link. He thought about Rachel sitting in Robin's class in September. Launching her plot.

I caught a husband for you and a murderer for him.

He was closing in on something. He could feel the confusion in his brain clearing, like fog on the lake.

Stride heard the whine of tires striking the steel deck of the bridge. He was startled to see a red Volkswagen speeding from the Point, with a dark-haired girl behind the wheel. She grinned at him as she roared by. He had a wild thought that it might be Rachel. Even knowing she was dead, he thought she could find a way to haunt him.

But it wasn't Rachel's car. It wasn't . . .

. . . the Blood Bug.

Stride suddenly could see through the fog. And he knew. Rachel had been sending him a message all along.

51

Eleven hundred feet in the air, atop the saucerlike crown of the Stratosphere tower, the temperature was a comfortable fifteen degrees cooler than the Strip below. When Stride stepped out onto the open-air observation platform, he felt a disconcerting vibration under his feet as the tower swayed with the turbulent air. He had never been particularly afraid of heights, but being so far up, on what felt like an exposed catwalk, was enough to make him dizzy.

"Try the tower," Cordy had told him.

Serena once told Cordy that when she couldn't sleep, she sometimes drove to the

Stratosphere and spent a few hours staring out at the city.

In the three weeks Stride had been gone, they had talked occasionally by phone, but he still wondered if the electricity would be there when they saw each other again. He worried that the few days they had spent together would already have been eclipsed in her mind.

Looking out on the panorama of Las Vegas, he asked himself if he could come to like this town, which was so unlike anything he had known. It was hard to take a creature of the wilderness and drop him in the neon jungle. But he wasn't sure he wanted to live in Duluth anymore. He had done his time, enough for a full pension, and this was his chance to make a break with the past. Plus, as of last week, he had learned that Maggie was pregnant and that her husband had prevailed upon her to hang up her shield. The prospect of doing his old job without her seemed empty.

He found he could walk by the edge and look down without a sense of vertigo. He followed the platform to his right, which led him on a course overlooking the eastern half of the city, free of the long stretch of glittering casinos. As he made his way to the south side, he saw the hypnotic grandeur of the Strip, jutting into the desert like a bent laser beam. At first, he saw only a dazzling ribbon of colors, devoid of detail. But the more he stared, the more he found himself focusing on individual details, like the emerald glow of the MGM Grand or the superstructure of the faux Eiffel Tower at Paris. He was so taken by the view that he spent several moments before realizing that he wasn't alone.

Serena stood a few feet away, watching him with a smile. She wore black jeans and a white mock turtleneck. He couldn't help but remember that Rachel was wearing almost the same outfit on the night she disappeared. With her black hair and athletic body, Serena must have looked very much as Rachel did then, atop the bridge over the canal. It gave him a little bit of sympathy, understanding how easily Robin, Graeme, Kevin, and everyone else could have been seduced by Rachel. Serena, with the same beauty, had that kind of power over him.

Why does a man do anything? Robin asked. *A woman.*

With a quiet grace, she came and put her arms around his back and pressed her cool cheek tenderly against his face, which was flushed and warm. He reached up and stroked her dark hair. Holding her felt natural, as if they had been doing it for years. He never wanted to let go, and for a long while, it felt as if they never would. They could stand there, wrapped around each other in the breezy night, forever. The electricity was still there, as vibrant as it had been at the start.

"You came back," she said, with a hint of surprise in her voice.

"I told you I would."

"I know. But promises don't always mean a lot in this city."

He let go and studied her, becoming familiar with her face again. "You looked good on television," he said.

Serena grinned. "You're such a charmer."

Two of the Minneapolis network affiliates had sent reporters to Las Vegas to do stories about Rachel's death. They interviewed Serena and Cordy, took footage inside and out at the strip club where Rachel had worked, and did live feeds from the open spot in the desert where Robin's trailer had been parked. The broken-down trailer had already been towed to the junk yard and its pest-ridden contents burned.

The television crews had no photograph of Jerky Bob to put on the air. Stride had seen to it that the only known photograph was lost during the investigation. So it was up to Serena to describe him, which she did. He was a vagrant. A nowhere man. There were a lot of them in Vegas, most of them mentally ill, and this one had nursed an obsession until it grew violent. Rachel had the bad luck to be the girl he couldn't let go.

That was her story, and she was sticking to it.

"They picked up your line, you know," Stride said. " 'Rachel Killed By "Nowhere Man" ' That was the headline in the paper."

"I like it."

"So what if it isn't true," he murmured.

"We talked about this," Serena said. "You had to protect her."

He placed his hands gingerly on the shield that prevented jumpers and peered downward, feeling dizzy again at the height. Serena joined him, laying a hand on his back.

"What else could you do?" she asked.

"I know. But I'm sorry I put you in the middle of it. I made you lie for me."

"That was my choice," Serena told him. She saw he was ready to say more, and she put a finger over his lips. "It's over and done, Jonny. End of story."

"Not quite the end," he said.

He took a breath and thought about how to tell her the rest. He still blamed himself for not seeing the truth earlier, even though it would have made no difference. The deed was done.

Serena watched him, waiting.

"There's still the relationship between Rachel and Graeme," he said. "Something happened—something that made them blood enemies."

"We know they were having sex," Serena said. "Rachel wanted to stop. Graeme didn't. I've been there, Jonny. If he raped her, or if he tried to, that's enough to make a girl like Rachel get revenge."

"Yes, it is. But Graeme got his revenge first."

Graeme watched his hand tremble as he held a glass of brandy up to the light. He brought the drink to his lips and took a

sip, hoping the alcohol would settle his nerves. The fumes filled his nose, and the brandy burned his dry throat. He swirled the liquor in the glass and took another swallow. But the quivering in his fingers refused to be quieted. He felt his desire rise.

Emily was at a church retreat in St. Paul. Rachel was in her room, waiting, knowing he would come. Graeme put the brandy down and slipped up the steps and down the hall to her bedroom door. He moved stealthily, measuring each step on the carpet to avoid a creak that would alarm her. A light came from under the door. He pictured Rachel on her bed, staring up at the ceiling with her head on the pillow. Thinking about the many times they had made love.

He twisted the knob silently and pushed. The door was locked.

"Rachel," he called out, just loud enough for her to hear. "You know how much I need you."

Nothing. She was inside, listening, but not saying a word.

"We're made for each other, Rachel," he told her. "You can't run away from that. We're like two sides of the same soul."

He knew she was there. The lingering silence began to erode his control. He found himself clenching and unclenching his fists and breathing harshly through his nose.

"Open the door, Rachel," he insisted, his voice quavering. "I promise I won't hurt you. But I need to talk to you."

His promise was a lie, and they both knew it. If she opened the door, he wouldn't be able to control himself. He needed to touch her and be inside her, whatever it took. The thought of her naked body made him sweat and tremble with longing.

"Rachel!" he shouted, anger creeping into his voice. He pounded the door with his fist, unable to restrain himself. "I need you!"

He threw his shoulder against the door with a jarring thud. He was willing to break it down to get inside. But it was a solid old house, and the oak door didn't budge.

"Let me in!" he screamed.

He laid his cheek against the door and

listened. Rachel's voice, when it came, was so close it startled him. She was right on the other side of the door, separated from him by only an inch of heavy wood.

"I'll let you in if you want, Graeme," Rachel said. Her voice was like honey, without the slightest hint of emotion or venom. "If you need to rape me, you can rape me."

"I won't," he murmured.

"It's all right, Graeme. I understand. You have needs."

"Yes," he told her. "Yes, I need you so much. I want it to be like it was."

"And I'm telling you that you can have me."

He hardly dared to breathe. The thought of making love to her again overwhelmed him. "You'll let me?"

"I will. But let me tell you what will happen then."

Something in Rachel's tone made his flesh creep with unease.

"If you come inside and touch me again, I'm going to take a butcher knife to you, and I'm going to cut off your balls. Got it? And then I'm going to cut off your cock. That's a promise. Are you listening? Do you understand? You'll never sleep another night in this house without wondering when I'm going to dismember you. And don't even think about having your little darling reattached. Because once I cut it off, I'm going to flush it down the toilet where it belongs."

Graeme sank to his knees, terrified. Nausea gripped his stomach.

"Do you believe me, Graeme?" Rachel asked. "Do you believe I'll do it?"

He tried to talk but choked on the words.

"I can't hear you, Graeme."

"Yes, yes, I believe you!"

And he did.

"So tell me, do you still want to come inside?" Rachel asked.

Graeme fled without answering her. He had never felt so destroyed. She had proved once again that she was the one who held the real power. He returned downstairs and paced in the den, adrift. The trouble was that he was still enormously aroused. His penis was rock hard, and his desire for her was so strong that he wanted to go back upstairs and

fuck her anyway, even knowing the consequences. But he knew Rachel wasn't
lying. She would do to him exactly what
she promised.

He felt himself drawn toward something ugly and familiar, like a star caught
in the inexorable gravity of a black hole.
He told himself that he wanted to pull
away, but the truth was that he needed it,
wanted it, would do anything for it. He
tried to be calm, but his fingers were jittery again, and sweat gathered at his
armpits and on his skin like a clammy
film. He felt something stirring in his
soul, a door opening, a shadowy figure
awakening.

Please, no, he pleaded with the monster inside.

But it wasn't listening. It played with
him like a child with a doll, making his
limbs move and telling him what to do.

Rachel, this is your fault.

"Go," the monster rumbled, sounding
so unlike a monster, so like himself.

Sounding so . . . immoral.

Graeme grabbed his keys and went out
through the front door. The air was fragile. On an August night, it shouldn't have

been dark so early, but the shroud of storm clouds overhead left the western sky almost black. The shifting wind made the oak branches whip angrily.

He made it almost to the detached garage before realizing the way was blocked. Rachel had parked directly across the two doors, trapping his van inside. Graeme cursed. When he glanced up at her bedroom window overhead, he saw her standing there, watching him with an icy smile. The very glimpse of her set his pulse racing. But he scowled, stretching his face muscles tight. His eyes were furious black dots. He kicked her rear fender, hard enough to leave a dent.

He stood outside, thinking furiously. Raindrops began to leave dark splotches on his clothes. Then he had an idea. The thought of it made him grin up at Rachel in the window. She frowned, reading his mind.

He stormed back into the house and panted as he ran up the stairs. In his bedroom, he rifled through Emily's dresser, dumping jewelry cases and cosmetics on the floor. He pawed to the far back of the drawers, groping through the mess. Finally, he heard a jangle as his fingers touched them. He pulled them out, his excitement growing. Emily's old spare keys.

He snatched them up and ran back outside, slamming the door shut behind him. He looked back up at Rachel's window, but she was gone. At the car, he fumbled with the keys. The rain made his fingers slippery, and he dropped them on the driveway. He bent down, grabbing the key ring, and shoved one key into the lock. It turned. The car door opened.

Nervous, Graeme looked around. He was alone.

"Drive," the monster growled. "Hunt."

He gripped the wheel so fiercely that it grew sticky from the sweat on his palms. Nuisance rain spat on his windshield, a mist that the wipers couldn't seem to wipe away. He sought out the back roads. His need was even more urgent being in the car, where the smell of Rachel was everywhere. She might as well have been seated next to him, teasing him with her cold green eyes. The memory of having sex with her was so intense he could still feel her fingers gliding over his skin.

"Hunt."

He headed uphill from Lakeside, quickly leaving the developed areas behind him as he climbed. Within five miles, he was driving through a deserted stretch bordered closely by stands of birch trees on either side of the highway. It was now pouring and completely dark, forcing him to slow down and peer through his headlights to see.

He drifted onto the right-hand shoulder. At the last second, he made out a girl jogging on the shoulder, directly ahead of him, distinct from the shadows of the trees. He braked and swerved the wheel sharply to steer around her, catching a glimpse of fear in the girl's eyes as she saw the car and dove off the road to avoid it.

Graeme pulled off and stopped, leaving the motor running. He hurried back and found the girl picking herself up and brushing dirt and mud from her skin. Her features were difficult to distinguish in the darkness, but she appeared to be about Rachel's age, with long chestnut hair tied in a ponytail. She had an athletic build and was dressed in tight shorts and a sports bra.

"I'm so sorry," Graeme said. "Are you all right?"

The girl took a few steps, favoring one ankle. "I'm okay. Probably just a sprain."

His eyes adjusted enough for him to make her out more clearly. She was young and very attractive, with a sweet vulnerability as she perched gingerly on her good ankle, strands of hair falling loose from her ponytail, her clothes and skin soaked by the rain.

"Come on, let me drive you home," Graeme said, holding out an arm to help her walk.

He smiled, reassuring her, hating himself for what he was doing. It's not me. It's the monster. There's a difference.

She took his arm, steadying herself. He was conscious of her touch. Her body was close enough to envelop him in an aroma of sweat and rain. He unlocked and opened the rear door, taking a quick glance up and down the deserted road.

"Why don't you sit in back so you can keep your ankle elevated?" he suggested.

The girl scooted inside. He leaned in, watching her get settled. The dome light illuminated her, sitting with her head propped against the opposite window. Her moist face had a rosy glow from her long run. Her eyes were bright. She stretched out her right leg on the seat and let the other dangle on the floor of the car. He saw her muscled calves and thighs and traced the Lycra where it met in a V at her crotch. Her chest rose and fell with her heavy breathing, and he watched her breasts swell. She smiled shyly.

"I'm getting the seats all wet," the girl said.

"It's all right," Graeme replied. He let the moment linger a little too long, and her smile eroded into a nervous laugh. A hint of uncertainty clouded her eyes. Suddenly, he felt that she could see through him and recognize his intentions.

Graeme shut the door and climbed into the front seat. He looked back and gave her a winning smile. "I have to make one stop, then we'll head back to town. Okay?"

"Oh. Sure." The girl bit her lower lip. He could see questions forming in her mind and the first glimmer of fear.

Put her at ease.

"I'm Graeme," he said. "What's your name?"

"Kerry," the girl said, squeezing some of the dampness from her hair. "Kerry McGrath."

Serena's eyes were lost somewhere, focused beyond the city. He knew it was Graeme she could see in her brain. Trolling the back roads, hunting the way a tiger hunts. Graeme, coming upon an innocent teenage girl whose only sin was to go running at the wrong time and in the wrong place.

"Are you sure?" she asked.

Stride took a deep breath and nodded. "Graeme killed Kerry. Rachel knew. That was the beginning."

"But after Rachel disappeared, your team went over Graeme's van with a microscope. It's hard to believe he didn't leave something behind."

"He did," Stride said. "We were just looking in the wrong place."

Serena's brow furled in confusion. Then she exhaled in disgust as she put it together. "That son of a bitch. He used Rachel's car."

"Exactly," Stride said. "That was what we missed all along. I remember listening to the testimony at Graeme's trial and thinking there was something I hadn't caught. It was right there in front of me, and I never made the connection. Kevin and Emily both testified about Graeme buying Rachel a new car to replace the old hand-me-down from her mother. I should have recognized the timeline—the red VW, purchased almost immediately after Kerry disappeared. And what did Rachel call it? The Blood Bug. Oh, yeah, she knew. She was going to pay him back—her way."

"Did you trace the car?" Serena asked.

"We did. We tracked down the new owners in Minneapolis. We found a strand of hair and minute traces of blood in the backseat that we matched to Kerry and semen we matched to Graeme. I told the McGraths. They were pleased to learn that, in an odd way, justice had already been served. At least they know now that Kerry's killer didn't get away."

"Were there any others?" Serena asked.

"You know how it is. These guys don't usually do it just once. We're looking into other missing teenagers that could be linked to Graeme."

Serena hugged herself and shivered, but when Stride looked at her face, he realized she wasn't cold. She rubbed the flesh of her arms, as if trying to wash away a stain.

"I'm not sure there's so much difference between me and Rachel," she said. "I was abused, too. I wanted revenge."

"Rachel wasn't completely innocent," Stride reminded her. "She was playing a dangerous game."

"Don't judge her too harshly, Jonny. Until you've been alone with the monster, you don't know what you'll do." She shivered again, glancing over her shoulder. "I feel haunted."

"I don't believe in ghosts," Stride said.

Or did he?

For all he knew, they were surrounded by ghosts, pushing and shoving to get past them on the narrow platform. There were good spirits, like Cindy, whispering that he had done the right thing by falling for Serena, and spirits in limbo, like Rachel, smiling in dark irony at all the profound changes she had wrought in his life. Maybe there were evil spirits, too, like Graeme, raising gooseflesh on Serena's skin and making her as scared as the girl she was when she was alone with her own monster.

Stride lifted Serena's chin to stare into her soulful green eyes. With the back of his hand, he caressed the soft skin on her cheek. He tried to be strong for her, a man who would dispel her nightmares, someone she could walk next to, or lean on, whichever she chose. As they stared at each other, her face softened, and the fear fled. At that moment, he knew they were alone on the roof of the world, without any spirits at all except their own.

"There are no ghosts," he told her firmly, wanting her to believe him.

Serena's lips turned upward in a smile. "I have no right to ask you this," she said, "but it would be nice if you could stay here a while."

"I was thinking that, too."

She leaned into him and kissed him, moving her mouth passionately. Below them, the city glowed.

"Welcome to Vegas, baby," she murmured.

ACKNOWLEDGMENTS

Many people made this book a reality. To Ali Gunn in London and her wonderful team at Curtis Brown—Carol Jackson, Diana Mackay, Tally Garner, Stephanie Thwaites, and many more—thanks for all your passion in supporting my book and my career. And the same thanks to Deborah Schneider in New York. You all changed my life.

Marion Donaldson at Headline and Jennifer Weis at St. Martin's Press have been the most passionate, thoughtful editors that any author could hope for.

Robert Bond, London's finest intellectual

property attorney, is the man who knows everyone. Thanks, Robert. Alison, if I haven't told you before, that spreadsheet of yours is a great idea.

Novelist Ron Handberg and his editor, Jack Caravela, provided guidance that helped me at a crucial phase of editing.

To my many wonderful friends at Faegre & Benson—and in particular the readers among the lawyers and staff who encouraged me—I'm very grateful. You're a terrific team. To my good friends and readers in the Twin Cities business community—Tony Carideo, Jay Novak, Lynn Casey, and many others—thanks for all your good wishes and good ideas.

A special word of thanks to two mentors in my life: Joyce Bartky, who told me to sit in a corner and write; and the late Tom McNamee, whose wisdom and advice changed my career in ways that led me to where I am today.

To Barb and Jerry, for taking such good care of Disney when we had to be away. To Janean, for reading all my earlier works and waiting patiently (sort of) for a copy of this one. To Janice, for your guidance and insight. To Keith and Judy, those crazy English. You're all wonderful friends.

The people of Duluth will have to forgive me for the evil deeds I have written into their beautiful city. (I'm sure the people of Las Vegas are used to it.)

Finally, and most important, I owe my success to my wife, Marcia, who has always believed in me through more than twenty years together, and to my family: my parents, brother, cousins, aunts, and uncles, who are still cheering me on, and those like Bea, Frank, Jo, and Neal, who are smiling down from above.

www.bfreemanbooks.com

If you want a little more of the stories behind the characters in this book, go to my Web site at www.bfreemanbooks.com. I have posted some bonus flashbacks.

While you're there, feel free to send me an e-mail to let me know how you liked the book. I will do my very best to reply to all letters. You can also use the Web site to send information about the book to your friends. And you can register for my mailing list to receive a notice when my next book is in stores and get a sneak preview.

THE UNDERGROUND RAILROAD

When Joseph told me about Teresa's phone call, and about their meeting that night in the sculpture garden, I couldn't help but think of my own brief encounter with her the month before. I didn't know then what was starting. Or perhaps I did. Perhaps I picked up enough of the clues to be less than surprised.

I often run away to the wilderness of Black Oak Park, the great forest which looms near our small town and seems sometimes to possess it. There I sketch, paint and think in solitude. Sometimes, wandering higher and higher, I fantasize that this time I will not return. But these are fleeting things, longings, yearnings. Most of the time, really, it is glorious to be alive.

On one of my excursions to the park I saw Teresa. I had hiked alone until the afternoon was almost gone, through the quiet of the thickest forest, to the point where a small meadow led to Octavia Lake. The view there near sunset, the expanse of blue water with the hills framed behind it, never failed to seem alive to me. That day it was, alive with childish laughter. My first sight from the trees was a young boy, seven or eight, running by the shore with his hair jumping up and down, his mouth hanging in a silly smile. I followed him and watched him run up to his mother, who knelt down, beaming, and pressed her nose against his.

I knew her, of course (in Black Oak everyone knows everyone). But I had rarely spoken to her and surely never seen her in this light. Teresa Benton's reputation ran before her, an oddity, a newcomer, although that could be quietly said about anyone not born here. She had no real friends (at least none shared with me), but she did have Blake Benton as a husband, plus a son from a previous marriage. No one seeing her here would have supposed she needed much more.

Teresa took her son's hand and guided him to the edge of the lake, where she crouched down and pointed out across the water to where a heron was lifting off, its wings curved into a giant arch. The boy squealed with excitement, then covered his eyes as the bird flew closer and closer. It rose higher and disappeared far above me. I saw the boy crouch in the sand and pry up a flat rock, then skip it twice, three times across the surface of the lake. Teresa clapped and laughed.

She wandered away as her son continued to dig up rocks from the beach. I saw her run both hands through her hair. In those moments, I thought I had rarely seen someone look so free, as if her vision of the hills were much grander than my own idle fantasies, as if indeed she might scoop her child up and dance away. Here was someone I would paint, her black hair messy and flowing in the breeze, her billowing dress a splash of yellow. I even felt an odd pang of envy, staring at a different life from my own and wondering—was it more intense? Did she see or do or feel things I did not? Even odder, I remember thinking, one day she will flee. Escape, like my idle dreams.

When a cold wind blew through the forest down to the lake, I shivered. Teresa looked up, not seeing me in the shadows. She stared over the swaying treetops at the sky, to where the sun had now vanished and left a deepening, darkening blue.

The universe seemed to close in on us. This would be the moment, I imagined, for a ghost to appear. A timely thought, because just then I heard a noise and turned to see something in the blackness move thirty yards away. No ghost, though—a man, stepping into the waning light of the clearing. The specter was Blake Benton, one of the few physicians in town (just as Joseph was one of a few lawyers), and more important now, Teresa's husband.

Blake stood well over six feet, with wavy blond hair and intense blue eyes, a contrast to the clipped black cut and medium build my husband Joseph carried. I had coveted him once (every girl had) a very long time ago, when my imagination ran wilder than my reason. That fire left no sparks at all. I knew, though, that several local women felt cheated three years ago when Blake married Teresa, a stranger who had seemingly wandered off a train and into his arms. Very romantic. But not popular to steal the most eligible bachelor in a small town.

I felt guilty eavesdropping. As Blake approached Teresa from behind, I expected him to slip up quietly, put his arms around her, startle her and kiss her. Teresa spoiled his surprise. Some instinct caused her to turn, and she saw her husband a few feet away. A strange moment. It may have been the shock, not to be alone in such a desolate location, but Teresa recoiled, her small body seeming to shrink even further as I watched her. Even the relief and relaxation I waited for did not come. I was not close enough to see her eyes, but something had gone awry. Her son froze, too, not moving a muscle, a rock still lodged in his hand where he had been about to toss it. Then voices. I couldn't hear words, only fading tones like whispers. What was happening here?

I didn't understand. I stared in utter confusion at all three of them, as if watching a play that had taken a bizarre twist. None of the emotions matched my expectations. Instead here was tension, anger, fear, all simmering and bubbling to the surface. It made no sense. Their whispers became like arrows or guns, and the more I looked, the more I saw Teresa wilt, losing her spirit. And still her son never moved, afraid maybe that one word, one motion, would cause a catastrophe. But what?

For a while I was paralyzed, too. But I could not stay that way. Suddenly I knew it was very important that those people not be alone. I was witnessing something intimate, and intimacy here bore a danger I didn't fathom. Everyone had to put on a mask again. So I plastered a smile on my face and burst from the trees: "Hello!"

I don't know if they welcomed or resented me, but just as I thought, the tension melted. They all smiled like nothing had happened here. Was I wrong? I looked for an answer in Teresa's eyes, but she wouldn't look at me. She turned away after a murmured greeting, bowed her head, and hurried to her son.

It left a mystery lingering in the back of my mind. Then Joseph called, and the mystery finally made sense. Or did it only begin again?

Joseph entered the sculpture garden from the southwest. The garden formed an enormous wheel, two paths cutting across it, another path stretching in a circle around the inner grounds. Each spoke ended at the fountain, a fabulous complex bordered by porpoises spouting at frogs, surrounding a reef where a well-endowed mermaid lay perennially bathed by geysers spraying up from hidden crevices in the rocks.

He passed through a mythological gallery, watched by nymphs and gods and deer. Their frozen alabaster brooded in the pale moon glow, faces profiled in silhouette, arms pointing into the skeletal bushes of early spring. They had all been captured in motion, as if trapped by a spell that would one day relent and allow them to re-awaken. Joseph, no dreaming romantic, shivered when he saw a shadow detach itself from the cluster of statues ahead of him. Coming closer, he realized this was the person he had come to meet.

Standing nervously by the fountain was the woman whose voice, half-weak, half-whispered, had drawn him here. Her hands clutched a white purse, held in front of her like a shield. She had a black leather coat draped over her shoulders. Under it Joseph saw a silk lavender blouse and a simple blue skirt. She was slim and small, a wisp of a woman, but as attractive as she was frail, with dark hair past her shoulders and warm brown eyes. Her face had the sculpted narrow lines of any of the more striking goddesses erected in the gardens. Behind her, wild waters danced.

"Hello, Mr. Birch," the woman said quietly. Her voice echoed like a soft bell, barely audible over the rush of the fountain. "I appreciate your coming here on so little notice, with so little explanation. My name is Teresa Benton."

Joseph nodded. "I know. You're Blake's wife."

He had picked the wrong introduction. Teresa's brown eyes widened, and she tripped over her words. "Oh, you know my husband?"

"Black Oak is a small town," Joseph said. "You knew me enough to call me. I know you enough to know who you are. But that's all."

"I see. Even in three years, I guess I haven't adjusted to the ways of a town instead of a city."

Joseph smiled. "Still you knew that coming openly to my office wouldn't go unnoticed."

"That's true," Teresa admitted.

"But in some ways it's riskier if anyone wanders by. So maybe you should tell me how I can help you."

Teresa closed her eyes and nodded slowly. Joseph felt guilty, as if even this slight pressure had been too much. But when Teresa focused her eyes on him again, she had become calmer and stronger. She had come this far, and she had chosen to see it through. "Can I trust you, Mr. Birch?"

Joseph reached out, placing a firm hand on her shoulder. "Let's sit down." He guided her to a cast-iron bench, its back shaped to form the pattern of two black roses. When they had sat down on the cold metal, Joseph took one of Teresa's hands. Her palm was warm. "I can see that something has you frightened and concerned. I hope I'll be able to do something for you. But regardless, what you tell me now is between us."

His sensitivity convinced her. Teresa smiled. Slipping out from her anxious features came her bewitching beauty again. He felt her whole soul reaching out to him, investing in him her hopes and desires. The sudden rush of emotion in her face disconcerted him, so complete was the change.

She had an overwhelming need to believe in someone.

"That's a great relief," she murmured. "I've thought about calling you for a long time." Teresa glanced off at the fountain. "Does she look free to you, that mermaid? She's not, you know. I come here when I can, when I'm not in the big park, and sit and watch her. She's trapped there, no less than me."

"I'm afraid I don't understand," Joseph said.

Teresa nodded sadly. "Mr. Birch, I need to divorce my husband."

"I see."

"I never thought I'd be saying this."

"A divorce can be amicable, if both parties realize it's inevitable," Joseph said. "And even in the messy ones, for all the pain, eventually you come out on the other side."

"It's not so simple, I'm afraid." She stood up restlessly, mesmerized by the jets of water again. Teresa unlatched her purse and slid out a photograph. She handed it to Joseph, who saw a picture of a boy, perhaps four years old, playing in a swing, his hair flying.

"That's Bobby. My son. He'll be eight next

month now. That was taken a few years ago."

"He looks like a sweet boy."

"Yes, he is. He's the reason I have to do this. If it were just me, I would probably stay. But for Bobby..."

Joseph watched her, not interrupting. Her thoughts and emotions spilled out randomly, like cards plucked from a deck, some high, some low. She seemed to be watching her life in her mind's eye, a sad old movie, played over and over again.

"Three years ago, I thought I was saved. Finding Blake lifted me out of a black hole. My first husband had died, you see, and I had never held a real job. We had hardly any savings, and when it ran out—well, we were on the edge." She held up two bent fingers, a fraction of an inch apart. "This close, that's how near it was. This close to giving it all up. We were homeless, drifting."

"How did you meet Blake?" Joseph asked.

"Bobby and I were on a train. Someone had given me a little money. I heard them call the Black Oak station, and I knew about Black Oak Park, you see. That vast, wonderful space. I knew nothing about the town or anything else, just the park. On the spur of the moment, I decided I wanted to see it. And it was wonderful. Bobby and I spent hours by the lake, on the trails, wandering everywhere. But then I tripped and broke my ankle."

Teresa smiled, finding something ironic in the event—either her own carelessness, her luck, or the way simple things changed lives.

"Bobby had to run and get help. They carried me out and took me to a doctor."

"Blake."

"Yes. I was in desperate need, and I guess a star guided me to Blake, or that's what I thought then. He must have sensed I had no way to pay him, and nowhere to go."

Joseph could understand Blake's realization, because he had already felt Teresa's great need himself. She projected a sweet, vulnerable sensuality, an odd paradox.

"At first it was wonderful," she continued. "I needed help, he offered it. For the first few months, I thought we were the perfect couple, that I had finally re-captured part of what I had lost when my first husband died. The trouble was, as I got my confidence back, Blake resented it. I began to realize he wanted me weak and helpless, that as long as that was the role I played, he would lavish his love on me. And that's what I did, as long as I could, but the net just kept tightening. I couldn't go anywhere without him being jealous and suspicious. He would throw rages, go into strange fits. And worse." She stopped and looked away.

Joseph frowned. "This is difficult to ask, but do you have any proof to back up your story? Witnesses? Anything else?"

Teresa hesitated. She began to undo the buttons of her blouse. She stopped at the base of her bra and pulled aside one of the lavender folds. On the pale swell of her breast, rising and falling with her breath, Joseph saw a thin line of scar tissue. He glimpsed, too, a slim crescent of the dark half-moon of her nipple above the lacy fringe of her bra.

"He smashed a plate," Teresa explained as she fixed her blouse. "One of the pieces flew out and cut me."

"Is there more?" Joseph asked quietly. "Other physical evidence?"

Teresa nodded. "Yes. Other nights, other scars. Or bruises. They go away, of course, on the outside anyway."

"How long has this been happening?"

"Well, it keeps getting worse. It started with a few isolated incidents about a year ago. It's every week now, sometimes every day."

"You'll be asked why you chose to stay," he said.

Teresa sighed, closing her eyes. "I know." She pursed her lips, as if she had already asked herself this question over and over and still had no answer. "I could just say it was for Bobby, couldn't I? Because I thought leaving would hurt him, after what we had suffered before. It isn't all true, though. The truth is, I don't know. I still love him. I don't know what kind of future I have without him. It's just that, after yesterday, I realized it couldn't go on as it had."

"What happened?"

"I went and shopped in the town for a few hours. When I returned, Blake wasn't mad. He was calm, almost smug. Bobby had a massive welt on his cheek. He wouldn't explain it, and Blake said he had fallen in the yard. But I knew. It chilled me to the bone, Mr. Birch. You see, he's found a new weapon. Whenever I leave, I know Bobby won't be safe. I'm terrified. I have to free us, Mr. Birch. I have to escape." She stared at him with her soulful eyes, now welling up with tears. "Will you help me?"

I knew he would, of course, but Joseph had chosen an unpopular cause.

Blake Benton had spent his whole life in the town of Black Oak. He had delivered many of the children who spent their afternoons playing near the mermaid fountain in the town square. Teresa lived with the disadvantage of still being the stranger here, and she was telling the townspeople something they didn't want to hear or believe. The rumors of abuse spread quickly but were quickly discounted. Then the counter-rumors began, where Blake's considerable wealth became the real issue. She had arrived penniless, they whispered, and now she wanted to flee with his money. I understood. I knew the people at their best, but in this fight they were forced to choose. They chose one of their own.

I believed they were making a mistake. Years ago I discovered how easily a strong and attractive man could cross an ugly line, but I had the good fortune of escaping before I suffered any real harm. It was the glimpse of Blake and Teresa in Black Oak

Park—that odd moment I cannot forget—
which echoed my own experience.

But who could I tell? They would not believe me either, not now. Instead, in the
weeks that followed, I felt my neighbors placing Joseph and me on the wrong side of an
invisible line. Maybe if Joseph had not been
so righteous in her defense, they would have
believed he had taken the case out of some
obscure legal obligation. He had no choice,
they would say. But this was not Joseph's
way. Everyone knew the truth, that he had
genuinely taken her side because he believed in her.

The proceedings went smoothly at first.
Joseph obtained a court order to remove
Teresa and Bobby legally from Blake's
house until the hearing, with sufficient man-
dated support to allow her to live. For a brief
period, at least, she was free. That tempo-
rary escape was small comfort, though.
Everywhere she went, mean looks followed
her.

About the same time, Blake's lawyer
launched a devilish counter-attack.

I was in Joseph's office when he took the
call. As he listened, his eyes hardened angrily. When he hung up, he immediately

called Teresa and asked her to join us. He told me about it while we waited. It was nasty indeed. I suspect Teresa had read the tone in Joseph's voice, because when she arrived, she hovered reluctantly in the doorway and had to be coaxed in. I offered to leave, but she insisted I stay.

Joseph came around in front of his desk and guided her into the overstuffed chair. He stayed near her, leaning back on the desk, balancing his palms on the smooth mahogany. I drifted to the sofa by the window and sat down.

Teresa fidgeted, uncomfortable in the office setting (or was it because of me?). Her eyes darted back and forth between us. She grabbed a strand of hair and massaged it nervously between her fingers. Several times she smoothed her black trenchcoat and tugged it down below her knees.

"It's not a nice process, is it?" she asked softly.

Joseph shook his head. "No. No, it brings out the worst in people, I'm afraid. I know it's hard on you. And Bobby."

Teresa smiled humorlessly. "I didn't have a choice, you know that. Even so, I'm not sure I'd do it over again if I could go back."

Teresa bit her lip and continued, her voice cracking. "You said you had news?"

"I do."

"So is it good or bad?"

"I'm not sure it's that simple," Joseph began.

"In other words, bad?" Teresa laughed and stared at the ceiling. "Do you know what a friend told me once? She told me to play the lottery. She said luck comes to some people in huge doses, the good and the bad, and sooner or later I'd have to strike it rich. I actually bought a ticket. What's funny is, I missed the jackpot by one number. Can you believe it? One number. What does that mean, do you suppose?"

Joseph groped for words. He reached a hand toward her, then pulled it back. I looked away. "Blake has elected not to contest the divorce."

Teresa's eyes registered a new hope, tinged by disbelief. The glimmer of a smile crossed her face, then disappeared as Joseph raised his hand to stop her. The other shoe dropped. She wasn't prepared.

"However, I'm afraid he is counter-suing. He wants to get custody of Bobby."

I winced. Even knowing the news, and

how it might affect her, I had no desire to see its results. Never had I seen such instant, crushing devastation. It was obvious that even in her worst fantasies, her nightmares of all the consequences of the path she had chosen, she had never imagined this. Joseph may as well have been a doctor, breaking the results of a lab test that left her in a battle for her life.

Trembling, Teresa asked weakly, "Why?"

I didn't even know if she was talking to Joseph. Perhaps she expected an answer from the walls or the sky, some explanation for her life. Why? Like an echo. She must have asked it many times.

"Overtly for financial considerations," Joseph replied evenly. "He's claiming he can provide a more stable home environment."

"He's not even Blake's son," Teresa whispered. "He barely knows him, or talks to him. My God, the man is cruel. It's extortion. Go back to him, drop the divorce, or I lose my son."

Joseph clenched the sides of the desk. His knuckles were white. "That seems to be his strategy."

I found myself staring at both of them, lawyer and client, like an apparition they couldn't see. They were too absorbed now to notice me anyway. For someone who didn't wear his passions on his sleeve, Joseph's involvement in this woman's plight was surprisingly intense. I had seen him handle case after case for years, sometimes caught in violent or emotional disputes, but he had never crossed this line before. As the tide of opinion turned against him, as he found himself her lone defender, he began to let his emotions cloud the judgment that saved him in court. He believed in her so much that I saw him grow blind to the dangers.

Teresa meanwhile teetered on the edge of an abyss. I think she saw the future coming, more clearly than Joseph. In hindsight, I imagine she knew right then, as we all sat there, that her gamble was lost.

Joseph had no such doubts. "I don't think you should be overly concerned," he continued. "It's a crude tactic but a desperate one. These things are decided in the courtroom, remember, not in the streets. Judgments come from facts, not gossip."

"Do they really?" Teresa wondered.

"Believe me."

He reassured himself with this little speech, and maybe some of his confidence penetrated Teresa's soul. It gave her something to cling to. She had trusted him with her life; perhaps, after all, he could deliver.

I wasn't so sure. Joseph had the confidence that comes with experience, but I wondered if he understood the battle he had joined. I didn't tell him of my reservations, my instincts. They arose from nothing I could prove or talk about. Partly I saw something in Teresa's eyes (a weakness to be exploited, a secret to be exposed), and partly I remembered the coldness of her husband. I did not believe Blake was the kind of man who would give up readily, or who would play this game without the hand he needed to win.

The day of the hearing proved uglier than I imagined. I sat behind Joseph and watched the courtroom fill with gossips and curiosity-seekers, those with a morbid fascination in the suffering of others. Teresa sat next to Joseph, her hands folded in front of her, wearing a light blue flowered dress. I could see her face in profile, a face frozen in fear, no stronger than a dandelion puff in a meadow, on the verge of scattering at the first breath of wind. By contrast my husband's confident eyes showed the fortitude of a rock. But it took so little wind really, and what could a rock do to save a flower?

I saw Blake at the opposite table, and what I saw confirmed all my fears. Without glancing across the divide, Blake stared into space, unconcerned, uncaring, unafraid. His whole demeanor, from the close-shaved jaw to the lines of his designer suit to the neat layering in his hair, bespoke utter calm and patience. This was the patience, I thought, of a lion following the bloody tracks of a wounded gazelle, secure in the knowledge that time is a friend and will ultimately bring victory.

In reality he needed little patience.

Teresa took the stand. My husband guided her through her story, rationally, thoroughly, laying a foundation of brick to build the same image in everyone's mind: That here was a caring, abused mother, fighting for her freedom and her future, at the hands of a man whose temper and desires could not be controlled. So easy, I thought, as Joseph laid each brick. So true, so right. And then he sat down, as pleased with himself as he had every right to be, and up popped

Blake's lawyer, the big bad wolf, huffing, puffing, blowing Teresa's house down.

Is it true? Is it true?

Three little words, one little question. Oh, Joseph, you never asked, did you? Why now, why the blind spot on this one? What have you not told me? But it wouldn't have mattered.

Is it true?

"Is it true, Mrs. Benton, that four years ago you spent two months in a drug rehabilitation center after your second arrest on charges of theft? Is it true you were temporarily removed from custody of your child? Is it true, Mrs. Benton? Is it true?"

The buzz of the courtroom stopped in shocked silence, all this too macabre even for the ghouls here. A grim smile of triumph curled onto Blake's lips. On Joseph's face, I saw his confidence, his faith, his principles, crumble around him, as he realized for the first time that justice would not prevail here.

And Teresa. She didn't answer. Is it true? She sat there like a statue, her mouth going slack, her eyes dazed and disbelieving. She had retreated into a nether-world, driven by the certainty that the past had won—that the most important part of her life would be stripped away—that maybe madness lay in any direction she chose now.

I wondered what this said about any of us as human beings, and in due course, I would find out.

When Teresa came to our back door several weeks later, I barely recognized her. She came at night through the yard, a bonnet shrouding her head to protect her from the spring rains and perhaps also from the stares of our neighbors. Her black hair, wet and unkempt, fell in loose strands across her face. Her cheeks were gaunt, her neck and wrists thin. I wondered when she had last eaten. Nonetheless Teresa retained a certain dignity, proud in her despair, maybe even more attractive now that hardship had gripped her soul again and etched a troubled reality in her features.

"I'm sorry," she whispered guiltily. "I didn't know where else to go."

I shook my head. "You did the right thing."

I took her coat and replaced it with a blanket, which I wrapped around her shoulders as she sipped hot coffee at our kitchen table. When I found some crackers and cheese, she tried to hide her hunger, and I pretended not to notice the speed with which she ate piece after piece.

Joseph came into the kitchen, glasses pushed to the edge of his nose as he perused a thick brief. He wore a gray V-neck cardigan I had found for him on his last birthday. Joseph noticed Teresa with surprise and concern. I had been downstairs when she arrived and hadn't had time yet to call him from his upstairs office. Teresa blossomed as she saw my husband. I felt awkward, as if the reality of my life were too normal, too happy, as if I were a shrew to resent Joseph's part in this tragedy. And did I resent it? Did I resent her? Joseph, too, looked awkward. For him, two opposite worlds had suddenly joined. Here I was, warm and secure, his equal; here she was, vulnerable, beautiful not just in her face but in the way she needed him.

"I didn't know where to contact you." Joseph scolded her like a child. "I was worried. I haven't heard from you since the hearing."

Teresa avoided his eyes. "I'm sorry. I'm sorry about not telling you about the past. I thought it was over, but I guess I can't escape it. No one ever understands the kind of bottomless pit you face when you're alone, or how easy it is to slip down when you want more than anything to climb out."

"That isn't important. What's important is, how are you now?"

"No." Teresa shook her head, intent on punishing herself. "It is important. It's my fault." From each eye a tear mingled with the rain on her cheeks. "And I've lost my child because of it."

"We're appealing the case."

Teresa smiled weakly. "You're sweet to fight for me." She caught my eye, and the smile faded. "But it's a waste of time, isn't it? They know me, who I am, what I am. Or what I was—but it doesn't matter to anyone else. That's fine. I don't ask for anything better. It's Bobby."

"Have you seen him?" I asked her. "Is he all right?"

"Two afternoons a week," she murmured. "Under lock and key. Blake's always there, watching me. It's still clear, isn't it? Go back to him, the door's open, my son is there. And Bobby needs me. He hardly says a word, never smiles. He's dying on the inside."

Joseph and I said nothing. There was little to say.

"I'm thinking of doing it," Teresa concluded, her voice hollow. "I'm going back to him."

"No!" Joseph retorted angrily. "Teresa, don't do this. You don't have any illusions. Putting yourself back in his web won't make it any better for Bobby."

"At least we'd be together. He'd have me."

"Blake would have both of you."

Teresa hesitated. She glanced at the little things around the room: spice rack, wooden shelf lined with photographs, a calendar on the wall. Everything that was us, Joseph and me, stared at her and reminded her of what she didn't have. She flicked her eyes at me sullenly, aware of the chasm between us. I understood. We could argue with her about good and evil, right and wrong, but never from her perspective. Joseph didn't want her to put her head back in the tiger's mouth. But he didn't live in the jungle.

"I've taken too much from you already," she decided finally. Teresa stood up and gathered her coat. "I haven't even been able to pay you. Maybe I can remedy that, too."

"Don't be foolish," Joseph said.

Teresa smiled. "Thank you." She was anxious to be gone now, as if in one short visit she had reconciled herself with a terrible choice. Without letting us stop her, she hurried back into the rain.

Who knows what motivates a person? I didn't analyze my own reasons too carefully (don't go looking for something, my father told me, unless you're prepared to find it). Instead, when Teresa left us alone, the two of us in our warm kitchen, I spoke right from my heart. "Joseph, we must help her," I said.

But Joseph didn't hear me. His mind had sailed ahead, sifting through precedents and appeals. He tore apart his memory until he began to massage his forehead to rub down the pain. I knew the answer already: If there had been a way out in his law books, he would have found it weeks ago. He had run out of tricks, but his humanity and his morality still stared him in the face.

"Is there a way?" I asked.

Joseph went and poured a cup of coffee. "No." He paused, hardly able to say the next words. "And yes. There's only one way. It occurred to me a few weeks ago, but I never even considered it until now. But how can I do it?" Joseph stopped. So would anyone, on a cliff at night, about to jump, hoping for a river below.

"Do you remember the old fairy tale?" he asked me idly. Joseph took a sip from the mug and watched the rain fall in streams through the glow of our porch light. "A son and his father lived in a seaside village. The father was a seaman, and he used to go off for months at a time, out trading riches in far-off lands. Every time he came back, he would ask his son, 'While I was gone, boy, did you look into the eyes of the devil?' The boy would say, 'No, sir.' 'That's good,' the father always replied, 'because no matter the cause, that is the one thing you must never do.' And the boy grew up strong and honorable, looking forward to the brief days with his father as the sweetest times of his life. Except one day the ship returned, but his father did not."

"Joseph," I said. But he looked away and kept talking.

"The men on the ship told the boy his father had been spirited away by a wizard. So like the father, the son went to sea to find him. He visited port after port, and in every

BRIAN FREEMAN

town he asked after his father. He talked to the poor and the powerful, the religious and the magical, and no one could help him, no one could tell him anything, no one could show him the way. And when he had nearly given up, he met a blind man in the most distant of villages, an old man in a tattered robe and black glasses, with a dented tin cup rattling with a few coins. The boy almost didn't ask, because what could a blind man tell him? But to his amazement, the blind man knew his father immediately. He could show the son just where his father was, if only the boy would do one thing."

I knew how this ended. Seriously, I repeated, "We must help her."

Joseph found the courage to stare at me. He laughed, the kind of laugh of someone about to cry. "And the blind man took off his glasses and told him, 'First, look into my eyes.'"

"Dr. Benton!" A muffled, agitated voice crackled over the phone line.

Blake Benton balanced the antique receiver on his shoulder. "Yes?" he answered calmly. Panicked calls were commonplace in his evenings over the years.

"I'm down in Bounlea!"

"Bounlea, yes. Can you speak slowly and clearly please? I can barely make you out."

Bounlea, twenty miles south of Black Oak, had no doctors or medical facilities inside the meager blocks of the town. The doctors of Black Oak serviced the few residents among them.

"It's Annie Scriver, Dr. Benton. I'm going into labor!"

Outside rain tapped on the chambered windows of Benton's den. He heard the sound of pacing footsteps in Bobby's room upstairs. Blake sighed wearily. "I see. Who is your regular doctor?"

"Dr. Thompson. He's out of town this weekend. I'm scared." The voice cut off into a bellow of pain.

"Take a deep breath and relax, Mrs. Scriver. How frequent are the contractions?"

"I haven't timed them. It seems like they're one on top of another!"

"All right, can your husband drive you to the hospital?"

"I don't have a husband, Dr. Benton."

Blake paused. For a brief moment, the chilly voice sounded familiar. "I see. Do you think you can drive yourself?"

The woman sobbed, "No, no!"

"Don't excite yourself," Blake retorted firmly. "I'll be there. Lie down and relax. I'll be there in twenty minutes. Give me your address."

"15 Violet Drive. A white Rambler. Hurry, please!"

I hung up the phone. I had slipped only once, and I hoped it was not enough to betray me.

My part was done. Now it was Joseph's turn.

Were we on the side of the angels tonight? Or was Mephistopheles staring back from the mirror? Was I looking into his eyes?

It seemed to Teresa that they drove forever. She had no idea how far it really was, only that the cluster of houses in the town disappeared and the spectre of Black Oak Park loomed for miles and miles on the north side of the road. Even that, too, disappeared (she thought), and they found themselves in an even deeper frontier, moonless and foreign. She saw strange shapes in the shadows, strange beasts. Next to her Joseph sat

silently. He didn't look at her, perhaps to follow the black line of the road, or perhaps to
avoid her eyes. She thought this was a new
route for him, too, and maybe he was as un-
sure of what the night held as she was.

Bobby lay asleep in the back seat. They
had parked in the rainy cover of Blake's
street, almost invisible in the cloak of night
and fog. When Blake's car turned out of his
driveway toward Bounlea, Teresa crept
across the street, eyeing the nearby houses
for the silhouettes of neighbors peering into
the avenue, and reclaimed her bewildered
son. Teresa could tell him little, for she was
bewildered, too. Joseph had divulged very
little of his plan, only that tonight she and
Bobby would escape. As they drove and
drove, she wondered where this newest escape would lead her.

They made only one stop. It came nearly
an hour after they left Black Oak far behind
them. A yellow light beamed above the road
ahead of the car, and suddenly Teresa realized they had reached the crossing of an old
railroad track. Joseph drew to a stop beneath the solitary light. He got out of the car.
Teresa heard his steps crunch on the dirt as
he walked to the trunk and popped it open.

She got out, too, to listen to the stark silence and feel the crisp air on her face. The railway, like the road, came from nowhere and returned there, nothing but a crease in the endless rows of trees. She saw nothing and heard nothing. The rusted joints on the warning lights looked as if they had long since corroded, as if no trains had thundered by here in years. But Joseph had other ideas. He pulled a blaze orange flag from the trunk, then spent two or three minutes wedging it securely into a rotting post by the tracks. When it unfurled, it cast a sharp neon glow that must have been as visible as a fire in the piercing headlight of a train. If a train were to come.

"Will you tell me now?" she said. Her voice, breaking the silence, sounded loud.

Joseph hesitated. He stared at the flag, fluttering gently in the weak breeze. "Soon."

That was all. They returned to the car and drove again, back through the forest, twisting and turning, all alone on the road. Teresa began to feel scared. She had not had time to listen to her feelings in the midst of the intrigue, but now, staring into the nothingness, she felt she was staring into her future. With each mile she felt more disconnected. It did not seem to have an ending. She knew what she had left, but where was she going? She wondered, too, if the past would catch up with her there (where?), as it had in Black Oak. Were some things inescapable?

Quietly, Teresa sobbed, surprising herself. She didn't want Joseph to hear her, but he glanced and saw the shine of tears on her cheeks. All her uncertainties had spilled over.

"It's a new beginning," he said softly. Then after a pause: "Have you heard of the Underground Railroad?"

Teresa wiped her eyes. Confused, she stared at Joseph. "Wasn't that during the Civil War? The route for slaves out of the South?"

Joseph nodded. "There's a modern equivalent," he said.

"I don't understand."

"An underground. For abused women and children. A way out. It's an illegal network, a sort of shadow protection program that helps women disappear, start new lives under new names. You'll be safe. No one will know where you are. I won't. Certainly Blake won't."

The magnitude of this scheme settled in

slowly. Joseph was right to call it a shadow program, for she was leaving amid the shadows, vanishing like a shadow. Teresa thought about losing her identity, blending into the darkness, and the image held both comfort and fear for her. She would be safe, but she had no illusions that she would be free. But freedom felt like a luxury now.

Somewhere in the dark curves, Joseph found a narrow dirt road. For another mile, they crept through a wilderness that seemed to brush up against the car. Then the trees thinned, and an old farmhouse rose like a vague silhouette against the black sky. The car bumped and bucked in deep ruts as Joseph guided them along the driveway to the fallen front steps.

No one had lived there for many years. Most of the windows upstairs and downstairs were broken, with large gaps where wind, rain, and snow blew inside. Fragments of siding, remnants of several years of storms, lay in the overgrown yard. It had been beautiful once, a grand Victorian painted bright rose, set amid a clipped lawn and bushes growing with white berries. The rose had faded and peeled now, and the landscaping had begun a slow repossession of the house. Whoever had deserted it had left emptiness behind for miles, an unvisited corner of the world. But Teresa noticed a small slope a short distance from the house and the same crease in the forest that marked a railway cutting across the land.

"So it stops here?" she said.

"Yes. We have about an hour."

Joseph stopped and headed for the steps, picking his way carefully. The front door loosened wide cobwebs as he pushed it in. The hinges screeched, sharply enough that both of them jumped, expecting people to run at them from the shadows. No one did. Inside a damp chill pervaded, a smell of rotting wood, an echo of ghostly voices.

Teresa carried Bobby inside and laid him on an old bench in what must have been the living room. Then Teresa and Joseph stood nervously on the wide, open floor. As their eyes adjusted to the darkness, they saw each other's faces in new detail, with the nuances of eyes and lips.

"How did you hear about this?" Teresa asked awkwardly. "How did you make contact?"

"There are some things that come your way as a lawyer that you never dream of using. But you don't destroy them, either. I peeled it away layer by layer. After the first contact, it was all anonymous. They didn't know me, I didn't know them. All they knew was you. They did their own research. Last week I discovered they had approved you."

"Another trial," Teresa said. "A jury of my peers?" She smiled. It changed her emotions somehow, to know that others had already passed judgment and believed her. And to know, too, that she might not be thoroughly alone. That in one form or another there would be welcoming arms for both of them.

Bobby slept, the way only children can, uncomfortably, in the cold, in the midst of one more sea-change in his young life. He curled up on the hard bench, knees pulled up almost to his chin. He would sleep while Teresa and Joseph talked softly, while Teresa carried him onto the train—sleep until the sunshine of a new day and a new world. Teresa watched her son's quiet slumber. She watched Joseph, too, whose face betrayed his doubts.

Teresa sensed his emotions when she turned away from Bobby and found Joseph's confused eyes. It was a dangerous moment.

"I don't imagine you've ever done this before. Or am I wrong? Am I the latest in a long
line saved by the angel of Black Oak?"

"You're the first."

"Yes, I know. It isn't enough to thank you. I
can't even convince you you've done the
right thing."

Joseph winced. "Don't misinterpret. It's
not from any reluctance to help you."

"But to help me this far," Teresa said. "To
break the rules."

"I live my life by rules."

Teresa reached out shyly, touching
Joseph's cheek. "And now that you've broken them for me, how does that change your
life?"

For Joseph, she knew, this was a question within a question, an echo hanging between them, asking too many things. He
opened his mouth and said nothing. Behind
Joseph, a wisp of fog drifted through the
cracked window and floated above them,
glowing in the flickering light. She smiled at
him and tried to read his mind. He had
jumped into the breakers for her, not knowing how to swim, and as he saved her, he
drowned himself. He struggled through a
watery nothingness, no anchor, no escape,

no rules. Perhaps her smile could rescue him.

"Why did you?" Teresa said finally.

"I wanted you and Bobby to be safe."

"But it's so risky for you."

Joseph shrugged. "I took precautions. Lawyers understand alibis, after all. If it becomes necessary, my wife and I can prove we were home together tonight."

"I see." Teresa paused, and her voice became a whisper. "But you're not."

"No."

Bobby whimpered, shifting in his sleep. Teresa knelt and stroked his face. "Teresa flees," she murmured ironically. Her eyes filled with an uncertain longing. "I don't know if I'm strong enough."

"You are."

"You want me to be. But tomorrow you won't be there, if I'm weaker than you imagine."

For a moment Teresa had a fantasy, blooming out of the chill and night. The cold house seemed warm. She pictured Joseph's strong arms and wanted him to hold her. As long as he held her, she thought, as long as the train didn't come, as long as they spent an infinite night together in the abandoned building, then the future and past didn't matter. She pictured a kind of frozen eternity here.

"How long?" Teresa said.

Joseph said, "We still have a few minutes."

Teresa came closer.

I didn't ask Joseph if Teresa kissed him goodbye, or even if he kissed her, just as I had not asked about the late nights and missed dinners over the past six months. I didn't need to ask, because in my heart I trusted Joseph, to be true to his own life regardless of temptations.   Surely he was tempted.   Because I knew that Teresa had fallen in love with Joseph.

I saw it in her eyes, the flush in her cheeks, the sound of her voice. Teresa needed to be in love. As surely as day followed night, she would find a man and flower in his shadow. At least in my man she had hit it right.

He was the kind of honorable gentleman she needed if she would not find her own strength—someone to scoop her up, or put his arm around her shoulder, or tell her to come in from the rain and dry her hair. He could do everything for her, give everything to her, not for power but for love, because she wanted him to, needed him to. And in return she would offer herself in the bargain, let her damp clothes fall away, let him ravish her in the pale light.

It's funny. To me Joseph was never a hero. Ours was a comfortable love: come home from the office late; I'll be up. Sit with me by the fire. Would you like a glass of wine? Tell me about the case; I'll tell you about my day. We would be doing that for sixty years, I knew, and I would be as happy in the sixtieth as I had been in the first.

Then I began, these past months, to see him through Teresa's eyes. What a shock. That was the problem all along: I was jealous, not of their being lovers (for I did not believe they were), but of the way she saw Joseph, of the part he played in her life, a part I had not seen in him for me. This was all different. I was angry because he was her savior, her white knight. To me he was a friend, someone who knew me like I knew him, quiet, funny, a man to cherish. Yet had I missed something? My man of principle had broken the law.

He said little when he returned late that

night. I asked him if the train had come, and he nodded, distracted. So she had gone. The pieces of our lives were back in place. Although something would always be different now, not better, not worse.

I let him struggle with his thoughts. There was no point in asking what he still had never explained, why he had gone so far for her—no point, because I knew. Not for her alone, but for us. For me—because I wanted it. My hero.

Joseph stood by the window. He swirled a glass of red wine in his hand idly and stared into the darkness of our garden. What a handsome man he was, tall and strong and caring. He had saved Teresa. And I thought, He'll make love to me tonight.